I0674552

The Highwayman's Lady

Melba Moon

Published by MFM Books, 2025.

Table of Contents

Cover Design Melba Moon
Art work Depositphoto
Interior Design: Melba Moon
Editors: Mary Marvella

This novel was first published in serial format in 2022 on Kindle Vella.

Dedication

As always, for EWM.
Also with thanks to my daughter, Belinda Shane for her unfailing support and confidence in her momma.

Chapter One

THE ENGLISH COUNTRYSIDE MARCH 1844:
The overcast night made travel treacherous. The darkness reached out inky arms to encase the lone rider as he guided his horse carefully along the woodland path. The rider came out on a hillside overlooking the main coach road.

A sudden wind gusting from the valley below caused the rider's black cape to billow around him like the sails of a ghost ship. Clutching the reins tighter, he paused for a moment, listening to the sounds of the night around him. In the distance, the rumble of a fast-moving coach alerted him that his prey neared.

Breathing deeply of the cold evening air, the man cursed the unfamiliar climate and pulled his cloak tighter against the chill. He slipped a black silk mask from his pocket and quickly covered his face. Then, clucking softly to his mount, a giant black beast, he resumed his slow trek through the thick forest.

Stopping again, he listened intently, his senses picking up the presence of another person even before he heard the low whistle of a bobwhite calling to its mate. He returned the whistle, and the bird responded in kind.

Slowly, he urged the stallion forward. He stopped as a figure detached itself from the shadows of the trees ahead.

"All's ready?"

"Aye, it is," the figure answered.

"Stay hidden. No sense both of us taking chances," the masked rider reminded the figure as he urged his horse nearer the roadside. There, a soft fog swirled in patches like steam rising from witch's brew.

"Keep me covered. We don't know what his lordship will do."

"Be my pleasure to send the bastard to 'is maker." He patted the pistol tucked in his belt. "Won't take much reason, at all. Milord makes one false move and will be in 'ell before daylight."

"Steady, friend. The time's not right, yet. His lordship will get all that's coming to him."

"Right ye are about that."

"Now quickly hide yourself. The coach is coming."

"I'll be 'ere lad, if ye should 'ave need o' me." The figure shifted nervously, one hand clutching the butt of the pistol in his belt. "If aught goes wrong, make 'aste to the cave. I'll meet ye there."

The rumble grew louder. The creak of harness and rattle of wheels filled the heavy night air as the cumbersome vehicle careened recklessly around a bend and bore down on where the nightrider waited.

A flickering pool of moonlight illuminated the roadway, outlining the shape of a large tree trunk blocking the way.

The driver stood on the brake and pulled back on the reins with all his might as his curses mingled with the protest of the frightened horses.

For a moment it seemed the coach would not stop but would barrel on, causing untold damage to both men and horses.

At last, the team reared, their hooves pawing empty air as the driver finally managed bring the coach to a halt.

The masked rider urged his mount into the roadway beside the stalled coach.

"Stand and deliver!" he shouted as he trained his pistol on the driver.

"I'll deliver nothing to the likes of you," the driver answered, reaching for the musket that leaned against the seat between him and the footman riding beside him.

"Touch it and die." The highwayman's voice was low and harsh. His weapon was aimed at the center of the driver's chest.

"Driver, why have we stopped?" an impatient voice demanded from behind the drawn curtains of the coach. "What's going on?"

"It's a highwayman, milord," the driver answered. His attention never left the gun barrel trained upon his chest.

"Toss down that gun, friend, and you'll live to drive for his lordship another day."

Carefully the driver obeyed the command.

The highwayman urged his mount nearer the window of the coach. With the butt of his gun, he pounded on the door of the coach. "You in there, out now, and be quick about it."

The door slowly opened, and the passengers, a middle-aged man with graying hair and an aging trollop, stepped out.

The man's face was red with rage and the woman's white with fear.

"How dare you stop my coach! Do you know who I am? I'll see you dancing upon the gallows for this outrage."

"Will you now, gov'na? And I'll see you in hell before I'm done," the highwayman's voice lowered as he leaned down and brought the revolver even with the earl's chest.

His lordship took a step backward and pressed against the coach.

The highwayman chuckled at his lordship's apparent loss of bravado and pressed his advantage. "Just who might ye be, gov'na?"

"I," said his lordship, drawing himself up to his full height, "am the Earl of Wyndridge."

"Well now, yer lordship, it's purely impressed I am. If you'll be so kind as to give me the contents of your purse, I'll take myself out of your way, and you can continue with your journey."

"Impertinent fool, whelp of a cur, be gone with you while you still can," the earl snarled.

"I'm neither a fool nor a cur. Be careful that tongue of yours doesn't cost you your life." The gun moved closer to its target, pressing against the fine material of the earl's waistcoat.

"Your money or your life. It makes no difference to me one way or the other."

"Please, my lord, do as he says," the frightened woman whimpered at the earl's side.

"You've nothing to fear from me," the highwayman said to the woman. "I wouldn't harm a lady."

"Lady? She's no lady, I'd sooner give you her than my purse," the old man sputtered.

"Then I'll just relieve you of both. Now, your purse, old fool. I tire of this game," the highwayman cocked his pistol.

Lord Wyndridge slowly removed his purse and tossed it to the highwayman. A deep scowl crossed his harsh features. "You'll pay for this outrage. I'll have every man on my estate looking for you," Lord Wyndridge threatened. "And when they find you, I shall take great pleasure in watching you hang."

"Ah, but you have to catch me first, milord," the highwayman answered cockily, reaching up to pull a long black feather from his hat. With a flourish, he presented it to his lordship, who paled visibly at the sight.

"By your leave, milord," the rogue grinned into the earl's stricken face.

The highwayman tucked his gun into his belt. He leaned down and with one arm lifted the frightened woman onto the horse in front of him.

Turning toward the shadow shrouded trees just beyond the roadway, he gave an almost imperceptible nod, then without another word to the outraged earl, the highwayman was gone.

FOR A LONG MOMENT, his lordship stared at the feather in his hand. An expression of near horror deepened the lines of his face. It didn't mean anything. *It couldn't. It happened so long ago no one could possibly remember.*

"Get that bloody tree out of the way at once!" Earl Wyndridge bellowed at the coach driver and his men when at last he had recovered himself.

"Yes, milord," the driver answered.

"I want that cur caught immediately!" He twisted the feather savagely between his hands.

Lord Wyndridge turned his attention back to his men, who had done nothing to save him. "What's taking so long? Are you fools trying to give the blackguard time to leave the country? Hurry, I say." The earl stood with his hands folded behind him, glaring at the men struggling to move the log from the roadway.

"It's no use, milord," the driver finally acknowledged the hopelessness of their moving the log unaided. "He must have used his horse to pull it into place."

"Then use one of ours to remove it, imbecile."

Earl Wyndridge continued to pace while his men worked to free one of the horses from its traces. Finally, the tree was pulled aside, and the horse was again buckled into its harness.

"Hurry, quickly, I say. We must be on his trail before it grows cold. Put the whip to the horses. We'll be on his tail fifty strong by dawn." With the nimbleness of a much younger man, his lordship swung himself up into the coach.

Leaning from the coach window, he continued his blustering tirade as the vehicle lumbered off. "I'll leave no stone unturned until I find that blackguard. He'll see just who he's dealing with!" his lordship shouted, shaking a clenched fist in the air. With a last spurt of expletives, the coach sprang away, careening down the narrow road toward Wyndridge Hall.

For a moment, all was quiet. A lone figure, shrouded in the forest's deep cloak, stood staring after the departed coach. Hatred burned in the chest of the man. A deep smoldering rage that had been banked for many years sparked and sprang to life.

"'e's the same, evil clear through and through. Not changed for naught, just older like meself." His voice carried on the wind for no one to hear.

"I'm back, yer bloody lordship, and by me pledge, I'll see ye in 'ell." Finally, he turned and walked through the dark night to where his horse was tethered.

London, 1844

"NO, IT CAN'T BE TRUE," Lady Spring Lansing insisted as she paced her late father's study.

Mr. Brownstone, her late father's solicitor, shook his head as he turned back to the papers strewn on the polished surface of the heavy oak desk.

"I'm sorry, milady, but I'm afraid it is quite true. I have checked all the papers given to me by Lord Wyndridge. They are perfectly legal. The claim he holds against your father's estate is staggering."

"But what are we to do?"

"His lordship now holds title to this townhouse," Mr. Brownstone gave a sweeping gesture with his wrinkled hand. "He also holds notes of credit against Lansing Hall. In short, all of Lord Lansing's holdings are at peril. Even if we sell your mother's jewels, it will not be enough to pay off such massive debts. The family will be left destitute."

"No, Mama must not learn of this." Spring sank into the chair across from Mr. Brownstone. "There must be something we can do?"

"Surely you cannot mean to keep word of this from Lady Lansing?" Mr. Brownstone said incredulously. "I'm sure your father never meant for you to bear this burden alone."

"Father never intended me to bear this burden at all, but he is gone, so it's up to me to sort this mess through. Mama must be spared at all costs. The shock would be too much for her. She's not been well since Papa..."

"But milady, she will certainly be aware of what's happened when she is forced to vacate her home." Mr. Brownstone studied the beautiful face of the young woman across from him. *How very like her father she is, how spirited and loyal to her family.*

He shook his head slowly. "I see no way in which we can keep this grave circumstance from her for more than a few days, at most. His lordship will have papers delivered any day now to notify you of his ownership. You have no choice but to tell your mother."

"I will not." Spring took a deep breath and folded her hands in her lap, pleating the fine muslin of her gown. "There is one other way. Lord Wyndridge has offered ..." Spring felt the words catch in her throat and could not seem to force them past the lump lodged there.

"Yes?"

Spring cleared her throat and began again. "Lord Wyndridge has offered to relinquish his claim against Papa's holdings if I agree to become the Countess of Wyndridge."

"Milady," Mr. Brownstone's kind eyes widened in alarm. "Surely you are not considering his suit?"

"I have no choice. I cannot stand by and see my family turned out into the street."

"But the man is older than your father, rest his soul."

"Be that as it may, his lordship has made the offer, and I can do naught but accept." Lady Spring rose and crossed to the window looking out across the bleakness of the city street, all gray and foggy, mirroring the hopeless despair her life had become.

She could hardly credit all that had come to pass in the short space of six months; even two weeks ago she had been blissfully ignorant of this last plight fate had foisted upon her. Sighing, she turned back toward Mr. Brownstone.

"You will see that the necessary steps are taken to see Mama's interest are protected? I do not think I can trust his lordship to keep his word."

"Oh, the misery of it all! And Milord had so much confidence in this investment he'd made in the colonies. It is almost as if Lord Wyndridge had advanced warning of the disastrous end to silk farming."

"You will send word to his lordship that I have accepted his proposal. I shall endeavor to convince Mama that this match is one of my choosing. With your help she need never guess the real purpose behind it."

"Milady, are you sure this is what you wish to do? If we consult your mother—"

"No." Spring cut him off sharply. "The decision has been made. Mama must be spared and the twins, what would their prospects be if it became known there was no dowry for them?"

Spring sat in the empty study long after Mr. Brownstone had taken his leave. She felt a cold, insipid chill that spread through her system, turning her blood to ice in her veins. What had she gotten herself into? How could she bear to marry a man older than her own father? *Oh, Papa*, she cried silently. *What is to become of me?*

The English Countryside

THE HIGHWAYMAN SHIFTED in the saddle. He could feel the woman trembling in his arms. An aging harlot was lucky to find such as the earl as a protector. Now she would have no one. Still, she was much better off without the protection of a man like Lord Wyndridge, a man who'd offer her as booty in place of his purse.

Well, you've got her now, the highwayman admonished himself silently as he rode on down the road. *What do you plan to do with her?*

He now regretted the impulse that led him to taunt his lordship by taking the woman. But there was no help for it now. What was done was done.

"I won't harm you," he reassured the frightened woman. "Where do you live?"

"The earl kept me at his house in London, but now he says I need to be nearer the country estate. What with his getting a new bride and all, he'd not be staying in London any longer. Can't say that I envy her, either. His lordship has a mean streak to him when he's been drinking."

"And do you know the name of this bride his lordship's found?"

"Not off-hand, I don't. But she'll be coming down soon enough. The wedding's to be in a fortnight's time. His lordship said I should stay at the manor until she arrived. Now, I don't know where I'll go.

The highwayman pulled the earl's purse from his vest and placed it in the woman's hand.

"That should take care of you for a long time to come." He turned the stallion back in the direction of the main coach road. "I'll leave you at the Inn. It isn't far, and you can stay there until the coach comes by."

"Thank you, sir," the woman exclaimed as her fingers curled around the fat purse in her hand.

"Discard the purse least someone should recognize it," he cautioned as she slid from the large horse in the yard of the inn. The masked figure put heels to the stallion's flanks as the woman disappeared into the inn.

Fresh sea air filled his nostrils, bringing a familiar longing, reminding him of home. He longed to go home, but he must complete his quest first.

He guided his mount carefully along the narrow path toward his lair. The undergrowth was thick on either side of him. It held sudden death for the unwary traveler who forced his way through with no regard for what lay on the other side. But he knew and was forewarned.

The steep craggy cliffs were no mystery to him, just as the sound of the surf breaking on rocks far below held no surprise.

Further on, the path turned abruptly and started downward at a nearly vertical slant, but the sure-footed stallion did not hesitate at the task his master had set for him.

Moonlight glistened on a tranquil sea as they made their way along the soft sandy beach.

The highwayman urged his mount across the expanse of white and into the surf, where they cantered along, uncaring of the tracks swiftly washed away as the surf swept the beach clean.

Suddenly the stallion raised his head and whinnied, tossing his midnight mane in the sea breeze.

"Right you are, boy." The rider patted the stallion's neck and tugged ever so slightly on the reins so that the animal turned away from the surf and headed across the beach. When they neared the steep wall of the cliff, the rider slid from the animal's back, letting the reins dangle freely toward the sand at his feet.

He strode quickly to the growth of brush and bramble and pulled it aside until the mouth of a cave was visible. Clicking softly to the horse, he held the brush aside for the animal to enter the cavern.

The stallion trotted into the cave with his master following him. Inside, the cave took several twists and turns before finally widening to a cavernous room where a make-shift corral had been fashioned.

The air was damp and dank. It smelled slightly of horse and the scent of an oil lantern. The walls and floor of the room were of rock and earth, covered in places by a dark substance the man avoided at all costs. Flocks of bats had been in residence when he and his friend had first entered the cave.

He opened the gate of the corral and patted the stallion's rump, "In you go, Diablo."

Standing contentedly in the middle of the corral, a sorrel-colored mare lifted her head, whinnied and trotted over to the man as he closed the gate behind the stallion. Stretching her neck over the crude fence, she nuzzled at the man's clothing.

"You've not had your sweet. Did he forget again?" the man asked as he pulled a lump of sugar from his pocket and offered it to the mare.

"I did no forget. She's greedy, that one is," the old man spoke from the mouth of the cave.

The highwayman smiled. "So, you made it back. All's well?"

"Aye, that it is. Did ye see to yer tracks?"

"No, I've just arrived. I wanted to be sure Diablo was safely locked away."

"'E'd be up to no good left on 'is own." The old man cast a derisive gaze toward the horse. "I'll be seeing to the tracks meself then, I saw ye coming along the water's edge. It should no take a trice to sweep away yer tracks."

"Be sure the mouth of the cave is well hidden. We don't want any unexpected visitors," the highwayman cautioned, causing a grumble as the older man hurried from the cave, leaving his young companion alone with the horses.

The highwayman stroked the neck of the mare. "Miss me, girl?" He produced yet another lump of sugar and held it out for the mare. "Or was it just your sweet tooth that missed me?" he added as the mare used her lips to gently take the sugar from his hand. Her reward achieved, the mare trotted away to stand beside the stallion looking on with tolerant superiority.

The man's gaze swept the lamp lit cavern, searching out familiar items. A cot stood to one side across the room from the corral. A crude table was propped against the wall of the cave. A pile of fresh, sweet-smelling hay and a bag of feed for the horses sat near a curve in the wall.

At the back of the room, the cave narrowed again to a mere tunnel and plunged deeper into the cliff.

Crossing the crude rock-strewn floor, he lifted the wooden lid from one of two water barrels. With a long-handled gourd hollowed out for drinking, he dipped into the water and brought it toward his mouth. Only then did he realize he still wore the black silk mask. He quickly loosened the material and tucked it away inside the pocket of his coat. Then he quenched his thirst with water from the gourd.

Filling a wooden pail with water, he carried it back to the corral and waited while the horses drank their fill. Then he dipped a brush into the bucket and began to scrub the stallion's chest. The stallion shied away from the cold water, but a gentle word calmed him, so he stood quietly as his master washed his chest and right foreleg.

"Steady boy, just a bit more." He gentled the large animal.

"None 'll find this place now what didn't know o' it aforehand," the older man said when he returned. "Did I tell ye 'is bloody lordship was still whooping and hollering of what he'd do with ye when the coach rounded out of sight? Madder 'an 'ell 'e was."

"But he'll have to catch us first. Won't he Diablo?" the younger man responded as he finished his work with the horse and dropped the brush into the pail of water.

"Drew, 'is lordship be a mean 'un. Ye best be careful of 'im. 'E's not changed a bit, 'e hasn't."

"I know, old friend, and I will be careful. I promise you that. We've not come all this way to let Lord Wyndridge win again.

"'ad 'im in me sights, I did," the older man continued. "Old Tob could have dropped 'im where 'e stood. 'E deserved it, 'e did."

"Then we'd be no better than he. It'll take time, but we'll get the proof we need. In the meantime, I intend to make life very uncomfortable for Lord Wyndridge."

"Aye, 'e didn't seem any pleased with parting with that fat purse. 'Ow much blunt did 'e 'ave on 'im?"

"I never counted it."

"Well then, give it over and let's 'ave a look."

"I....I haven't got it."

"Ye mean ye lost it? Surely yer not that damn foolhardy, lad."

"Actually, I gave it to the lady."

"Lady? What lady?" The man's brows drew together as he gave a pained moan. "No, lad, ye didn't!"

"It seemed the honest thing to do. She'd lost her protector because of us, and she had no way to support herself. Besides, we've no need for his money."

"No way to support 'erself? Ha!" the older man gave a derisive laugh. "Drew, me boy, I think yer education at that fancy school yer grandpa sent ye to was somewhat lacking."

"But she really seemed grateful for the money."

"Sure, and I guess I'd be grateful for a fortune dropping in me lap, too. Those o' 'er kind always land on their feet. She probably laughed all the way back to 'is lordship." He frowned again as another thought occurred to him. "She did'na see ye face, did she, lad?"

Chapter Two

T he Lansing home, London

ALL NIGHT SPRING WRESTLED with the problem of how to break the news to her mother of her coming marriage.

Finally, in the wee hours of the morning as the first pink streaks of dawn shone on the distant horizon, she'd hit upon a plan. She wouldn't be the first woman to marry for the social position her husband could afford her.

As the Countess of Wyndridge, her place in society would be assured. If she could convince her mother she desired that social prominence above all else, then she need never learn the true reasons for her marriage.

With a few carefully placed hints, the groundwork would be in place. When the time came to break the news, her mother would not question her decision. After all, hadn't Grandmother made just such a marriage? Why should she be expected to marry for love? How many people did?

It's not as if I'm in love with anyone. Spring heaved a deep sigh. At nineteen, Lady Spring Melanie Lansing was quite untouched by love.

She'd never seen a man who could claim her heart, never met one she'd wanted to spend the rest of her life with.

Oh, yes, she'd had dreams of a wonderful, loving relationship such as Mama and Papa had shared, but that would never be.

She could never love the earl the way her mother had loved her father, and he would never be the adoring husband Sir Geoffrey Lyons Lansing had been.

Spring pushed back the heavy comforter and swung her bare feet to the carpet. Padding silently across the chilled room, she stood gazing down at the street below.

The city still slept. Fog swirled ghost-like in the thin beams cast by the gaslight at the corner, giving the street an ethereal appearance that made Spring shivered in apprehension.

Dropping the drapery back into place, she returned to her bed and tried to capture the elusive sleep that had eluded her all through the night. She shivered as she curled into a tight ball, clutching her pillow to her chest.

"Get up, oh do get up!" a gamine voice penetrated her slumber. "Must you sleep all day?" A demanding hand shook her shoulder as the bed beneath her began to tremble and then to bounce, threatening to toss her onto the floor.

"Do stop that, Rebecca," a genteel voice admonished. "It's not at all ladylike to bounce on the bed in that way. Tell her, Spring. It's quite unbecoming, isn't it?"

"Oh pooh!" the gamine voice answered as the bouncing stopped. "You're quite a stick in the mud, Winifred. Spring doesn't mind if I bounce on her bed. She always lets me."

Spring looked up at her younger sisters affectionately. Identical twins, they looked as much alike as two black eyed peas, yet their personalities were quite different.

Spring called Rebecca—the frivolous and gay minx who was always giggling and playing pranks— Beckie. While Winifred, with her perfect manners to rival any lady of Queen Victoria's court, was serious minded and always took the deportment lessons Miss Grey imposed upon them straight to heart. She would always be Winifred.

"Can't you act your age?" Winifred chided Rebecca as she resumed her bouncing on Spring's bed.

"You're no fun at all. I wish Spring and I were twins, then I could go to the ball, too!" Rebecca answered, sticking out her tongue at her twin.

Rebecca stopped bouncing and began to tug at one of Spring's arms as Winifred pulled on the other. "Oh, do get up, Spring. Grandmother's here with your gown for the ball, and Mama promised we could watch you try it on. They're waiting in Mama's parlor. Do hurry," Beckie demanded as she increased her pressure on Spring's arm.

As usual with the twins, they were set upon opposite courses with Rebecca pulling in one direction and Winifred tugging in the other. Spring playfully resisted their tug of war as love for her younger siblings well up inside her. She endured their tug of war, caught between them like a pulley-bone.

Happy and carefree, the twins were unaware of the cloud that hung over their future. All the splendid balls and parties that their thirteen-year-old hearts longed for might be denied them.

She looked at Rebecca and knew that she could not bear to see that laughing free spirit that dwelled within her flicker and die out. And what of Winifred, with her precise manners and plans for a perfect future?

Though she never spoke of it, Spring understood that Winifred dreamed of attending court and being presented to the Queen. Their fate now rested in Spring's hands.

There was no one else to look out for them now that Papa was gone. The task fell to Spring, and she would not let them down. She did not take her responsibility to her sisters lightly.

"Am I a branch to be bent and broken between you?" Spring protested. "Cease, or you'll have my elbows drooping to my knees."

When the twins relaxed their hold, Spring took advantage of the moment to pull them down on the bed beside her. They lay at her sides, one giggling and squealing while the other protested at having her hair mussed.

For a moment, Spring lay with her arms wrapped tightly around the twins. *How safe and content they are in their innocent world.* Was it really such a short time ago that she had been just as naive?

It seemed like years since the day Papa was killed in that carriage accident and Spring had been thrust, ready or not, into the adult world.

No sense crying after the moon. Spring sighed, pushing at the twins, urging them up.

"Up you go, Loves. And send Mary to help me dress."

For a moment, Rebecca's exuberance was contained as she cuddled in the warmth of her sister's embrace, then she was free and bouncing upon the bed once more.

"Do hurry, Spring." Rebecca tossed the mop of black curls out of her face. Her hoyden behavior had wrecked the careful coiffure Miss Grey insisted on. Sticking out her tongue, she reminded Spring, "Grandmother is waiting. The gown she's brought for you is just the most beautiful creation I've ever seen." With a flounce, Beckie bounded off the bed and headed for the door.

Winifred left Spring's side and followed her twin. At the doorway, she stopped and cast a wistful glance back toward Spring.

"Maybe Grandmother will let me try on the gown. I wish I were going to the ball. Oh, Spring, I'm just so sure you're going to meet the most wonderful beau at the ball!"

AT THE BOAR'S HEAD Inn

NEVER HAD HIS LORDSHIP, Marcus Tollersley, Earl of Wyndridge been so angry and frustrated. All night his men had combed the countryside, but not so much as a trace of the highwayman had been found. Rage boiled within him. How dare this cur come into his shire and prey upon him. His fingers found the crushed remains of the feather in his coat pocket and curled around them as if it were the throat of the culprit he had sought all night.

He narrowed his eyes, remembering the thread of apprehension that had wound itself around him as the highwayman handed him the feather. It was nothing. No one had remembered or mentioned such a thing in years. He would put it from his mind and concentrate on catching the bandit.

My men and I need food and something stronger to take the chill from our bones. Marcus directed the small party of men accompanying him toward the Boar's Head Inn.

Throwing open the door of the taproom, Lord Wyndridge stomped in, followed by his men knocking mud off their boots on the way inside. All eyes turned toward the earl and his men.

At once, Molly was subdued. "What can I get for your Lordship?"

"Food, wench, and make it quick. We're on the trail of a highwayman who stopped my coach last night." His lordship took a seat at a table across from the colonial. "Ale, woman! A dram to route the chill from our bones."

Molly hurried across the taproom to do the earl's bidding and quickly returned with his tankard of ale. "We heard about the robbery. Miss Ross stayed the night here with us," Molly said timidly.

"Ross, here? Where is she? Summon her at once. She may can identify this cur."

"She's gone, she is," Molly warmed to her subject, missing the anger that flagged upon the earl's face. "Took the coach this morning, she did."

The earl crashed his fist on the roughhewn table in front of him and turned savagely on the innkeeper. "Smith, you should have kept her here," Lord Wyndridge railed at the cowering innkeeper.

"There was naught I could do to stop her. The wench had the fare, milord."

"Where'd she get it?"

"T'was him, the highwayman, he gave it to her," Molly answered with a wide grin.

"I would know what this blackguard did to her," his lordship insisted in a sputter.

"Nothing save kiss her." Molly ignored the rage which seemed to choke his lordship. "And she looked as if she'd enjoy more of the same. Seemed quite taken by the man, she did."

"Still your tongue, wench," Lord Wyndridge warned. "I'll see this scoundrel hanging from the gallows, then I'll wager you'll not be so taken with him."

The American watched the exchange with great interest. He studied the older man over the mug of coffee he held before him. He'd traveled a long way to meet his lordship, and he had no intentions of being put off. Setting his mug on the table, he rose and approached the earl's table.

"Lord Wyndridge," the young man began in a smooth, deep voice filled with the slow drawl of his homeland. He fixed his gaze evenly on his lordship. "If I could have a moment of your time, sir."

"What's that?" the earl asked, for the first time noticing the younger man. "No time, we're about a search, didn't you hear what I said?"

"But, Sir," the stranger's voice held a thread of steel, the strength determination. "I've traveled a long way to trade with you, all the way from America to purchase the finest horse flesh. I was told you were the man to see."

"America? Horses?" Lord Wyndridge asked, looking closely at the stranger for the first time. "I've the best breeding stock in England or Europe, for that matter. To find better you'd have to go to Arabia."

"Wyndridge's stables are known around the world. I'm sure you have what I'm looking for," the stranger answered.

"To be sure. But I've no time for horse trading now. There's a highwayman in the area."

"Then perhaps I could call at Wyndridge Hall later, when my Lord has more time," the young man suggested, taking a small card from his breast pocket and presenting it to the earl. "Jonathan Andrew Sinclair, at you service, sir."

"Of course, of course, see me later, but we must be off now before the blackguard is out of the area."

"I shall be visiting with my uncle, Lord Meldon. Perhaps you know him? My aunt is expecting me in London shortly, but when I return, I shall call at Wyndridge Hall, with your permission, sir."

"Of course, of course," Earl Wyndridge answered, focusing on the card the younger man placed in his hand. Jonathan Andrew Sinclair, of America.

Jonathan Sinclair sat at his table long after the earl and his men had left the inn. He smiled, thankful he had his mother's brown-black eyes and raven hair.

There was little in his appearance to remind one of his father except his temper, his determination, and his strong, stubborn chin. And now that chin was set in a determined line, the slightly square jaw jutting out in determination.

Finally, he ordered a tankard of ale, ignoring the invitation of Molly's rounded breasts exposed by the deep cut of her blouse as they brushed softly against his arm. He had no time for wenches, even one as comely as Molly.

Jonathan had work to do, things to see to. The horses he'd acquired in Scotland must be cared for until he was ready to sail for home. Then there was the business in London to be settled. Impatience deepened the frown that creased Jonathan's brow. He shifted in his seat, running one strong tanned hand through his hair. The barrister he'd hired should have had some news for him by now.

Draining the last of the ale, Jonathan rose and crossed to the bar where the innkeeper was busy drying the tankards used by Wyndridge's men. He tossed a handful of gold coins onto the counter beside the man. "Hold my room. I'll be away for a while. I've some business in London."

Tobias McDonald looked up as Jonathan entered the room, wondering at the glower that seemed to turn the lad's features into the devil's own. *Had his back up, that's for sure.* Tobias watched Jonathan pace the room.

"'E be 'is father's son all right," Tobias muttered, noting the stubborn jut of Jonathan's chin.

Jonathan crossed to the window and stood staring out across the English countryside that should have been his home but was so alien to him. He felt he'd never get used to the weather. It was an abomination. He'd been in England for nearly two months and had settled nothing.

With a sudden longing, he thought of home. Here winter still hung on with a grip like death upon the land, but back home it'd be spring. The Georgia countryside would be bursting into bloom by now. His mother's flower garden would be a riot of yellow crowned jonquils.

Jonathan shook off the thoughts of home that sought to make his determination waver. He had a mission, a quest, so he would not be swayed by sweet memories of home.

"Pack a bag, we ride for London within the hour," Jonathan said as he turned away from the window and its bleakness that seemed to cast a coldness into his very soul.

His gaze met that of the man who'd been as much a father to him as any man.

"Ye tire of waiting to hear from 'im, then?" Tobias asked.

"He should have sent word by now. It's been a fortnight." Jonathan crossed back to the window as Tobias began to gather their belongings. "Besides, I promised Aunt Sarah I'd return in time for the ball she's planning."

"Will ye be taking the new 'orses?"

"No, we'll leave them here. We've paid well for their board."

"Aye, that we 'ave."

"Then don't worry. They will survive. You selected the paddock yourself, remember?"

"Aye, that I did," Tobias answered, but his voice held little conviction.

"What's wrong?" Jonathan asked, knowing well the intonation that lowered his friend's voice.

"I do'na like the idea o' leaving Diablo. 'E's a spirited 'un and bent on trouble. If 'e should escape 'is stall, 'e'd be outta there in a flash."

"Then calm your fears. Where I go, Diablo goes, remember?"

THE LANSING HOUSEHOLD

WITH THE ASSISTANCE of her maid, Spring had quickly dressed and followed her sisters to their mother's sitting room.

The drapes were pulled back, allowing the morning sun to stream into the room. As it filtered across the mauve furnishing, Spring noted how it highlighted the vividness of her grandmother's striking coloring while throwing into sharp contrast the shallowness of her mother's pale complexion.

Seated next to the dowager Countess, Lady Lansing appeared quite fragile. Spring paused for a moment in the doorway, studying her mother's appearance. Every day she seemed to slip a little further away from them, as if by her own will she sought to join her husband.

Lady Lansing coughed delicately into a lace handkerchief held in her thin hand. Spring made a mental note to send for Doctor Long.

Worrying the tender flesh of her bottom lip as she studied her mother's beloved face, Spring convinced herself that her decision of the night before was the only solution to their problem.

"Dear, do come and see the gown Mum has brought for you," Lady Lansing summoned with a limpid smile.

"Are you feeling better today, Mama?" Spring inquired, hurrying across the room, anxious to please her parent. "I do believe you've more color in your cheeks." Spring lied, noting that the pallor of her mother's complexion was even more pronounced.

"Why yes, my dear, I do feel—" Lady Lansing was interrupted as a spasm of coughing engulfed her. "Better today," she finished when the spell had passed.

A worried glance passed between Spring and her grandmother before she forced a smile to her lips and moved to kneel at her mother's side. The thought of losing yet another parent terrified her. How would they go on without Mama to guide them? No, it would not happen, Spring decided, squaring her shoulders. She simply would not allow it. She would keep this last damning circumstance secret, and her mother would slowly regain her strength.

"Mama, I do wish you could go to the ball. Maybe I shouldn't go." Spring looked at her mother doubtfully, hating the thought of leaving her for even the few hours necessary to accompany Grandmother to the ball. "There will be other balls."

"Nonsense, you must go and have a wonderful time. When you return, you must tell me all about the wonderful young men you've met."

"Perhaps I shall find one with a grand title like Grandmother did. I think I should quite like to be a Duchess or a Countess."

"But, my pet," Lady Phoebe intently studied her granddaughter's face, her eyes sharp as they roamed over Spring's face. "I thought you wanted make a love match. What's all this talk of titles? You've never been interested in them before."

Spring cast a glance at her sisters, seeking help that was not forthcoming. The twins were busy oohing and ahhing over the lovely ball gown. No help there. They'd not heard one word that had been said. Maybe it would not be quite as simple as she'd thought to convince her mother. At any rate, the ground had now been broken, the idea planted. When her plans to marry the earl became known, it wouldn't be so much of a shock, Spring hoped.

"Spring, dearest, do try on the gown," Lady Lansing insisted, waving a limp hand in her daughter's direction. "The color is perfect. I'm sure it shall be lovely on you."

Spring took the gown from the velvet lined box and hurried into the dressing room with the twins close behind her. Mary was waiting to help her into the full-skirted, jade, silk gown. As style dictated, the sleeves were off the shoulders, leaving a creamy expanse of snowy skin exposed, while the modified V-neck rode low on her full breasts. From the narrow waist, which accented Spring's minute waistline, yard upon yard of sublime green silk billowed out in its full skirt.

The twins were awestruck. Spring hardly dared believe her own eyes as she examined her own image in the large three-way mirror. Mary beamed with pride as Spring pirouetted this way and that.

"Lordy, milady, you look just like your mama the night she met your papa," Mary exclaimed with a sigh. "And she was acclaimed to be the most beautiful woman in England. Weren't a one what could touch her in looks. Had all the dandies calling upon her, she did. But she wasn't interested in a one of 'em after meeting your papa. Love at first sight, it was." Mary finished with a contented sigh.

"See, I told you," Winifred chimed, quite pleased with herself. "This ball shall be magical. Prince Charming will see you and fall madly in love with you."

They made their way back into Lady Lansing's sitting room as Beckie took up the story.

"Only you can't stay, you have to leave the ball at precisely midnight or something dreadful will happen," Beckie completed the tale.

"Beckie, I'm not Cinderella. I shan't turn into a pumpkin at midnight!" Spring objected. *And it's not Prince Charming that I need but a white knight come to rescue me from my fate.*

Stopping before her mother and grandmother, Spring waited expectantly to hear their opinion of the gown. Her hands smoothed the rich satin lovingly as she looked from her mother's face to her grandmother's face and back again.

"Lovely, my dear. Simply beautiful, don't you think so, Mum?" Lady Lansing asked.

"Breathtaking," Lady Phoebe answered, patting her daughter's hand. "The dress is a copy of one the Queen wore just a few months ago. Do you like it?"

"Yes, the gown is perfect. The perfect foil for Spring's beauty," Lady Lansing answered, her eyes misting as she gazed lovingly at her daughter.

Seeing the tears well in her mother's blue eyes, Spring was bereft. "Mama, are you sure? It's only been six months since papa..." Spring couldn't bring herself to say the word aloud in her mother's presence. "Perhaps it would be better if I did not attend?"

"Nonsense, dearest," her mother reassured her. "You cannot stay in mourning forever. Lately you've done nothing but seclude yourself with papa's man of business, and it's high time you resumed your own life. It is quite proper for you to accompany your grandmother." Lady Lansing lifted the delicate lace handkerchief to her lips as another spell of coughing engulfed her.

"If you're quite sure?" Spring hesitated and watched her mother's face carefully. "I 'll only be away for a few hours, at the most."

"Yes, yes, my pet." Lady Lansing favored her oldest daughter with one of her dazzling smiles, and for a moment she seemed almost like her old self again. "You must not worry about us. We shall be quite all right while you're away. Now, do turn so that I may see how splendidly the gown becomes you."

Chapter Three

A n American in London

LONDON WAS THE SAME bustling, crowded city Jonathan had seen when he'd first arrived in England. Compared to home, which was relatively young as the age of cities went, London was ancient.

The city held a strange charm, a sense of mystery, of daring. Jonathan narrowed his gaze, seeing only the cobblestone street ahead of him, refusing to allow the romanticism of London's rich history to sway his course.

He had to remember his quest, his reasons for being in London, in England. He must not fail. *The debt owed is too great, the reasons too dear*. Jonathan guided Diablo through the crowded streets, dodging puddles of filth that had been cast down from second story windows.

The smell of smoke hung heavy on the evening air, mixing with the scent of offal that ran in the gutters, but Jonathan barely noticed as he trudged on deep in thought.

By now Thomas Bailey must have some idea of the lay of things. Would his quest be easy, or would he have to fight for what was rightfully his? It didn't matter. They had come to right an old wrong, and right it they would.

Lord and Lady Meldon were out when Jonathan and Tobias arrived at the town house to be admitted by Toombs, the Meldon's stony-faced butler. Tobias snorted as the man cast a doubtful eye in his direction and followed close behind Jonathan.

"Needs to be taken down a peg, that one does," Tobias muttered.

With a soft laugh, Jonathan led the way up the marble staircase to the suite of rooms given over for their use.

"You'll have no time to worry about giving Toombs a set down. There's much to be done."

Tobias snorted and moved across the room to place Jonathan's hastily packed valise on the chest at the foot of the heavy four-poster bed.

"T'wouldn't take long to set 'im straight, I'd be thinking," Tobias grumbled as he took his own valise into the smaller dressing room that served as his bedroom.

Moving to the dresser, Jonathan poured water from the large pitcher into the basin and quickly refreshed himself before he changed into clean garments. He turned away from the mirror just as Tobias returned to the room.

"I should not be long at Bailey's office," Jonathan said while Tobias began to unpack the remaining valise.

"Ye'll be careful?" Tobias said, pausing over his task for a moment.

Jonathan smiled at his friend's concern as he shrugged into a finely tailored coat. "And you'll not be baiting Toombs while I'm gone."

"Would'na think o' it," Tobias answered.

"If you should have need of me, you know where to find me, but I doubt this will take long," Jonathan said as he left the room.

A short while later, the elderly solicitor hustled Jonathan into his inner office and quickly closed the heavy wooden door behind them before speaking.

"We must be sure no one hears any of this. There are those who would pay much for the knowledge of your presence in England," Thomas Bailey cautioned.

"You make it sound as if I am a spy intent on stealing secrets from the royal court," Jonathan said with a laugh, dropping his lean frame into the heavy leather chair across from Bailey's desk.

"You might be safer if you were." The elderly man shook his head. "You must take this matter seriously," Bailey warned somberly. "These are serious charges that you are about to bring against one of the richest men in England. He is a very powerful man."

"He is also a murderer."

"You have no proof of that, my boy. You must be cautious, or all will be lost. If we are to be successful in establishing your claim, then it is essential that we do so in secret."

Seating himself behind his large oak desk, the barrister began thumbing through a sheaf of papers he'd taken from the desk drawer.

"Now, let me see. As yes, the captain." The old man placed wire framed spectacles on his nose then peered at Jonathan over their rim. "We've been unable to locate the good captain, but rest assured we're still looking. It takes time, you see. We must not arouse suspicion. If the wrong person were to get wind of the lay of things, we'd not have a prayer of success. For now, no one must know of the real reasons for your visit."

"As you wish," Jonathan answered as he took his leave of Mr. Bailey. The wheels of justice moved slowly, much too slowly to suit Jonathan Andrew Sinclair.

At the door, Jonathan turned back toward Thomas Bailey, studying him for a moment before he spoke. "There is one more thing."

"Yes?"

"Wyndridge plans to take a bride, I want to know her name."

WYNDRIDGE HALL

EARL WYNDRIDGE SMILED. His scheme was going according to plan. He'd not doubted that it would.

Staring at the letter in his hand, the lord smoothed it on the desktop. Brownstone's message said no more than what he'd expected. After all, what choice did the chit have? Let them make their contract, once the marriage had taken place everything that belonged to Lady Spring Lansing would be under his control. His plan was working perfectly. Nothing would stand in his way.

"Bring round the coach, we leave for London within the hour," Lord Wyndridge shouted as he headed for the stairs to change his clothing.

"Mrs. Graves," his lordship bellowed again from the hall leading to his suite of rooms on the second floor. "The vicar is to be notified of my intent to be wed upon my return. The bride will arrive within a fortnight. See that everything is made ready."

"Yes, Milord," the grim housekeeper answered in an emotionless monotone as she emerged from a room on the right side of the hall, carrying a stack of crisp white linens. The woman watched as Lord Wyndridge passed on down the hall and disappeared into the doorway of his suite.

The stern lines that made Mrs. Graves' face appear like a weathered facade deepened as a frown gathered upon her brow. A bride, was it? *Poor woman has no idea what she was getting herself into.* She placed the neatly folded stack on the shelf in the linen closet. But at least peace would descend upon the household again with His Lordship absent.

LADY MELDON'S BALL

JONATHAN VALIANTLY tried to suppress a yawn as he stood at his aunt's side in the receiving line. He'd been presented to so many of Lady Meldon's dear friends and Lord Meldon's business associates that he'd long since lost count and held little hope of recalling names for all the people filling the large glittering ballroom.

There were a few more prominent names that had stuck in his mind, yet once the room had begun to fill it had become impossible to put those few names with the proper faces.

Hopefully, when his friends, Baron Rinehardt and Geoffrey Collins arrived, they would be able to slip quietly away and go to White's for a game of Hazards. Anything would be better than spending the entire evening greeting his aunt's friends.

The expertly tied cravat at his neck felt like it was growing tighter by the moment, and he longed to quit the ballroom and search out Tobias, who'd been absent for the better part of the day. But convention demanded that he stay at his aunt's side, dutifully being introduced to London's elite who'd gathered in honor of his visit.

His cool gaze swept the ballroom, resting for a moment on a raven-haired beauty whose name had not escaped Jonathan. Lady Susan Billings had given Jonathan a bold stare before she'd followed her older husband across the room.

Even now, Jonathan could feel those sultry eyes on him, but he refused to return her torrid gaze. He had no time to offer comfort to the bored young wife of the elderly Lord Billings, not now, at any rate.

The sheen of jade satin caught Jonathan's attention as two more guests were announced. His gaze swept slowly up from the green slippers that seemed to barely skim the polished marble steps, past a sea of jade to a face so delicately lovely that Jonathan was transfixed. Jonathan felt his breath leave his body in a great gasp, as if someone had hit him soundly in the middle while he took in the radiant vision descending the steps. He had to force himself to breathe evenly, to take command of his senses as the beautiful young woman approached. Try as he might, he could not break the spell enveloping him.

He wanted to hold her, to kiss those softly shaped lips and bury his face in the golden flame of hair surrounding her lovely oval face. Her skin, like the finest bisque China, was fair and smooth over perfectly turned features. She was without rival as far as Jonathan could see. Even the lovely Lady Susan paled by comparison.

Remarkable. Jonathan watched the beauty slowly approach the side of a silver-haired, yet still attractive matron. She was, without question, the most exquisite creature Jonathan had ever seen. Suddenly, the thought of an evening spent with his friends at White's was infinitely less appealing.

The gleaming ballroom swirled with color while the Ton enjoyed the Season. Standing beside her grandmother, Spring took it all in. The dozens of debutants being introduced sought suitable matches, each trying to outdo the other as they paraded around the ballroom. Spring took a deep breath and tried to calm herself as they stood calmly waiting to be announced. It seemed all eyes had turned toward them.

A thrill of excitement coursed through Spring while she and her grandmother descended into the large ballroom aglow with a thousand candles.

The receiving line was long, and Spring felt nervous as she cast her gaze around the room in search of familiar faces. Across the room, she spotted Lady Susan Billings holding court with all the dandies paying court to the beauty who had married the aging Lord Billings two seasons ago. Rumor had it the marriage had been arranged to secure the financial security of her family. At the time,

Spring had thought it quite scandalous, but now she understood and felt kindlier toward Lady Susan.

Spring's gaze flitted past her host and hostess to the tall dark man standing beside Lady Sarah. Her knees turned to molten wax. She could hear her own pulse racing in her ears as her gaze encountered one of midnight intensity. She was drowning in a vortex of inexperience and longing as her gaze locked with his.

The world around them melted away when their eyes met across the distance. Never had Spring felt a more compelling gaze. She felt trapped by the midnight intensity of his eyes holding hers. A small tingle began low in the pit of her stomach and spread so that her entire body was alive in a way she had never experienced before.

For a moment, the prismatic mirror of his eyes reflected such longing that Spring felt it like a soft touch upon her heated skin. She trembled, unable to break away from his gaze.

Too late, she reminded herself, even as her grandmother caught her arm and pulled her closer to the dark countenance that would forever after haunt her dreams. She was lost in the power of his gaze, drowning in the unknown sensations swirling between.

This was what I wanted, wasn't it? To experience the thrill of meeting a dashing young man who would steal my heart away. To enjoy, if only for a few days, the pleasure of having my season? Memories to cherish during the bleak times to come.

Spring forced herself to smile brightly and straightened her small frame. This was her evening to shine. She would not think of the impending doom awaiting her. For tonight, she would be happy and carefree.

Closing her eyes, Spring took a deep breath, trying to bring under control the rioting emotions assailing her. She was overreacting, responding to the hopelessness of the life that stretched ahead of her. She'd never met this man before, and once she married Lord Wyndridge, she would never see him again.

"Jonathan, may I present my granddaughter, Lady Spring Melanie Lansing," the countess was saying, "Spring, this is Jonathan Andrew Sinclair, nephew to my dearest friend, Lady Sarah. Jonathan has only recently arrived from America."

"Most charmed to meet you, Mr. Sinclair," Spring said.

Holding out her glove clad hand, Spring centered her gaze on the ruffled silk of his white shirtfront.

He'd come here from the other side of the world, and her grandmother had hopes of some attachment growing between them?

What possible harm could it do to flirt just a little, to enjoy his attention for a short time?

"The pleasure is mine, I assure you, my lady," he returned, taking the hand she offered in a firm grasp and raising it to his lips, sending small volcanic eruptions all along her arm.

Even through the soft fabric of her glove, her hand burned with liquid flames where his lips had touched. The grasp of his tanned hand was an exquisite torture, yet she was loathe to break the contact.

Somehow, she'd known it would be like this when he touched her. With an effort of gigantic proportions, Spring raised her eyes to his while she gently pulled her hand from his grasp.

His eyes, deep lustrous brown almost to the point of black, had changed, and Spring could read no messages written in their depths. Despite what she'd thought she'd read in them seconds ago, now they held only the gleam of a man admiring a woman he found desirable.

It was only my imagination, Spring reassured herself as her grandmother led her away from the receiving line and across the ballroom floor where couples were beginning to dance.

Even before Lady Phoebe had found them a place to sit, Baron Rallyforth, a longtime acquaintance of Spring's father, was at their side beseeching Lady Phoebe for the pleasure of leading Spring out for the next set.

"You must ask my granddaughter," Lady Phoebe teasingly told Rallyforth.

Gallantly, he turned his attention to Spring, sweeping her a bow and flashing her a charming smile. "Lady Spring, please honor me with the next dance?"

For a moment, Spring's gaze searched the ballroom. Her eyes found the tall, dark figure as he led the lovely Lady Billings onto the dance floor. Her earlier congeniality toward Lady Susan evaporated.

For a moment, Spring felt a sensation not unlike pain in the region of her heart while she watched the couple.

"My lady?"

Spring forced a bright smile and exclaimed enthusiastically. "Your name will be the first on my card!"

Wasn't this what she'd come for, what she'd wanted? She'd hoped to enjoy the excitement of the season before the earl forced her into a life she could not bear to think of.

With eyes brightened by more than excitement, and a smile that didn't quite reach her eyes, Spring accepted Rallyforth's invitation, placing his name at the top of the card she held.

When Rallyforth returned to claim her for his dance, Spring went willingly onto the floor. Her body, with its natural gracefulness, moved through the steps of the dance effortlessly.

She smiled and nodded, hoping she was making the right responses to his words, but her gaze ever traveled across the room to the tall, wide shouldered form of Jonathan Sinclair.

Jonathan leaned against the wall near the French doors that opened out onto the balcony. His arms were folded across his broad chest, and his dark eyes seemed to smolder as they followed Spring's progress around the dance floor with her partner. She could feel his intent gaze on her even when her back was to him. She found it unnerving yet strangely exciting.

"Lady Spring, I swear you have broken my heart. I fear I shall never love another. How can you do this to me?" Rallyforth's protest brought her attention back to him as they moved with the flow of the music.

"How, pray tell, have I broken your heart?" Spring inquired as they continued to dance, but her gaze wandered across the swirl of colorful gowns and brilliantly dressed gentlemen to find a tall dark stranger.

"Your beauty has quite blinded me to all others. I am but your willing slave," Rallyforth gave her his most charming smile. "I shall never recover. Perhaps, I should join the foreign legion to forget you," he protested.

"I don't think Lady Jane Woodwind would care for that idea over much. Did I not hear that you were together last week at the opera?" Spring asked, laughing up into his handsome face.

Rallyforth smiled broadly. "She is a pale substitute for your beauty, my dear," he answered, resorting to his usual charm to get him out of a pinch.

"I'm sure she's capable of making your heart quite whole again."

"You underestimate your charms, my dear. I remain forever your devoted servant," Rallyforth said as he returned her to her grandmother.

No sooner had Rallyforth returned her to her grandmother than another young dandy was there to claim his dance and yet another offering to fetch her a cooling drink when Spring protested tiredness. She smiled up at the young man and accepted the glass he offered her.

When the music began for another set, she allowed him to lead her out on to the floor.

Still, she felt Jonathan's gaze on her. Excitement seemed to be building within her to a fevered pitch, making it hard to concentrate on the steps of the dance. She tripped and, protesting tiredness, pleaded with her partner to return to her grandmother.

Waiting at Lady Phoebe's side was the American. He watched with dark intensity as they approached. Jonathan's slight bow to young gallant was clearly a dismissal, and the latter quickly retreated as if realizing when he was out manned.

"Lady Phoebe has promised me your next dance," Jonathan said as his gaze rested on Spring, causing her pulse to skip a beat then begin again at a rapid rate.

"Run along and enjoy your dance, children," the countess said, tapping Jonathan's arm gently with her fan.

The music had changed. The glorious strains of a waltz flitted across the candle lit ballroom. Jonathan took Spring into his arms, and they floated around the ballroom.

The satin of her gown billowed like a jade sail behind them as Jonathan held her in the prison of his arms and whirled her expertly around the ballroom. Spring forgot the world around them as she experienced the heat of his arm at her waist. He held her discreetly, yet his hand at the small of her back sent messages of suppressed passion to assault her near befuddled mind.

It was only when the coolness of the night air touched her inflamed skin that Spring realized he'd maneuvered them out onto the balcony. The music sounded soft and far away, yet still he continued holding her in his arms as they moved in perfect time to the faintly drifting strains.

He studied her face as a thirsting man looks upon an oasis. Spring was transfixed by the power of his gaze as it swept her features. What sort of sorcerer was he that he held such sway over her? What was this spell he had cast upon her to make her long for his arms around her when she knew she should pull away?

"I've found you at last." The words seemed to come to her from far away as she stared hypnotically into the black abyss of his eyes.

What possible harm to pretend just for tonight that life could be different for her, to allow herself to experience just the slightest bit of the life that was to be denied her?

For tonight, she would forget Lord Wyndridge. For tonight, she would allow herself to experience the wonder of being desired by a man like Jonathan Sinclair.

His presence exacted such tremulous emotions within Spring that she dared not name them. She felt a strange fear, an intense longing, and the most bittersweet pain. She wanted this experience as she had wanted no other. Slowly, as if in a dream, she moved closer.

"You are exquisite," he breathed close to her ear, his warm breath fanning the soft golden tendrils that clung to the nape of her neck.

How wondrous it would be to hear such words and know they were sincere. Still, if that possibility was to be denied to her, she could at least savor the moment. Closing her eyes again, Spring leaned closer, feeling the heat emanating from his strong lean body. Lifting her face, she offered her lips.

For a moment, Jonathan hesitated. What was the minx playing at? Did she hope to add him to the trail of beaus hanging after her all evening? By offering a chaste kiss in the moonlight, did she expect her conquest would be complete?

Well, she was offering, but it was no chaste kiss that Jonathan had in mind. If the minx wanted to play the game, then she'd jolly well pay the piper. His arms tightened around her, pulling her against the hard wall of his chest.

Her eyes opened in surprise just as Jonathan's head descended toward her.

Jonathan closed the distance between their lips. He claimed her mouth with a thoroughness that sought to imprint his essence upon her and make her pay for the little game she'd set out to play. But the payment was not entirely Spring's. The taste of her was heaven and hell. Heaven in feel of her in his arms, hell in that he dared not take more.

Surprised when his arms tightened around her, Spring opened her eyes. For a fleeting second, she saw his dark, intense eyes as his head moved closer. When his lips claimed hers, the whole world spun wildly out of control. He was not supposed to kiss her this way, was not supposed to hold her this tightly against his lean, hard body.

She knew she should resist his impassioned kiss, and for a moment her small hands fluttered against the fabric covering his chest then stilled as pure instinct took over. Her fingers curled into the material, clinging to him like a lifeline as her world spun, careening out of control.

Spring was sure she would die there in his arms. Her body liquefied, held stable only by the jade satin of her gown and the strength of his arms around her. She had never felt like this, never experienced the burning that now engulfed her entire being. Spring was inundated with the strange new sensations that his lips evoked. Never had she imagined a kiss could be like this. A kiss? No, this was no mere kiss. This was possession. He had claimed her heart, body and soul, hypnotic sorcerer that he was. She clung to him, offering her lips as sacrifice, trusting him blindly as only a true innocent could.

Spring was trembling violently when finally he released her. She was an innocent, yet with this man she felt like a wanton. She wanted to learn, to experience, to give to him things she had never shared with any man. She could not understand the impact his presence had on her. She had flirted and toyed with all the young men in her circle of acquaintances, yet not one had ever aroused her the way Jonathan Sinclair had.

When Spring shivered, Jonathan was instantly attentive. Removing his coat, he placed it around her shoulders, then took his crisp white handkerchief out to gently blot away her tears. He led her down the steps and into the garden where he sought the shelter of a dormant rose arbor to protect them from the evening's chill.

The crystalline blue of her eyes drew him inexplicably to their enchanting depths. He smoothed a lock of gold from her pale cheek while he studied her beautiful face. She was exquisite. More beautiful than either Aunt Sarah or Uncle Charles had insisted. Her light golden eyebrows arched delicately over wide clear eyes of the palest shade of blue. Her lips, full and luscious now from the demands of his kisses, normally formed the most delightful cupid's bow. Her nose was small and narrow. Her skin held the beauty of the finest bone China, her cheeks the bloom of summer's rarest rose. She was perfection.

Jonathan forced thoughts of her beauty away. He had no time for romance. He had a mission. He must not be swayed from that mission, no matter how lovely the diversion.

"Better now?" he asked when the tears no longer slid down her smooth cheeks.

"Y—yes," she answered in a small quivering voice.

"I'm sorry," he apologized. "I didn't mean to frighten you, but I became quite carried away by your beauty."

They both knew there had been more to it than that.

"I'm fine now," Spring answered, trying to steady her voice. "I don't know what came over me. It's not that I haven't been kissed before." *But never like that.*

"Of course not," he agreed solemnly.

Spring looked up to see a teasing gleam in his dark eyes.

"I must go—inside—now," Spring stammered in confusion. "Grandmother will be searching for me."

"Not before you promise that I may see you again, my lady," Jonathan insisted.

Spring was fascinated by his slow drawl. "May I call on you tomorrow afternoon?"

A few days of stolen bliss? A memory to cherish during the dark years that stretched before her. How could she resist? She had almost two weeks before she was due to leave for Wyndridge. What harm would it do to see him just once more?

She nodded.

Later, after she had gone, Lady Sarah could tell him the truth. Spring turned and fled back into the crowded ballroom.

Chapter Four

Through the dark streets of London, the Lansing coach traveled with Spring huddled in one corner, brooding over her predicament. The shadowy images outside the coach window could offer no help, no relief.

Disgusted, Spring pulled the dark curtains closed against the dark, drab images of a London, so like her future, without benefit of sunlight or hope. She sank deeper into the corner. What could she do?

Why had fate been so cruel? She had just met the most fascinating, exciting man in the world. Spring groaned inwardly, feeling Lord Wyndridge's trap tightening around her. How could she go through with her promise to wed a man she could never love? But what could she do? Lord Wyndridge held all the advantages. She held none.

It just was not fair. She should have listened to her first instincts and stayed home. She would not have found herself infatuated with Jonathan Andrew Sinclair.

Spring's hands clenched into tight fists in her lap as she railed against the impasse to which fate had brought her.

Her family's happiness or her own, there was no question in Spring's mind which one must take precedence.

In the flickering light cast by the small lamp in the coach, Lady Phoebe watched her granddaughter fight an internal battle. *What could possibly be troubling the girl*? Lady Phoebe searched the shadows of Spring's lovely face. In this last year since her father's death, the child had taken everything so seriously, as if she bore the weight of the world on her small shoulders. Spring had not been herself for months. What had become of that smiling, carefree young sprite? Lady Phoebe squared her shoulders and decided to take the situation in hand.

"What is it, child? Won't you tell Grandmother what is troubling you?"

With a soft sigh Spring lowered her gaze to her clenched hands. "What am I to do?"

Lady Phoebe reached across to smooth the small frown that creased her granddaughter's forehead before lowering her hand to clasp one of Spring's clenched hands. Still Spring did not speak.

"What's this, my pet?" Lady Phoebe lifted Spring's chin to study her strained expression. "What is the cause of this little frown I've been seeing all evening? Did you not enjoy the ball? You were quite the smashing hit, you know. No one could hold a candle to you, my pet."

"Grandmother," Spring said, her hand clasping the thin, wrinkled one of the dowager. "What's it like to fall in love?"

Lady Phoebe smiled a small secret smile. "Love, my pet, is not unlike catching a cold. You feel hot, then cold, lightheaded and quite faint." Lady Phoebe laughed softly.

"Young love is the most beautiful thing in the world. Of course, your young gentleman will love you back. How can he help it? You're my granddaughter." Lady Phoebe chuckled, delighted at the apparent outcome of the scheme she and Lady Sarah had plotted.

Patting Spring's hand, she continued. "You must be patient. These things take time, you know."

Spring wanted to strike out at the fates that had brought her to this state. It just was not fair.

"But there is no time. I have promised to wed the Earl of Wyndridge. Even now the arrangements are being made. Within a fortnight I shall be the Countess of Wyndridge." Spring refused to give in to the tears gathered in her eyes. She would not allow her grandmother to see how very painful this disclosure had been for her.

Lady Phoebe shook her head as if to clear her mind. "Pray continue." Lady Phoebe pinned her granddaughter with a stern gaze. "Explain yourself this instant! What arrangements are being made? It would seem you have omitted some particularly crucial details." Lady Phoebe searched Spring's face carefully in the dim light.

Spring dropped her gaze to her clenched hands. She could find no words to explain.

"Why have you promised to marry Lord Wyndridge? What nonsense is this?"

Fighting for control, Spring took a deep breath and raised her gaze to meet her grandmother's. It was not easy to explain how she had let her family down and failed to uphold the trust her father had placed in her.

Lady Phoebe moved to sit beside Spring and placed her thin arm around her granddaughter's shoulders. Intuition told her there was more to this story than her granddaughter was telling.

"I think," Lady Phoebe began in slow measured tones booking no resistance. "It is time you explained to me just exactly what is going on."

Taking a deep breath, Spring told her story. Her bottom lip trembled with the effort to control the emotions assailing her as she explained the events that had transpired between her and the Earl of Wyndridge.

"The old fool, surely he does not think we will allow this marriage to take place," Lady Phoebe demanded when at last the tale was told.

"It must, I have no choice. Mama has been so frail since losing Papa. This would kill her." Giving a resigned sigh, Spring at last raised troubled eyes to those of her grandparent. "And what of the twins?

What chance would they have were it to become known that the Lansings were left without a feather to fly with?"

"Surely, there is something to be done. We must have time to think, to plan. We will think of something," Lady Phoebe insisted.

"There is no time. Wyndridge has agreed to the terms Papa's barrister set forth. The wedding shall take place within a fortnight," Spring answered. "I have no choice. Marriage to the earl is the only way to ensure a secure future for Mama and the twins. Papa expected me to take care of them, and I shall."

"Not to the extent of becoming shackled to an odious beast like the Earl of Wyndridge. My dear, the man is old enough to be your father." Lady Phoebe placed one thin finger against the still smooth skin of her cheek. Her brow wrinkled as she studied the situation her granddaughter had just outlined for her.

"It matters not. I shall marry the earl."

Lady Phoebe smoothed the lace handkerchief she held in her lap, her fingers tracing the embroidered initial at one corner. A secretive smile curled her lips. "I think not."

"Grandmother—"

"We shall send Lord Wyndridge your regrets. That is all there is to it," Lady Phoebe insisted.

"No, it's the debts, don't you see?" Spring insisted. "Papa had investments he expected to pay off handsomely. Instead, everything has come up wrong, so there isn't anything left. Only the debts, so many of them, and the earl has bought them up. He is going to take everything, even Lansing Hall, and put us into the street. Unless... Unless..."

"We must tell your mother."

"It would kill Mama, and I don't think I could bear to lose her, too. And the twins must have their season. No, there is no other way. I must marry the earl."

"What exactly has he promised you?" Lady Phoebe asked quietly.

"It's done all legal and proper. Papa's man of business oversaw everything. As a marriage settlement, Mama is to receive the deed to Lansing Hall and the notes on Papa's other properties will be paid. All the debts will be settled, and Mama will receive a yearly allowance. Promise you will not tell Mama," Spring beseeched.

"Yes, against my better judgment," Lady Phoebe reluctantly agreed. "Melanie has not been strong since Geoffrey..." Lady Phoebe smoothed the handkerchief in her lap. "There must be another way, something else we can do."

"No, Grandmother." Spring's eyes clouded with despair. "There is no other way." Spring sighed. "I wish had never gone to the ball," Spring said sadly. "If only he had not come."

"There is no way to change your mind about this marriage?"

"I must think of Mama and the twins."

Phoebe smoothed her granddaughter's golden curls. "My brave little pet, don't give up hope. We still have a few days. Let Grandmother worry over it for a while."

The Meldon Home

When Lady Sarah arose early and joined Jonathan for breakfast, he was delighted and tenderly plied his aunt with questions about Lady Spring Melanie Lansing.

Lady Sarah answered his questions with relish, adding even more tidbits of knowledge about the beautiful miss who had bewitched him the night before. Lady Sarah fairly bubbled over with praise for her friend's granddaughter.

Suddenly, Jonathan laughed loudly then leaned over to plant a kiss on his aunt's forehead. "You had it planned, didn't you?" he asked with another laugh.

"Whatever do you mean, Jonathan?" Lady Sarah asked with feigned innocence.

"Don't play coy with me, Aunt. You know very well what I mean," Jonathan answered with mock sternness.

"I'm sure that I don't know at all what you mean, Jonathan. You must explain yourself."

"I mean, dear Aunt, that you've been playing the matchmaker, again." Jonathan touched the tip of his aunt's nose with an accusing finger. "Tell me, was the countess in on your little scheme, or did you plot all by yourself?"

"Now Jonathan—"

"No, you'll not convince me otherwise," he interrupted her. "But I can't say I mind, this time. I find Lady Spring quite enchanting. Far more interesting than the fragile chit you sent to Riverside last summer. Did you really think I would be interested in Sophie?" Jonathan asked doubtfully.

"Well, father had said it was time you thought of settling down, and I quite thought Sophie would do at the time."

"And a word from Grandfather was all it took, was it not?"

"I see now that Sophie was all wrong for you dear, but Spring—"

"No, you don't. No more matchmaking." Jonathan cut her off.

Lady Sarah smiled at her nephew, thinking what a grand couple he and Spring had made on the dance floor the night before. Oh, to be young and in love. What fine children these two would produce, Lady Sarah finished her idle happily.

Jonathan did not fool her for a moment. She had seen the way his gaze had followed the lovely Lady Spring all evening, the way his jaw had set firmly each time Baron Rallyforth had approached the girl. He might not be aware of it yet, but her handsome nephew had fallen for Lady Phoebe's granddaughter with all the swiftness that his father had his mother.

Lady Sarah watched him as he finished his meal. The boy seemed less preoccupied and more relaxed than he had since arriving in

England. Lady Sarah smiled happily. *Just wait until Phoebe hears the news.*

The appearance of Toombs, the butler, in the dining room doorway ended Lady Sarah's appraisal of Jonathan's handsome features.

"Yes?" Lady Sarah turned toward the stern featured man.

"A Mr. Thomas Bailey to see Mr. Jonathan, my lady," Toombs said stiffly, looking down his nose at his employer's American guest.

"Show him to the library," Lady Sarah ordered.

Folding his napkin and placing it beside his plate, Jonathan rose from the table. "Excuse me, Aunt. A business matter." Jonathan hurried from the dining room.

The honorable Thomas Bailey stood before the large fireplace, studying the portrait of Lady Sarah Meldon as Jonathan entered the room. He turned at the sound of the younger man's approach.

"Your aunt is a very beautiful woman," Bailey said.

Jonathan crossed the room, flicking a glance at the portrait of a youthful Lady Sarah. "Remarkably so," Jonathan agreed then got right to the point. "You had something important to discuss, Mr. Bailey?"

Thomas Bailey cleared his throat. "Yes, I've come upon some interesting information I thought it best I tell you as soon as possible."

"Yes?"

"You know his lordship has returned to London?"

Jonathan nodded. He had paid well to have his lordship's London town house watched.

"Yes, well, I've just learned the reason for his hasty return."

Lady Sarah had never seen a darker look on her nephew's handsome face than when he walked calmly from the library and announced he and his companion were leaving as soon as possible.

At Jonathan's curt command, Tobias quickly saddled both horses and led them up to the back door of Lord Meldon's home just as Jonathan bounded out the door with Lady Sarah following close behind.

In the fever that gripped him, Jonathan ignored the bag of food Lady Sarah had quickly gathered for them when she had learned of their planned departure.

"Lad, what 'as lit such a fire under ye?" Tobias grumbled as he watched Jonathan swing onto Diablo's back.

Once again, Lady Sarah held out the bag, but Jonathan had wheeled the stallion around and was halfway out of the yard by then.

"I'll look after the lad, always 'ave," Tobias reassured as he reached for the bag that Lady Sarah held.

"We must reach the Boar's Head before night's fall."

"Keep ye shirt on, lad. These old bones be tired. Have a care for me age," Tobias grumbled as they hastened through the streets of London.

"Old bones, is it? I'll leave your old bones here in London to gather dust, if you like. His Lordship's bride arrives at Wyndridge Hall on the morrow. Best we be back at the inn before then. We wouldn't want to miss our invitation to the wedding, would we?"

Given his head, Diablo reached the inn all of six hours before the familiar clatter and jangle of harness from the courtyard announced the arrival of Earl Wyndridge's coach.

Jonathan sat nursing his tankard of ale and brooding. How could she marry Lord Wyndridge? Was it because of the wealth and power he possessed as the Earl of Wyndridge?

Was the chit willing to sell herself for the social position Lord Wyndridge could afford her?

And what of her life if Marcus could no longer provide her with that social prestige? Would she turn from him to another protector? Intense anger ate at Jonathan. *Curse her for the deceitful wench she is.*

How could she respond so ardently to his kisses when she was pledged to marry Lord Wyndridge?

Jonathan remembered the feel of her lithe young body against his and the way her pulse had raced when he had kissed her. There had been something between them, something strong, vital, and alive. Hadn't those kisses meant anything to her?

His brows drawn together, Jonathan stared into the near empty tankard in his hands before raising his gaze. Through the smoke darkened window, he watched as the passengers traveling in the Wyndridge coach disembarked. He was not concerned in the least that he would be discovered.

A lady of quality never ventured unescorted into the taproom of a wayside inn. No, his quarry would seek her refreshment in the comfort of one of the small private dining rooms provided for that purpose.

When Molly approached his table, Jonathan purposely showed keen interest in the way her full bosom thrust threateningly at the low neckline of her shift.

"Could I be getting you another dram?" the barmaid inquired, letting one lush breast brush Jonathan's arm as she reached for the empty tankard sitting upon the table.

"No, it's been a long day, and I'm rather tired. I shall retire to my room," Jonathan answered, rising from his chair and swaying slightly.

Molly quickly reached out to steady him. "Here, let me help ye," she offered, pulling his arm around her shoulders and pressing her ample breasts against the wall of his chest.

Putting much of his weight on her, Jonathan allowed her to help him toward the stairs. As they reached the top, he stumbled and pulled Molly down on top of him. She squealed with delight as his fingers found the round, softness of her breasts.

"So that be the way of it, eh?" she asked as she struggled to help him rise. "Well, just you wait 'til I get ye ta' ye room."

Jonathan allowed her to help him to his feet. Then, still leaning heavily upon her, continued along the narrow hall until they reached his room. He pretended to search his pockets for the key but pulled out a gold coin instead. He tucked the coin into the deep crevice between the mounds of Molly's breasts.

She smiled her pleasure, "I'd be going with ye without the money, I would. Such a fine one ye are, and here I was thinking that ye did not like me. But it just took ye a while to get ye courage up, eh? Well, don't be worrying now, Molly will show ye a real good time," she promised as she took the key he finally produced and quickly unlocked the door.

Darkness shrouded the room as with Molly in tow Jonathan crossed bare the wooden floor and collapsed upon the bed. He pulled the serving wench across him and ran his hands over her voluptuous curves. She was pretty enough, but still something held him back. Mumbling incoherently in her ear, Jonathan allowed his hands to gradually slow their exploration of her body, then finally still, he pretended to fall into a heavy sleep.

After some moments, Molly stirred, shaking him, trying to rouse him, at which Jonathan snored loudly. Finally giving up the effort, she slid from beneath his weight of his arm and slipped from the bed.

"More's the pity. Looking forward to pleasuring ye, I was," she said as she stood looking down at his prone form. "Had me eye on ye ever since ye arrived, I have. A man what can't hold his ale should no be a drinking it," Molly complained as she fished the coin from her bosom and tested it between her teeth. "I'll be thanking ye for this," she muttered as she returned the coin to its hiding spot and left the room.

Two riders left the forest and headed along the coach road in the direction of Wyndridge hall. That they were up to no good was evidenced by the fact that they wore black masks to hide their faces.

The taller and thinner of the two wore a black cloak, while his companion wore a curious fur coat.

"Since when are we interested in 'is lordship's bride?" asked the shorter of the two as they rode quietly along the road.

"Since the time I decided to abduct her," the highwayman answered.

"Abduct? Be ye daft? 'Is lordship will see ye 'anged drawn and quartered, 'e will. 'E'll spread ye body to the four corners of England as they did in the old days."

"Yes, but he's got to catch me first, and I don't plan to allow him do that," the highwayman answered with a grin.

"Took yer sweet time leaving that room," the shorter man complained as he dismounted and stood beside his companion.

"I'm here now, just needed to be sure the wench believed my act. It's going quite well," the highwayman told his accomplice.

"Well as it's gonna be. This be the devil's own business, I tell ye," the man muttered, shaking his head.

"But it was your idea to make him pay, was it not, old friend?"

"'is Lordship, yes. But not the lady. She's done nothing for us to 'arm 'er."

"Harm her?" The highwayman appeared offended by the idea. "Nae, I shall not harm her, more like save her from a fate worse than death."

"Ye be sure the lady's not staying the night at the inn?"

"Quite certain," the first answered. "Take my word for it."

Chapter Five

The small private dining room was quaint but adequate for their needs. The food served by the innkeeper consisted of a rich hare soup, mutton cutlets with tangy sauce, bread, and cheese.

Spring pushed the food around on her plate. Each bite seemed to grow as she chewed. Her appetite deserted her in face of the looming wedding. Even Lady Phoebe's treasured presence did not help to dispel the despair that engulfed Spring.

The innkeeper hovered about, making sure Lady Phoebe and Spring were pleased with the meal he served them.

"Ye will be sure to tell his lordship we took good care of ye?"

Lady Phoebe inclined her head slightly. "I shall inform his lordship of your service to us. Please let the coachman know we will be leaving at once. My granddaughter and I wish to arrive at Wyndridge Hall as soon as possible."

"Yes, my lady." The innkeeper scurried away.

After changing the horses, the coachman ate a quick meal of mutton, bread, and cheese. Then he hurried to see to his passenger's comfort. Less than an hour later, they were quickly back on the road.

Evening had fallen, and everything was now cast in deepening shadow, the passing countryside hardly discernible. *No more than an hour*, the driver had said as they had left the inn. Spring shifted on the seat, trying to find a more comfortable position but decided it was hopeless and gave up.

She had wanted to spend the night at the inn where they had stopped for a late dinner, but Lady Phoebe had insisted they continue their journey. Greatly vexed, Spring had thought her grandparent most unreasonable. Still, Spring knew her grandmother held her best interest at heart; hadn't she insisted on accompanying her? With a deep sigh, Spring turned away from the coach window.

When her father died a little over a year ago, Spring had been grief stricken as the rest of the family had been, but she had felt confident that they would survive even without Lord Lansing's guiding hand.

Six months ago things had begun to go wrong; the last straw had been the ultimatum Lord Wyndridge had issued. Anger flared in her eyes as she thought of the irrevocable turn her life had made. Shrugging, Spring closed the curtains against the darkness outside and continued to brood on her circumstances.

She had tried to tell herself she was not responsible for what had happened, that there was nothing she could have done to stop the earl from gaining the upper hand. It was almost as if he had planned their downfall, had somehow been able to orchestrate it all. Spring slowly shook her head, thinking it hardly possible.

Stretching her tired legs in the cramped space, Spring longed for the pleasure of a hot bath and her own bed. She glanced at her grandmother, who appeared to be resting comfortably on the seat across from her.

How could she remain so calm? Grandmother was not the one who would soon be marrying Lord Wyndridge. Spring tried to shake the feeling that her grandmother had somehow let her down. She knew it was wrong for her to feel that way. What was it she had expected Grandmother to do? Her grandmother could not perform miracles, and that was the only thing that could save her now.

The knot in the pit of Spring's stomach seemed to tighten when she envisioned her future. With a determined shrug of her slim shoulders, Spring pushed away the torrent of thoughts plaguing her. *I should follow grandmother's example and get some rest.* Spring studied her companion. Lady Phoebe had again settled into a light doze as her head lolled with the rocking of the coach.

Would Lord Wyndridge be waiting for them? Fervently, Spring prayed not. She would much rather postpone meeting her future bridegroom for as long as possible.

How different she would have felt if she were to wed Jonathan Sinclair. Spring felt the knot in her stomach tighten, twisting almost painfully.

Soon there would be no escaping the fate awaiting her. *I need a white knight to take me away on his charger. But there is no knight in shining armor waiting to rescue this damsel in distress.*

The Main Coach Road

The highwayman had chosen his spot carefully for the overhanging heavy oaks and the narrowness of the roadway. Here the road curved and twisted so that the coach would have to slow its speed. Here he would launch his assault.

Time had not allowed them the preference of using a felled tree to stop the coach. They dared not risk having other travelers come upon their machinations and sound the alarm, especially since Wyndridge's coach now had an armed guard riding beside the coachman.

Having been stopped by a highwayman once, the coach was more than likely to run down anyone trying to stop it. The highwayman had no wish to be run down by the matched team drawing the earl's coach.

Instead, he handed the stallion's reins to his companion and swung himself from the saddle up onto the low hanging branches of a large oak with limbs hung over the roadway. As his accomplice urged both horses back into the cover of the shadowed roadside, the highwayman crept carefully along the large limb and crouched low, awaiting the arrival of his quarry.

"This time try to be more original. Sounded like one of Miss Mattie's novels the last time, ye did," the man holding the horses said with a snort. "Stand and deliver! Near shot ye meself, I did!" he complained as the highwayman flashed him a quick grin.

The clatter of hooves and jangle of harness heralded the approach of a coach. Approaching the narrow curving road, the coachman slowed the horses.

The highwayman steadied himself on the limb, waiting until his accomplice identified the coach as Wyndridge's, then propelled himself downward and onto its top when it passed slowly beneath his perch.

Neither the driver nor the armed guard riding beside him detected the slight jolt as the highwayman's weight hit squarely on the polished wood behind them.

With hardly a second spared to gain his footing, the highwayman then crept forward and pressed the barrel of his pistol into the guard's back.

"Throw down your weapon, friend," the highwayman grated, his words a coarse whisper above the noise of the lumbering coach.

SPRING WORRIED OVER her grandmother's lack of stamina. She should not have allowed the dear lady to accompany her. Not that she could have stopped her once she had realized Lord Wyndridge had demanded Spring depart immediately for Wyndridge Hall.

Lady Phoebe had insisted on accompanying her granddaughter for moral support. Spring glanced toward her napping companion through lowered lashes, wishing she could escape into the oblivion of sleep, as well.

Lady Phoebe had tried to stay awake to offer solace to her granddaughter. But the lady, no longer young, had finally succumbed to the fatigue of their journey.

Spring smiled ruefully as the swaying of the coach slowed then stilled. Her mind snapped to attention as her ears tuned to the silence from outside.

Lady Phoebe stirred, uttering something between a moan and a snort, then lifted her head from its uncomfortable position against the velvet lined wall. Her eyes focused questioningly on Spring.

"So, we've arrived?" Lady Phoebe asked as she straightened the crumpled silk of her skirt.

"I'm not sure. It's so quiet..." Spring answered, reaching toward the gold velvet curtains covering the window beside her. "and dark I can't see a thing. Surely there—"

Suddenly the coach rocked, its springs creaking, and she heard the sounds of a scuffle. When the motion of the coach had subsided, Spring again reached to push the curtain aside and peered into the darkness.

Where is the coach's lantern? Why isn't it lit? She tried to see through the night that closed around them.

In answer to her unspoken question, a figure materialized from the darkness. Dressed entirely in black, the figure was bathed in a pool of yellow light cast from the lantern held in his hand. He moved quickly to the side of the coach and hung the lantern on the hook beside the coachman's seat before turning back toward Spring.

"A Highwayman!" she gasped when she saw the black silk mask covering the tall figure's face.

When a large hand clad in black leather reached for the latch on the carriage door, Spring shrank back against the gold cushions.

Lady Phoebe moved forward to protect her granddaughter, signaling that Spring should remain quiet.

"We are but defenseless women. Leave us alone," Lady Phoebe ordered, positioning herself between Spring and the menacing form that now stood in the open doorway of the coach.

The highwayman pushed Lady Phoebe gently out of his way and reached for Spring. His leather encased hand closed tightly around Spring's wrist.

She fought the firm grip pulling her closer and closer to his black clad form.

She sensed the strength of iron in his grip, yet strangely it was not painful, merely determined.

Struggle though she might, Spring could not break the hold the highwayman had on her.

Finally, she was forced to place her hands against the figure's chest to keep her body from being crushed against his. Her effort was futile when she pressed her palms against the hard muscles of his chest, seeking to keep her a measure of decency between them. When she lost the struggle, her breasts crushed against the hard wall of his chest.

Changing her avenue of attack, she reached up, her fingers grasping the smooth black silk of his mask. Her fingers tingled at the contact. The smooth material spread warmth from the heat of the firm flesh beneath it.

She continued to struggle in his arms. He looked like a great black bird of prey, Spring decided as she took in the flowing black cloak and matching silk mask covering the top half of his face.

"Let me go," Spring demanded. Her voice trembled far more than she would have liked. She fought down the scream that rose in her throat. "Take your hands off me this instant, you... you insufferable, masked bandit!"

She struggled as he pulled her slowly closer and closer to the door of the coach. Reaching up, Spring tried to scratch the face that was so close to hers that she could feel his warm breath on her face. His breath was not unpleasant but rather tickled at a memory that quickly skittered away. Her fingers clawed but encountered the smooth surface of silk rather than his skin.

With little effort, the highwayman captured her hands before any damage was done to either the mask or his features hidden beneath it.

Despite her resistance, the man's arms locked around her and swept her from the coach and into his embrace.

All Spring's efforts to kick and struggle were useless against the superior strength of the man holding her manacled against his chest. He strode silently to the massive black horse that appeared from nowhere and placed Spring upon the giant beast's back. Not sparing her a second to try for an escape, the man swung himself into the saddle behind her.

Again his strong arms claimed her as their prisoner, holding her tightly against the firmness of his chest. His thighs were hard against her buttocks. The heat of embarrassment flooded her cheeks at the intimate contact.

She'd never been this close to a man before, never felt the power of masculine muscle pressing intimately against her bottom. She squirmed, trying to lessen the contact but only managed to make it worse.

The heat in her face increased as the rising evidence that her captor was all male pressed against the soft roundness of her backside through the layers of her skirts.

"Barbarian, bully, ruffian, let me go," Spring gasped in outrage as the realization dawned on her how precarious was her position.

"Unhand my granddaughter, you ruffian!" Lady Phoebe, who had stepped from the coach, demanded, holding the only weapon within her reach, a silk parasol, and wielding it threateningly. "Take our jewels, if you must, but leave us be. We've done you no harm."

The highwayman moved back out of reach of the blows Lady Phoebe sought to land on him. He held Spring tightly yet not brutishly as his arm around her waist pinned her firmly against him.

The stallion protested with a loud snort as one blow found its way to the animal's flank, but the highwayman held the horse in check. He skillfully backed the stallion away from the woman wielding her parasol like a club.

Now Spring could see there were two of them. The other man held a large pistol. The gun was trained on the earl's driver and guard who stood helplessly in the roadway.

"Unhand her, I say," Lady Phoebe demanded, again advancing on the highwayman. "She's naught but an innocent child."

"The future Countess of Wyndridge a mere child?" he taunted, confidently backing the stallion out of range of Lady Phoebe's wild blows.

"You won't get away with this," Lady Phoebe warned, advancing on the highwayman.

Turning the stallion and again backing away from Lady Phoebe's weapon, the highwayman answered, "Give 'is lordship a message," the highwayman began in his raspy voice, but suddenly his voice, though still a low whisper, lost its clipped intonations. "Tell him, I covet only that which he calls his own."

At last Lady Phoebe realized that nothing she said would make any difference to the man. He'd decided to kidnap her granddaughter, and there was naught she could do. Still she continued her protests. "But you can't do this," Lady Phoebe moaned weakly as she raised one hand to her head and crumbled daintily into a swoon on the ground.

Spring was terrified now. She had been sure that her determined, strong-willed grandparent could manage the situation. No harm would befall her while in her grandmother's care, or so she had thought. Frantic, Spring renewed her struggles, knowing she was now at the mercy of the highwayman.

Putting his heels to the flanks of the stallion, the highwayman urged it away from the pool of light cast by the lantern.

Spring strained against the arms holding her. Her nails dug into the black leather covering the hands gripping the reins in front of her. She leaned as far to the side as his grip would allow, peering back at the pool of dim yellow light cast by the coach's lantern.

The second highwayman had left his vigil and now followed close behind them, the hooves of his horse flying as he urged it to catch the black giant. But it was the crumpled figure of her grandmother, lying as still as death on the roadway beside the carriage that held her attention.

Spring urged her to move, to show some sign that she still lived. What if... the thought was beyond bearing, so Spring pushed it away.

Finally, the lantern was no more than a glimmer of fairy light in the darkness that surrounded them, and Spring gave up the effort to see her grandmother.

She was alone, on her own, quite defenseless against the superior strength of the black clad demon who held her.

The giant beast upon which they rode thundered down the roadway. His hooves pounded dangerously over the rutted ground. Anyone who fell beneath those thundering hooves would surely be killed instantly.

While they were mounted, she dared not try to escape the arms holding her safely away from those thundering hooves.

Shuddering at the knowledge of her own vulnerability, Spring refused to give in to the fear threatening to claim her. As long as she breathed, she would fight!

Chapter Six

His lordship, Marcus Tollersley, the Earl of Wyndridge, reached up to bang the ivory handle of the cane he held against the roof of the rented equipage he rode in.

At the driver's answering shout, the earl commanded again. "Hurry, I say! We're less than an hour behind them now."

Lord Wyndridge rolled the ivory tipped cane between his hands, his mind on the pleasure he anticipated at the young chit's expense. He would soon teach her to obey his orders.

And it would take even less time for him to send that mettlesome old baggage on her way. Defy his orders, would they? He would soon teach them with whom they were dealing.

He had been enraged on learning that Lady Phoebe had insisted she accompany her granddaughter.

The lessons he had planned for his young wife were better learned in private, without the presence of any of her family.

Wyndridge ruled with an iron hand on his estate. Not one hand would be lifted to stop anything he did. No one would risk his ire to help the young chit, but Lady Phoebe was a different story.

This last victory was to be the crowning achievement in his planned revenge against those who had long ago spurned him in favor of his brother.

Even as a child, he had known his parents favored his brother. Their mother had doted on Edward, sparing little affection for Marcus. Hatred burned violently within him at the memory. But they had never guessed that he knew the truth. Lord Wyndridge's fingers tightened on the cane as he remembered.

"Faster, driver," the earl shouted over the rattle of the coach. "We must overtake them."

Poised upon the edge of the seat, Lord Wyndridge again twirled his cane while he contemplated the success of his plan.

The hired equipage barreled around a curve in the narrow roadway. The driver stood on the brake, cursing when he saw the coach stalled in the roadway ahead. His lordship was thrown forward, nearly losing his seat as the coach tumbled to a violent stop. Irate, the earl threw open the curtain and stuck his head out the window to berate the careless driver.

"Appears to have been an accident, milord," the driver called down, anticipating his passenger's response to this new delay.

Lord Wyndridge quickly opened the coach door and swung himself down, complaining of the inconvenience.

Just ahead of them in the roadway was a stranded coach. In the dim light of its lantern, his lordship saw a man holding the prone form of a woman in his arms.

It took a few seconds for the earl's eyes to adjust to the lack of light, but soon he recognized the familiar shape of the Wyndridge coat of arms on the stalled vehicle.

"What's happened here?" Wyndridge demanded, rushing up and looking quickly inside the empty coach before he turned on the quaking coachman.

"'Twas the highwayman, milord."

"Blood hell, man? Did I not tell you not to stop for anything?"

"He jumped us from behind, milord," the driver tried to explain. "Fell on us from out of the trees, he did."

"And your other passenger, the future Countess, where is she?" Wyndridge demanded.

"He took the lady, milord." the driver explained, dropping his gaze to the ground.

"You did nothing to stop him? What kind of incompetence is this?"

"There were two of them, milord. One held us at gun point while the other took the lady from the coach. Her Ladyship tried to stop them from taking the lady and just look what they have done to her," the driver answered, indicating the unconscious form of the dowager Countess.

"Where is Peters?" Wyndridge demanded for the first time missing the other coach attendant.

"He's gone after the horses, milord. The highwayman cut them loose to stop us from going for help. Left her ladyship here to die, they did."

As if on cue, Lady Phoebe moaned softly and began to struggle out of the arms of the man who had held her cradled for the better part of an hour.

"My pet, what have they done with you?" Lady Phoebe mumbled when she opened her eyes and tried to focus on the shadowy figures around her.

As the lady regained her composure, the driver seemed to remember that he may have overstepped his place by touching the countess, even if she were in distress. He quickly moved away from her, not sure what her response might be.

"Here, man," Lady Phoebe demanded in her usual brisk tone. "Help me up. Don't just stand there gawking at me."

The driver stepped back to the lady's side and helped her stand, holding her arms gently as the dowager sought to steady herself. Lady Phoebe's gaze fell on the earl.

"You!" Lady Phoebe lashed out at the earl. "This is all your fault. They have taken my granddaughter, and it's all your doing. If anything happens to Spring, I will see that the Queen hears of what you've done." Lady Phoebe struck out at the earl with her right hand, but he caught it before any harm was done.

The earl's eyes narrowed as he saw the long, black feather clutched in her hand. Slowly, he pried her fingers from the shiny feather and drew it through his hand, staring at it intently.

"Where did that come from?" Lady Phoebe asked as she gazed at the long black feather.

"The highwayman put it in your hand, milady," the driver answered. "After he'd set the horses loose, he came over and took the feather from his hat and put it in your hand after you'd fainted milady."

"Did he indeed?" Lady Phoebe said, outraged at the assault on her defenseless person.

The steady clip clop of hooves from down the coach road announced the return of Peters with the runaway team.

Within moments, the rented coach had been dismissed, Lady Phoebe installed back into the Wyndridge coach, and, with the earl sitting facing her, the entourage continued its journey.

Wyndridge sat deep in thought as he pulled the black feather continually through his hand. A seething anger boiled inside him. He hated to be bested by any man, and especially by a specter from the past.

He would catch this highwayman, and then he would take pleasure in watching the man die a slow, prolonged death.

Make a target of the Earl of Wyndridge, would he?

Somehow, Marcus knew this highwayman was no ordinary bandit, that he wanted more than to lighten his pockets every chance he got. It was as if he gained pleasure from humiliating and persecuting him.

Lady Phoebe fanned herself, worrying over the fate of her granddaughter. What had become of her? Where had they taken her? What was it that the villain had said?

Give his lordship a message. Yes, he had said that, but what had the message been? Lady Phoebe closed her eyes trying to picture the highwayman in her mind.

Suddenly he loomed there, just as frightening as he had been in person. The words he had spoken rang through her mind as if he spoke them again.

"Tell his lordship I covet only that which he calls his." Lady Phoebe eyes flew open. "The highwayman said that, those were his words."

"Damned, cur!" Earl Wyndridge roared striking his cane against the seat beside Lady Phoebe. "This time I won't give up the search until I've captured him, and then he'll know a taste of my wrath."

Lady Phoebe jumped as the cane resounded upon the seat beside her.

"But what about my granddaughter?" Lady Phoebe demanded. "I insist you find her at once. When I think of her at the mercy of those men...."

Lady Phoebe began to fan herself rapidly. "Oh dear, I feel quite faint," she said as the coach continued its journey. "I must insist that you send for the doctor immediately when we reach Wyndridge Hall."

The highwayman slowed his large steed to a walk, unafraid of capture now that they were far away from the coach road. Spring tensed in fear.

What did he intend to do with her? Why had he abducted her? She had no money, no jewels save the earl's betrothal ring on her finger. With that she would have gladly parted.

What was it the highwayman had said? Spring trembled with fear as she remembered. "Only that which the earl calls his."

Fighting to contain her mounting fear, Spring cached her strength for another attempt at freeing herself from her captor, but the grip pinning her against the hard, muscular chest was unrelenting. It was useless since her strength was as nothing against the power in the arms that imprisoned her.

Continuing her struggle, Spring managed to twist herself around so that she faced the man holding her. In the pale moonlight, she could see the determined, stubborn jut of his jawline. His face below the mask was clean shaven and deeply tanned. The eyes behind their satin shield were dark yet snapped with fire when they met Spring's.

Reaching up, she caught the mask, seeking to remove it, but her attempt was stayed by the grip of a black clad hand. Spring trembled as his dark gaze bore into her, willing her to surrender.

Something about the man's eyes left Spring breathless, even as she trembled with an unnamed fear.

They entered a small clearing, and the highwayman reined in the stallion. He sat quietly for a moment, listening to the night sounds of the woods around them before he turned to his companion.

"Double back to see if anyone is on our trail," he ordered. His hold on Spring remained firm.

With a silent nod, the other highwayman turned his horse and left without a word.

Her captor dismounted then lifted her to stand beside him. "You must be tired, but it's not far now. Soon you can rest."

Spring stiffened as his hand caressed her shoulder with undue familiarity. She trembled at his touch. A lump of fear rose in her throat, but she fought it down.

"What do you want from me?" she asked, dreading the answer. "I have naught of value save this ring given me by Lord Wyndridge. You may have it," she said, pulling the ring from her finger and placing it in his hand.

When he said nothing, Spring stammered, "I... I..." then began again. "Lord Wyndridge will pay handsomely for my safe return. I'm sure you have need of the money. His lordship will pay you."

"Indeed?" the highwayman said with an insulting sneer.

His dark gaze studied her in the moonlight, seeking to read what was written in her heart. Spring had to fight the impulse to turn away from his soul-searching eyes.

His eyes behind the mask took on a dangerous glint.

What had he discovered in those few moments? When he spoke again, Spring felt her breath catch and knot painfully in her chest.

"You'd prefer being returned to Lord Wyndridge, foul creature that he is?"

His words tore painfully at Spring's conscience. Wrapping herself in her stubborn pride, she lifted her chin and spoke as haughtily as she could under the circumstances. "Should I prefer the attentions of a common highwayman who shall see his days end on the gallows?"

The cool leather of his gloved hand caressed the soft skin of her throat tenderly, sending a chill along her spine.

"'Ere be plenty would find me touch not unpleasing," her masked abductor challenged in his strange coarse voice, the clipped pronunciation leaving Spring confused at the change in his manner of speech.

"I shall never be one of them, for my heart belongs to another," Spring answered indignantly.

As if in anger, his hand tangled in the curls at her nape, arching her neck. Lowering his head until there was hardly any space between them, he whispered, his lips caressing hers as he spoke, "Careful of throwing out such challenges, my lady. Some men can't resist a dare."

His firm mouth covered hers, moving urgently against her lips, demanding a response. His teeth found her tender flesh and nibbled delicately. The tip of his tongue sought entry to the recesses of her mouth. His hand tangled deeper into her hair and held her steadfast against his tender attack.

Never had Spring been so thoroughly kissed. She was drowning, swept away in a wild, swirling maelstrom of emotions she had never imagined possible. Her body trembled under the onslaught of his kiss.

An overwhelming response built within her, and Spring fought hard to crush it down. She was not some wanton who responded to the touch of just any man. She was Lady Spring Lansing, gently reared and well-schooled in how to react to all manner of circumstances, but nothing Miss Grey had ever taught her had prepared Spring for her overwhelming response to the highwayman's kiss.

The taste and feel of him were almost familiar, a shadowy remembered thing as the kiss went on and on, draining every ounce of resistance from her. Torrid thoughts flashed through Spring's mind as he kissed her, herself in Jonathan's arms, the ardent response of her body pressed against Jonathan's, the exciting, unfamiliar fire that consumed her when Jonathan touched her.

Spring felt the sting of tears in her eyes as she realized it was the remembered touch of Jonathan she was responding to and not this dangerous, callous bandit who held her in his arms. Her traitorous body was reliving the responses it had so willingly and freely given Jonathan.

In doing so, she was betraying both Jonathan and herself. She did not want to respond to this man, did not want to feel his hands on her, his body pressed against hers. Somehow, when Jonathan had held her and kissed her, she had known it was right, was meant to be. But not this, never this!

The image of Jonathan gave Spring the strength to resist, to fight the arms that held her. She pushed against the hard wall of his chest, seeking to break the intimate contact, but still he held her pinned against him. His mouth twisted over hers, demanding a final surrender from her. Spring fought back in the most basic, primitive way left to her, sinking her teeth into the softness of the lips ravishing her. The warm, salty taste of blood filled her mouth as the highwayman cursed and slackened his grip on her.

He raised a hand to his mouth, fingers gently assessing the blood left from her attack. Free for the moment, Spring realized it was now or never. She could feel the heat of anger radiating from him. If she did not escape now, this instant, she was lost.

Now was no time to act the demure young lady. Too much was at stake. With firm resolve, her actions were swift and effective. Using a move she had once seen employed by a kitchen maid to unman an overly amorous stable boy, Spring brought her knee up sharply into the highwayman's groin. At the same time, she pushed hard against his chest.

Uttering a loud curse, he bent double in pain, and Spring broke away from him.

"Damnation! Hellish vixen!" His words followed her as Spring lifted her skirts and fled to the safety of the dark woods. "Just wait'll I get my hands on you!"

Chapter Seven

Blindly Spring ran, branches and briars scratched her tender flesh and tore at the soft material of her gown. Her heart pounded against her rib cage like a frightened bird she had once seen trapped in her grandmother's solarium.

That bird had battered itself against the glass until finally it had fallen lifeless to the floor.

Spring's lungs ached from the effort to provide oxygen to her tortured limbs. She could hear nothing now save the heated rush of her own blood echoing in her ears as it surged violently through her veins.

If I can allude my abductor, I have a chance. Her foot caught on a gnarled root and sent her sprawling toward the dark woodland floor.

When her head hit solidly against a small boulder, a thousand stars exploded behind her eyelids. The world went dark around her. She sank silently into oblivion.

The gloom of the night sky taunted Jonathan with his inability to find the vixen who had rendered him temporarily stunned and made her daring escape through the darkening woods.

Jonathan cursed the provocation that had brought about his downfall and allowed Spring to escape his grasp. He had intended to assure her of her safety in his care. Really, he had, but something about her avowed love for another had put the burr under his saddle well and proper. He could not stop himself from trying to wipe all thought of his uncle from her mind.

Jonathan cursed the darkness around him as he searched for Spring, calling himself all manner of fool for bringing her to this danger. For an instant, he had seen the faint glimmer of her golden hair just ahead of him.

One moment she was there, almost within his grasp, the next she had vanished completely. Jonathan stared around himself in disbelief.

Now, with Spring lost and alone somewhere in the darkness, prey to whatever fate might befall her, he could not help but reproach himself. Had his motives been so noble, after all?

Indeed, was he that much better than his uncle? What, exactly, had he intended to do with her once he got her out of Wyndridge's clutches?

The sound of the woods surrounded him, unbroken by the presence of another such as himself. He strained his ears for any sound that would tell him the direction Spring had taken.

She could not have simply vanished into thin air. Frantic, he narrowed his gaze, trying to penetrate the darkness around him.

"My Lady," he shouted. "God's teeth, answer me, woman!" He swore under his breath.

"Spring."

No response came to his shouts of her name. He knew, of course, that thinking her life in danger, Spring would not answer.

Yet still he tried again and again as he pushed through the dense undergrowth.

As the minutes stretched into half an hour and then that into a whole, a deep sense of dread took hold of Jonathan.

He had to find her, to protect her from anything that might hurt her.

Because of him, she was out there alone, and it would be his fault if any harm befell her.

Abandoning caution, Jonathan continued to push his way through the dense growth of bramble and brush. *Surely, Spring did not come this way.* She would have become helplessly tangled in the briars that slashed at his black cloak and ripped at his trousers as he struggled to push his way through them.

The damp night air smelled of salt and sea. The sound of the surf pounding relentlessly against the shore rode upon the wind.

Knowing he was nearing the cliffs overlooking the sea, Jonathan urged himself to use caution, but he pushed through the last barrier of bramble and stepped through to find his feet anchored firmly in nothingness.

Grappling wildly at the growth that somehow managed to survive on the craggy cliff face, Jonathan managed to break his fall toward the rocks below.

Slowly, he pulled himself up the face of the cliff. The wind caught his cloak, sending it billowing like a sail, threatening to carry him away from his precarious hand hold and hurl him outward and down to certain death. Wrapping one arm around the stubby tree that had become his lifeline, Jonathan quickly undid the fastening of the cloak and it fluttered away into the darkness below.

A sudden chilling fear filled Jonathan. He struggled to pull himself back up the sheer face of the cliff.

Spring. His mind railed against the idea that she might have suffered the fate which had very nearly claimed him.

Frantic, he struggled to master the elements trying to destroy him. He damned her for escaping and himself for bringing her to this. He ranted to the wind whipping wildly around him.

And then he prayed, something Jonathan seldom did. Prayers not for himself but for Spring.

"Dear God, let her live. I'll return her to her grandmother. Just let her live." It was not a bargain easily made, but it was one he fully intended to keep.

After a prolonged struggle, Jonathan pulled himself to safety and made his way along the rim of the cliff to a path that made a steep and treacherous descent to the beach.

He was familiar with this section of the beach, for it was here Tobias had located the cave that served as Diablo's stable.

As he scoured the beach, searching for Spring, Jonathan berated himself. He should have told her who he was as soon as they were away from the coach. Why had he waited?

Jonathan knew the answer to that. His pride had been pricked by her words of love for another. He had wanted to make her acknowledge the strange attraction sparking between them the moment their eyes had met. Had wanted to make her desire him as he desired her.

Instead, he had frightened her, and she had run away. Now both were paying dearly for his foolish pride.

Just possibly, he had lost her forever. The thought sent a chill all the way through him. Terror such as he had never known gripped him. If Spring had come to harm the fault was his. He should have called Marcus out and killed him to free her.

Sheer desperation kept Jonathan going all night. He put aside the highwayman's guise then stabled Diablo in the cave before returning once more to search for Spring.

He combed the rocky stretch of sand bathed in the pale moonlight, watching the way the surf broke over the rocks. Was that something there in the shadows? No, just a reflection from a passing cloud.

When he found no trace of Spring on the beach, Jonathan returned to the woods and searched for her. He called to her, but there was no answer. Frantic now, he refused to give up the search and made the tortuous trek back to the beach. He walked along the water's edge, dodging the surf now and again. Still, he found nothing.

Finally, just before dawn, Jonathan made his way back to the cave where Diablo was stabled.

He took the cup of coffee Tobias offered him and sat on the low cot with the warm mug held between his hands.

"They'll be missing ye at the inn, mayhap ye should be getting back. Leave me to look for milady."

"No!" Jonathan exploded. "It's my fault she's here. I will find her and take her back where she belongs!"

"And what are ye going to do 'bout the innkeeper?" Tobias asked as he threw an armful of sweet-smelling hay into the stall with the stallion.

"I don't care about the innkeeper," Jonathan said flatly. "I have to find the Spring."

"Reckon as 'ow they might've 'eard something. 'is lordship's men might 'ave already found the lady," Tobias suggested.

Relief flooded through Jonathan.

"Of course." He took a bucket and began to wash the lampblack from Diablo's coat. "She probably found her way back to the road and the coach picked her up. I must go back to the inn. They will have news of what's happened to her."

"Ye be careful, now, lad," Tobias cautioned as Jonathan made ready to leave. "Don't go taking any more fool chances. The wench's not worth getting killed for."

Jonathan left the cave, clasping the fragile hope that somehow Spring had managed to make her way either back to the earl's coach or to the inn. He refused to consider the other possibilities as he turned Diablo back toward the inn and gave him his head.

All was quiet outside the inn when Jonathan stealthily put Diablo into a stall and crept toward the window at the back of the inn where he had exited hours earlier.

Dawn's first pink fingers had begun to flex on the distant horizon as Jonathan levered himself back through the window. The room was chilled, the fire that had burned in the grate had died, but Jonathan hardly noticed as he stripped off his clothing and donned fresh ones.

Jonathan looked at his haggard reflection in the mirror and winced at the red-rimmed eyes and day's growth of beard. He ran his fingers through his hair, carefully removing a twig which clung there.

The inn came alive as he stood there. From the sounds, Jonathan decided the queen's guard or Wyndridge's men had arrived. And since he was sure the queen was not in the area, Jonathan surmised it must be Wyndridge's men. Impatient to learn of Spring, he paused only to tuck his revolver into the waist of his trousers and don his coat before he hurried out of his room.

"Make haste, Molly," Lord Wyndridge's coachman shouted as Jonathan made his way down the stairs. "We have but a minute. His lordship's likely to have our heads, as it is."

Molly handed the man a mug, dodging the swipe of his hand directed at her bottom as she hurried over to Jonathan where he had taken a seat at his usual table.

"What's all the ruckus about?" Jonathan asked as he focused on Molly's smiling face.

"Ye missed all the excitement, ye did. Stopped here for dinner, she did, just after ye'd gone to yer room. Unfortunate thing should have stayed the night, but her lady grandmother would not hear of it. Now she's been kidnaped by the highwayman."

Jonathan felt hope slowly dying in his chest.

"No wonder his lordship's in such a rage. First Miss Ross and now the lady traveling in his lordship's coach. Guess the highwayman must have been taken with her, didn't even bother with her grandmother's jewels." Molly moved closer. Her breasts brushed against Jonathan's arm as she set a cup of coffee on the table in front of him. "Just lifted her onto that big beast and rode off with her, he did."

"His lordship must have found the lady by now, I'm sure," Jonathan ventured.

"No," Molly answered, leaning closer. "The highwayman spirited her way, he did. Like as not the lady will want to remain with him. He's a handsome devil, he is. Saw him meself, I did." Molly patted her hair and pretended to straighten her gown, successfully pulling the neckline of her blouse lower on her full bosom. "Got an eye for the ladies, that one has."

Jonathan bristled. What had he done? He had never stopped to think of the damage that would be done to Spring's reputation. All the gossips in London would have a lark at Spring's expense. It was his fault. He had brought this upon her.

"Surely, the lady will be found unharmed."

"Had to summon the doctor for Lady Phoebe, they did. Suffering from shock, she is."

Jonathan blanched at the news then recovered himself. "Not the Lady Phoebe Lansing?" he asked, and Molly nodded. "Lady Phoebe is my aunt's closest friend. You cannot mean it is her granddaughter that's been abducted, surely?"

"The very same," Molly imparted her knowledge with smug authority.

"But this can't be. I saw them in London only two days ago. How is it Lady Phoebe and her granddaughter came to be here?"

"Coming for the wedding, they were. She's to be his lordship's new Countess," Molly shared her carefully garnered information.

"Lady Phoebe?"

"No, of course not." Molly giggled. She placed a finger beside her full, pouted lips and stared at Jonathan thoughtfully. "Lady Spring, that's her name," Molly appeared much satisfied with her ability to remember the lady's name.

"Milord has a sharp eye for the ladies. It is the Lady Spring that's to be his lordship's bride."

"Surely they must have found the girl by now," Jonathan said again.

"The highwayman vanished into the night with her. They'll not catch that one. Not this time. Some say as how he's more ghost than man." Molly again smoothed her hair and tugged at her blouse. "He looked like real enough to me."

Jonathan pushed the coffee away untouched.

"I have to help," he said as he stood and turned toward the innkeeper. "Where did this abduction occur?"

"They'd just left the inn when he struck, hardly more than a stone's throw down the road," the innkeeper answered. His lordship's offering a year's wage to the man that takes the highwayman."

Spring was still out there alone. Determined to find her, Jonathan strode to the door. "Lady Phoebe's granddaughter must be found. I must help."

A new sense of urgency fired Jonathan. Where was Spring? If she had come to harm, it was his doing.

Urgently he set off down the coach road. The dust had hardly settled from the passage of the earl's men when he arrived at the spot where the highwayman had stopped the coach.

Jonathan sat listening for a moment then urged Diablo down the roadway and turned into the woods at the same spot he had taken the night before. He followed the trail of their passage with unerring skill.

When he reached the clearing where he had stopped the night before, he dismounted and began to push his way through the dense undergrowth.

He found the spot where he had lost sight of her and expanded his search from there. She would not fear Jonathan Sinclair as she had the highwayman. When she heard him calling her, she would come out of hiding. He would find her, he would! He had to!

Chapter Eight

Spring struggled through the darkness that surrounded her, feeling stiff and sore. Her head ached terribly, and the bed she lay upon felt damp and lumpy.

She flexed her fingers, curling them into the counterpane and instead found them tangled in leaves and vines. She gasped as memory came flooding back.

The highwayman!

All the terror of her kidnapping came flooding back. She curled into a tight ball to quiet the shudders overtaking her.

Spring huddled in her cramped hiding spot for what seemed like hours, listening. Afraid he would come back, afraid he would find her. But all she heard was the chirp of crickets and the call of an owl.

Something moved in the undergrowth near her, and Spring nearly screamed, but she clenched her teeth against the sound, determined not to give herself away. The rustling came again, and Spring shivered uncontrollably. Suppose it were a snake, a rat, or some other loathsome creature.

Carefully, as quietly as possible, Spring stood and extricated herself from the tangle of bramble surrounding her. Her skirt caught on a thorn bush, and the fabric ripped as she tried to free herself.

She blinked, her eyes trying to adjust to the sparkling shafts of morning light glimmering between the dense foliage.

Standing as still as a doe poised for flight, she listened for any sound of danger. Satisfied that for the moment she was alone, she began to push her way through the tangled growth. Unsure which way to go, Spring continued in the direction of her flight the night before.

The woodland ended abruptly, giving way to a coarse overgrowth of Bell Heather, that ended on a high ragged cliff not much farther on.

Far below, Spring heard the sea lapping on rocks scattered along the craggy beach. She took a deep breath, filling her lungs with the fresh, salt-tinged air.

Shivering, Spring studied the steep drop. Had she not fallen but continued to run blindly through the night, she would have ended up on those rocks so far below. Her eyes followed her line of thought. She trembled as her gaze swept the desolate, rock-strewn beach.

Far below, where the ragged rocks gave way and the tide washed against the sand, something swirled in the froth, stirring a memory.

Again, the sea rushed up to the beach, and this time deposited its sodden burden higher on the bleached sand. Spring stared at the water-soaked object as an uncontrollable trembling shook her slight frame.

Searching, Spring found a steep and dangerous trail of sorts, winding its way down to the rocky beach.

Without hesitation, Spring lifted her tattered skirts and started down the narrow path. She clutched at vines and branches to anchor herself to the treacherous path. Her feet in delicate slippers ached from the sting of sharp rocks.

At a particularly narrow ledge, she grasped a large, braided vine to keep her balance, only to feel it give way in her hand. Spring teetered on the ledge, certain she was about to pitch to her death on the rocks below, but she managed to secure a hold on another vine and continued her decent.

Finally at the bottom, she lifted her skirts and flew toward the spot where she had seen last the tide toss the object. Black material swirled in the tide as the sea threatened to pull it away. With a cry, Spring hurried toward the sodden heap on the beach.

He must have gone over the cliff in the darkness. Spring dropped to her knees beside the sodden black cloak. Her fingers trembled as she reached out to touch the wet fabric. Its coldness chilled her to the very bone.

She had not wanted this to happen; she had only wanted to escape, to get away. Spring trembled as she thought of the highwayman. How tragic to end like this, but perhaps the sea was better than the hangman's noose...

She shivered again and reached to pull the sodden cloak from the surf.

Tugging at the edge of the material, Spring tried to prepare herself for the worst. She had never seen a drowned man. Would it be horribly grotesque? Had he suffered terribly as the dark water had closed over him that final time?

Again, the tide tugged at its burden. Spring, determined not to allow it to reclaim the sodden mass, pulled at the cloak with all her strength.

Like an Indian Tracker

Jonathan followed the trail left by their passage the night before with the stealth of an Indian tracker. Despite having scoured the countryside all night, Lord Wyndridge's men had failed to find the trail which Jonathan now followed unerringly.

At the small clearing Jonathan dismounted and continued on foot, finding a twig bent here and a branch broken there. His boot caught on an up-thrust root and Jonathan reached out to steady himself but drew back quickly when he encountered the spikes of a thorn bush.

He cursed softly as he lifted his injured hand to his lips. Just then a few tattered strands of cloth skewered by the thorn bush caught his attention.

He touched the material gingerly. It was the same shade of brown as the traveling gown that Spring had been wearing the night before.

Stepping closer he reached to gently remove the scrap from the thorn which pinned it. He rubbed his fingers over the material, certain it was from Spring's gown.

Carefully, he searched for further evidence of Spring's passing, and it was then he noticed the dark stain upon a small boulder nearby.

He leaned closer touching his fingers to the spot; knowing with certainty that it was dried blood.

Matted into the dark stain was a few strains of long golden hair; Jonathan touched them reverently.

The thorn bush was large and thick, if Spring had rolled beneath its branches, he could easily have missed her in the darkness, Jonathan thought as he studied the scene.

She might have even been knocked unconscious. That would certainly explain how she had vanished so completely. But where was she now?

Moving in a wide circle radiating from the thorn bush, Jonathan searched the surrounding area.

Finally, he found more bent twigs and smiled as he picked up her trail. He would find her!

Remembering the night before and his narrow escape at the cliff's sharp drop, Jonathan used caution as he followed the trail through the undergrowth. The air freshened with the salty sting of the sea.

Jonathan's heartbeat became a rapid tattoo in his ears as he followed the trail to the cliff's edge where last night he had pushed through the undergrowth and stepped off into nothing.

He moved away from the cliff's edge and headed toward the path that led down to the beach. With an increasing sense of urgency, Jonathan traversed the dangerous path.

Moments later, he was almost afraid to believe the fragile picture which greeted him.

Seaweed, black, slimy, and completely disagreeable, but no highwayman. Spring shuddered, as a sigh of relief escaped her constricted throat. She stared at the sodden mass.

She should have known better. The highwayman was bold and daring, it would take more than a cliff and the sea to stop him.

The surf swept around her pulling at her skirts, the cold seeped into her bones. Spring shivered. Would she never feel warm and safe again? She wondered as she clutched the sodden cloak to her thin frame.

Without warning, firm hands grasped Spring's shoulders and hauled her forcefully to her feet. She screamed at being so roughly handled, and with flailing limbs fought the hands that turned her. With all her strength Spring resisted the arms seeking to imprison her, until suddenly she stared up into blazing dark eyes.

"Jonathan," Spring gasped breathlessly, as strong arms clasped her against a hard masculine chest.

Jonathan's hand traced a red welt along her cheek where a branch had scratched her. "What has happened to you?"

"Oh, Jonathan it was horrible," Spring wailed throwing herself into his arms. "A... a ... highwayman stopped the coach and he... he..., grandmother fainted, and he just left her there on the road. I tried to get away from him, but he held me and... and he kissed me." A tear gathered at the corner of one eye and traced a path down her dirt-stained face. Soon another followed.

"You're safe now, my darling," Jonathan soothed as he wiped a tear from her cheek.

"Last night when he stopped in the forest up there," Spring pointed toward the cliff. "We were... talking, and I escaped." Spring blushed as she remembered the real method by which she had secured her freedom.

"But where have you been all night? Surely not here on the beach?" Jonathan pulled her closer, wrapping his arms around her. He held her close and gave thanks for having found her.

"In the woods. I fell and hit my head. The highwayman must have passed right by me in the darkness." A shudder ran through her slender body. "If I hadn't fallen, I'd have gone over the cliff like the highwayman..."

Jonathan held her trembling body against him, hardly daring to loosen his grip for fear that she was not real. He felt her shiver and yet her body felt hot to the touch. Her body melded itself to his as if with a mind of its own, her hands clung to him as if she would never let go, and Jonathan found the idea not at all unappealing.

How was it all the other women who had sought to bind him to them had only made him seek his freedom so much the more, yet Spring's arms around him set his heart pounding and made him want her more than ever?

Warm tears soaked his shirt front as Jonathan cradled her in his arms. When he lifted her in his arms, she tightened her arms around his neck and snuggled her cheek against the hollow of his shoulder. He strode quickly toward the cave. He removed his arm from beneath her legs and allowed her feet to slide gently to the cavern floor.

She swayed when his arms left her, but Jonathan's hand was there instantly to steady her.

He would keep his promise. He would return her to Lady Phoebe. He would but not yet. He moved to help her out of her wet gown. He held the blanket and wrapped her slender naked frame in it, feeling a tightening in his loins. Knowing he must put space between them or succumb to the vital need to make love to her threatening to overpower him, Jonathan gathered her sodden garments and strode from the cave.

He spread her gown and undergarments to dry in the morning sun on the brush outside the cave. Returning moments later, he knew that all the length and breadth of England was not enough to keep him from wanting her, from making love to her.

She lay huddled on the cot, the blanket tightly clasped around her slender frame. Violent trembling shook her as chills racked her fragile body. Her eyes gazing up at him were feverishly bright.

Damnation, was this God's way of reminding him of his vow? Fetching a cup of tepid water, Jonathan bathed her face with his handkerchief. Spring closed her eyes and drifted into a troubled sleep, twisting and tossing about wildly as if she fought some demon.

In her wild thrashing, she repeatedly pushed the blanket away from her exposing her naked breasts to Jonathan's tortured gaze. The thought of ravishment crossed his mind as he soothed her with the coolness of his damp handkerchief. Her body responded to his touch, breasts becoming taut, nipples pouting provocatively against his hand. How he longed to hold her and caress those twin peaks. But he would not take advantage of her. It was his fault she was in this state and he would not injure her further by taking what her fevered body so tauntingly offered.

"'Tis more than even any man could bear," Jonathan muttered as he again pulled the blanket up to cover Spring's nude body.

"Jonathan?" Spring called softly.

"Yes, Love?"

"So glad you're here," she whispered. "Hold me, I'm so cold."

Her urgent plea was his undoing. He could withstand his own need, but not hers. Carefully Jonathan slid his weight onto the cot beside her and pulled her into his embrace. The sweet scent of her filled his nostrils, making the aching need in his loins almost unbearable.

Just for a while. He pulled her slender form tightly against him. His hands sought her body beneath the coarse blanket, caressing, warming, giving freely of the heat of his own body. Her skin was like warm silk beneath his hands. Her hair glowed with golden fire in the lamplight.

Holding her close against him, Jonathan kissed her mouth, her eyes, her cheeks. One hand found a haven on her breasts just before exhaustion and loss of sleep claimed him.

In her dream the hand on her breasts stirred, fingers slightly squeezing, and Spring responded to their gentle teasing pressing herself closer. A strange tingle began in her right breast, concentrating in the taut nipple then radiating outward to the rest of her body.

A new quivering tightness began in her belly and lower. Spring moaned and moved closer to him. The arm at her waist tightened, pulling her against the muscular length of his all-male frame.

Spring's eyes flew open. This was no dream!

The man at her side was real. One arm was beneath her and circled her slim waist, the other placed bold claim on her breast. Her body entwined intimately with his beneath the coarse blanket covering them. The weight of one of his legs thrown across hers made her his prisoner.

Spring was filled with terror as memories of the long night came flooding back. Then came the memory of Jonathan finding her on the beach. Jonathan, her rescuer, her savior. Her heart swelled with love for him.

She felt a flush creeping over her as she remembered how she had boldly asked him to hold her. And what else had she asked for in the shocked aftermath of nearly losing her life at the hands of the highwayman? For the life of her, Spring could remember nothing after Jonathan had taken her in his arms.

Spring was very sure,however, she would remember in great detail if Jonathan had made love to her. At the thought of being with Jonathan like that, Spring again felt the strange tugging in her lower belly. An intense yearning for something more filled her. What would it matter if they made love? The highwayman would have taken her if she had not managed to escape. Marcus would take her when she became his bride.

Her virginity should be hers alone to give and should not be taken from her by a man she did not love. The thought of going to Marcus as a virgin was repugnant to Spring. If she must give herself to a man, then let it be one of her own choosing, not one wicked enough to force himself on her.

And truly, had not her heart already chosen Jonathan? Did not at this very moment a strong, demanding love flow through her for this man? And if everyone thought she had been ravished by the highwayman, he could hardly come forward to deny it, could he? Might the wedding be called off because of it?

Spring moved shyly against him, unsure how to make her wishes known. Her hand moved to his chest, assessing its firm muscular hardness. She raised her eyes to his face and found midnight eyes studying her intently. Spring felt her flush deepen and spread over her as his hand moved gently at her breast. His questioning gaze never left her face.

Spring took a deep breath, for she was suddenly breathless as she stared into his gaze. Finally, unable to bear the heated longing in his eyes any longer, she closed her eyes.

"Love me, please."

"I shall, always." He pulled her tighter against him.

"Now, I want you to love me now, Jonathan."

He thought he could not possibly have heard her right. "Make love to you?" he questioned.

"Yes, please."

"You don't know what you're saying. It must be the fever." He could not believe he had heard her right. Jonathan felt her forehead and found it not overly hot.

Spring was beginning to feel angry and not a little frustrated. "I know exactly what I'm saying, and I'm quite recovered from the chill, and I want you to—"

Groaning, Jonathan crushed her to him, praying she would not hate him later for what she had asked him to do. He was only a man, after all. And, God help him, he could not resist the sweet temptation of her body pressing urgently against his.

All Jonathan could think of was the woman in his arms and how badly he wanted her. He wanted to be inside her, to feel the warmth of her surrounding him. He could not get enough of the feel of her in his arms. They were so close that a single pin prick would have drawn blood from both, yet he wanted to be closer still.

Suddenly, his clothing was a restriction he could not afford. He moved away from her and flung the garments from his body, uncaring of where they landed. In seconds he was back holding her, caressing her, loving her. He wanted her, heart, body, and soul. She had to belong to him, be his and his alone. He ached with wanting her, the pain was near unbearable.

Jonathan tightened his arms around Spring. He laid his forehead against hers, trying to calm his racing heart. He had come so close to losing her he had been terrified. But now she was safe in his arms, and he would never let her go.

Let Marcus keep the estate, the money, and the title as long as I have Spring.

Jonathan again lowered his lips to hers and found her trembling, eager for his kiss. She was so open, so innocent, so giving. With a groan of pleasure, he deepened the kiss. He pressed himself closer against her, letting her feel his need. She was his. He would take her home to America. They would forget England and the Earl of Wyndridge. He had come seeking revenge but had found a love to last for all time.

Spring responded to his touch from the very center of her being. She wanted his kisses, wanted his hands on her, filling her with longing and need. Everywhere he touched small fires kindled and radiated outward and inward, setting off a raging furnace inside her that she could not control.

Carefully, with nimble fingers, he stoked those flames, urging them ever higher until Spring felt her entire being consumed by his golden flames.

She reveled in the exquisite torture that his hands moving along her spine wrought. His lips twisted over hers, his tongue playing gently over her lips, seeking entry to the secrets of her mouth. With a sigh of submission, Spring parted her lips and gave herself up to his invasion of her mouth. Her tongue played tag and touch me not with his. First coaxing and tempting then coy and shy.

Shifting her in his arms, Jonathan moved so that one of his legs slipped between her knees and parted her thighs. He gathered her closer and planted hundreds of small pleading kisses on her lips, her eyelids, her cheeks, her chin, and forehead. Then his tongue found the shell of an ear and traced a delicate pattern there.

A shiver of longing raced through Spring.

She moved instinctively closer to him and felt his leg brush the secret spot between her thighs. The unfamiliar tightening in her belly grew.

"I feel I could die of wanting you," Jonathan whispered against her throat. "My body aches to possess you, to make you truly mine."

With a shiver of desire, Spring pressed closer to him, urging him to take what he would. His hand moved down to caress the silken mounds of her breasts, and his lips followed their heated path. Never had Spring felt anything quite so exquisite as the touch of his tongue as it scorched her with the heat of his passion. She felt she must be branded, marked forever by his searing touch.

She could not stop her untutored body from responding wantonly to the practiced moves of his lovemaking, so she gave herself up to the pleasure his touch wrought.

With a gasp, she clutched at the blanket beside her as his marauding touch moved lower still. Small butterfly kisses marked his passing along her rib cage, past her naval and across her belly and lower still. She felt herself tense when his hand slipped to the tangle of golden curls at the juncture of her thighs.

For an instant, sanity threatened to return, and then his lips followed the path his hands had plotted. All coherent thought escaped her.

His tongue was a hot, questing blade seeking to open the secret center of her. His fingertips moved over her in the most deliciously seductive way. Arching toward him, she moaned her pleasure as he discovered the very core of her. His tongue taunted and teased the passion engorged bud it found there, bringing her need for him to fever pitch.

She thrashed and moaned beneath him, begging for release from the gentle torture his lips so subtly applied. When finally he moved above her, she welcomed his weight.

"Just a bit more, Love," he coaxed as he sought to spread her legs to better accommodate him. He hovered above her, letting her feel the hot questing shaft of his manhood against her entrance. For a long moment he hesitated, searching the passion darkened depths of her lovely eyes.

"I don't want to hurt you, my darling," he whispered, brushing small butterfly kisses across her lips. "But there is always pain the first time."

He had known from the first time their eyes met that this moment would come. Yet now, he could not bear the thought of causing her even a moment's pain.

"That which you seek is mine only to give," Spring answered in a husky whisper. She raised her knees and braced her feet against the coarse material of the cot as she felt the throbbing shaft pressing against her. "I give my gift to you, Jonathan, only you," she said and thrust her hips upward, receiving the full thrust of his manhood as he instinctively responded to her movement.

Pain tore through her, making her body jerk convulsively. The deed well done, Spring fell back to the cot, gasping for breath. How could she stand a lifetime of this? How could any woman?

"Little one, you should have waited. It would have been easier more slowly done." When he moved slightly within her, Spring winced at the pain. "It will not always be like this. It gets easier, I promise." He kissed her and held her, waiting until the tension left her body. Then he began to move.

Slowly the pain receded, replaced by a growing need to be closer to Jonathan. Spring moved her arms to his shoulders and held him tightly to her. Her body trembled beneath his., Slowly the heated pain cooled, and a deep smoldering need set in. Spring was not sure what she wanted, but it mattered not, for Jonathan seemed to know.

Gently he moved, pressing her deeper into the cot as he stoked the flames that rose within her again. His hands moved over her breasts, molding the throbbing nipples between his thumb and finger before he lowered his head to suckle them gently.

Spring could feel the pull of his lips all the way to her toes that curled into the cot. Her nails raked his shoulders as she moaned and writhed beneath him.

"Jonathan, please, oh... I feel, Jonathan! What is happening..." Her words became an incoherent mumble as he increased the rhythm of his hips, sending his pulsating manhood deeper into the core of her. He completely filled her, moving deeper with each powerful thrust.

His lips found hers. His tongue played in and out of her parted lips in the same heated tempo as his quick thrust. Spring matched her movements to his, seeking to learn from him of the passion he showered upon her. The pain was but a faint memory now, chased away by the glowing pleasure that his loving cast over her.

She spun out of control. The glow became so brilliant she thought surely they would be consumed by it. Instead, it burst above them into a thousand shooting stars and fell around them in multicolor waves. Wave after wave of pleasure assailed her as her body answered the tremulous demand of Jonathan's. His body tensed. Every muscle coiled tightly as Jonathan thrust deeply inside her one last time.

His release was warm inside her, and Spring welcomed it, her legs holding him when he would have moved away.

Finally, he moved partially off her, leaving their lower bodies still entwined. At her protest of even this small separation, he pulled her into his arms and pillowed her head on his shoulder. Jonathan pulled the blanket over them, and finally, with Spring wrapped securely in his arms, they slept.

Chapter Nine

It was early afternoon when Jonathan awoke. For a moment he lay gazing at Spring's face. She was so beautiful, he thought as he watched her sleeping. Then his gaze slid lower to where the blanket had fallen away from her shoulder down to expose one creamy breast. He could not resist the temptation her flesh offered.

He lowered his head to nibble greedily at her nipple, tasting and savoring her unique flavor. Jonathan's hands skimmed over the soft curves of her breasts, smoothing over the silken skin. Lower and lower his fingertips quested, seeking to memorize the treasures of her body. When his fingers encountered the soft curls at the juncture of her thighs, his breath caught painfully in his chest. Still, his hands ventured on, followed closely by his lips.

Instantly her body responded to the labors of his teeth and tongue. Spring stretched languidly then pressed herself closer against him. Her body came alive under his touch, responding to him with such sweet, innocent abandon it took his breath away. He never wanted to leave her. He wanted to be here with her always, in her arms, inside her, touching the flames of passion she so willingly shared.

Jonathan's hands played over her body while his lips followed the path of his fingertips as they traced over her silky skin. His body responded to hers. His manhood, hard and pulsing, thrust against her hips.

Much later, Jonathan wearily got up and gathered his scattered clothing. For one so young and inexperienced, the depths of her passion astounded him.

It was as if she wanted to experience everything at once. Jonathan was no lightweight, so he could hold his own with the best of them, but the vixen had worn him out. Yet even now, he knew it would take only a glance from her, a stroke of her untrained hand to make him ready to take her again.

Jonathan's heart swelled with love for her. He felt a fierce possessiveness. She was his. She belonged to him. He would not share her with another man, ever. The thought of another man touching Spring made Jonathan see red. He would kill any man who dared to touch her, to harm her.

She was his soulmate. He had known the first time their eyes had met that it would come to this.

Suddenly, he felt an intense longing for home. He wanted to take Spring there, to see her eyes light with joy when she saw the beauty of his home. *She will love Riverside, just as I do.* He studied her lovely features.

Jonathan pushed thoughts of home aside as another concern reared in his mind. It was well past time for Tobias to have returned. If he did not arrive soon, Jonathan would have to go in search of him.

He pushed those thoughts away as his gaze returned to Spring. He smiled softly at her. His hand smoothed a long golden strand away from her face.

"You will love Riverside," Jonathan said as he looked around the earthen floor in search of his other boot.

"Riverside?"

"My home. Sinclair Hall lies but a stone's throw from the river. Its lush green yards run right down to the riverbank." He found the missing boot and pulled it on.

"You'll love it. My grandfather built it for my grandmother when he took her there from Charleston," Jonathan continued without noticing how quiet Spring suddenly became.

"We'll take the barge up the Savannah, and Grandmother will have a carriage waiting at the wharf. You can see the river from the veranda," Jonathan continued, caught up the vivid images of home. "It's so beautiful and peaceful you'll love it just as I do."

Spring closed her eyes against the tears that threatened. How she longed to do the things Jonathan spoke of. She would willingly follow Jonathan to the end of the earth, if only she were free to do so. But those wondrous joys Jonathan had described would never happen, for her fate had been sealed before she met him. Sadly, she watched Jonathan dress.

"I can't imagine what's keeping Tobias," Jonathan said as he rose from the cot after pulling on his boots.

"Tobias?"

Jonathan ignored her question, caught up in his own thoughts. "Your clothing should be dry. I'll fetch it." Jonathan left the cave as Spring stood and wrapped the blanket sarong style around herself.

She moved over to the stable to rub the nose of the large black stallion penned there. Spring ran her hand over his sleek, gleaming coat. He reminded her of the highwayman's steed. Except for the large white blaze on his chest, he looked much the same.

"Careful, he doesn't take kindly to strangers," Jonathan cautioned as he entered the cave with her garments.

"But you like me, don't you, boy?" Spring said scratching the stallion between his ears as he nuzzled at her blanket. "What's his name?"

"Diablo," Jonathan supplied.

"Are you really such a devil?" she teased, still scratching his head.

Before she realized what he was about, Diablo caught the edge of the blanket in his teeth and gave it a jerk.

When Spring lost her grip on the blanket, the horse backed to the other side of the stall with it held in his teeth. She was left holding on to air as she stood nude before Jonathan. Diablo waved his prize in the air and gave a whinny that sounded almost like a chuckle.

Spring laughed, quite unaffected by her nudity when Jonathan stepped to her side and handed her clothing to her.

"I did warn you to be wary of him," Jonathan chuckled.

Spring felt warmth spread through her as Jonathan's gaze flickered over her body. Instead of feeling embarrassed by the glow of desire that lit sparks of fire in his brown eyes, Spring longed to respond to that desire.

An answering need quickened within her, causing her belly to tighten and her breasts to tingle. *How could the merest touch of Jonathan's gaze kindle such strange fires in her blood?* She accepted her clothing.

When Jonathan whistled, the stallion trotted toward him, the blanket still clasped between his teeth. "I'm afraid he's use to having his own way."

"Just like his master," Spring quipped as she pulled on her undergarments.

Struggling into her gown, Spring presented Jonathan with her back. The tiny mother of pearl buttons were a chore to do up when you could see them, but when they were behind one's back, they were impossible. Jonathan easily dealt with the buttons for her. Then he turned her around and planted a tender kiss on her lips.

"I will not be long. I have arrangements to make for our voyage to America, and Tobias must see to the horses."

"You will take Diablo to America with you?" Spring asked incredulously, "but how?"

Jonathan moved to the stall and he clicked softly to the large horse. "You're a seasoned traveler, aren't you, boy?"

"You brought him with you?"

"Yes, he was trained from a colt to swim out to a waiting ship. From there it's easy to lower a sling and lift him aboard," Jonathan stroked the sleek neck of the large stallion. "We're a pair, aren't we, Diablo."

Jonathan led Diablo from his stall. Spring stood watching him, following his movements. She shivered and wrapped her arms around herself feeling suddenly chilled. He mounted and then leaned down to capture her chin in his hand. His lips brushed hers again, and then he was gone.

Looking down at her soiled crumpled gown, Spring tried to tidy herself, but the effort was futile, at best. It was stained and ripped in several places, and the color was beginning to fade from exposure to salt water. What did it matter? When Jonathan returned, she would be gone.

Shivering again from the chill that seemed to have seeped into her very soul, Spring looked around the cave one last time. She could not remain here, regardless of how much she wished otherwise.

Wyndridge still had his hold over her. Nothing had changed, yet nothing would ever be quite the same. She had to go. If she didn't, Wyndridge would make good his threats.

Her heart ached with love for Jonathan. She had felt alive and vital when he touched her. She remembered his every word, every stroke of his fingers, every touch of his lips. Her body felt warm with desire when she remembered the taste and feel of him. Memories were all she would have to get her through the time ahead. She wrapped her arms tightly around herself hugging Jonathan's memory to her.

Duty was strong within her. She had an obligation to her family. She could not throw away their happiness and security for love of Jonathan.

If only he had come sooner. If she was already Jonathan's wife, Wyndridge would not have dared make such demands upon her. But it had not happened that way. She was not Jonathan's wife and never would be.

A coldness settled around her heart as she faced the loss of Jonathan's love. He would not understand her leaving. He would hate her as much as she hated herself for leaving him.

She would follow the shoreline, Spring decided as she emerged from the limestone cavern where Jonathan had left her. Surely it would be only a matter of time before someone came along to help her.

She trudged along as if in a trance, uncaring that the water licked at the hem of her gown and ruined her slippers.

She was beyond caring, beyond feeling. Nothing mattered anymore. Nothing would ever matter anymore.

Spring heard hoof beats pounding in the surf behind her, and for a moment she hoped wildly that it might be Jonathan come to claim her. But, when she turned toward the sound, she recognized the colors of the Wyndridge livery. The little hope that had remained was dashed like the pounding of the surf upon the rocks.

For one fleeting moment the idea of flight came to her. There might yet be time for her to avoid capture, but then her foot came down on a hard sharp object buried just beneath the sand. A hot pain shot through her foot as the shell cut through the soft fabric of her slipper and into the tender flesh of her foot. With a gasp of pain, Spring sank to the sand.

The first image Spring had of Wyndridge was a dark gray, imposing structure, all dark shadows and cold stone. There was no warmth to the massive stone structure, more a castle than the manor house Spring had expected.

The rider who had lifted her into the saddle in front of him stiffened as they neared the manor. His movements as he swung down from their mount then handed her down were quite circumspect. Almost as if he feared retribution if his actions were considered otherwise. Spring thanked the man for rescuing her then turned toward the massive front door, but her injured foot protested having the slightest weight upon it.

After a moment's hesitation, the man lifted Spring in his arms and turned toward the heavy stone steps leading up to the massive oak doors.

"My pet!" Lady Phoebe wailed. "Thanks be to God! You're safe!" She launched herself at her granddaughter, nearly sending the coachman toppling over backward with Spring still in his arms. "I've been so worried."

"I'm quite well. Actually, except for a sprained ankle, I'm no worse for the ordeal I've been through," Spring reassured her grandmother, though she felt an overwhelming weakness seeping over her. She ached in every part of her body.

"Your room is ready, and you'll be wanting a bath, of course," Lady Phoebe fussed over her as the coachman carried her up the stairs.

"Indeed, I can think of nothing more soothing than a bath at the moment," Spring said thinking Jonathan's arms around her would be more comforting than a thousand baths.

Spring closed eyes and let her head loll back in exhaustion.

"No, not that room," Lady Phoebe directed. "The next one, by my room." The man followed Lady Phoebe's directions and turned into the room at the end of the long hall. He carefully lowered Spring into a chair and quickly left the room, leaving her to Phoebe's tender ministration.

"We'll just get you into a nice warm bath and then into bed." Lady Phoebe motioned for the maid who lingered nearby. "Fetch water. Be sure it is warm."

Spring waited, watching a young lad carry in pail after pail of warm water until the copper tub was filled.

Relaxing against the rim of the large tub, Spring allowed her head to rest against it as the maid gently lathered her body. She would forget everything that had happened.

All except Jonathan. That secret she would always hold locked deep within her heart.

Jonathan. Her heart filled with love as thoughts of him brought a rosy glow to her skin where he had loved her.

After Spring's bath, the maid helped her from the tub and wrapped her in the folds of a towel warm from the heat of the fireplace. Yet, despite the warmth of the fire, Spring shivered.

Finally, dressed in one of her own nightgowns, Spring sat in a chair near the fire. She gingerly placed her injured foot on a small stool and sank back into the comfort of the large chair with a deep sigh.

"I'll fetch milady," the maid excused herself.

"You do feel better now, don't you, my pet?" Lady Phoebe asked as she returned to Spring's side. "Perhaps some tea would make you feel more the thing."

"Yes, Grandmother." Spring closed her eyes feeling tired and drained.

The young maid returned. "Excuse me, milady." The girl stopped in the doorway, twisting her hands in her apron. "The Doctor Morgan has arrived."

"Send him up at once," Lady Phoebe insisted, and moments later, a tall, silver-haired man stepped into the room.

"The doctor should examine you at once," Lady Phoebe insisted as she noted the cut that had reopened on Spring's foot. "Aaron, come this instant. The child has been injured."

"Now my pet, Doctor Morgan is here to help you," Lady Phoebe said as Spring turned away when the doctor approached her.

"I... I'm just so tired, couldn't I just go to bed, please?"

"Of course, my dear," Doctor Morgan answered patting her hand gently. "But we must tend your injury right away to keep infection from setting in."

Spring turned away from the kindness in his eyes as gently inspected her foot. When his fingers tenderly tested the wound, Spring gasped at the pain shooting through it. She bit into the soft flesh of her bottom lip while he gently probed the wound with an instrument he'd taken from his medical bag.

When waves of nausea rose to swamp her, Spring closed her eyes in an effort to fight them down.

"There, it should feel better now," Doctor Morgan said as he extracted a piece of broken shell from the wound.

He washed the wound with fresh water brought by a servant and poured a solution from a small vial over it before he applied a clean white bandage.

"You must stay off your feet for a few days to give the wound time to heal. Keep it clean and dry. It should heal without any problem. Your ankle will be sore for a while, but nothing's broken."

Aaron Morgan gently lifted Spring in his arms and carried her to the bed that had been turned down. He placed Spring on the bed and then turned to her grandmother.

A look passed between them, and Lady Phoebe lowered her eyes, pressed her handkerchief to her lips and quickly left the room.

"His lordship," the doctor paused for a moment, cleared his throat then continued. "has requested that I give you a complete examination to assure you have not suffered further injury."

Yet another degradation for which Wyndridge would pay, Spring vowed. Were she a man, she would call him out and shoot him down like the cur he was. But then, were she a man, she would not be in this situation in the first place.

She wrapped her arms tightly around herself and grieved silently for Jonathan. She squeezed her eyes shut against the tears that threatened. She would not feel sorry for herself, she would not.

"I will inform his lordship what has happened. I am sure that under the circumstances it will make no difference in how his lordship regards you." He patted her hand reassuringly. "I doubt there's much chance of a child resulting from this."

Spring turned wide eyes back toward the doctor. "A child?"

The possibility had never occurred to her. What if she had conceived? What if she were to bear Jonathan's child? Surely Marcus would turn her away then. He would not want her once he learned that she was no longer pure. Finally, Spring drifted into a fevered and troubled sleep.

When Spring awoke, Lady Phoebe sat silently beside her bed. Her grandmother stared at the handkerchief, which she twisted in her trembling hands, her eyes red rimmed from weeping.

"My sweet child. How brave you are," Lady Phoebe whispered.

Spring wanted to tell her not to weep for her, for she had suffered more indignities from Doctor Morgan than she had from the highwayman, but she knew she could not. It would serve her purposes much better if they thought her disgrace had come at the hand of the highwayman, who could hardly come forward to deny it.

"It's all right. You're safe now. Grandmother won't let anyone harm you again," Lady Phoebe murmured, trying to reassure her.

Spring found Lady Phoebe's words less than reassuring. Since her grandmother had been unable to prevent either Wyndridge's plot or the highwayman from carrying her off, she very much doubted her ladyship would be able to protect her from the wrath of Lord Wyndridge now.

Had things been different, she would have gladly confessed her secret to her grandmother. But, as it were, she dared not. Still, it rankled that she could not tell her grandmother that she had not really been harmed by the highwayman, that she had given herself freely to Jonathan because she loved him. Her grandmother would have understood. Spring was certain of it, yet if her plan had any hope of success, she had to make her grandmother believe she had been mistreated by the highwayman. Later, Spring promised herself, she would tell her grandmother the truth.

Chapter Ten

After hours of a fruitless search, Lord Wyndridge returned home, his dark mood barely relieved by the news of Spring's rescue. Hardly sparing a look toward the cowering servant who opened the door for him, he stalked toward the library.

He filled a glass with brandy, drained it in one gulp and sent it crashing into the large stone fireplace. The crash of breaking glass echoed throughout the silent house, as did his lordship's voice a moment later.

"Morgan, get me Morgan!" he bellowed as he pulled on the bell rope behind his chair.

The sound of scurrying feet could be heard as a servant hurried to do his master's bidding. Within minutes Doctor Morgan knocked at the library door.

"Come in, blast it," his lordship shouted, reaching again for the brandy decanter.

"You wanted to see me?"

Lord Wyndridge downed another glass of brandy and then took a seat in the leather chair behind his heavy wooden desk. He scowled at the doctor through narrowed eyes, as if trying to see inside the man.

"You've examined the girl?"

"I've examined Lady Spring, yes."

"And?"

"She has been feverish most of the day but appears to be better now. She has suffered a severely sprained ankle and a deep cut on her foot, but it should heal given time, provided infection does not set in."

"Blast it all man! Do you think I am concerned about a sprained ankle and a cut on her foot? Did that cur defile her?"

Aaron Morgan looked around the room as if wishing to avoid direct eyes contact with the earl.

"Damnation, man," Wyndridge shouted, bringing his large fist down on the desk with bone crushing intensity. "Give me a straight answer!" he demanded.

"She is not a virgin," Aaron Morgan voice was low as he answered, his face carefully neutral. He would not add to the lady's humiliation.

Lord Wyndridge howled with rage. His face turned motley red, and the veins at his temples throbbed with the force of his fury. He again pounded his fists on the desk with such force that the paper weight on it bounced with each blow.

"Your lordship, this was none of the lady's doing." Aaron Morgan entreated, "You understand that, of course, what has happened should not affect your feelings for Lady Spring. She is still the same girl you wished to marry."

"After she's become the highwayman's whore?" Lord Wyndridge grated out between clenched teeth.

"But, milord, the lady cannot be blamed for..."

"He did this to disgrace me! He will pay dearly for this, do you hear? I will not stop until he is tracked down and the hangman's noose is tightened about his neck." Lord Wyndridge's voice raged deeply with savage emotion.

"No one must know he's had the chit."

"The countess has been told of her granddaughter's condition, of course," Aaron Morgan stated quietly.

"Yes, well that can't be helped. The old harpy would insist on knowing. But she will not tell anyone. She'll not want to see the chit's reputation torn asunder."

"Lady Phoebe is quite understandably concerned for her granddaughter's health and welfare," Aaron Morgan defended the countess against what he saw as the earl's unwarranted attack.

"I will see the chit now."

"Lady Spring is sleeping. Her ladyship is sitting with her. I shall ask Lady Phoebe to send for you when her granddaughter awakens."

Lord Wyndridge reached for the riding crop he had thrown onto the desk when he had come into the room. His hand tightened on it so that the knuckles stood out white against the darker skin of his hand. He stood, sending his chair toppling over backward in his haste. Stalking around the desk, he stood glaring at Aaron Morgan. The riding crop hissed through the air, cutting the silence of the room with a sharp retort as it repeatedly stuck the top of the earl's black riding boots.

No one tells me what to do, no one. Wyndridge continued to pound his riding crop against the polished leather of his boot. He was the Earl of Wyndridge, and, in his domain, his word was law. The sooner Aaron Morgan learned that the better for him. If he wanted to see the chit, he would see her.

At the Boar's Head Inn

"Found her, he did. Knew his lordship wouldn't stop until the lady were found," Molly said as she entered the taproom, drying her hands with the stained apron tied about her waist.

Jonathan turned from the bar where he had been settling his account with the innkeeper to stare at Molly with narrowed eyes. What was the woman going on about now?

"Had it straight from his lordship's man, I did." Molly stopped in front of Jonathan and leaned closer so that her full breasts tested the restraints of her bodice.

"Found her a wandering along the beach, they did. Said as how the highwayman were dead, the lady said he had gone over the cliff. But I do not believe that, not for a minute. Like as not, he was disgusted with the lily-white lady and let her go." Molly preened, smoothing the coarse material of her blouse over her full bosom. "He needs a real woman, he does."

"They've found Lady Phoebe's granddaughter?"

Jonathan felt a tightening in his chest. Why had she left the cave? He had told her to stay put, that he would return to take her to America with him.

Hadn't she cared for him even a little? Bitterness settled over Jonathan. She had chosen the earl's social position over his love for her. How could he have misjudged her so completely? Jonathan's hand clenched on the small coin purse in his hand. For a moment he felt as if he might throw up.

"Here now, just said as they did, didn't I?" Molly answered with a twist of her hips as she leaned across to wipe a puddle of ale from the bar beside Jonathan.

"The shame of it all, unfortunate thing, and her such a fine lady and all."

Molly's words finally penetrated Jonathan's train of thought. He stared at her incredulously. "What?"

"The highwayman had his way with her, is what I were told," Molly whispered in a hushed voice.

Jonathan's hands clenched into fists. So, she had blamed her loss of innocence on the highwayman. How convenient.

Did she think Earl Wyndridge too old to properly initiate her into the rite of love and so bestowed that privilege upon me?

And who would be her next lover? Jonathan threw a handful of coins on the counter and took his leave of the taproom.

How could he have so completely misjudged her? Was it possible she had not been the innocent he had thought her? No, that was not possible. He had had the indisputable proof. But why?

Dusk was just falling when Jonathan returned to the cave and found Tobias waiting for him. He led the stallion into his coral and quickly gave him fresh water and hay before turning troubled eyes toward his old friend. The last visages of hope that Jonathan had stubbornly clung had withered and died.

"She's gone, then?"

"Aye, lad."

Retrieving a brush from a large boulder that made up one side of Diablo's pen, Jonathan let himself into the coral and set to work brushing the horse's sleek coat.

He worked rapidly, letting the force of his labor take away some of the rage that had built within him.

"Saw 'er walking 'long the beach, but 'is lordship's men were on 'er before I could reach 'er," Tobias said, watching Jonathan curry the stallion with near savage strokes.

"Be ye trying to take the hide off 'im, lad?" Tobias asked, recognizing the tightly leashed anger fueling Jonathan's movements.

He had known this was a fool's errand the lad had set out on, but there had been no stopping him, and now just look where they had wound up. *Much better we'd left the lady alone and kept to our mission.* Tobias snorted.

"Will we be going back to the inn?" Tobias asked as he turned back to the campfire he had been tending when Jonathan entered the cave.

"No."

Tobias stopped with the coffee pot he was holding suspended in mid-air and stared at Jonathan for a few seconds before hanging the pot back over the flames.

"Then ye'll stay here?"

"For tonight," Jonathan answered.

Taking a seat beside the fire with Tobias, Jonathan poured himself a cup of coffee and sat staring into the fire. Tobias watched his friend closely, noting the quiet brooding engulfing him.

Producing bread, meat and beans from their supplies, Tobias quickly set about preparing their meal. When the food was ready, he watched in consternation as Jonathan stirred it around on his tin plate.

Trouble was brewing. Tobias studied his friend closely. He could feel it in his bones. Once the lad decided what to do next, there would be hell to pay., *Just mark me words, there will.*

How will Spring react when Jonathan Sinclair arrives at Wyndridge Hall? Jonathan settled into the blankets of his bedroll.

Well, he would soon find out, because he was about to pay Lord Wyndridge a long overdue visit. But first, he would send Tobias to London with instructions for Thomas Bailey.

The next morning

"Ye can't mean to do it, lad," Tobias McDonald insisted as he watched Jonathan saddling Diablo.

"What better way to learn what's going on?"

"But to go riding into his hands? Are ye daft?" Tobias continued, even more insistent. "Don't ye ken what 'e'd do ta ye if 'e even suspected ye?"

"It's a chance I'm willing to take. Besides, no one knows the identity of the highwayman."

"Not even the lady?"

"The lady thinks the highwayman dead. She'd not betray me even if she knew."

"Can ye be sure 'o 'it?"

"I am going," Jonathan said with finality as he mounted Diablo. "I must."

"Ye'll not be swayed then?"

"This is something I must do. You should understand that, at least."

A momentary look of hatred crossed Tobias' features, then he slowly shook his head. "Aye, reckon I do."

Chapter Eleven

Finally, the fog began to clear from Spring's mind so she could concentrate. Still, she felt confused and disoriented. Her body felt weighted, and even the slightest movement was too much for her. She was drained, completely without energy, and there was nothing she wanted quite so much as to sleep.

Darkness beckoned, a peaceful abyss where there was no thought, no feeling, no danger; only the solitude of darkness that sought to enfold her and hold her in its embrace. Instinctively she realized she must fight the darkness, that giving in would mean being trapped there for all time. Spring wanted to live.

With her gaze fixed on the flickering flames in the grate across the room, she struggled to avoid slipping back into the darkness. *How long has it been? Was it minutes, hours, or days since she had been brought to Wyndridge?* Time had held no meaning in the darkness from which she had just escaped, but now, as reason returned, Spring wondered.

Her body slowly responded to her strength of will. After a time, she was able to lift her arms still longer, and the weights shed from her legs so that she could raise her knees.

Finally, as the weakness abated, she was able to turn on her side to face the fire. The effort cost her dearly, and for a moment she felt drained. With the last dredges of her strength, she curled into a comforting position with her knees nearly touching her chin and continued watching the fire. The golden flames flickered in the growing dusk of the room, casting strange shadows over the wall.

She felt utterly alone. Where was Jonathan? Had he searched for her when he returned to the cave and found her gone?

Instinctively, Spring knew that Jonathan would not give up easily on their love. That thought was comforting. Spring's thoughts turned to her family. What were they doing? How was her mother? Thoughts of Jonathan and her family brought a fierce determination for survival to Spring. She would not let them down.

When a door creaked, Spring turned toward the sound. A hint of a smile touched her lips as she recognized her grandmother's silhouette in the doorway.

"You're awake!"

Lady Phoebe crossed the room and sat on the bed beside Spring. She took one of Spring's hands in one of her own and gently squeezed it. With gentle fingers, she stroked Spring's forehead, and Spring moved closer to their remembered tenderness of childhood.

"At last, the fever's gone. My pet, I have been so worried! But now you are going to be fine, Doctor Morgan will see to it. I have the utmost confidence in Aaron," Lady Phoebe gushed with relief.

"How long have I been asleep?" Spring inquired as Lady Phoebe paused to catch her breath.

A frown etched Lady Phoebe's brow while she continued to stroke Spring's cheek gently.

"There, there," she soothed. "Don't' worry, you needed to rest. It has done you good, I am sure. Why you look better already."

"How long?"

Lady Phoebe looked away nervously. Clearly, she did not want to divulge the information which Spring sought.

"How long?" Spring prompted again, struggling to sit up.

"Two days," Lady Phoebe answered reluctantly. "Now, now, you must rest," Lady Phoebe said, pressing Spring back upon the pillows. "You must not exert yourself. The doctor has said you must rest."

Two days! Spring thought in bewilderment. What could have caused such a lapse? She had felt fine when her grandmother put her to bed, tired but then not so tired that she would sleep for two entire days. And why did she feel so weak and drained, almost as if she were recovering from a lengthy illness.

"I'll get the doctor. He will be pleased to see you so greatly improved. We have been quite beside ourselves with worry," Lady Phoebe insisted as she left the room to fetch the doctor.

Relaxing against the pillows, which her grandmother had fluffed behind her, Spring surveyed her surroundings.

The room was elaborately furnished with heavy baroque furniture. The bed itself filled one corner of the room and was heavily carved with ornate figures and hung with velvet curtains.

These were not the type of furnishing Spring would have chosen for herself. She shivered at the oppressive atmosphere that the heavy, ornate furnishing cast.

When the door creaked open again, Spring turned toward it expectantly. Her breath froze in her throat as she recognized Lord Wyndridge in the fading light.

Quickly closing her eyes and praying he had not seen her, Spring pretended to sleep. Maybe if she pretended to sleep, he would leave her room.

His footsteps echoed against the stone floor as Spring held her breath, waiting. When he fumbled with something on the table at her bedside, she struggled to hold in check the shiver rising within her at his nearness. Knowing that he stood over her and not being able to see what he was doing set her nerves on edge.

Finally, opening her eyes a sliver she peered between thick lashes toward the earl. What was he doing? She wondered an instant before light flared brightly in her eyes, answering her unspoken question.

The sudden light hurt her eyes, so she closed them tightly against it. Her breath ached in her chest as the earl held the flame nearer to her face. She could feel the warmth of the flame as its light flickered over her features.

With a cruel grip, a cold hand clasped her chin and forced her face fully toward the candle's light. Spring gasped at his reptilian touch upon her skin. The breath she had been holding left her lungs in a rush, making the candle sputter in its onslaught. Startled, her eyes flew open and focused wide upon the hated vestige of the Earl of Wyndridge.

"Highwayman's whore," Earl Wyndridge ground out between clenched teeth as his fingers tightened painfully upon her chin.

Spring tried to lift her head proudly, but his grip held her pinned with his bony fingers. Still, she refused to lower her gaze, meeting his evenly, defiantly.

"Have you no shame, whore?" Wyndridge sneered, his fingers biting into her tender flesh.

"Tis no different than the role you wish me to play. Forced wife or whore, I see no difference."

In one swift movement, the earl loosened his grip on her, drew back his hand and struck Spring full across the cheek. She recoiled under the blow, tasting the saltiness of her own blood in her mouth.

"Bastard."

"And you, my little trollop, shall learn your role well before I'm done with you. Shall I have you continue to play the whore?"

Spring had known Wyndridge was a cruel, hate filled man, but she had never dreamed of the depths of his vileness. Calling upon all her courage, Spring rounded on him, her eyes glittering dangerously.

"Play your whore? I think not. Do you think me some mere village chit you can take then cast aside? Must I remind you that I am the daughter of an earl, and my mother was once Lady-in-waiting to the Queen. I have no fear that you will not do right by me, my lord. It was by your contrivance that I was brought to this state. If you no longer want me to wife, then free me and all my father's holding with me!"

For a moment Wyndridge was taken back by Spring's open challenge, then his eyes narrowed to thin icy slits, his face set into hard lines, and he gave a dry, evil laugh.

"So, you could scamper safely away with your mettlesome grandmother?" his voice fell into the empty silence of the darkened room like grains of sand into an open grave. "No, my little whore, it will not be nearly so easy for you. Not nearly so. The wedding will take place as soon as the doctor says you are fit. You'll not escape me, my dear."

When the earl reached out to trace the reddening welt on her cheek, Spring shrank away from his icy hand, as if his touch could mark her soul. He could not treat her like this. She would not stand for it. She had no recourse as far as the marriage, but she would be damned if she would stand for this.

Determined, she sat up in the bed and stared evenly at the earl, her eyes filled with all the hatred and loathing she felt for him as she defied him with her gaze. She would not shrivel before him, nor would she beg. His lordship would soon find that in dealing with Lady Spring Lansing, he would reap such as he had sown.

"I am here because you saw fit to bring me here. You will treat me as befits my station. I shall not countenance less."

"Therein lies the problem, my lady. What exactly is the position of a highwayman's whore? On her back, I would presume." When Wyndridge's cold gaze slid slowly over her form beneath the bedcovers, Spring had to suppress a shiver.

Curling her hands into tight fists, Spring prepared another heated torrent to fling at his head when the door was thrown open and Lady Phoebe sailed in with Doctor Morgan in tow.

Suddenly conscious of the burning welt upon her cheek, Spring turned face toward the shadows, but not before Aaron Morgan's keen eyes had noted the reddening mark. Spring watched the doctor's gaze shift from her to Wyndridge and back again. It appeared that in that instant he made up his mind about something, for his lips thinned and a grim scowl darkened his usually pleasant features. Heat rushed to Spring's face as she felt his gaze on her face. The imprint of the earl's hand seemed to burn more intently on her skin.

She silently thanked the doctor when he took her grandmother's arm and gently urged her back toward the door.

"I need to examine my patient. Perhaps you could have a tray prepared for her? I am sure she must be quite famished," Aaron suggested to ease the lady's expulsion.

When her ladyship had gone, Aaron turned his attention toward Lord Wyndridge.

"My lord?"

When Wyndridge failed to respond to the doctor's hint, he began again, more forcefully.

"If you will excuse us, my lord?"

For a moment it seemed Lord Wyndridge would refuse the doctor's request. His gaze narrowed on Spring, his light eyes glittering with icy crystals.

"The highwayman shall be caught and will pay dearly for his transgressions, my dear. Anyone that conspires against me pays very dearly in the end, never doubt that. I shall not stop until this highwayman is dead." His lordship turned and left the room.

Spring shivered. She closed her eyes for a moment, struggling for composure.

The touch of the doctor's hand brought her eyes open instantly. He gently assessed the angry welt upon her cheek. Spring blinked back unshed tears. *I will not cry. I will not.* She raised her chin proudly.

"He struck you. "

There was no need for Spring to respond to his statement, so she focused her attention on the flames burning in the grate.

Silently the doctor moved away. Spring kept her eyes on the flames, feeling hatred eating at her like the hungry flames devouring the logs in the grate.

She heard water splashing into the wash bowl on a stand against the far wall. A moment later, Aaron Morgan returned to press a cold cloth against her cheek.

"You'll have a bruise tomorrow," he said, holding the soothing cloth against her injured cheek.

"It's nothing," Spring answered, finally meeting the doctor's gaze.

Next, he carefully examined her injured foot, washing the wound gently and applying a pungent salve before wrapping it with a clean bandage. When he had finished, he moved back to the head of the bed where he felt her forehead.

"The fever's gone," he said and smiled reassuringly. "You're much better tonight. By tomorrow you should be well on the road to recovery. Still, you need to rest." Aaron Morgan pulled the door closed behind him and went in search of Lady Phoebe.

Lady Phoebe brought the tray containing a rich broth, bread, cheese, and a glass of milk over and placed it on the bedside table. She tucked pillows behind Spring's back and fluffed them so that they supported her in a sitting position. Then she shook out the crisp linen napkin and placed it on Spring's lap.

"Here you go, my dear," Lady Phoebe coaxed as she spooned up the broth and offered it to Spring.

Wrinkling her nose at the greasy broth, Spring looked down at it doubtfully.

"I'm not an invalid. Could I not have something else?"

"You don't want to overtax your system, my dear. The doctor wants you to be careful and continue to rest for a few days. Come, this will help you to regain your strength. "

Spring managed to force down several spoons of the greasy broth to appease her grandmother then refused any more. Instead, she reached for the cheese and bread, nibbling at it hungrily as she sipped the warm milk.

Lady Phoebe pursed her lips, going on about the benefits of the broth. But steadfastly Spring refused any more of the rich, greasy brew with its faint woodsy taste.

"I received a letter from your momma. Young Mister Sinclair has been asking after your health. He came calling, hoping to court you."

"Jonathan came?" Spring's pulse began to race.

"Oh, yes, my dear. The young man was quite taken with you. Why, if you had not taken to this confounded plan of yours to marry the earl, I am quite convinced he would have offered for you. His family is quite presentable, you know, even if he does not have a title. Still, there is a title on his aunt's side, you know. And I am convinced he is quite wealthy. He would have been a fine match. A fine match."

"Grandmother, I know you had high hopes of joining our family to Lady Sarah's, but it just cannot be. I do what I must. However distasteful I find the earl, I will marry him. There is no other way. My father inadvertently brought this misfortune upon us, and it remains for me to make it right. If father had listened to reason in the beginning, this need not have happened. But no, he thought he knew best." Spring took a deep breath. "I encouraged him, and now I must pay the price."

"My dear, I'm sure this is not your doing. There must have been other mischief afoot. It's not right that you should have to pay such a dear price. "

"No, Grandmother, it was my doing. Mr. Brownstone warned father against the investment, but he and I would not listen. I encouraged father to make the investment, don't you see? This is my fault and mine alone.

"Still, I can hardly bear to see you sacrifice yourself because of it. Surely there must be something to be done..." Lady Phoebe continued to fret over her granddaughter like a setting hen with only one egg.

Spring resolutely tried to push thoughts of her coming marriage aside as she concentrated on her meal. There was nothing to be done about it. No way out, so it was best that she not dwell upon it. If she did, she might break down completely, and she did not want her grandmother to know just how distressing she found this marriage to the earl.

By the time she had finished the last of her bread, cheese and milk, Spring's eyelids were beginning to droop. Her strength, which had been fragile, to say the least, now deserted her, and the cup almost slipped from her fingers as she reached to replace it on the tray. Spring welcomed the darkness pulling her back into its grasp. In the darkness there was peace, in the darkness there was escape. Finally, with a sigh, she closed her eyes and let it claim her.

Lady Phoebe stood watching the sleeping form of her oldest grandchild and smiled a sad little smile. *Such a brave little thing.* She brushed a tangled curl away from Spring's forehead.

"Sleep, my sweet, while grandmother thinks about what's to be done. "

Long after Lady Phoebe had left her, Spring thought about her words. If a speedy recovery from her ordeal would hasten her marriage to Wyndridge, she would see that her progress was slow and drawn out. Even a few days' respite would be worth the pretense. Thinking of ways to put off her wedding day, Spring drifted off to sleep.

The faint glow of a candle burning on the dressing table across the room cast shadows about the room when Spring awakened. Her head ached dully, and her throat felt scratchy and dry. She tried to sit up, but the throbbing at her temples became much worse. Weakly Spring fell back to the bed with a low moan.

"So, you're awake?" Lady Phoebe spoke from the shadows. She hurried to her granddaughter's bedside and placed a cool hand against Spring's forehead.

"The fever has returned. It is no wonder, what with all you have been through," Lady Phoebe's voice broke slightly. "Just lie back while I get the doctor. "

Spring did not want to take the foul-tasting medicine her grandmother and the good doctor forced down her throat. She did not want to get better. Getting better would mean hastening her marriage, and Spring dreaded the thought of it.

The days passed, and her ankle improved, the swelling went down as did her fever, yet still, Spring languished in bed. Even if Wyndridge was not fooled by her complaints of poor health, he left her to them and concentrated his efforts on finding the highwayman.

"Pet, it's been nearly a week. The doctor says your ankle is quite better. Don't you think it is time you left these four walls?" Phoebe indicated her disdain for the room with a grand flourish of her hand.

"No. I cannot. Not yet," Spring answered.

Pretending to doze, Spring watched Lady Phoebe gather her needlework and take a seat close beside her bed.

"Everyone has been very concerned about you. Surely you could let them see that you've recovered?"

Spring opened her eyes and studied her grandmother for a moment. "And have everyone watching me? Whispering behind my back about what happened?"

Spring had given the matter much thought of late, and her bravado was wearing thin. She did not know how much more she could stand.

Chapter Twelve

It was just past noon when the letter arrived from London. Wyndridge, seated alone in the library, studied it with narrowed eyes.

Benedict Edward Goodwood made short work of explaining what had transpired. Wyndridge seethed with anger. How dare anyone make claims against what belonged to him.

This suit before the Chancery was a mere formality, a nuisance to be handled post-haste. The court order freezing all the holdings of the Wyndridge estate. as well as his own personal bank accounts, might prove a little more troublesome.

He had no doubt that his sources would discover the identity of the young whelp seeking to lay claim to the Wyndridge title. And once found, he would be dealt with severely.

A small smile played on the earl's straight lips as he anticipated that deed. So, Edward was still trying to best him? Even from his grave his brother sought to thwart him. But Edward would lose. He always lost.

For a moment Marcus thought of this supposed nephew he had never met. Under different circumstances, he might have acknowledged the boy, might have even accepted him as his heir. Then this business with the Lansing chit would not be necessary.

But now, because of all the lies, this would have to be dealt with and swiftly. He would leave for London immediately. The sooner the matter was settled, the better.

A knock sounded at the door. Wyndridge looked up from the letter in his hand, annoyed at the interruption.

"Yes? "

The door opened slowly. "A visitor, milord," the butler announced. "Jonathan Sinclair. He said you were expecting him, milord."

"Sinclair, what? Expecting him?" Wyndridge answered. "Oh yes, horses, he wants to buy horses. Show him in and have the coach prepared. I leave for London within the hour."

"Very well, milord."

The butler pulled the door closed behind him and hurried to retrieve the guest.

Jonathan stood in the wide hall, staring up at the many portraits that lined the stone walls. Ancestors, his ancestors. Strange, he felt no connection to any of the faces in the pictures.

The only connection he felt was to the woman who had so recently come into his life and even now might be his aunt.

Jonathan refused to entertain the idea. The wedding had not taken place. He would have heard, if it had.

"If you will come this way, milord will see you now."

Jonathan turned and followed the man without a word. Where was Lady Spring Lansing?

Lord Wyndridge was seated behind a massive desk in the library when Jonathan strode into the room. He studied a letter on the desk before him and did not look up as Jonathan was ushered into the room. Jonathan stood quietly for a moment, letting his gaze become familiar with the room.

He turned to study the books that lined a shelf to the right side of the room. Obviously, the letter was particularly important. Jonathan smiled. He would not interrupt.

Finally, Wyndridge folded the letter and tucked it into the pocket of his vest. Jonathan smiled again. When Lord Wyndridge looked up, their eyes met and held for a moment.

"You're interested in horses? "

Jonathan nodded.

"My stables are the best in England."

"So, I've heard."

"I've business to deal with in London. I shall be gone for a few days. You may stay here and acquaint yourself with my stock, if you like. You may have use of my stables while I am gone. When I return, we can talk business."

"Most generous of you, my lord."

Wyndridge pulled the bell rope behind the desk. A maid hurried in.

"Milord? "

"See that a room is prepared for Mr. Sinclair."

"At once, milord," the woman answered nervously, then backed out of room and hurried away to do her master's bidding.

"AT LEAST, SEE JONATHAN Sinclair," Phoebe continued. "He is quite beside himself with worry, although he tried not to let his lordship see it over much."

"Jonathan?" Spring gasped. "He's here?"

"Yes, he came to look over some horses Wyndridge has, but when he learned of your misuse by the highwayman, he demanded his lordship allow him to help with the search while his lordship tends to business in London."

Jonathan is here. Spring felt her heart begin to race. She had thought it was the fevered dream that made her think Jonathan was here. But no, he came after her.

Why had he come? Would he tell her grandmother what had transpired between them? Why could he not have just returned to America and left her to her fate?

"He had business with his lordship, but when he heard of your misfortune, he came straight away to offer his support."

"Indeed?" *Had he come for her?*

But she must not even consider it. If his lordship ever suspected it had been Jonathan and not the highwayman who had aided in her fall from grace, he would kill him.

"They've been out every day combing the countryside for the bandit," Phoebe continued. "Not that they've found a trace of him."

"He's dead! Why won't they just let it rest!" Spring insisted, her words sharpened more by the knowledge of Jonathan's presence than she wanted her grandmother to know.

"If you'd just speak to Jonathan—" Phoebe began, but Spring cut her off.

"No, I won't see him. I do not want to see anyone," Spring buried her face in her pillow.

Jonathan was here, at Wyndridge Hall. He had followed her as she had known in her heart that he would. She clutched that knowledge to herself, letting it warm the cold region where her heart resided. Jonathan was nearby.

She hardly touched her dinner when her grandmother brought it to her. She pushed the food round on her plate as her mind churned and images of Jonathan played out in her memories. She pictured him as he found her on the beach, the longing and care etched on his face. The intensity of his eyes on her as he made her his own.

She felt heat infuse her face as the memory of Jonathan's touch inspired a tingling awareness in her body. Thoughts of Jonathan were a welcome diversion from her self-imposed exile. She was loath to leave her refuge and face marriage to his lordship.

"Dearest, are you feeling unwell?" Lady Phoebe touched her hand to Spring's forehead. "Should I send for the doctor? You appear quite flushed."

"I'm fine, Grandmother." Spring tried to will the flush away. "There is no need to send for the doctor."

Lady Phoebe puttered around, rearranging the items on the bedside table. She straightened the covers of Spring's bed. She fluffed the pillows and then moved to the fireplace where the last of the embers glowed faintly in their bed of ash.

"I am fine, grandmother. Don't fret over me so."

Once her grandmother took the tray with the barely touched food and left, Spring settled down, pulling the covers up tight around herself. The room was chilled, but she didn't bother asking to have the fire trimmed. Instead, she curled into a tight ball and willed her mind to calm. Finally, she slept.

Spring awoke with a start. The room was bathed in darkness. The candle she had left burning at her bedside had long since died, and the fire in the grate was no more than faintly glowing embers. *What time is it?* She looked toward the window where a curtain fluttered in the night breeze.

Was grandmother hoping she would catch her death of cold? Why had she opened the window? Spring pushed back the thick coverlet and slid her feet to the floor. With unsteady steps, she started toward the window. When something moved in the deep shadows beside the window, Spring's hand flew to her throat. A dark shape detached itself from the darkness and stepped toward her.

The highwayman, her mind screamed as she slid soundlessly toward the cold floor.

Jonathan caught Spring's limp body in his arms before she hit the cold floor. He had not meant to frighten her, but he had been desperate to see for himself that she was not in danger, not as seriously ill as he feared.

He lifted her slight form in his arms. Cradling her close against his chest, he lowered his cheek to hers, reveling in the fact that her skin was cool to the touch. Jonathan carried her to the bed and placed her carefully on it.

He then searched in the drawer of the bedside table, found a candle, and lit before placing it upon the bedside table. He moved it a bit closer, turning it low so that it cast slight flickering shadows across the still form on the bed.

Taking her in his arms, he gently pushed the long-tangled strains of hair away from her face as he cradled her in his arms and softly caressed her cheek.

How he had longed to hold her like this, safe against his heart forever. But he knew he must not. Soon she would awaken and sound the alarm at finding him in her room.

A moment later, Spring stirred in his arms, coming slowly to alertness. With a soft moan, she moved in his arms, for an instant snuggling deeper into the comfort of his embrace.

When she took a deep breath, he thought he caught his name on her lips as she exhaled.

In the candlelight, he watched as her eyelids flickered slightly then opened. Her eyes were clear and blue as they focused on his features above her.

"You came back," she whispered. Her hand trembled as she reached up to touch the silk mask covering his face.

He caught her hand before she could remove the mask but instead brought it to his lips. Her fingers were chilled and trembled slightly as he placed a gentle kiss on each fingertip.

"Was there any doubt that I would, my lady?"

Spring wondered at the calmness that engulfed her. She should cringe in fear for her life. She should scream for someone to rescue her from the highwayman again. She did neither.

"I thought you were dead."

"Not before I make his lordship pay for all the wrongs he has done my family."

"But why must I pay this debt and not his lordship?" Spring asked as she studied the black caped figure. Her strength was returning gradually and with it a healthy sense of indignation.

"Surely, I, who has suffered much at the hand of Earl Wyndridge, with still worse to come, should not be forced to pay for his sins against your family."

"My Lady, I came tonight merely to assure myself that you had not suffered undue harm in our last encounter," his voice was a strange rasping whisper.

"I am fine, just a touch of fever from the chill night air. The doctor says I shall be quite recovered in no time. Now that you've assuaged your conscious, you may leave the way you came, whatever that may have been." Spring removed herself from the comforting embrace of his arms then moved away from him, pulling the bed coverings about her in a prim manner.

"Be gone now, before someone discovers your presence."

"Now that I have assured myself of your recovered health, I would be on to another matter."

Spring's eyes narrowed slightly as she stared at the masked intruder. "What matter?"

"I have heard the most disquieting rumors and accusations against myself, and I would know why you have made them? Are you so anxious for my demise that you would as soon it be as the despoiler of innocent young women as a highwayman?"

Spring lowered her head as a subtle pink stain crept up her neck and bloomed in her cheeks.

"I thought you dead," she defended herself. "I thought only to protect myself from the Earl of Wyndridge. No further harm could have befallen you. You were supposed to be dead!"

A sardonic smile suddenly creased his face below the mask, lifting one corner of his firm mouth.

"In that case," he whispered. "My lady." His words were both possessive and disquieting. He reached out and gently traced the outline of her cheek then lifted her head to stare deeply into her eyes.

"Know that any service I could render you I freely give. I would gladly face the triple tree for the merest taste of your lips, gladly die your willing servant for even the rumor of one night spent in your arms," he said in a seductive whisper as he moved closer.

Spring watched in hypnotic fascination as he moved slowly nearer. Her gaze held transfixed by the dark gleam of his eyes beneath the mask, she did not try to move away, nor did she turn away as his lips descended to hers.

His touch was gentle, tenderly so. When he encountered no resistance, he became bolder, more demanding. His hands for a moment hovered in the air beside her then closed on her shoulders bringing her mouth harder against his. Her eyes slowly closed of a will all their own.

He tilted his head slightly, letting his lips playfully attack hers. The moist tip of his tongue darted demandingly at one corner of her mouth. Skillfully, he coaxed her to open to him. Shifting his position, he achieved complete access to her mouth. His tongue testing, tasting the secrets of her mouth.

The first bold thrust of his tongue between her teeth left Spring breathless and trembling. The headiness of his kiss held a strange drugging quality that robbed her of the will to resist and left her with senses reeling.

When she regained control of her shaken equilibrium and slowly opened her eyes, she was alone in the middle of the large bed. He had gone as silently as he had come. Spring shivered, feeling suddenly chilled and very much alone. With one last glance around the room, she blew out the candle and slid beneath the covers.

Darting shafts of sunlight spilled across the bed where Spring lay. She watched them spread a lacy pattern across the coverlet. The heavy brocade draperies were pulled back, so only a sheer lace curtain served to diffuse the sun's full strength.

Someone had been in and tidied her bedchamber while she slept, Spring observed as she glanced around her. She stretched languidly, feeling much more herself than she had in days.

She longed to be free of her prison, to walk in the garden and feel the warmth of the sun upon her skin, but still she faced the prospect of marriage to Lord Wyndridge.

It was necessary to keep up her pretense, for she could not abide the alternative. Marriage to his lordship was unthinkable after what she had shared with Jonathan. How could she endure the touch of Lord Wyndridge, of any man, after Jonathan's?

Slowly Spring raised her hand to her lips, as a slow heat spread on her cheeks at the memory of her nocturnal visitor. Had he really been here last night, or had it only been a dream? Her fingers traced the outline of her lips, remembering the pressure of his mouth on hers. How was it possible that her body responded so passionately to the highwayman when she loved only Jonathan?

Had the dreamlike quality of his visit played tricks on her senses and made her think for a moment it was Jonathan's arms holding her? But what of later? How could her body be so traitorous? It was Jonathan she loved, Jonathan she longed to be with.

Feeling restless, Spring walked to the window. Where was he? Her gaze drifted from the garden directly beneath her window to the stables visible in the distance.

In the several days since Lord Wyndridge had departed for London, Jonathan had repeatedly requested permission to visit her, but she had steadfastly denied his request.

Lady Phoebe had become quite vexed with her, yet still Spring could not bring herself to see Jonathan. How could she face him when she had given herself to him so freely yet rebuffed his proposal of marriage in favor of an alliance with Lord Wyndridge? He did not know of the hold Lord Wyndridge held over her family. What must he think of her? Spring cringed as the thought of Jonathan's condemnation filled her mind.

What was he to think? She could not bring herself to tell him the truth, could not abide that he should think both she and her father were complete fools for having been taken in by Lord Wyndridge. Sharing that shame was even less palatable than being thought a social climber.

Spring squared her shoulders, wrapping her battered pride closely around herself. Let him think what he would. She had an obligation to her father, to her family. She would not let them down.

Still, she condemned herself for her response to the highwayman. How was it possible that she felt so drawn to him? Why had she allowed him to kiss her with no resistance? Loving Jonathan as desperately as she did, how could her body respond so traitorously to the highwayman's embrace?

Deep in contemplation, Spring started when the door of her chamber opened slowly and her grandmother peered in, smiling broadly when she saw her granddaughter was awake.

"How are you this morning, my pet?" Lady Phoebe inquired, rushing on without giving Spring a chance to answer. "I declare, the bloom has returned to your cheeks, my love. You look very much the thing. Shall I ring for a tray? Surely you must be famished. I could use a cup of tea myself," Lady Phoebe rattled on, not giving her granddaughter a chance to say a word.

Spring waited patiently until her grandmother finally paused to draw a breath, then she hurriedly interrupted before Lady Phoebe could get her second wind.

"I feel much better this morning, quite rested, in fact. And I find my appetite has returned."

"Good, good." Lady Phoebe pulled the bell rope. "I took the liberty of having a tray prepared. It should be delivered shortly."

Spring smiled at her grandmother.

"I am obliged to ask again today if you might not allow Jonathan to visit. He is quite concerned about you."

"No, I..." Spring began, only to falter. "Please tell Jonathan I appreciate his concern, but I am still to overcome to receive guests."

"Surely you could see him for a moment?"

Spring raised one hand to her forehead dramatically. "No, I couldn't face him. Not after the shame that has befallen me. What must he think of me?"

Lady Phoebe was at once sympathetic.

"There, there my pet. No one knows of what has happened." Lady Phoebe patted Spring's hand gently.

Dabbing gently at her eyes with a lace edged handkerchief, Spring continued, "How can you think that the secret will be safe. The whole countryside knows my disgrace."

Never had Spring thought to carry the charade so far. Usually, when Lady Phoebe saw her granddaughter was not willing to consent to Jonathan's visit, she gave up.

Spring felt guilty at the shameful way she was abusing the highwaymen, especially after his visit last night. But she could not face Jonathan, not now, not yet.

"There now, of course you don't have to see him, I'll convey your regrets and offer some excuse. Don't fret, my love."

Chapter Thirteen

Lord Wyndridge stared at his barrister with hatred . His face burned with anger,eet red, and veins protruded on his neck, as his fist crashed down upon the desk.

"How dare this cur make claims against what is rightfully mine."

"But my lord—" Benedict Edward Goodwood began, only to have Wyndridge cut him off.

"Find him! I don't care how much it costs! Do you hear?" Lord Wyndridge pounded on the desk again, causing the barrister to jump.

"Yes, my lord."

"You will find this cur who dares to claim what is rightfully mine. I will deal with him in my own fashion." Wyndridge paced the small office.

"But surely—"

"I tire of this waiting. The courts take too long. Why should they even listen to this preposterous tale?"

"But surely, my lord," the barrister began again. "This matter is better managed through legal channels." He paused for a moment to marshal his thoughts before he continued. "If uh... if some unfortunate accident should befall the young man, might not suspicion be cast in your direction?"

"Unfortunate accidents befall people every day. Why should I be held responsible? Even if he is Edward's bastard, my brother left no legitimate issue, so he has no claim upon the estate of his sire."

"But, my lord, they claim to have in their possession the ship's log which records a marriage while at sea. Is it possible that this could be truc?"

Lord Wyndridge blanched. All color drained from his face. "And the captain, what has he to say about it? You have questioned him, no doubt." Lord Wyndridge asked, watching carefully for the man's reaction.

"Impossible, the man's dead. He was found with his throat slit."

"You see? Isn't that proof enough? He could not convince the captain to lie for him, so he killed him. Why has the constable not arrested this blackguard?"

Lord Wyndridge crossed the room and leaned on the desk. The gold tipped cane in his hand nearly touched Goodwood's nose. "Find him—and soon."

JONATHAN WAITED IMPATIENTLY for Lady Phoebe at the bottom of the stairs. How long did she intend to remain closeted up there with the girl? Surely, she remembered he was waiting for Spring's answer. The Lady did not appear addled, but quite sharp, never missing a trick.

No, it was not that she had forgotten. Jonathan swore under his breath. The hoyden had yet again refused to see him. Lady Phoebe was avoiding telling him for as long as possible.

For a moment, he considered knocking on Spring's door and demanding to be allowed in. What a howl that would set up! No, he would just have to bide his time. Surely before long she would give in and agree to see him.

Jonathan's face brightened when he heard the sound of a door closing somewhere on the floor above him. He watched the head of the stairs expectantly. But the look on Lady Phoebe's face when she appeared told him Spring had yet again refused his request.

"Damnation," Jonathan swore beneath his breath.

In a temper, he took himself off to the stables. It was either that or totally disgrace himself by forcing his way in to see her. He had thought that seeing her last night would have put to rest the gnawing that ate at him, but those few moments he had spent with her in the early morning hours had only heightened his need to see her, to be with her, to hold her.

Drat the girl. What was wrong with her? Why did she keep putting him off when she had all but welcomed that rogue into her bedchamber?

What kind of woman would welcome a bandit into her bed in the middle of the night, would marry a man old enough to be her father, and yet kept the man who genuinely loved her barred from her side? Jonathan chaffed at the restraint. He wanted to be with her, to talk with her, to hold her, to make love to her. At least he had been able to reassure himself of her return to health with his late-night visit. But that was little consolation when still she refused to allow him to visit her.

Jonathan saddled Diablo and headed toward the caves where Tobias should be waiting. He would put all thoughts of Spring out of his mind and concentrate on the business that had brought them to England.

Thinking of his last exchange with Tobias before he had left for Wyndridge, Jonathan smiled. Tobias had been quite vocal in his objections to this plan.

"Aye don't like it," Tobias had said flatly. "Aye can see ye'll no be changing yer mind. So, aye will just save me breath, but aye intend to keep watch for 'is lordship. No telling when 'e's like to return."

Tobias had brushed aside Jonathan's objections and continued, "Ye must be careful. Old Tob will be giving you a signal, so ye'll know when 'e's approaching. If he catches the highwayman, all we've worked for would be lost, ye know that."

Jonathan had watched Tobias from across the cave as he spoke and thought how lucky he was to have his friendship and loyalty. A fatherless boy could not have had a better friend than Tobias had been to him. It was such a little thing he requested, and Jonathan was powerless to refuse him.

"I'll be careful," Jonathan had promised. "And I'll listen for your signal."

Now, with his plans made, Jonathan could hardly wait for the house to fall quiet so he could put them into action.

He had taken dinner with the good doctor who had explained Lady Phoebe was taking her meal with her granddaughter. Jonathan had inquired after Spring's health and been told she was much improved but still felt too weak to join them downstairs.

For a moment, Jonathan had felt disquieted at this information. She had seemed quite recovered when he had last seen her, but perhaps he had been mistaken. No matter, soon he would see for himself.

Jonathan retired early, impatient to set his plan in motion. Once alone in his room, he listened for the sounds of the household to quiet.

To busy himself, he studied his hand-drawn sketch of the secret passageway that honey-combed the manor and studied it by lamp light. He had mapped every passage, had assessed each secret panel, and had found several on each floor.

On the pretense of liking the morning sun, he had managed to arrange to be moved to a room on the second floor that contained a secret panel.

When Jonathan had visited Spring before, he had scaled the side of the manor and climbed in through her window. It had been risky, but he was desperate to see her and reassure himself that she was recovering. All had gone well, but when he left her room, a stable hand crossing the yard had nearly discovered him.

Jonathan knew better than to try that route again. While pondering the problem, he had remembered tales from his childhood about secret passageways in an old manor house that Tobias had regaled him with. Jonathan decided to explore and found Wyndridge Hall indeed had secret passages.

He had explored that morning and set his plan in motion. It was not too difficult a feat, but it did require that he wait until the household was abed, so no one was likely to be up to hear his footsteps.

Impatient, Jonathan gathered an assortment of candles then opened the secret passage and stepped inside. He quickly lit one of the candles and held it aloft, searching the passageway. He found the black trousers, shirt, cape, and mask of the highwayman folded neatly on a wooden crate that he had found in the passageway.

He lowered the candle to the crate, closed the secret panel behind him and reached for the highwayman's costume. Once he was dressed for his part, Jonathan first made his way down into the lower regions of the house, where he checked to see that the servants had retired.

Once satisfied that the household had settled in for the night, Jonathan began his journey back along the narrow passage. By the flickering candlelight, Jonathan followed the passageway upward, pausing now and again to listen.

When he reached Lady Phoebe's chamber, Jonathan stopped for a moment, listening for any sound of movement from within, but only silence greeted his keen ears.

Spring's room, located on the opposite side of the house from Lady Phoebe's, required going up to the third floor and then crossing to the other side of the house and then back down to the second floor.

The walls of Wyndridge Hall were a maze, like a rabbit warren. It had taken Jonathan hours of exploration to plan his route to Spring's room.

He continued along the passage, up narrow steps that led to the third floor. At the end of the passage, he emerged and crossed to the other side of the house. He found the room he thought was directly above Springs and slipped inside.

Jonathan had been in the room earlier today and was certain it was unoccupied. The room had not been used for quite some time, judging from the lack of cinders in the grate and a fine film of dust covering the furniture.

Apparently, Lord Wyndridge's housekeeper is no more concerned with tidiness than she is with setting a decent table. Jonathan crossed the room and drew the bolt on the door, locking it from the inside. He deftly worked the spring mechanism that slid the secret panel back and slipped silently into the hidden passage.

Jonathan blessed the architect's love for symmetry and simplicity as he nimbly followed the narrow stairs down to the second floor and easily lifted the latch on the secret panel that opened into Spring's room.

Spring settled down to read her book but soon found it impossible to concentrate. Thoughts of Jonathan crowded her mind and chased away all hope of following the printed words and putting together a coherent sentence. That her grandmother had selected the work of John Locke made it no easier to concentrate.

Any other time Spring would have been delighted at the opportunity to read John Locke's theories. Her father had seen that she was well familiar with the enlightened ideas of Locke. Had encouraged her to read all the works of those men of his period who had heralded social change, even though it was quite unseemly for a girl to know of such ideas, let alone speak of them.

Again and again her mind returned to Jonathan. Had he read Locke's treatises? Did he realize Lock's theories offered the basis from which America's Thomas Jefferson had taken his principles of freedom and equality? She would love to discuss those ideals with Jonathan!

Her father, despite his loyalty to England and the crown, had held great admiration for the experiment in democracy that America had embarked on. Something of an amateur historian, he had never tired of debating the issue, and Spring had often served as his sounding board. How she had enjoyed those sessions. How she missed them.

The book slipped slowly from her fingers as Spring's eyes closed and she drifted into a dream filled sleep. Jonathan was there, laughing with her, talking with her, urging her to follow him out into the sunshine to enjoy the few stolen moments they had together.

Trusting him, she followed, reaching out to him, urging him closer. But when he took her into his arms, he suddenly changed and became Lord Wyndridge. The tyrant taunted her cruelly for her foolish attachment to Jonathan. He held her tightly in his arms, and she thrashed about wildly, trying to escape the hateful grasp, but his arms were unyielding.

Suddenly, someone was there challenging Lord Wyndridge's claim on her, pulling her easily from his lordship's grip and into the safe haven of his arms.

Spring looked up to see who her benefactor had been and encountered the smiling face of the highwayman.

It took several moments for Spring to realize that her dream had faded away with her rescue by the highwayman, but the highwayman had not. She blinked several times, thinking the black cloaked figure no more than a lingering specter of her dream, that as sleep pushed away from her dream clouded mind, he would dissipate.

He did not. Neither did he loosen his hold on her.

Strangely, she felt no fear. She knew deep inside that he meant her no harm. If he had meant to harm her, he could have done so long before now.

Finally, she realized he was indeed real and not a dream figure. Spring placed her hands flat upon his chest, for just an instant noting the slight tensing of powerful male muscles before she pushed him away. As clarity returned, she sought to put as much space between them as possible.

She did not understand the strange clamoring his proximity set up in her unschooled body, but she knew instinctively that to be close to him was dangerous because of her own traitorous body.

She must think of Jonathan. She must remember their love. Strengthened by the memory of Jonathan, and greatly chastened by her unbridled response to the highwayman, she turned furious eyes upon him.

"Rogue! What are you doing here?"

"Rescuing damsels from the grips of nightmares and late-night demons. Can you deny that, for a moment, you were exceedingly glad to see me, my lady?" he quipped. Spring blushed that he had read her so accurately.

"I was..." Spring stammered, "no such thing."

"My lady, to tell the lie does not become you." He traced the line of her cheek with his fingertip. "See, even by candlelight the truth is easily read in your face."

Spring pushed his hand aside and moved farther away from him, gathering the bedclothes more closely around her. She watched as he lifted the volume from where it had fallen and began to leaf through it.

"A very admirable work, my lady," he said when he returned his gaze to hers. "but surely not a subject to interest a lovely young woman. Would you not prefer one of the new fiction novels everyone finds so popular?"

Spring stiffened. How dare he relegate her to the rank of insipid female who could not possibly understand the more gentlemanly subjects of politics and freedom. Angered, she snatched the book from his hands.

"My choice of reading material is of no concern to you," she stated testily.

"Ah, but everything about you is of interest to me, my lady," he answered, reaching to slowly pry each of her fingers away from the book.

When he had recovered the book, he began again turning the pages. "Do you believe in these inalienable rights Locke speaks so highly of?" he finally asked.

Spring stared at him, amazed. Was it possible that the rogue not only had the ability to read but had read such lofty subjects as Locke's Treatises? Seeing her apparent doubt, the highwayman flipped through the pages found a certain passage then began to read:

"Men being, as has been said, by nature all free, equal, and independent, no one can be put out of this estate and subjected to the political power of another without his own consent..."

Those words spoken in his strange raspy whisper sounded almost ethereal. Spring shivered, feeling as if someone had walked across her grave.

"Are you real? How came you here? Do you really exist, or are you a specter conjured up of my own need?" Spring whispered as he closed the book.

"Touch me, my lady." He moved closer. "See that I am flesh and blood. A man at your biding, your eager servant, my lady. What need have you that I might fulfill?" He moved closer still. With one hand he tucked an errant strand of golden hair behind her ear. With the other he lifted her right hand and planted a kiss in its palm.

Spring stared into the dark eyes behind the mask, her gaze held mesmerized by his intense eyes.

A slow flame began in her palm where his lips had touched and raced along the nerve endings of her hand and arms, spreading in ever widening circles, until her entire body felt sensitized by his touch.

"Which demons are there that I may chase away, my lady?" he whispered, still holding her right hand. He caught the other and pulled her slowly closer.

"Tis not a demon but a flesh and blood rogue who plagues me," Spring answered with a soft laugh. "How can you chase him away when you are one and the same?"

"But, my lady, 'twas not fear that I saw in your eyes just now but relief that I had rescued you from some terrible fate. How can you seek so easily now to wish me away?"

Spring sobered, as his playful words reminded her of her plight. She pulled her hands away from his and folded them in her lap. She broke her gaze away from his and studied her folded hands.

"Nothing can save me from my fate," she whispered.

At once Jonathan sensed her withdrawal and cursed himself for his impatience. He must gain her confidence before he could expect her to confide in him. If he moved too fast, he would destroy the only chance he stood of learning the truth.

Casting around, he urgently sought some way to return the ease of communication which had passed between them moments earlier. Finally, his gaze fell on the book that had fallen to the coverlet between them. Lifting it once more, he sought to put their conversation back on firmer ground.

"How is it that a gently reared lady is familiar with the work of John Locke?" he asked in his throaty whisper.

Gazing at him suspiciously, she refused to be drawn back into conversation. He was dangerous, leading her along, tricking her into revealing too much about herself. Would he somehow use it against her? Was that his game?

Refusing to give up, he tried again. "What do you suppose Locke had in mind when he wrote those words? Many of his words are found in the work of Thomas Jefferson, you know."

Had he invaded my very thoughts as well as my bedchamber? Spring lifted her gaze to meet his. How was it that he echoed the very thoughts that had filled her mind just before she had fallen asleep? Spring could no longer resist the bait he had used.

"How is it a common highwayman is familiar with John Locke?" she countered as she turned the question back on him.

Stalemate. He acknowledged with a slight smile that slowly widened into a grin.

"I have not always been a highwayman, my lady. It is of strict necessity that I find myself so."

Spring felt sudden sympathy at his frank answer. "But surely you could have found a position to support yourself without resorting to a life of crime?"

"Tis not money I seek, my lady, but revenge."

"Revenge?" Spring stiffened at the word. "What have I done that you should seek revenge against me?"

"Not against you, my lady," he answered in his strange raspy whisper. "'Tis Lord Wyndridge who must pay. Murder carries a very high price."

"Murder?"

He watched her closely, wondering just how much he dared reveal. *Should I trust her? Would she tell Wyndridge?* One must bestow trust to gain trust, he decided as he gazed deeply into the spellbinding azure of her wide eyes.

"Aye, murder."

Spring gasped. She had known that Lord Wyndridge was ruthless and devious, but a murderer, as well? Yes, she could believe that of him, as well. The man was evil. He would stop at nothing to achieve his ends, as she well knew.

"Who?" Spring asked quietly, never doubting the guilt cast by the dark specter seated beside her.

"My father." At her small cry of distress, he continued quickly. "It happened years ago. I've only recently learned the entire story and have come to settle the score."

If Lord Wyndridge were gone... Spring crushed down the faint glimmer of hope beginning in her mind. She could not accept her freedom at the expense of another.

"Surely, you must realize murder is not the answer. It would make you no better than Lord Wyndridge. Revenge serves no constructive purpose. It is such a negative force it sours and sullies all that it touches."

He watched her intently, searching her features, wondering if he had trusted her too much. She might warn Wyndridge of the danger, might betray the trust he had placed in her. It would make no difference to the outcome of his plans. He would still have his revenge, but how would it affect his feelings for her if she did?

"Lord Wyndridge owes a great debt," he said at last. "One way or another, it will be paid. Just remember that, my lady."

Chapter Fourteen

The coldness of his voice made Spring's blood run cold. She had never heard so much anger or determination in a man's voice before.

Hesitant, she reached out to stroke his face below the black satin mask, wishing to somehow take away part of the pain she heard in his voice.

She sighed as a tear formed in the corner of one eye and ran unchecked down her face. She knew a great deal about debts that must be paid, regardless of the suffering it inflicted. *Does he?* She studied the dark eyes behind the smooth mask.

"Lord Wyndridge has much to answer for," Spring whispered. "but I very much doubt he'll answer for anything in this life."

"He'll pay."

Spring shivered slightly at the resolve in his whisper. Did he realize that in seeking his revenge the payment might very well be his own?

"Is that why you stopped the coach? Because it belonged to Lord Wyndridge?" she asked holding his gaze intently.

He nodded.

"And you kidnaped me because I am to wed his lordship?"

Again he nodded.

"Why?"

"He wanted you, I determined that he should not have you," he stated flatly.

"And now?"

"He shall not have you, my lady." He moved closer, closing one hand gently around her throat as the other tangled in her hair. "Not as long as I live and breathe, my lady."

The sweet warmth of his breath fanned her cheek as he moved closer. His gaze never left hers until he was so close that her eyes refused to focus on his features any longer.

His nearness sent her senses tumbling. Her mind careened out of control as her body responded to his nearness. Instinctively her body leaned slightly toward his. Her eyes closed more out of self-defense than surrender, but it did not matter, for when his lips touched hers, she was lost to reason.

With his hand in her hair, he urged her head back slightly so that he had better access to her mouth. His tongue slid smoothly over the outline of her lips then determinedly sought entrance to her mouth.

With a low moan, Spring surrendered, and he took possession of her mouth. Her senses swirled out of control as his tongue plundered the secret places of her mouth then moved on to explore the soft tender spot just behind her earlobe.

His touch left a trail of fire as he planted tender kisses down the column of her throat and on down to where the firm mounds of her breasts pressed pleadingly against the soft material of her nightgown.

It was as if her body remembered his touch and responded with a mind of its own. Her breasts rose under his attention. Their peaks became hard rosebuds of desire as his lips captured them through the soft material of her gown.

A slow fire spread from her belly downward as he captured first one then the other between his teeth.

"Jonathan." The word escaped her parted lips almost of its own volition.

Sanity returned with the impact of water drawn from a mountain spring. She stiffened in his arms then began to struggle. Heat flooded her face as mortification at what she had almost done, had almost allowed him to do set in. How could she be so wanton? Was she cursed that her body responded so to a stranger?

He allowed her to escape but held on to one of the ribbons at the neckline of her gown. Slowly he twisted it around his finger, making it clear that she had not escaped but only been granted a slight reprieve.

"Your lips may lie and tell me no, my lady," he said with a slow smile. "but your body speaks only the truth when it responds to my touch and tells me yes." His teeth flashed white in the candlelight.

"Do not mistake me for a gentleman such as your Jonathan. I am not so chivalrous as he."

Despite his words to the contrary, he did not press the issue but allowed her to move away while he slowly unwound the ribbon.

Desperate, she sought to marshal her defenses. She straightened her nightgown and tidied her hair, avoiding looking at her nocturnal visitor as long as she possibly could. When at last she lifted her gaze, empty space greeted her.

Even without looking for him, she knew he was gone. The atmosphere of the room had changed, the electricity that marked his arrival had dissipated, and all was again as it had been before. Only the slight motion of the draperies at the window gave any sign that he had been there.

Thinking he must have left by way of the window, Spring padded across the cold stone floor to the window but found it firmly closed. For a long moment she stood staring into the darkness of the garden below. Was that a movement there in the shadows? No, only a tree limb swaying in the early morning breeze.

Baffled, Spring pulled the heavy draperies shut and returned to bed.

She slept peacefully with only the occasional intrusion of Jonathan or the highwayman into her dreams, but both vowed to keep the earl at bay. Jonathan and the highwayman merged into one image having the highwayman's dark visage and Jonathan's smooth voice. With that strange specter standing guard in her dreams, Spring drifted in her contented dream state.

Lady Phoebe and Aaron Morgan visited Spring later that morning and, encouraged to find her in such good cheer, urged her to join them downstairs.

"Jonathan is eager to see you, my dear," Lady Phoebe gently reminded as she fussed over Spring.

"No, not yet," Spring refused firmly.

Left alone when her grandmother went to request a breakfast tray prepared, Spring moved to a chair near the window. She watched with envy as Jonathan left for a morning ride. How she longed to ride across the meadows and hillsides as Jonathan did every day.

It was so boring to remain closeted in her room hour after hour, day after day. She considered leaving the haven of her room while Jonathan was gone but discounted the idea. No doubt the staff would be called upon to make a full report to Lord Wyndridge upon his return. Since her only hope of postponing the wedding lay in the continued guise of illness, she dared not take the chance.

The pattern for the next several days followed the same path. The days she spent alone or with Lady Phoebe to keep her company. Left alone, she would sit by the window and watch for Jonathan.

At night, she read by candlelight and waited for her nocturnal visitor. The loss of sleep when she tried to stay awake to discover how he gained entrance to her room caused faint purple shadows beneath her eyes, which added credence to her continued convalescence.

Yet with all her vigilance, he waited until she finally drifted off to sleep before he made his appearance. The stealth with which he came and went gave his visits an ethereal quality that caused Spring to almost believe he was no more than her overactive imagination working in the vacuum of her seclusion. Finally, one night she vowed to tell him as much.

He awakened her with a kiss and presented her with a book he deemed more suitable for her than *Locke's Thesis on Government*.

"Are you a ghost or some figment of my imagination that you come and go so secretly I can neither see nor hear you?"

"Nay, my lady," he answered with a gentle laugh. The soft whisper of his voice washed over her.

"I have tried to stay awake, yet you never arrive until I've fallen asleep, and when you leave you always weave your spell about me to distract me, so when I look up you are gone." Spring studied the coverlet for a moment before raising troubled eyes to her visitor.

"I think you must surely be a ghost come to haunt me," she accused.

"I am flesh and blood, my lady," he answered in his strange whispery voice. "made more so by your beauty. Shall I prove to you I am man not ghost?"

"Yes," Spring answered, daring him. "I would have the proof."

Before she guessed his intent, he wrapped her in his embrace and pulled her close against the firmness of his chest. His lips closed over hers to silence her protest that this was not what constituted proof.

She had wanted him to divulge his method of arrival and exit of her chamber, not slake his lustful appetite upon her.

As always, when he touched her, her body responded in a thousand little rivulets of fire spreading through her veins inflaming her senses as they went. She fought unsuccessfully against the response and felt rather than heard him chuckle at her feeble resistance.

His hands traveled over her body, playing it like a finely tuned instrument, bringing a keen awareness and aching need for more. For just a few moments, she allowed herself to respond to his touch, to return his kiss, to dream about what could never be, that she could be the highwayman's lady.

Then she forced herself from his embrace and picked up the book he had brought her. How fitting that he had brought her a tale of true love lost. Did he realize how prophetic the work was? Was that the reason he had given it to her?

At times, it baffled her how sensitive and intuitive he appeared. His conduct, so out of character for the rogue he was, caused her to have trouble remembering just what he was.

She knew so little about him, yet felt she knew everything that mattered. Just as had been the case with Jonathan, there appeared to be a special bond between them, one she failed to understand but could not deny existed.

He, too, appeared aware of the link between them and had come to accept it more easily than she. But then, by admitting his attraction to her, he was not betraying someone dear to him.

Spring was brought up short by the thought. Might he, after all, have a wife, children even, waiting somewhere for him when his mission of vengeance ended?

The idea that he might have a wife was extremely unpalatable. Suddenly, it was especially important that she knew all those answers. Still clutching the book, she crossed her arms protectively over her chest and raised troubled eyes to the highwayman.

"Is this some game you play? Why do you come here? Is there not some gentle wife awaiting your return?"

"Nae, my lady. 'Tis your beauty that draws me," he said dramatically. "Like a moth to the flame. Others pale beside your beauty. There is no one who holds my heart save you."

Spring tossed the book away from her as if it had burned her skin. "Why do you so torment me. You know I love another!"

"And would wed yet another?" he challenged.

"I have no choice in the matter. The die has been cast. There is no turning back," she answered defiantly.

"You have but to tell me what needs be done to free you, and it shall be done."

Spring stared at him incredulously.

"Free me?" she demanded. "You think you could do that when my grandmother's barrister could not?"

"With but one squeeze of my finger," came the softly whispered response. "You have but to give the word, my lady."

"Murder is not the answer. Even were the earl to die, my debt would not be canceled, my family would still be left destitute," Spring answered.

When he remained silent, she continued.

"Don't you see I must marry the earl? He holds power over everything, my father's entire estate. The only way out is by this marriage, Wyndridge has seen it so. Even were his lordship to die, I would not be free of the hell he has created for me."

He took her into his arms and sought to comfort her with the only means available to him, gentle kisses and whispered vows of undying devotion. Finally, she slept in his arms.

When she awoke alone in her bedroom, tears welled up in her eyes and slid silently down her cheeks. There was no hope of a life with Jonathan. He would never accept her as less than his wife, but perhaps the highwayman might not have such high principles.

Even with her plan to leave Wyndridge as soon as all the legal requirements of their contract were met, she would still be unsuitable as bride for Jonathan. His family would expect his wife to be above reproach. She could not expect him to still want her once she was legally tied to Wyndridge.

It would not be easy for her to escape from the prison that Wyndridge planned for her, but she would find a way. The image of the highwayman crept into her mind, and she knew fate had thrown them together for this reason. Did not the highwayman find his way in and out of her room at will? If he could, then she could also. He might even be persuaded to take her with him.

Suddenly, a new determination filled her. She did not understand how it was possible, but what she felt for this rogue, this bandit, was just as strong, just as urgent as what she felt for Jonathan. *How is it possible that I love both of them*? She searched for an answer in the turmoil of her thoughts.

In the back of her mind, a seed had taken root some time ago and now burst forth with singular clarity. She remembered the highwayman's eyes. Yes, they held the same fire when they touched her as Jonathan's had. He might have fooled her eyes and ears, but her body, her soul had known him. Even in his disguise they had responded to him. What a fool he must think her, playing such games with her.

Indignation well up inside her. She would teach him to toy with her. Highwayman indeed. Rogue was more like it. Deceitful, conniving, rutting rogue. Suddenly, it pleased her to have revealed her plight to him. Let him see what he thought of her newest plan. Impatiently, she waited for night to come.

Knowing he would not arrive until she was asleep, Spring planned to thwart his surveillance of her. She was not certain how he knew what she was doing, but she was certain that he somehow knew every move she made. Had he even watched as she dressed? No wonder he found it so hard to keep his hands off her.

She opened the drapes, allowing moonlight to suffuse the room. Then she quickly rearranged the furniture in the room, moving a chair and small table into the middle of the room. Satisfied with her handy work, she closed the drapes so that only a small sliver fell across the room. Unlike previous nights when the candle at her bedside remained burning, Spring blew it out. With the room in darkness, it would be harder for him to tell if she were sleeping.

Now, let him come. *I'll be ready for him.* She settled into a light sleep.

Sometime later she awakened. She felt no fear when she recognized his familiar dark form outlined in the moonlight from the opened window. With delight, she realized he had tripped over her chair in the darkness, and that sound had awakened her.

He approached the bed slowly. He had stopped to search for the lamp on the bedside table.

She sat up and reached across the bed to stay his hand when he would have lit the candle. Instead, she urged him to join her on the bed. She allowed the coverlet to fall to her lap leaving the thin nightgown her only protection.

She played her part. She moved nearer to him and reached up to touch his face, allowing her fingers to trace the smooth lines of the satin mask.

"I don't even know your name," she whispered seductively. There, now just let him lie to her.

"Drew," the raspy whisper answered.

Drat the man. She had given him a chance, but now he would pay the price. Spring allowed one finger to slip beneath the edge of the mask to caress his cheek in slow seductive circles. *So much for honesty.*

If he wanted to play games, then she would oblige him.

"Do you believe in fate, Drew?" she asked in a throaty whisper.

"No."

"You're wrong," she answered. "Somethings are just meant to be. It doesn't matter how much we fight it."

She moved closer, pressing her breasts against the firm wall of his chest and reached up to place a soft kiss at the corner of his lips. "If it's fate, it will happen. There's just no stopping it."

She felt him tense as she ran a hand along the firm muscles of his upper arm. A heady power filled her as she again touched her mouth to his, this time letting her tongue trace the outline of his lips. Delighted, she felt the low groan that he tried to stifle deep in his chest.

"I've tried to fight it, but I can't help myself, Drew. When you come to me, I can't remember Jonathan. You replace him in my thoughts until I can't separate you." She felt a slight tremor in the male flesh beneath her hands and delighted in the distress that her words caused.

"I can't deny what your touch does to me any longer." She waited for a moment then delivered her final salvo. "Love me, Drew."

At first, Spring thought she had won, that he was about to denounce her for the faithless wanton he thought her.

She could feel the effort of will he exerted to restrain his body from responding to the urgent pull of her arms. How she would laugh at his denouncement when she removed his mask and threw his accusation back into his face. Merrily, she planned how she would taunt him with her knowledge of his identity all along.

Then his arms came around her, crushing her to him as his lips burned fire along her throat. He pressed her down among the pillows of the bed. His hands moved skillfully over her body as his lips claimed hers. He eased the soft gown from her body and left her defenseless against his plundering lips and hands.

He kissed her again and again, long drugging kisses between which he called her name repeatedly and professed his undying love for her, his urgent need for her.

Spring sank into utter turmoil, her mind totally aghast at what was happening. Yet her body reveled in it. In an instant of sanity, before all reason was driven from her by the touch of his hands and lips upon her body, Spring reached up and caught the mask. She would have her proof.

"No, no, my sweet," he whispered as with a gentle laugh he pulled her hand away from the mask.

He moved slowly along her body, planting tiny, teasing kisses as he went. His touch ignited an unquenchable flame of desire. Everywhere he touched, a new fire sprang up.

She was mindless with her need to touch him, to return caress for caress, when he finally released her hands and urged her arms around him. Her hands trembled slightly as she spread them across the wide expanse of his back, feeling the sensitive play of muscles beneath her fingertips.

In the instant before he claimed her, she whispered his name. "Jonathan."

For she knew just as surely as her body had known that it was Jonathan's arms holding her, Jonathan's lips claiming hers, Jonathan's body that now making hers whole. Even if he had denied her the truth, his body could no more lie than could hers. She knew him, and she welcomed him with a fierceness to match his own.

With each thrust, he drove her nearer to the pinnacle, closer to the edge of the abyss awaiting them until together they tumbled over the edge. She matched each powerful stroke, welcoming him, taking him into herself and forging a bond with him that could never be broken. He was the other half of her whole, the soulmate who had come to her from so far away and so long ago.

When finally they both tumbled back to reality, their bodies still entwined, limbs glistening with perspiration, Spring wondered vaguely when he had removed his clothing, for all he now wore was the black satin mask. Contented and too sweetly tired for it to be more than a passing thought, she lay her head upon his hard muscular shoulder and drifted off to sleep.

Chapter Fifteen

For what seemed like hours, Jonathan had lain watching the gentle rise and fall of perfect, rose-tipped breasts with each breath Spring drew. Though his need for her should be sated, he found holding her sleeping form in his arms aroused a sensation that ran much deeper and stronger than mere physical need bordering upon spiritual.

He had almost been taken in by the minx when she had begun her scheme.

Luckily, he had realized in time what she was about and had turned it to his own advantage. She knew who he was, did she? Jonathan chuckled.

After these last hours spent in his arms, he held little doubt that she had convinced herself she was right. In the moonlight, he noted the contented little smile slightly curving her lips and the soft sighs that escaped her lips ever so often.

He smiled. When she had declared her desire for the highwayman, he had in that moment felt a murderous jealousy of the rogue, but how could one be jealous of oneself?

The urgent call of an owl brought Jonathan's thoughts up short. When he first heard the call an owl from the garden beneath Spring's window, Jonathan thought it was no more than a dream. But the second call, more urgent this time, alerted him to danger. He slid from the bed and donned his clothing as rapidly as possible. As he reached for his shoes, it came again.

"Damnation," he cursed as he hurriedly pulled on one shoe and reached for the other.

"What is it?" Spring asked, sitting up.

"Wyndridge, returns. I must leave before he arrives."

SPRING SCRAMBLED ACROSS the bed and retrieved her discarded nightgown from the floor. She quickly pulled it over her head then turned back to him with words of caution upon her lips.

He was gone. She hurried toward the window but tripped in the darkness over the small table, lost her balance and went sprawling to the floor.

By the time she finally gained the window, the highwayman was nowhere to be seen. Once again, he left her to wonder at his method of departure.

She studied the shadows of the garden then looked out toward the stable yard. There, was that a movement in the shadows? She waited as a cloud passed over the moon, casting the yard into deeper shadow. When the moon came out again, she thought she saw the flutter of a cape at the corner of the stable, but it might have been a trick of the moonlight.

In the stable yard, the Wyndridge coach came to a lumbering halt, its lanterns rocking wildly as the driver struggled to control the excited team.

Shouts arose from the stable yard. At first Spring thought it was only Wyndridge returning but soon realized the excitement was directed toward the darkness beyond the coach.

A premonition of impending disaster led Spring to abandon the sanctuary of her room.

Quickly donning her dressing gown, she hurried from the room. She arrived on the first-floor landing in time to hear a wild-eyed groom raise the alarm in the sleeping household.

"Milord's home, and he's captured the highwayman!"

When he spotted Spring on the landing, he stopped and began to babble excitedly. "But I weren't scared, not me. Like a giant black bird, he came swooping down on me. Saw him myself slipping around the stable yard. Now they got 'em, too!"

"What?"

"They've caught the highwayman, milady," the lad exclaimed.

Spring felt cold fear grip her heart. "The highwayman?"

"Aye," he answered. "They have 'em pinned down behind the stable in some trees. It's only a matter of time now. His lordship sent me to alert the household."

Spring turned and ran back up the stairs, her only thought that Jonathan was in danger, and she must help. Would he have a gun in his room?

She hurried past her own room toward Jonathan's. When she had become convinced Jonathan was her midnight visitor, Spring had asked her grandmother which room Jonathan was using, thinking there might be a secret passage that he used to enter her room. She had searched unsuccessfully for such a passage and finally had given up.

Without knocking, she threw open the door and burst inside expecting the room to be empty. Instead, she found Jonathan neatly tucked into his bed.

Confusion ripped through her and then mortification. If Jonathan were here asleep in his room, then who was it pinned down behind the stable? Worse yet, who had been in her bed only a few moments earlier?

"Oh, God," Spring groaned, crossing to the bed. "Wake up," she cried, "Oh please, wake up. Something terrible has happened."

Instantly his eyes opened, and he sat up. His eyes traveled over her, taking in her state of disarray. Gently he cradled her in his arms trying to soothe her.

"What's wrong?"

"You must help me, it's all my fault. Lord Wyndridge has returned..." She drew a deep breath and pressed on. "The highwayman—"

Jonathan cut her off. "Now, my dear, I'm sure the chap's quite out of his lordship's reach by now."

"No, no," she cried. "You don't understand, he was here, and now Lord Wyndridge has returned, and they have him trapped behind the stable."

Jonathan's grip tightened upon her shoulders. "Who?"

"The highwayman, he came... to see me," Spring tried to explain. "You must help, he's...." She bordered on hysterical. "They will kill him. We must do something."

"There, now," Jonathan tried to calm her. "I'm sure it's no more than a bad dream. The highwayman couldn't be within miles of here, you have nothing to fear."

"No," Spring insisted, pulling out of his arms. "He was here, in my room. Somehow he knew Lord Wyndridge was returning, so he left.

Jonathan stiffened. "I hardly think Lord Wyndridge will need my help to catch one highwayman."

"One of the stable hands saw him in the stable yard, and now they will catch him. You must help." Spring pounded on Jonathan's chest. "You've got to help him get away."

Jonathan moved away from her, throwing the bedcovers off. Spring realized in embarrassment that he was nude, but she had no time for embarrassment, a man's life was as stake.

"There's no time to explain now. They will kill him. We must help."

Jonathan reached for his trousers, neatly folded at the foot of his bed.

"Go back to your room and lock the door. I will do what I can to help," he told her as he pushed her gently toward the door.

"Let me go with you," she insisted. "You might need help."

"No, stay here. It will be safer."

"I will follow, so you may as well let me come along," Spring threatened.

For a moment, as their eyes met and held, she thought he meant to refuse, but stubbornly, Spring held her ground, refusing to look away. It took all her courage to return his fierce glare, and finally, with a curse, he gave in.

"Meet me in the library in five minutes," he said. His hand cupped her chin as he stared deeply into her eyes. "Five minutes, or I leave without you."

Pushing her out the door, he closed it behind her then hurriedly pulled on the remainder of his clothing. He located his revolver in his luggage and tucked it beneath his belt before opening the secret panel and slipping into the dark passage.

He paused at the library, considering leaving Spring behind, but decided against it. The girl was just stubborn enough to make good on her threat and follow him.

It would be better if he knew exactly where she was. Then he could keep an eye on her. Through the narrow crack that allowed a limited view of the library, Jonathan could see her pacing the room. She had changed into a black dress and covered her golden hair with a matching kerchief.

With deft fingers, he worked the counterbalance mechanism, and the secret panel slid noiselessly open.

"Come on."

Spring did not think twice but followed the hushed command. She moved through the open panel and into the narrow passage where it was necessary to stand very close to Jonathan or be out of the faint glow of candlelight.

They traversed the passage quickly, down a set of steep, damp steps and came out into a subterranean passageway. It was dark, dank, and smelled of decay. The sound of small scurrying feet filled the darkness just beyond the candle's reach. Spring suppressed a shudder and moved closer to Jonathan.

Abruptly they reached the end of the tunnel, and Jonathan signaled for her to be silent as he snuffed the candle, leaving them in total darkness. She could hear him moving in the darkness. For an instant panic filled her as she imagined him leaving her alone there. Then she saw stars overhead and felt the chilly night air rush into the narrow passageway.

With his finger to her lips to urge caution, Jonathan pulled Spring out of the narrow opening between two large boulders and into the moonlight. Spring saw they had emerged into the boulder strewn field just behind the stable yard.

All around them, Spring could hear Lord Wyndridge's men closing in.

"He's got to be in there somewhere," Wyndridge shouted. "He can't have gotten far on foot. Keep looking."

Jonathan pushed her down behind a rock as two men passed close by. Only when he was sure they were gone did he allow her to get up.

The boulders, which Jonathan had at first thought to be a natural grouping like many others he had seen around the English countryside, had been strategically located to hide the entrance to the subterranean passage.

From the darkness beside Spring came the sound of an owl and only Jonathan's hand over her mouth kept her from crying out in alarm at its nearness.

Within seconds, a second owl responded, and Jonathan quickly began moving in the direction of the call, pulling Spring along.

"What's that?" one man called.

"Damned owl," another answered.

"Keep looking," Wyndridge shouted.

Moments later, they found the highwayman propped against one of the large boulders. A Dark stain had spread over his shoulder.

"Do you think you can stand?" Jonathan asked.

"Aye, with a little help."

"We must get you away from here. Your horse?"

"Over there..." Just answering seemed to take all the remaining strength the man had. "in the trees.

"What's that?" a man shouted close by, and the three held their breath.

The owl called again.

"Damned fool bird again," came the reply, and the man moved on.

"Look sharp, he could be anywhere."

"Can't see nothing. It's too dark now that the clouds have moved in."

The wounded man was growing weaker with each passing moment. The dark stain grew increasingly larger. Even if they were successful in getting him to his horse, Jonathan knew he would not be able to ride alone.

"I'll lure them away while you help him to escape," Jonathan whispered urgently.

"He'll need your help to walk," Spring answered. "You might even have to carry him. He's near passing out now."

Jonathan checked the man's pulse and found it weak, going into shock, he had seen it happen before.

"Stay with him, I'll get his horse."

Jonathan left her huddled there with the highwayman. Spring was frantic that the wounded man might moan or move and give away their position.

Lord Wyndridge's men were everywhere. Any sound would bring them down on their heads for sure. Spring leaned closer to whisper a word of caution but realized the wounded man had lapsed into unconsciousness.

Temptation filled her as she touched the silk mask covering his face. Gently, she lifted it and leaned closer, straining into the darkness to see his features. Her fingers dropped the mask back in place as shock coursed through her.

She drew back aghast. My god, how could I have made such a mistake?"

Chapter Sixteen

As much as she longed to remain with Jonathan, Spring knew she had to be the one to lead the men away. Already the highwayman had lost consciousness from loss of blood. His only hope was in getting attention to his wound as quickly as possible.

Jonathan would be able to carry the wounded man to safety. She would not. Determined, she pulled the cape from around his shoulders and placed it around her own. She checked the highwayman and saw he was still unconscious. At least he would not moan and give away their location.

Silently, Jonathan returned and, in an instant, realized her intent. "I won't let you go," he insisted.

"I must," she replied. "If he isn't cared for soon, he will die. If Lord Wyndridge takes him, he will die. We cannot let that happen. Don't you see? It's my fault he is here."

She raised up on tiptoe and kissed Jonathan. His hands tightened on her shoulders, and he shook her slightly.

"It's not your fault. None of this is your fault. He knew the risks when he came here."

"You don't understand," Spring answered softly. "and I don't have time to explain. He grows weaker with each passing minute. I must go. Please, just take care of him."

Spring broke away from Jonathan, spinning from him before he could stop her.

Mounting the highwayman's horse with Jonathan ordering her not to do it, Spring gave a quick kick to its side and urged it away, not bothering with stealth. The alarm went up.

"There, over there," a man shouted. "He's getting away."

Aaron Morgan returned to his bedroom after going downstairs to check on the noise in the courtyard. He entered his bedroom and came up short when he saw Jonathan Sinclair standing beside the window, staring in the direction which Wyndridge and his men had disappeared.

"Close the door," Jonathan ordered, and Morgan complied.

Jonathan turned toward the doctor, searching his eyes intently for a moment before he spoke.

"It appears, Doctor Morgan," Jonathan said returning his gaze to the countryside beyond the manor house. "I have no choice but to trust you. Lady Spring's life, and the life of my best friend depend upon it."

"What do you mean?"

"You must help me, just as you have helped Lady Phoebe. We fight the same battle."

"I'm sure I don't know what you're talking about," Morgan hedged.

"Lady Phoebe can be quite persuasive, can she not? She has told you, I believe, that this marriage between her granddaughter and Lord Wyndridge must not take place. For that reason, you have been administering some type of potion to Spring to insure she does not recover too rapidly from her illness, have you not?"

"Why that's...."

"Please, doctor, we have no time for pretense," Jonathan cut him off. "I mention it only to gain your confidence. There is little time. You will need instruments for treating a bullet wound. Make haste, man," Jonathan urged. "We might already be too late to save him."

"Lord Wyndridge may have need of my services when he returns. I must not leave."

At the doctor's protest, Jonathan continued, "There is another who needs you more at the moment. Lady Spring has risked her life to save his. I don't think she would wish you to forfeit it now."

"But I must insist..."

Cursing, Jonathan pulled the gun from his belt. "Doctor, I really don't have time to argue the point. Get your things, we must hurry. Spring has led Wyndridge and his men away. I must to go find her. But first you need to see to my friend."

They quickly traversed the maze of passages to a subterranean room. When Doctor Morgan saw the man with a crimson stain spreading ominously across his right shoulder, he quickly took charge of the situation.

"Hold the light here so that I can see," Morgan demanded.

Jonathan lifted the lantern that he had left burning near his friend.

"No, higher. Yes, that's good."

Working quickly, the doctor cut away the soiled shirt using a small knife he had removed from his medical case.

"Hold the lantern closer," he urged, taking more instruments from his medical case.

For a moment, Doctor Morgan examined the wound, probing gently for the bullet. A groan of pain escaped the unconscious man as he pushed deeper into the wound in search of the bullet. Finally, the doctor gave a grunt of satisfaction and lifted the bullet from the wound with forceps.

"The wound must be cauterized to stop the bleeding," Morgan said. "Or he will bleed to death."

To Jonathan it seemed like hours that the doctor held the knife blade in the flame, turning it slowly over and over in the flame. Once it glowed red, the doctor removed it from the flame and motioned toward the wounded man.

"Hold him, this will hurt like hell."

Jonathan held Tobias' shoulders as the searing sound and smell of hot metal against human flesh filled the air. Tobias jerked convulsively, and Jonathan gave silent thanks that his friend was unconscious.

"Stay here and take care of him, I must go and find Lady Spring," Jonathan whispered and disappeared down the passageway.

A sense of urgency engulfed him. Guilt at his inability to protect both his lady and his friend ate at him. He would find her, he would. Jonathan sought to assuage the guilt flowing through his system.

HER PURSUERS WERE CLOSE behind her. She paused for an instant, the shape of her caped figure clearly outlined in the moonlight. Hearing the shouts of Wyndridge's men, she felt urgency surround her like a tangible thing.

By now, Jonathan had gotten the highwayman to safety, and now, she, too, must escape. She turned the horse sharply and urged it toward the woods, instinctively knowing that therein lay her best chance of eluding her pursuers.

The horse covered the distance quickly, and Spring was only yards from the thick, dark seclusion of the forest when she heard the loud report of a gun from behind her. A pain exploded in her head and spread instantly through her entire being, casting her into oblivion.

"I got 'im," shouted one of the riders. "Me, I did it. Milord, the reward is mine."

Lord Wyndridge tossed a small bag of coins in the air and caught it. "And you shall have it when we find the body, keep searching."

"'as to be here," the man grumbled. "I saw 'em fall. Took 'em clean off 'is horse, I did."

"Well, unless you help us find 'em, his lordship's not bloody likely to be giving you the money, so you'd best help search," another warned.

"Here," came a shout from another. "Bring the torches, I've found something."

"Out of my way," Lord Wyndridge demanded. "Let me through." He shouldered his way past the press of men surrounding the prone figure.

"He's done for," one man said with a low curse as he took the tip of his boot and rolled the black caped figure over.

Shocked silence fell over the group as torchlight fell upon the exposed features of the caped figure.

"Hell's bells," another man cursed.

"It's a bloody woman," yet another whispered.

Lord Wyndridge pushed them aside and knelt beside the prone figure. A deep scowl etched his features in the flickering torchlight as he reached for the mask and pulled it away. The men around him gasped in unison as the light played across the features of Spring's ashen face.

"What madness is this?" Lord Wyndridge shouted.

"I didn't know," the man who had claimed the kill whispered, fear showing plainly upon his face. "Is she dead?" he looked around him at the men who now stared at him. "Is she dead?" he repeated urgently.

"No," Wyndridge answered ominously. "But she will wish she were before I'm done with her."

One man shifted nervously while the others looked around as if wondering what they should do.

"Bring her," Wyndridge ordered as he mounted his horse.

So, the little pigeon had sought to escape me. Wyndridge fumed as he guided his horse back toward Wyndridge Hall. So much the better that she put up a fight. He would enjoy breaking her to his will so much the better.

"Take the girl to the chapel and lock her in the bell tower," Lord Wyndridge ordered as they entered the courtyard.

He would not be put off any longer. The marriage would take place at once. If she were well enough to flee, she was well enough to wed.

"Post a guard at the door and see that she does not escape."

DAWN WAS BREAKING WHEN Lord Wyndridge and his men returned to Wyndridge Hall. Jonathan watched the limp form of the girl in one of the riders' arms as they neared the courtyard.

He never should have allowed her to go. Jonathan berated himself as he watched from the window of his bedroom. He had thought she would be able to elude Lord Wyndridge and return to the secret passage without being captured.

It did no good to tell himself that she had insisted on helping. Guilt gnawed at him. He understood her concern for the highwayman was a direct result of his own duplicity. If she had died as a result, it would be his soul doomed to a lifetime of torment.

From the window, Jonathan watched as the men delivered Spring to the chapel while Lord Wyndridge continued to the manor house. At first, desperation gripping him, he feared the worst. Then the man who held her carefully handed her down to one who stood beside him. Together, they disappeared inside the chapel. Moments later. one of the men appeared at a window in the bell tower.

As Jonathan watched, the man closed and barred the window. Finally, one of the men came out of the chapel, but instead of leaving, he posted guards around the chapel and took a position beside the main door himself.

Jonathan felt an overwhelming relief. She was alive. He was certain of it. The earl would not bother to post guards were it otherwise. He must discover what Wyndridge's plans were. Jonathan opened the secret panel, checking the revolver he had tucked beneath his belt.

Wyndridge's single shot pistol would be no match for the revolver his friend had given him during his recent visit to Georgia. Now the important thing was to free Spring before Wyndridge could harm her. It would be a challenging task without Tobias' help, but he would manage.

Jonathan closed the panel and followed the passage down to the library, sensing that was where he would find Wyndridge. He paused in the passage and peered into Lady Phoebe's room where the old lady slept soundly, unaware of all that had happened or that her granddaughter was in danger. As he watched, the door of her room burst open and one of the maids hurried in.

Lady Phoebe sat up, wiping sleep from her eyes, looking greatly distressed at the intrusion.

"What's this fuss?"

"His lordship has returned. He requests you come to the library at once, milady."

Jonathan did not wait to hear her reply but continued along the passage. As he passed Aaron Morgan's room, he heard the same urgent message being delivered to the doctor. Jonathan descended the steep stairs and followed the passage to the panel in the library wall just behind Lord Wyndridge's desk. Through the narrow slit he could see Lord Wyndridge pacing back and forth behind his desk. His face was livid with rage as he turned on the maid who hurried into the room in response to his shout.

"Well, where are they?"

"They're coming, my lord," the girl answered, cowering near the door. Both Lady Phoebe and Doctor Morgan."

"Yes, and the other? Young Sinclair?"

"He was not in his room, my lord," the girl answered. "Nor the Lady Spring, I checked her room, milord."

Lord Wyndridge's fist crashed down on his desk with a powerful thud. "Enough! Away with you," he shouted.

The girl did not hesitate but backed quickly from the room and fled down the hallway in her haste to escape her master's wrath.

"Where is Sinclair?" Wyndridge whispered, turning toward the wall.

For an instant, Jonathan thought he must have somehow discovered his presence. His fingers tightened on the butt of the gun beneath his belt.

Wyndridge poured himself a glass of brandy from the decanter on his desk, drained its contents in one swift gulp then whirled and sent the glass crashing into the fireplace. His face a mask of enraged fury, he turned back to the desk.

"He won't win. I will kill him, just as surely as I had his father killed. But first I shall make them suffer. Both this pretender seeking to steal from me and this silly chit who thought to escape me."

Jonathan had to restrain himself from forcing his way into the room. He wanted to kill the man with his bare hands. Never had he hated anyone as much as he did his uncle in that moment.

Jonathan's hands clenched convulsively at his side. If he harmed Spring, there would be no place even in hell where his lordship could hide that he would not find him.

Jonathan's narrowed gaze flew to the doorway as Lady Phoebe entered amidst the rustle of her satin dressing gown.

"What is happening? Where is my granddaughter?" a furious Lady Phoebe demanded as she entered the room with Aaron Morgan trailing in her wake. "She is not in her room. What have you done with her?"

"It seems there has been another attempt to kidnap the lady, which I arrived just in time to foil," Lord Wyndridge explained.

At the gasp of outrage from Lady Phoebe, he continued. "For her protection, she is under guard in the bell tower of the chapel."

"What?" Lady Phoebe fanned herself, appearing quite faint.

"Is she all right?" Aaron Morgan asked, immediately concerned for the welfare of his patient.

"She is fine, I assure you. In fact, we have decided to proceed with the ceremony as soon as possible."

"But this is so sudden," Lady Phoebe protested. "I think it best the wedding be postponed. She might suffer a relapse because of this latest incident."

"As soon the vicar arrives, the ceremony will begin."

"I must agree with Lady Phoebe," Aaron Morgan interjected. "To be subjected to such stress after her recent ordeal can only have grave consequences. I must examine her at one to assure she is all right."

"Examine her if you must, then." Lord Wyndridge acceded. "But the ceremony will proceed in one hour, there will be no putting it off this time."

"One hour!" Lady Phoebe protested. "I cannot possibly be ready in that short of time. I must have at least two hours to dress."

"One hour, no more," Lord Wyndridge answered firmly.

"I must get my medical case," Aaron Morgan said, hurrying from the room.

Chapter Seventeen

Jonathan did not stay to hear any more of Lady Phoebe's protests but hurried back along the corridor.

"He has her," Jonathan said as Aaron Morgan entered the room.

"He has agreed to let me see her, since I've been treating her," Morgan said, reaching for the leather satchel on the dresser.

Jonathan leaned closer. "You must be discreet," Jonathan whispered as the doctor passed close beside him. "You must not reveal what you have seen. My lady's very life depends upon it."

When Morgan would have questioned further, Jonathan hedged. "There's no time to explain now. There is no time. Just tell her I have not forgotten my promise."

Jonathan followed the doctor from the room and quickly disappeared into his own room. *So much to be done.*

PAIN EXPLODED AND RAN down the length of her entire body. Spring wondered if she had died and landed in purgatory. With significant effort, she managed to open her eyes, blinking against the sunlight that streamed into the room in thin ribbons through a window covered by heavy wooden shutters. She tried to move but found the slightest movement made the pounding in her head increase.

Where am I? Why have I been brought here? Spring lifted her hand to a spot on her forehead where the pain radiated. Her fingers encountered a moist sticky substance. Spring lowered her hand to find it smeared with blood, her blood.

Frantic, Spring sought to remember what had happened to her but found that her memory shot through with holes. She wrinkled her brow, trying to remember more. The highwayman, it had something to do with the highwayman. If only the pain in her head would stop, she might be able to remember more.

Spring again tried to turn her head and found that this time it less painful. Cold chilled her, sinking deeply into her bones. A shiver ran through her. Wrapping her arms around her body, she struggled to sit up. Looking around her, she realized part of her discomfort came from the fact that she sprawled on the cold, stone floor of a shuttered room.

The room spun wildly around her as she lifted her head. She braced her body on her extended arms, willing the spinning to stop.

Spring sat up and looked around at the barren room. Nothing, only an empty room that echoed with the sound of her gasp. She pushed herself up and struggled to gain her feet, swaying slightly as she did. Across the room, the massive wooden door appeared quite impenetrable.

With hesitant steps Spring crossed the room and tried the latch but found it locked from the outside. Moving to the window, she paused to peer through the slits of the shutters. In the narrow space between the wide boards, she saw the courtyard of Wyndridge Hall, a different angle than the one she usually saw. Instead of looking out across the court to the small chapel and the stables beyond, a narrow view of Wyndridge itself greeted her. Directly beneath her, she saw the stone walkway that led to the chapel.

Memories rushed back to her. She gasped and her hand rose to her lips. "Jonathan," she whispered. Had he been successful in getting the wounded man safely away?, Her strength returned gradually, and she paced the narrow confines of her prison. The pounding in her head had lessened, settling into a dull throb just above her right eyebrow.

Moving back to the window, Spring positioned herself so that she had the best view afforded between the shutters. As she watched, Doctor Morgan left the manor and strode toward the chapel.

THE GIRL APPEARED A little the worse for wear. Doctor Aaron Morgan thought as he crossed the room and placed his case on the floor at Spring's feet. It was a good sign that she was conscious and quite lucid, as well, he observed as he looked closely at the girl.

"Bring a lamp," he commanded the man standing by the door.

Silently, the man turned and left pulling the door shut behind him. Moments later the door opened again, and the man returned holding the requested lamp.

Morgan looked around for a table but found none. Angered, Morgan berated the man, "Have you no decency? Bring a chair for milady, and I must have a table for my instruments, as well."

The man hesitated clearly unsure of the doctor's status to give orders. Morgan turned on the man, anger blazing in his narrowed eyes.

"Do as I have bid you, or I promise you it will not go easy with you when his lordship hears how you have abused milady."

Properly chastened, the man hurried away to do the doctor's bidding, leaving the lamp on the floor beside the doctor's case. In a matter of minutes, with the help of another man, he carried a small wooden table into the room.

Doctor Morgan placed his bag and the lamp on the table when the men returned with two chairs.

He gently pushed Spring down into one of the chairs. He slid the lamp closer and reached to remove the scrap of material she pressed against her forehead.

"Now, let's see what's happened to you."

He cleansed the wound carefully then held the lamp closer as he examined her eyes, instructing her to follow the light with her eyes as he moved the lamp back and forth in front of her face.

"Mmmm," he gave a noncommittal grunt as she followed the light. "How do you feel?"

"My head hurts."

He sighed, shaking his head. "Not without good cause, my lady." He checked her pulse, smiling when he found it normal. "If I didn't know better, I would think you had been grazed by a bullet."

Spring avoided his gaze. "I was... riding, and a tree limb..." She let her words drift away.

The doctor raised an eyebrow but did not question her statement.

"It would seem you and Jonathan are determined to keep me busy, milady."

"Jonathan?" Had he too been captured, wounded or worse? "You've seen Jonathan?"

Aaron Morgan lowered his voice to a whisper as he leaned closer. "He had a friend in need of my services."

Spring felt tremendous relief. Jonathan was safe, and the doctor had seen the highwayman. "How is his friend?"

"Weak, but he should recover." The doctor stood for a moment, searching through the contents of his medical case. "Ah-ha," he exclaimed, retrieving a small vile of yellow powder from the bottom of the case.

He tilted her head back slightly. "This might sting a little," he warned as he sprinkled the powder onto the wound. "He said to tell you he has not forgotten his promise, whatever that means, milady."

Tears sprang to her eyes, and Spring trembled, unsure whether to attribute them to the words he had spoken or the fire that spread along her nerve endings as the yellow powder contacted raw flesh. She quickly blinked them away.

"My lord has ordered the wedding ceremony to begin as soon as the vicar arrives. I'm afraid there will be no putting it off this time, milady."

Spring paled but held her head high. She had known that Wyndridge would not be put off once he discovered she had recovered from her illness. "I expected no less," she answered in a soft whisper.

She sat quietly while he finished tending her wound then wrapped a bandage around her head. The doctor's gentle touch offered little comfort as she felt his lordship's trap closing around her. While the doctor replaced his instruments in the case, Spring turned back to the window and continued her vigil. Any moment now, the vicar would arrive, and her fate would be sealed.

"My grandmother?"

"Lady Phoebe's protests were brushed aside. His lordship has also requested she return to London immediately following the ceremony."

Spring nodded. His lordship intended to isolate her from her family. Had her grandmother capitulated to his demand or refused? Spring doubted even her grandmother's strength of will would manage to stand up to the earl in his present state.

The arrival in the courtyard of Lord Wyndridge's coach and the loading of her grandmother's luggage confirmed her fears. Desolation swept through Spring.

She stiffened her backbone, sitting very straight in her chair as she watched her grandmother emerge from Wyndridge Hall and disappear inside the coach. Within moments, the coach door closed behind the countess, and Spring sank back into the chair, feeling even more alone and vulnerable.

What coercion had he used to force Lady Phoebe to abandon her? Spring knew her grandmother would not easily have been parted from her. What new threats had he made that she did not know of?

"Strength, my lady," Aaron Morgan encouraged as he patted her shoulder soothingly.

"I have very little strength left," Spring answered quietly.

The large coach bearing the Wyndridge crest departed, and another smaller, much less ornate equipage pulled into view. The vicar had arrived.

Am I not even to be allowed to change into something more suitable? She turned listless eyes toward the doctor. Perhaps it was fitting that she wore the black mourning dress for her wedding. This ceremony did signal, for all purposes, an end to life as she knew it.

"If milady will excuse me, my services are needed elsewhere. I shall, of course, be at your service should you have need of me," Doctor Morgan politely excused himself.

Spring held her head high, admonishing herself not to cry as the doctor moved toward the door.

"Thank you for coming, Doctor." She lowered her gaze to her hands in her lap. "And if you should see..." Spring hesitated, taking a deep breath. "Tell him I have not forgotten."

"Yes, my lady."

The resounding click from the latch holding the panel echoed in the silence of the secret passage. The panel creaked from lack of use as Jonathan opened the concealed portal and slipped into the countess' bed chamber. Now he just had to wait for Lady Phoebe to return. He sank into the chair in the corner to await her arrival.

Jonathan drummed his fingers on the arm of the chair. He had to persuade the countess to depart immediately and leave the rescue of Lady Spring to him. With the countess out of harm's way, Jonathan's focus could narrow to saving his love.

It had taken all his power of persuasion to sway the lady to his plan. But finally, the elder woman had placed a hand on his arm and studied him closely for a full moment and finally, with a sigh, she had agreed. As he left her room, she was calling for the maid to come help her pack.

Now, Jonathan made his way back through the secret passage and waited at his lordship's office. Standing near the panel that opened from the secret passage, Jonathan watched Lord Wyndridge through the tiny peep hole someone had conveniently made.

Wyndridge pulled a pouch from its hiding spot, replaced the strongbox and carefully locked the drawer before he left the office. So, his uncle had not trusted his entire fortune to the banks. He smiled as he thought of his uncle's consternation when next he opened the secret compartment.

It was tiresome to continue his battle against his uncle using his own fortune. How fortunate that these funds were not frozen along with the other assets of the Wyndridge Estate. He would use those secreted estate funds with immense pleasure to continue his persecution of Wyndridge. Impatient, he waited for his uncle to leave the room.

His mission accomplished, Jonathan soundlessly returned to the passage and closed the panel behind him. He quickly slipped a small block of wood into the spring mechanism, rendering it immobile.

Back in his own room, Jonathan hurried to the door and checked the hallway before moving stealthily along it to the doctor's room. Aaron Morgan stood near the bed. The doctor's valise sat open upon the coverlet.

"Your friend?" Morgan spoke without turning from the bed.

"Resting."

"That's good, he should remain quiet. His body needs time to mend. He's not as young as you."

"Not that he would appreciate hearing it," Jonathan agreed.

Jonathan crossed to the window and stood looking toward the chapel. Lord Wyndridge and the vicar stood just outside in conversation.

Soon Jonathan reassured himself. "My lady?"

"She is well but was distressed when she saw her grandmother leaving. She felt abandoned."

"We thought it best that Lady Phoebe go on ahead. My lady and I shall join her shortly in London," Jonathan answered turning to study the doctor for a moment before he continued.

"And now, my friend, will you help, or at least not hinder my efforts to rescue my lady?"

Aaron Morgan took stock of the young man standing before him. If Lady Phoebe thought enough of him to trust the life of her granddaughter in his hands, how could he do less? But in her desperation to prevent this marriage had the lady forgotten the reasons for it in the first place? He could not offer his full support until he was certain that was not the case.

"I understand there are certain financial complications that make this marriage necessary. I would not want to make things more difficult for the Lansing family by interfering when I do not know the entire story."

"It is precisely for their protection that this marriage must be prevented," Jonathan stated.

"But Lady Phoebe said—"

"I regret that I do not have time to fully explain. The ceremony is about to begin, and I intend to see it does not run its intended course. Suffice to say my lord is not what he claims to be. His title and inheritance are being contested. When he loses the case, he will be left destitute."

Aaron Morgan nodded gravely at the unexpected revelation. Then, with a swift glance toward the chapel, he made his decision. "Tell me what to do."

Chapter Eighteen

From the window Spring watched as Lord Wyndridge approached with the vicar. She felt his trap tighten around her. The oppressive weight of hopelessness crushed down upon her until she felt she must surely be destroyed by its sheer force. How could she continue to hope when her fate was about to be sealed?

Finally, out of sheer desperation, she fell back upon the plan which she had formulated earlier. Spring took a deep breath. She would go through with the ceremony. She must somehow find the strength to see the bargain through for her family's sake, but as soon as the ink was set to paper and her part of the agreement fulfilled, she would escape.

The key grating in the lock of the door behind her sent a chill of apprehension along her spine, threatening the hard-won determination with which she had stiffened her spine. For an instant, her courage almost faltered, then she reminded herself she was a Lansing, she would not shame her father's name by showing cowardice in the face of her enemies. Defiant, Spring turned to face her tormentor. She would not give Wyndridge the pleasure of seeing her fear. She pulled herself up to her full height and squared her shoulders; chin held at a defiant tilt, she turned to face her tormentor. She would not cower before him.

Having attained Aaron Morgan's assistance, Jonathan followed the tunnel which forked near the rear of the chapel and led to two separate entrances into the chapel. One ended just behind the altar, and the other behind a set of oak bookshelves in the chapel's small office.

Confident that his plan would work, Jonathan left the lamp he carried and a small block of wood beside the opening that led to the chapel office. Fishing a small stub of candle from his pocket, he touched it to the flame of the lamp and then made his way back to the panel behind the altar.

All the other entrances to the secret passages had been jammed except the one which led to the stable. He needed that one open for just a while longer.

From the small peephole beneath the altar, Jonathan watched as Aaron Morgan entered the chapel and stood near the large double doors at the rear of the chapel. Closer to the front of the chapel stood the vicar, dressed in severe black. He clutched a well-worn bible against his chest as he rocked anxiously back and forth.

Impatient, Jonathan waited. Where was Spring? He dared not make his move until she was within his reach.

Jonathan smiled a thin hard smile. Now the only men he would have to worry about were those already inside the chapel. By now, Morgan had slid the bolt in place on the large doors, and the men posted around the exterior of the chapel would be of no help to his uncle.

Jonathan slid his pistol from his belt. He silently thanked his friend for the gun, a prototype for the ones Colt had only recently begun to mass produce. For a moment, Jonathan's mind drifted back to home and the summer months when his friend had visited his home near Savannah. It had been a peaceful time, a time before he had become embittered by a sense of loss with the death of his beloved grandfather and driven by a quest for revenge with the revelation of the events surrounding the death of his father and his true identity.

Jonathan pulled the black mask from his pocket and covered his face. He was not particularly concerned with the legality of what he was about to do, because he knew his uncle deserved all he got and much more, but he did not intend to spend the next twenty years in an English goal or worse, dangling at the end of a hangman's rope.

After what seemed to Jonathan like hours, a small door near the rear of the chapel opened, and Spring lurched through with Lord Wyndridge close behind her. Aaron Morgan quickly stepped forward and took her arm to steady her when she stumbled at the rough handling. Jonathan's anger reached the flash point. He struggled to contain it.

"Allow me to help you," Aaron Morgan encouraged, placing himself between Spring and Lord Wyndridge.

He bent toward her and whispered as he hurried her up the aisle toward the altar. Patting her hand gently, he bade her to be brave for just a little longer. Soon, all would be well.

Turning from his dark scowling perusal of their progress along the aisle, Lord Wyndridge called to one of the three men who stood near the rear of the chapel.

"Thomas, come and stand witness along with Doctor Morgan."

"Your grandmother has returned to London," Wyndridge said as he joined them at the altar.

"She said there was nothing more she could do here. I am sure you will be seeing her again soon," Aaron Morgan reassured the pale young girl beside him.

When Thomas had joined them, Wyndridge ordered the ceremony to begin.

All eyes trained on him expectantly, the vicar opened his Bible. As if on cue, Spring slowly crumpled soundlessly to the floor. Without success, Doctor Morgan sought to revive her as everyone crowded around her.

Lord Wyndridge cursed loudly berating his men, "Keep your places."

"Too late, milord," the Highwayman spoke quietly from his position just behind the altar. His pistol, gleaming in the light filtering through the rose window behind him, aimed steadily at Wyndridge's heart.

"And now, if you'll just order your men to drop their weapons, we can complete our little exchange with no one the worse for it."

"You can't take all of us," Wyndridge answered.

"But I will take you first, milord. Never doubt that." The Highwayman cocked his pistol. "Your weapons?"

Still Lord Wyndridge hesitated. "I have no time to waste with your indecision. The weapons or your life, which shall it be, my lord?"

"Do as he says," Lord Wyndridge capitulated with a curse.

When the men had dropped their weapons, Jonathan ordered them to the rear of the chapel where they were to stand leaning against the stone wall with their hands above their heads.

"My lady?" The Highwayman extended a hand to the prostrate form at Lord Wyndridge's feet. He raised one hand to place the gun against Lord Wyndridge's temple while the other remained outstretched toward Spring.

"Have trust, my lady."

Slowly, Spring reached to take the hand extended to her. She did have trust, but what would become of her family when Lord Wyndridge collected his debts? If only he had waited a few moments later with the ceremony complete, she would have followed him to the ends of the earth. But how could she now?

With his help, she rose to her feet, drawing strength from the touch of his hand on her arm as he steadied her.

No sign of any weakness from his wound showed upon the hard virile lines of his body as he stood strong and tall beside her. Strength and vigor emanated from him, filling the air around her with a familiar tension. This was her masked visitor, but he was not the same masked man she had risked her life to save.

(NOT THE TIME FOR SLOWLY) he replayed the scene of her first abduction. Of course, there had been two of them. Why had she not remembered last night when she had found Jonathan in his room? His partner and accomplice had been the one cornered in the stable yard. The man had come to warn Jonathan of Wyndridge's return and had been spotted in the process.

Could she place her trust in him? Could she risk the future of her family with only his word that he sought the best for her? How could she trust him? How could she not?

Her heart insisted she must have faith in him. If he promised all would be well, then it would. With renewed confidence, she moved closer to his side.

With lightning speed, Jonathan raised his gun and brought it down against Lord Wyndridge's skull, rendering him unconscious. Spring watched in shock as his lordship sprawled upon the chapel floor. Then Jonathan trained the gun on the men at the rear of the chapel, daring them to interfere as he pushed Spring toward the small office to the left of the altar and quickly closed the door behind them.

Once he had turned the key in the lock, he quickly wedged a chair beneath the doorknob. He pushed open the shutters of the small window, allowing the morning breeze into the small office. Then, motioning for Spring to be silent, he quickly uncoiled a length of rope and snaked it out the window, until it hung suspended from the end securely wrapped and tied around the leg of the heavy wooden desk.

A protest that they could not escape with so many of his lordship's men surrounding the chapel died on her lips as the caped figure moved to the bookcase behind the paper strewn desk. With a deft movement of his nimble fingers, a secret panel slid silently open, emitting a rush of damp stagnant air.

Relief flooded Spring when she saw the dim glow of lamplight from the opening. He urged her into the passage and quickly followed. Holding her breath, she watched as he closed the panel and placed a small block of wood into place, jamming the intricate system of chains and pulleys that operated the heavy oak portal. His action rendered the mechanism inoperable from the office side.

The air hung heavily around them as Spring waited while he retrieved the lamp from the damp stone floor. Then, clasping her hand in a reassuring grasp, he urged her to follow him along the narrow passage. The dank, stagnant air pressed down upon them as they inched along the narrow corridor. Spring gave thanks for the meager light from the lantern.

Her fingers trembled slightly in the grip of the highwayman, and she moved closer to his side, seeking reassurance from his presence.

Just a few yards farther along, the passage merged with another, and her masked protector stopped to set in place another of the small wooden blocks, effectively jamming the panel that opened into the chapel. Flashing her a reassuring smile beneath the mask, he again took her hand, and they continued along the passage.

The light of the lantern cast strange dancing shadows that barely kept the darkness at bay. Spring welcomed the warmth of his hand holding hers in this strange underworld in which she found herself.

Her pulse raced faster as he pulled her closer to his side. His arm protectively around her, he guided her ever deeper into the labyrinth of tunnels that lead steadily lower into the very bowels of the earth. *Where are we going*? Spring followed the highwayman's urging with no resistance.

Strangely, she felt no fear at being in his power, only a strange sense of rightness, of being where she belonged. How could she be blamed for grasping this last reprieve fate had granted her?

Certainty infused her. She knew the identity of her masked avenger. The electrifying tingle that started where his hand caressed the sensitive skin of her palm and continued along her nerve endings radiating to inflame her very soul told her that it could be no other way.

Their bodies were attuned to one another. The silken mask could not disguise what her heart so readily recognized.

It was Jonathan, had always been Jonathan, and he had come, yet again, to rescue her.

The confusion that had blurred her reason lifted. She would follow her heart. She could not doubt that this was Jonathan, and yet something within her demanded that she seek this final confirmation.

Spring stopped.

The highwayman turned to her. "We must hurry."

"I must know for certain," she whispered as she reached for the mask.

TOO MUCH INTROSPECTION IN THIS SITUATION. Jonathan had thought himself prepared for the moment when Lady Spring Lansing discovered his duplicity. He felt she had guessed as much. He had not expected her to understand his need for deception or to condone his action. But he had maintained the fragile hope that she might somehow manage to understand. Never in his most pessimistic moments had he expected the lady to react as she had.

He had come to hate his alter-ego because the lady had developed a sincere attachment to the phantom.

It was, Jonathan thought, the very height of folly to find oneself jealous of oneself, and he did not quite understand how it had come about. Nevertheless, he was jealous of the affection that Spring showered upon the highwayman.

She had willingly risked her life for the highwayman. Jonathan gazed into tear misted eyes. It tore at his heart to see her unhappy. Tears shimmered at the tips of her lashes, threatening to spill down to the softness of her cheek. He stood transfixed as she lifted her hand to remove the mask.

In the tiny, all-encompassing world reflected in one tear, Jonathan saw the image of the highwayman. The image taunted him, filling his soul with emptiness and despair.

He had lost her to the elusive highwayman, a figment of his imagination, a phantom who had never really existed. It tore at his soul and rent his heart asunder. He had lost her.

Pain pierced his entire being to the core.

The voice of misery tightened its grip an excruciating turn upon his heart. How could he hope to compete with this phantom that her fantasies had created?

He remained but a man of flesh and blood, while the highwayman manifested all those things from which legends were made.

How could he best this phantom built of the romantic daydreams of a young girl? What foolishness he had set about when he had continued this facade. How dearly it cost him now that the truth stood out.

With trembling fingers, she pulled the mask away. Jonathan held his breath. She smiled, then lifted on tiptoe to place her lips briefly against his.

"The highwayman's lady thanks you for rescuing her, my love," she whispered as she moved closer into the shelter of his embrace so that he could feel the slow gentle thud of her heart against his chest.

Chapter Nineteen

The passage ahead reached out with darkness to surround them. Its inky gloom pushed aside only a meager distance by the lamp Jonathan held. Spring suppressed a shudder and moved a step closer to Jonathan's side, seeking to ward off the chill of the dark unknown with the warmth emanating from his body.

She was not afraid, she reassured herself valiantly as she drew comfort from Jonathan's tall, lean frame. The chilled air pulled at her, making his close proximity essential.

As if sensing her uncertainty, he looked down at her and pulled her tight against his side.

The tenderness that shone in his eyes in the lamplight caused her heart to double its pace.

"It's not much farther now," he reassured with the slow drawl she found so irresistible.

His arm tightened around her as they continued along the corridor. Spring welcomed his reassurance, drawing strength from his embrace. The warmth of his body helped to dispel the chill of the damp corridor. She fought to suppress a shiver. Her effort was almost successful.

They moved rapidly along the corridor. Jonathan seemed quite familiar with the labyrinth that totally confused Spring. Jonathan had traversed these passages many times, she realized as they followed the twists and turns of the passageway.

Trying to ignore the slight scurrying sounds in the darkness just beyond the reach of the lamplight, she instead fastened her gaze upon the small circle of light just ahead of them. Spring refused to focus on the darkness held feebly at bay by the yellow light.

The passage seemed to run on for miles, and Spring began to wonder why such elaborate passages had been built, in the first place.

"Why are they here?" Spring asked as a keen interest in her surroundings took control of her thoughts, blotting out the fear of the dark unknown.

"Pardon?" Jonathan paused, looking at Spring.

"These passages, why were they built? Do they date back to the time of the persecution?"

"Hardly a noble reason, my dear," he answered, his generous mouth spreading into a wide grin. "Smugglers, the Wyndridge fortune grew from ill-gotten gains."

When they turned a corner, a flickering light became visible at the end of the passage ahead of them. Taken aback by its sudden appearance, Spring's steps faltered.

"It's all right, love," he reassured. "There are no smugglers here now, haven't been for a long time. You don't have to be afraid. These natural caves were here long before the tunnels that connect them to the manor house were built. Because of the smugglers' need for secrecy, Wyndridge Hall perched high upon the cliff overlooking the sea. The entire coastline along this section of England is honeycombed with caves, natural shelter for the booty that the smugglers sought to hide. These particular caves haven't been used in nearly thirty years."

"How is it that you know so much about the area when you've only recently come here from America?" Spring questioned as they neared the light at the end of the passage.

"I grew up hearing tales of the smugglers and of the brothers who lived in the manor. One a rake and devil with the ladies who would take any dare thrust upon him. The other brother evil and always plotting against his older brother.

"It was like a fairytale. By the time I was six years old I knew the entire tale by heart. How the evil one had tricked his brother

and framed him for murder and finally arranged to have him killed."
He paused, staring fixedly into the darkness as his eyes narrowed in
remembrance.

"When my grandfather died, I came into possession of papers
that identified my father as the Earl of Wyndridge. It was then I
realized the story's importance, not just a child's story but the history
of my family.

"My uncle had conspired to kill my father." Jonathan kept up the
conversation, as if to distract her from their surroundings.

"How could you have learned so much from so far away?"

"My father's trusted servant who had been with him for years.
When my father fled England, the servant accompanied him."

"And so, you came to England to claim your inheritance," Spring
finished for him.

"Exactly."

"And?" Spring urged, sensing there was more as a deathly chill
spread along her spine.

"And to make him pay for the murder of my father."

A chill spread through Spring at the depth of hatred in his words.

The passage opened into a wider chamber filled with dim light
from a lamp sitting on the ground. She stared around herself, taking
in the sparse fixtures of the room. Her gaze skirted around the space
until it settled on a familiar form.

There, in the middle of the large, cavernous room, lay a man
upon a makeshift pallet of straw and blankets. He lay so still that at
first Spring thought he must be dead, but as they neared his pallet, he
lifted one hand in frail greeting.

Jonathan paused for a moment as he glanced from Spring to the
wounded man as if undecided what he should do next.

Finally, as if coming to a decision, he spoke. "Lady Spring
Lansing, may I present Tobias McDonald, mentor, friend and fellow
conspirator?"

"Tobias, the Lady Spring Lansing."

The wounded man nodded toward Spring. "Milady." The man ended on a wheeze.

"Do you think you can ride?" Jonathan asked.

"Aye."

"But—" Spring objected. "If the wound opens again, he could bleed to death."

"And 'is lordship will see to it if 'e finds me 'ere, milady."

"We have no choice," Jonathan responded. "We can't leave him here. It's only a matter of time until they begin to search the secret passages. The longer we delay, the greater the risk of being caught."

"Don't worry about me, milady. I've not finished my mission, and I won't be dying until I have."

"But surely—"

"There is no more time, we must go," Jonathan insisted. "Do you think you can stand with my help?"

"Aye, even if it kills me," the man answered grimly as Jonathan helped him to a standing position.

The sudden pallor of his skin and clenched lips told Spring just how greatly the movement cost the wounded man.

With Tobias leaning heavily on Jonathan's shoulder and Spring holding the lamp, they returned to the labyrinth of passages. Steps faltering, Spring followed the directions that Jonathan gave as they passed slowly along the corridor. tThe lamplight often cast strange shadows upon the damp stone walls as they passed, and Spring felt cold fear tightly coiling within her.

She would be strong. She would not be a burden to Jonathan. He had more than enough to worry about trying to get his friend away to safety. Still, when they emerged into another cavernous room and disturbed a flock of bats, she struggled to suppress the cry of distress that escaped her lips.

"Easy, love," Jonathan reassured. "The bats won't hurt you. Just follow their line of retreat. They're heading the same way we are. It's not much farther now."

Glancing doubtfully at Jonathan, Spring lifted the lamp higher and followed the course the flock of bats had taken.

The air became fresher, crisper, with the taste of salt to it, and she greedily filled her lungs with its freshness.

Moments later, they emerged into a natural limestone cave where Spring heard the ocean in the distance. Waves breaking upon the beach sounded an insistent tattoo that told Spring that they were nearing the end of their trek through the darkness. Instinctively, Spring moved toward the sound.

"Wait," Jonathan cautioned, halting her before she reached the mouth of the cave. "I must get the horses. You will be safe here. I will return as quickly as possible. You stay here with Tobias."

Carefully, Jonathan lowered the injured man to the floor of the cave and motioned for Spring to bring the lamp closer. She held the lamp nearer, its light reflecting upon the paleness of his skin and tiny dots of perspiration. His eyes closed and his mouth clenched into a thin hard line told of the toll upon his strength. The exertion had cost him dearly, but the red stain upon the bandage that covered his chest had not increased in size.

"I won't be long," Jonathan said as he left them.

To Spring, left alone with the injured man, the minutes ticked by with the slowness of eternity before Jonathan re-entered the cave, leading three saddled horses. Spring recognized the large stallion with the blaze on its forehead and chest that Jonathan had ridden on his morning treks while she had watched from her bedroom window. The second was the bay that she had ridden the night before, and the third a gelding she had never seen before.

"Your grandmother packed a few things for you. If you would like to change you can do so at the back of the cave. You will have privacy in the darkness."

Spring looked down at herself in despair. Her dress, tattered and torn in several places, sported dirt from her fall, not to mention all the cobwebs and dust gathered as they had traversed the narrow confines of the secret passage.

She touched a hand to her hair, feeling the loose tendrils that cascaded about her shoulders. What a sight she must present.

With a smile of thanks, Spring took the small bundle that Jonathan held and moved toward the darkness at the rear of the cave. She stopped just outside the ring of yellow light cast by the lamp and quickly changed into the gown she found inside the bundle.

Thoughts of a bath floated fleetingly through her mind, but she pushed them away. They had no time to spare for such niceties now. If the earl should catch them, she doubted very seriously any of them would escape with their lives.

Finally, she raked her fingers through her tangled hair, combed it into a loose ball at the nape of her neck and fastened it with her few remaining hair pins.

Tobias had mounted the gelding when she returned. Spring admired his strength and determination as he held the reins, determined to fend for himself, despite his pain.

Jonathan helped her to mount the grey mare, then he mounted Diablo and moved to the mouth of the cave. After checking to see that the beach remained deserted, Jonathan motioned for them to follow him.

For hours Spring guided her horse behind that of the injured man. Concern coiled in her chest as she watched Tobias sway in the saddle ahead of her. She feared at any moment that weakness would overcome him, and he would slide to the ground.

How much longer could the wounded man go on? Did not Jonathan realize the strain his friend was under? Did he not care? Was he willing to sacrifice his friend's life for this quest of vengeance?

At long last, Jonathan slowed Diablo, allowing Tobias to take the lead so that he was soon alongside Spring who rode just behind Tobias. He matched the pace of his mount to that of Spring's mare, then slowed a little, urging her to do the same. Tobias continued along at the same canter, pulling a little farther ahead of them with each passing moment.

Spring watched Jonathan scan the cliff above and ahead of them. Her gaze followed the sweep of his gaze along the jagged rocky crag for a moment then returned to study his familiar figure. Jonathan still wore the highwayman's black garb, although he had discarded the mask. He seemed oblivious to the danger his telling garb subjected him to.

"We should be well ahead of Wyndridge."

"Do you not think we could stop for a moment? Your friend must be exhausted."

"We dare not stop. His lordship doesn't care about fatigue. He won't stop," Jonathan answered.

They continued along in silence.

At last, they turned inland, moving away from the coast. With the grueling pace he had set, Spring continued to question Jonathan's concern for his friend's welfare. Surely, he must realize the wounded man could not continue at this pace. It was nothing short of a miracle that his wound had not reopened. But the red stain was no larger now than it had been when they first set out.

However, Spring could tell from his ashen coloring that the effort to remain in the saddle and conscious was taking a grave toll on the older man.

Exactly how much was Jonathan willing to sacrifice to this quest of vengeance? Would the life of his friend be too much, and would he be willing to forfeit his own life, as well?

"It's not much farther now," Tobias said as they walked their horses through the dark woodland.

"You're sure they'll have us?" Jonathan asked, guiding Diablo closer to the mare Spring rode.

"Aye." Tobias managed a slow grin. "Never would turn away a friend in need."

The path, overgrown with briars and brambles, caught at their clothing and hair. The trees grew tall and straight, reaching up to form a canopy high above that blocked out the sun.

They came upon a clearing with a small stone cottage weathered to a wintered gray. Jonathan signaled for them to remain in the cover of the trees while he approached the cottage alone.

Spring held her breath as Jonathan approached.

"Hello, Tobias sends his greetings," Jonathan shouted as he circled Diablo, keeping careful watch.

His greeting answered by a call from within, he dismounted and entered the small dwelling. Spring sat restlessly with her attention riveted on the building. She shifted in the saddle, tempted to follow Jonathan but realized such folly could put Jonathan's life in jeopardy.

Jonathan emerged from the cottage accompanied by a stoop-shouldered, gray haired woman of indeterminate age. *She might have been anywhere between sixty and ninety.* Spring studied the woman. A much younger woman followed behind them, wiping her hands on the apron tied around her waist.

As Spring watched, Jonathan paused for a moment, listening as the old woman spoke. Then his gaze swept the clearing carefully before he motioned for Spring and Tobias to join him.

Spring caught the reins of Tobias's mount and led it into the clearing, hoping that the man had the strength to remain mounted for just a little longer.

"Seems every time ye bring yerself home ye be all shot up, Toby," the old woman complained, reaching up to help Jonathan as he gently pulled Tobias from his mount.

"Aye does seem so, old woman," Tobias managed, leaning heavily on Jonathan.

Chapter Twenty

The old woman scurried before Jonathan carrying Tobias toward the cottage. At Jonathan's bidding, Spring relinquished the reins to both mounts to the young woman then followed Jonathan inside the cottage.

The interior of the cottage was dim and smelled of smoke and another aroma that caused Spring's mouth to water. It had been an exceedingly long time since she had eaten.

Taking a seat on a low bench near the fireplace, she watched Jonathan carefully lower the wounded man onto a narrow wooden cot in the corner of the cottage. She winced when a low moan escaped the older man ashen lips.

As Jonathan bent to care for his friend, the old woman pushed him aside, moving closer to the wounded man.

"I'll be taking care of Toby, milord," the old woman said as she studied the wounded man.

Spring watched the old woman retrieve various earthen jars from a storage shelf in the corner above the cot. Once she had assembled them to her satisfaction on the small table beside the cot, she began to remove the bandage covering Tobias's chest.

Jonathan paced nervously, stopping now and again to watch as the old woman ministered to his wounded friend.

"The doctor removed the bullet. He said if it doesn't set up infection, he should be fine in a few weeks' time," Jonathan said, as if to reassure himself as much as the woman tending Tobias.

"Then fine 'e'll be," she responded. Looking up as the young girl entered the cottage.

"Daughter, quick now, be about fixing milord and milady something to eat. There's enough stew for the three of them left from noonday." The young girl turned silently to do as bade.

"We've no time," Jonathan said. "We must get to London."

"Nonsense, ye'll eat before ye take yer leave, ye will, lad. Why just look at milady, near to fainting she is!"

Jonathan turned worried eyes toward Spring. "No, I am fine, really. We must go as quickly as possible," Spring sought to reassure him.

Jonathan crossed the room. Lifting a hand, he stroked Spring's cheek gently then pushed an errant curl behind her ear. His smile softened as he studied her face.

"We would be pleased to accept your hospitality, if it's not too much trouble, ma'am," Jonathan answered his southern draw more pronounced.

"Would not have offered if it were too much trouble, now, would I?"

The old woman nodded with satisfaction then turned back to her task. She liberally smeared Tobias's shoulder with the herb mixture then applied a clean dressing to the wound.

"The gray's lame. She probably has a stone in her hoof. I'll tend her if you'd like," the girl said as she filled a bowl from the pot hanging over the fire and handed it to Jonathan then turned to fill another for spring. "With a few days' rest, the tenderness will pass."

"Take the bay, instead," Tobias suggested, struggling to raise himself slightly from the bed.

"We cannot leave you here with a lame horse. You must have the bay. We can ride double on Diablo."

"Aye, that beast can carry both easily, for sure. Milady such a wisp other thing, the black will never notice the extra load." Tobias sighed heavily and gave up his painful efforts to lift his shoulder from the straw filled mattress.

Jonathan frowned when Tobias moved as if to try to sit up. "See that you behave, or the two of them will have you tied to the bed in the batting of an eye," Jonathan warned as he headed toward the door. With a reassuring smile, he disappeared outside.

Spring turned her attention to the bowl of stew and hard brown bread served her. After so many hours with no food, it tasted like the finest fare. She shuddered, remembering those long hours locked in the cold bell tower, chilled to the bone and thirsting for a drink. She broke the bread and dipped it into the rich stew, savoring the taste while eating with her fingers brazenly as she had watched Jonathan do.

"Ye've fussed over me enough, Mary," Tobias complained, pushing the woman's hand away when she would have forced yet another spoonful of broth down his throat. "See to milady. She has cuts and bruises enough to keep you busy. Now leave me be, old woman."

The woman turned her attention back to Spring, moving over to examine the gash on the forehead and the bruise on her cheek from a tree limb Spring had failed to duck. Muttering to herself about the misuse of one unable to defend herself, the old woman moved again to the shelf. Shifting several of the crocks aside, she took down four earthen jars. When she had mixed three of the herbs together, she placed the small bowl along with a small basin of water on the table beside Spring.

Spring sat with her hands folded in her lap. Gripping them tightly against the sharp stinging sensation as the woman first cleaned her wound then spread it liberally with the herbs she had mixed. She fought to keep from wincing as the woman cleaned the area where an angry purple bruise had spread across her temple and down to her cheek.

Still, the cool water against the bruised area of a cheek brought a welcome relief. Pushing the wild tangle of hair away from her face, Spring thought about what a mess she must appear. No one was likely to take her for lady Spring Lansing in her present state of disarray. Spring frowned. Having Jonathan see her in such a state was extremely distasteful but could not be helped.

"'Tis not so bad as you might think it is, milady. The scar will be mostly hidden by your hair, and you've only to pull a small curl down to cover the small part remaining," the woman said as she finished treating Spring's injuries and then cleared the table.

Slowly the old woman ambled over to a small chest that stood against one wall of the cottage. She opened it and reached inside. She returned carrying a small mirror and a comb that she handed to Spring.

"Ye'd be wanting to tidy yourself a bit before his lordship returns, I'd reckon."

Holding the mirror, Spring peered anxiously into the smoky glass, gingerly examining the damage done to her face. Relief flooded Spring to see that the damage, though incredibly painful, was very slight. She carefully removed the few remaining pins from her hair and tried as best she could to comb the tangles from its length.

When Jonathan returned, Spring was grateful for the few moments she had had to make repairs to her appearance. Jonathan had taken a moment to refresh himself and had changed into clothing more suited to travel. Once Jonathan had assured himself that Tobias was in good hands and well cared for, they took their leave.

They emerged from the forest quickly and began following a well-traveled carriage route. Jonathan held their mount to a gallop. Spring knew it was concern for his friend's safety that drove Jonathan to set the grueling pace. If apprehended, the farther they were from Tobias, the safer the wounded man would be.

When they had put many miles between themselves and Tobias, Jonathan slowed their mount to a walk. Diablo tossed his head and whinnied his protest at being reigned in. Jonathan stroked the animal's neck and clucked softly to him.

"Enjoyed that bit of exercise, did you?" Jonathan encouraged the stallion. "Patience, we have a long way to go, so you mustn't wear yourself out."

After a while, Spring loosened her grip at Jonathan waist, allowing her arms to relax so that her hands lay casually against the material of his trousers. Instantly she became aware of the unmistakable evidence of the effect of their proximity on certain areas of Jonathan anatomy. Spring quickly raised her hands back to their former position. Heat flooded her face when she felt a gentle chuckle rumble deep in Jonathan chest.

Laugh at her, would he? Spring seethed. Well, they would just see who had the last laugh.

Moving closer to his back, she fitted her body tightly against him and was rewarded by the slight stiffening of his spine. Smiling with satisfaction, Spring continued her assault. She turned her head to the side and lay her cheek gently against his right shoulder, making sure her breath feathered across the skin of his neck. Gradually she relaxed her grip and allowed her arms to slide slowly down, down until once again her hands rested against the tight material of his trousers. Sighing deeply, she pretended to sleep.

She delighted in his sudden intake of breath as Jonathan's posture became even stiffer and more rigid. With a contented smile, Spring snuggled closer.

She felt tension radiating from him as Jonathan struggled to control himself. Beneath her cheek she felt the subtle tightening of muscles straining against the soft material of his shirt. With an effort, she managed to breathe deeply and evenly, her reward, a low curse from Jonathan.

Encouraged, she snuggled closer and uttered a small mewling sound, eliciting another sharp intake of breath. Jonathan shifted in the saddle, seeking to ease his discomfort. Spring protested his movements with a soft moan and moved her hands ever so slightly.

"Damnation, woman," Jonathan grated, as if in pain.

"What?" Spring raised her head, innocently affecting a voice thick with sleep. "I must have dropped off. Did you say something, Jonathan?"

"Nothing," Jonathan answered curtly. "Go back to sleep."

Spring smiled, feeling vindicated. This time when she returned her head to the muscular pillow of Jonathan's shoulder, she allowed the fatigue to claim her.

Jonathan strained against the tight material of his trousers. He shifted uncomfortably, praying that Spring really was asleep. He was dangerously close to embarrassing himself as her pliant form molded itself to his back. When her hands had fallen a second time to the area where his manhood strained against the fabric of his trousers, just the weight of her hand had damn near unmanned him.

What exquisite torture it was feeling her supple body pressed firmly against his. The soft measure of a breath feathered against the back of his neck and sent tremors along his spine. Jonathan stiffened against the weakness her nearness engendered, wanting nothing at the moment quite so much as to hold Spring's naked body in his arms and lose his soul in the depths of her as their bodies became one.

Realizing the path his mind had taken could only lead to trouble, Jonathan pushed the thoughts away. With firm resolve, he forced the idea of Spring soft, warm, and willing in his arms out of his mind. He shook his head to clear the image. He must get his thoughts under control.

He must somehow tear his mind away from the dangerous track it had chosen to follow. He searched the roadway ahead of them. Their safety depended upon his keeping his wits about him. He could not allow his need for Spring to cloud his judgment. He had a mission to complete.

Finally, Spring's breathing settled into the slow easy rhythm that told Jonathan this time the minx really was asleep. With an extreme effort, he managed to put a lid on his raging need and slowly relaxed. He made a mental note to extract revenge for every torturous mile as soon as they were safely out of Wyndridge's reach.

She likes to play games, does she? Jonathan suppressed a chuckle. He could teach the hoyden a few things she would never guess about the game of love. *Just wait, my love.*

As they rode along, Jonathan began to plan his next assault to foil his uncle. The last message he had from Mr. Bailey had been good news. Things were moving rapidly, since the logbook and the marriage license were both now in the good barrister's hands. All the writs had been filed, and the case was to be brought before the Chancery court soon. The end was in sight. Once Jonathan's claim on his father's estate was substantiated in the courts, Marcus Tollersley would be stripped of both title and estates, leaving him destitute.

Thanks to the long conversations Spring had held with the highwayman when she poured out the sordid details of how Lord Wyndridge had forced her to agree to the marriage, Jonathan now had a plan. Armed with that knowledge, he knew exactly how to make his uncle's defeat complete.

Later, when the shadowy curtain of evening descended on the weary travelers, and a light mist began to fall, Jonathan urged Diablo into a canter. Up ahead, the gray shrouded outline of a roadside inn loomed in the darkness.

He had not planned to stop for the night, but with the threat of rain his anxiety mounted over Spring's health. They must stop. She had not long recovered from the fever, and he dared not take the chance that it might return. Resolved, Jonathan turned Diablo into the yard of the inn.

Spring shifted behind him, her arms tightening around Jonathan as Diablo slowed to a walk.

"We have reached an inn," Jonathan said when Spring lifted her head from his shoulder. "We will stop for the night."

"But—" Spring started to protest, but Jonathan cut her off.

"No, the weather's turning. It is likely to pour down any minute now. We cannot take the risk."

"Of course," she acquiesced.

When they stopped in the inn yard, Jonathan swung down from the saddle then reached up to lift Spring down. She swayed when her feet touched the ground for the first time in hours. Jonathan tightened his arms around her, steadying her against his chest.

Handing over the reins to a young lad, Jonathan escorted Spring toward the entrance to the inn. A sign swinging above the door squeaked its protest at a sudden gust of wind. Jonathan opened the door and all but carried Spring inside.

The first heavy drops of rain spattered the courtyard as they hurried inside. With Spring safely in the shelter of his arms, Jonathan swept away from the common room as he spoke to the innkeeper.

"My wife is very tired. We have been traveling since early morning. Do you have a room?"

The innkeeper, instantly solicitous, responded accordingly to the tone of authority in Jonathan's voice.

"Of course, milord," he sputtered rapidly. "We have a fine room for milady. Do you have baggage to unload?"

"No, we left home suddenly and had no time to pack. My father is gravely ill, and we must reach his side at once. Were it not for the storm which threatens we would have reached him before midnight. But I cannot risk my wife's health, so we must take refuge here."

Spring listened as the lie rolled easily from Jonathan's lips.

"Of course, of course, how terrible." The innkeeper tutted. "May I offer my wishes for your father's returned health, milord?"

"Alas, I'm afraid that all there is left to be done is to see his matters set to right, so he can rest in peace."

Spring shivered at the sudden coldness of Jonathan voice as he answered.

Chapter Twenty-One

For a moment, the innkeeper appeared taken aback by the suppressed anger of Jonathan's words, but he quickly recovered. "Yes, well, just let me get the key, and then I can show you to your room. Ye'll be wanting a tray sent up for my lady, no doubt. We have mutton stew and fresh baked bread. Baked it this morning, my wife did. None in these parts what can hold a candle to my Jenny in the kitchen."

"That sounds wonderful," Spring answered with a half-smile.

When the innkeeper had retrieved the key, they followed him up the narrow stairs to the back of a long hallway where he stopped and offered Jonathan the key to a heavy wooden door.

As Jonathan bent to unlock the door, Spring turned toward the end keeper. "May I have a pot of tea, please?"

"Certainly, milady, right away. Is there anything else milady?"

"A bath?"

"At once," he answered and hurried away to tend to her requests.

Spring could almost hear the man calculating the fat purse he would receive for all their needs.

The Golden Boar had once been a popular stopping point for coach traffic between Chichester and London, but with the coming of the railway it had fallen into decline. No longer did the coaches of the wealthy make their way leisurely through the forest of Kingsley Vale or stop at the inn for the night. Now, it was mostly the locals who frequented the inn, making it more of a tavern than an inn and the innkeeper more of a tavern keeper.

The sparsely furnished room, spotlessly clean, had clean linens on the bed. They smelled of fresh air and sunshine. Spring breathed a sigh of relief. Viewed from the outside, the inn was not the sort of place she would normally frequent. But she told herself resolutely they were lucky to have found shelter. Judging from the sounds breaking overhead, the storm had caught up with them with a vengeance.

Spring crossed to the window and pulled back the faded curtain, watching as the rain lashed in sheets across the thick dough panes of glass. She crossed her arms over her breasts, hugging herself tightly as she muttered her thanks for the shelter from the storm.

Transfixed, she watched lightning slash the sky, streaking across the now dark starless night with the viciousness of a crazed swordsman. She trembled as the thunder rolled closely upon the heels of the lightning, sounding like all the chariots of hell loosed in a deadly chase across the darkened sky.

With a shiver, Spring turned away from the window, putting distance between herself and the wild fury spending its anger against the window.

Jonathan worked to kindle a fire in the grate of the fireplace. Spring focused her attention on the long slender fingers of his hands as they moved over the wood. Her body tingled with awareness, remembering those hands upon her skin.

A light rapping sounded at the door as Jonathan coaxed a tiny flame to life under the small sticks of wood. He turned, leaving the fire to catch on its own accord as he crossed to the door.

A woman, rounded and plump, stood holding a tray containing a steaming teapot and two small, flowered China cups. The cups, though obviously expensive, matched neither one another, nor the teapot. The woman's round face broke into a wide smile as she curtsied toward Spring.

"Your tea, milady," the woman said, beaming happily at Spring. "'Tis a good night for it, too, it is, milady. Your bath water's warming. Will bring it up as soon as it's nice and hot, I will."

"Thank you," Spring whispered.

The woman smiled. "Name's Jenny Smith, milady. 'Tis pleased we are to have ye here. Has been a while since we had overnight guests such as yerself." She hurried over to the table near the fire and lowered the tray, then held a chair out invitingly for Spring.

Spring took her seat in the chair and waited while Jenny poured the fragrant tea. She inhaled deeply of its familiar, comforting aroma. She stirred a lump of sugar into the brew before lifting the cup to her lips.

Still holding the teapot in midair, the woman turned toward Jonathan. "A spot o' tea, milord? 'To chase away the chill.'"

"No, thank you," Jonathan answered as he moved to the window. He lifted the curtain to peer out into the storm's darkness. "I should check on Diablo." He crossed the room to stand beside Spring and placed one hand gently on her shoulder. "He'll be excited, so they may not be able to quiet him. He likes to run with the storm."

Jonathan's fingers massaged the tension from her shoulder. "It may take a while to get him settled."

Spring nodded, understanding that Jonathan intended she should have time to complete her bath before he returned.

When both Jonathan and Jenny had left, Spring sat quietly and sipped her tea, letting her mind worry over the events of the last day. She jumped nervously when the light tap came at the door. "Yes?"

"Yer bath, milady," Jenny called cheerfully.

The innkeeper brought in a large tin tub and filled it with bucket after bucket of steaming water while Jenny directed the proceedings. Spring suppressed a smile as she watched the woman supervise the filling of the tub. Jenny gently berated her husband when he declared the tub full enough by demanding more hot water.

The tub filled to her satisfaction, Jenny left the room but quickly returned with towels and a small cake of soap.

"'Tis not scented, milady, but 'tis decent quality, nonetheless. If ye want to sleep in your shift, milady, I could see to yer other things. Will dry quick enough by the kitchen fire, they will."

"I couldn't put you to such trouble," Spring answered.

"'Tis no trouble, milady. Be proud to do it, I would."

"My thanks then," Spring answered, realizing that to refuse the woman's offer would be ungracious.

When Jenny had departed, muttering to herself about finding just the thing for her ladyship, Spring stood in the center of the room, not certain what she should do. After a moment she started unpinning, her hair running her fingers through its tangled length to remove some of the myriad of snarls.

When a soft tapping at the door marked Jenny's return, Spring hesitantly bade her enter.

"I just happened to remember having this packed away, I did," Jenny said as smoothed the material of the garment she held in her hand before she placed the neatly embroidered nightgown on the bed.

"I couldn't possibly wear it," Spring protested.

"Of course, you can, milady." Jenny caressed the soft material again. "It gives me much pleasure to have you wear it."

"If you're quite sure?" Spring sensed that to refuse the gown would gravely wound the generous woman who had befriended her.

"Now, let's get you into that tub before the water gets cold."

Taking for granted Spring's need for the services of a lady's maid, Jenny moved to expertly assist with the bath. Once she had her charge settled in the tub, the woman moved confidently around the room, gathering the soiled clothing Spring had discarded. When Jenny had all the garments folded over her arm, she turned toward the door. As she reached for the handle, she paused, cocked her head to one side thoughtfully and said, "Almost forgot this." She held out a small ivory comb.

Jenny placed the comb on the small table beside the fire. With a satisfied smile, she turned and left the room.

Spring settled into the tub, reveling in the feel of the warm water against her tired flesh The muscles of her legs and back, tightly coiled from hours on horseback, slowly relaxed.

Much later, when the water had begun to chill, Spring plunged her head beneath this surface and emerged sputtering. She lathered her hair profusely. Her too aggressive enthusiasm with the soap allowed it to run down into her eyes. The strong soap burned. She tried to rinse away the soap but found the water too filled with soap to be of use. When she heard the door opening, Spring assumed Jenny had returned to help her and gave thanks for her thoughtfulness.

"Quickly," she said rising from the tub. "The rinse water, I've soap in my eyes."

The rinse water was cold. Very, very cold, so Spring sputtered out her distress as her body responded with lightning speed to the chill. Despite the shivers racing through her, she gave thanks for relief from the stinging soap in her eyes.

A towel was draped over her head, and Spring gratefully accepted the ministrations of gentle hands steadying her as she stepped from the tub. A second towel, warm from the fire, was wrapped around her, and Spring gave herself up to the pleasure of having her body vigorously toweled dry. With the first towel still covering her head and face, Spring found herself pushed gently toward the fire and urged to sit in the chair drawn close to the warmth of the fire.

Gentle hands guided and tended her lovingly. She gave herself over to the care of those hands, marveling at how tender and competent they were. The towel that covered her face and hair gently massaged, toweling the water away.

Slowly those gentle hands began to work at the snarls in her long golden tresses, tending one long silky section at a time. The tangles were gently worked free. Spring gave herself over to the tiredness that swept through her. Relaxing as those hands worked their magic, Spring allowed her head to rest against the chair's back as she enjoyed the gentle ministration of having her hair worked free of the snarls and tangles. The warmth of the fire lulled her, and soon she slipped into a peaceful sleep.

Like shining threads of spun gold, her long tresses slid through the comb in Jonathan's hand. He took a deep breath and tried to calm the response that rose within him. It had been bad enough when he had returned to the room and found Spring still in the bath, but when he had had to quickly discard the dinner tray on the bed and hurry to assist her it had sorely testing the limits of his restraint.

Jonathan had promised himself that he would not touch her again until they were properly married. It had seemed an easy enough task when he had made that resolution. He had anticipated achieving that goal without delay, but the unexpected storm had postponed their arrival in London. Now he faced the prospect of a night spent in sheer torture.

Jonathan could tell by the slow rhythmic rise and fall of her breasts beneath the towel that she had fallen asleep. He eyed the tub cautiously. It offered respite from his problem, if only temporarily.

Quickly he disrobed and immersed himself in the tub. The sudden chill of the water offered some relief to his difficulty, but soon he found the effect nullified by the subtle fragrance of Spring that lingered in the water. Uttering a curse, he quickly washed himself and left the tub.

Spring slept soundly in the chair. She had curled into it like a sleepy kitten, tucking one hand beneath her chin while the other gripped the edge of the towel. Jonathan's fingers touched the soft material of the nightgown spread across the foot of the bed but discarded the idea of trying to dress her. He could never manage without waking her.

Still, he should put her to bed. Jonathan let his gaze feast on the beautiful sight of her with her hair spread around her like the mantle of an Aztec God.

Touching the long tresses sparkling in the firelight, he found them nearly dry to the touch. He bent and lifted her tenderly in arms. She curled against his chest sleepily, one hand moving of its own accord to stroke taut muscle just above his heart. Fire raced through his veins as her fingertips caressed his skin gently then stilled.

Jonathan moved toward the bed with the sleeping woman in his arms. The covers had not been turned down, and worse yet, the dinner tray, with its covered dishes, still rested where he had placed it on the bed.

"Damnation," Jonathan cursed beneath his breath.

He studied the problem for a moment, discarding one thought after another and finding no solution. He could not, no matter how slight her weight, continue to stand holding her in his arms all night. His libido would not stand for it. Already the feel of her silken hair feathering against his skin was playing havoc with his self-control. Even if his strength did not desert him, his willpower surely would.

Slowly he slid her body down the length of his body, feeling a traitorous response as he did so. He held her pressed firmly against his chest with one arm as his breath lodged in his chest at the searing imprint of her breasts burned onto his skin through the towel. With a groan, he reached for the tray with his free hand and deposited it on the table near the bed.

Extremely pleased that he had managed what had been a very difficult task, Jonathan turned with renewed confidence to the bed and carefully turned down the covers.

The feel of satin skin beneath his fingers when he shifted her in his arms delivered Jonathan a sensory message more powerful than the report of a rifle. The towel covering his burden had given up its slight defense. With a sharp intake of breath, he turned back toward the bed, wondering just how much one man could endure before he lost complete control of his faculties. Good intentions and gentlemanly manners wore extremely thin.

Finally, he moved to carefully lower his burden to the bed. His senses were filled with the uniquely feminine smell of Spring. His skin tingled from the touch of her satin smoothness against his ruggedness. With a gentleness almost alien to one used to taking charge and rushing full speed ahead, he held her in his arms just above the mattress.

She giggled.

"That does it."

He dropped her. She bounced naked onto the mattress, now engulfed in a fit of giggles at his expense.

For a moment, he glared at her then he fell upon the bed beside her and doubled over with laughter.

When he regained control, Spring was on her knees beside him, the spun treasure of her hair a profusion of curls framing her slim body in a riotous tumble. Her eyes danced with amusement and more. She was glorious, splendid, spellbinding. And God, how he wanted her at that moment.

Reaching up, Jonathan caught her, tangling in his hand in the bounty of curls that surrounded her glowing face and pulling her slowly, slowly toward him.

When their lips touched, the storm that broke outside paled in comparison to the fury of their passion.

His hands caressed and molded her body like a blind man seeking to know and discover. Jonathan pressed her body ever closer to his, and she responded to every touch, every stroke as he branded her with his possession. Driven wild by his touch, Spring responded in kind, touching, exploring, learning, and relearning his body as he had hers, until he could stand no more of the exquisite torture.

Yes, still his body cried out for her touch, her warmth, her softness. The need to feel her warm and yielding beneath him drove all coherent thought from his mind as he lifted himself above her.

Their union held the wild thunder of storm driven waves, the blinding flash of lightning in the dead of night, and finally the calm, wondrous quiet of a fresh new morning.

Chapter Twenty-Two

The first pink streaks of dawn found them strangely rested and refreshed for all that they had only achieved a few hours of sleep. Contentment radiated from Spring as she watched Jonathan bathe and dress. He kissed her then announced he would go to prepare Diablo for their continued journey while Spring dressed and had breakfast.

With one last kiss and a meaningful glance toward the bed they had shared, Jonathan took his leave.

Left alone in their room, Spring quickly dressed and had just folded the unused nightgown when a light tap at the door announced the arrival of Jenny with her breakfast tray.

Jenny retrieved the dinner tray, and Spring thanked her for the delicious food, blushing as she remembered sitting naked in bed while Jonathan had fed her the rich tasty stew.

Once Jonathan had settled their account with the innkeeper, they resumed their journey

"It would have been faster to take the train from Brighton," Spring suggested when they had been on the road for several hours and the sun had climbed high in the sky.

"That's what Wyndridge would expect us to do," Jonathan answered. "He'll have someone watching the station."

"I hadn't thought of that." She turned to gaze up at Jonathan.

This time Jonathan had swung up into the saddle behind her and held her cradled against him. Spring relaxed, letting her back melt into his firm chest. The skirt of her dress rested midway of her shins, giving a glimpse of trim ankles where they rested on either side of their mount's wide body. After the horrors of the last few weeks,

Spring did not worry about showing her ankles. In fact, she doubted she'd ever place value on the mores of the Ton's narrow constructs again.

They headed northward, skirting Chichester, passing through the chalk valley and magical yew wood forests of Kingley Vale.

Jonathan preferred the woodland and was quite at home traveling through the well-kept forests. Spring noted how with unerring skill he kept them traveling northward through the thickest part of The Men's woodland and Thursley Heath, until at last their zigzag path brought them near London.

Jonathan dropped a kiss to the top of her head. "We will be in London before nightfall."

For a moment, his hand touched hers where they rested in her lap. Spring moved a little closer, her head pillowed in the valley between the strong muscles of his upper chest. She did not want their journey to end. This time alone with Jonathan had been the most exciting, wondrous experience of her life.

When they stopped at Box Hill, Spring gasped, enchanted by wild orchids and hundreds of butterflies. While Diablo grazed on the low cropped grass of the open downland, Spring gathered orchids and counted the varieties of butterflies.

Jonathan watched her, never letting her out of his sight as she gathered the delicate blossoms. He bent to pick one himself then tucked it gently behind her ear. She was touched by the gentleness of his attention to her, loving him more than she would have thought possible.

As they left the meadow behind and headed for London, Spring felt a strange sense of loss. It had been wonderful to be alone in the woodland with Jonathan.

"It's not much longer now," Jonathan said as they approached the outskirts of London.

"Grandmother must be very worried, I must go to her at once," Spring responded.

"No," Jonathan warned. "We can't take the risk."

"Then where shall we go?" Spring exclaimed.

"Don't worry, Love," Jonathan answered. "I have a plan."

"But my grandmother," Spring began.

"Will be informed of our arrival shortly. First, we have a stop to make," Jonathan reassured.

They crossed the Thames at Chelsea and continued north to Knightsbridge then turned eastward to Piccadilly. After a confusing series of twists and turns, they stopped at the courtyard of a small church. Jonathan dismounted then reached up to help Spring down.

"I sent a message to Mr. Brownstone informing him of our intentions, he will have taken care of all the arrangements."

"Jonathan," Spring said. "Why must we stop here? Surely, we should continue to Mr. Brownstone's office since he is expecting us?"

"We will, but first the ceremony must be taken care of."

"Ceremony?"

"Yes, my love," Jonathan answered, taking her hand. "You do wish to be my wife, do you not?"

Spring stared at Jonathan, her face a mirror of disbelief. He intended them to marry now, at this very moment? She stood transfixed, gazing up at Jonathan.

"Well?"

"Yes, definitely," Spring found her voice. "But Grandmother—" Spring began to protest again.

"Is fully aware of our intentions and has given her blessing. You will be seeing her soon enough, ask her."

"But—"

"Later, my love," Jonathan placed a gentle kiss on her lips. "Just trust me."

Trust him? Ah, yes, Spring answered silently. With my life, my love, my very soul.

Inside the small chapel, the solemn-faced clergyman wasted no time producing the papers for them to sign.

"The necessary steps have been taken by Mr. Brownstone. It is only a formality that you must sign these papers."

"Yes, but my wife wishes that we should exchange our vows in person, a matter of her personal preference, of course. I have explained that our marriage was perfectly legal. She insists, however, that she will not feel a proper wife until our vows are spoken in person."

"And right you are to feel such, my dear," the vicar responded, turning a reassuring smile toward Spring, as if noticing her for the first time.

"The ceremony?" Jonathan prompted, bringing the parson's attention back to the business at hand.

"Yes, yes," he answered taking up his book from the desk. "Now, let me see. Ah yes, here we are."

Spring managed to answer with the correct words in all the appropriate places as her mind swirled in a fog of confusion and a numbing coldness settled over her. What had she done? What would become of her family when Lord Wyndridge learned that she and Jonathan had married?

With his arm firmly at her waist, Jonathan directed Spring toward the door of the small chapel. Outside, Spring was surprised to see a coach emblazoned with Baron Rinehardt's coat of arms awaiting them.

At a sharp rap on the roof from Jonathan, the vehicle quickly moved away from the small stone church. Spring gripped the leather seat with both hands to steady herself as the coach lumbered out of the courtyard and picked up speed along the cobbled street.

"Everything is moving along according to plan. Don't worry, all will be fine," Jonathan reassured.

He lifted her hand to his lips and gently placed a kiss in its palm before closing each finger slowly so that the kiss remained trapped inside her clenched hand. Her skin tingled, and heat radiated along her spine.

Trust him? Did she have any choice now? For what it was worth, her fate and that of her family lay in his hands. She only prayed he took the responsibility as seriously as she had.

Jonathan placed his arm around her shoulders and pulled her gently into the shelter of his embrace. Spring settled contentedly into his arms, allowing her head to rest on his shoulder.

My husband, Jonathan Andrew Sinclair. Spring ran the words through her mind, savoring the effect they had on her senses. Everything would be all right now. Jonathan would make it so. Spring sighed contentedly. Just let Lord Wyndridge try to harm her now.

They would leave England behind, and all the trouble Marcus Tollersley had caused, as well. Her mother and the twins would come to live with them in America. There, the twins would make suitable matches, even without big dowries to recommend them.

Spring continued dreamily planning their future together as Jonathan's fingers gently massaged her right shoulder, slipping slowly down to her elbow then back up again. His touch warmed her, sending tingling sensations along her nerve endings and bringing her body alive in ways that only Jonathan's touch could. A soft whimper of desire escaped her lips as she pressed her body closer to the hard length of Jonathan's frame. Shifting slightly in the seat, leaning back against the velvet damask lined coach wall, he drew her fully into his embrace.

Jonathan lowered his head and ran his lips softly across her forehead then travelled a torturous path down to her earlobe.

"Soon, my darling wife." His voice held a wealth of promise as his lips moved the scant inches necessary to claim hers.

Spring melted into his embrace, offering Jonathan total possession of her mouth and greedily accepting his in return. She pressed closer, crushing her breasts between them, her heart beating a matching tattoo to the thunder of his against her chest. Her hands moved of their own volition to caress the smooth fabric of his waist coat while her finger made small wrinkles in the fine fabric as they clutched urgently at the material, as if seeking to touch the very essence of the man who was now her husband.

Finally, Jonathan lifted her so that she was sitting full upon his lap, and Spring gave a pleased moan as the evidence of his desire for her pressed urgently against the thin material of her pantalettes. She shifted her hips gently, felt his instant response, then began a slow systematic rotation, which brought a deep moan from Jonathan.

"For the love of God, woman," Jonathan pleaded.

"Yes, my darling?" Spring answered innocently with another rotation of her hips.

"Would you have me disgrace myself?"

"Never," she answered playfully, continuing her assault on his person.

"Then, unless you desire the first expression of our marital love to be in this coach, at this moment, you had better stop that immediately."

Spring slid gently off his lap and straightened her gown. She smiled, planning the second phase of her attack. He had, after all, begun this encounter. She had merely responded to his advances, which was what a wife was supposed to do, after all, wasn't it?

"Jonathan?"

"Yes, my love?" Jonathan answered in a voice slightly hoarse with suppressed desire.

"Have you ever made love in a coach?"

"No, but if you persist in this line of conversation, I'm quite sure the situation will be remedied very shortly."

Spring smiled, reveling in the feeling of power her effect upon Jonathan gave her.

"Jonathan, how long before we reach Mr. Brownstone's home?" Spring asked, placing one small hand on his thigh and with slow caressing movements traveled steadily upward.

"Long enough," Jonathan answered in a pained voice and shifted, seeking to relieve the discomfort of his tight trousers.

Spring's fingers continued their tantalizing upward path, stopping just a breath away from their ultimate goal. Spring felt a shudder pass through Jonathan's body.

"Witch," he accused as his arms tightened around her and he pressed her down upon the leather of the coach seat. "I warned you, minx, there was a limit to my endurance. Now we'll both pay the price of your impetuousness."

His lips found the soft mounds of her breasts where they swelled invitingly against the fabric of her bodice. His fingers quickly worked the laces of her corset, freeing her breasts to his eager mouth. Leaving her breasts to the tender care of his hands, his lips traveled up the long column of her throat to gently tug at the tender portion of her earlobe.

"And such a wondrous price it is," he whispered as his tongue began a thorough exploration of the shell of her ear.

Spring shivered as delightful spirals of desire cascaded over her. She pressed her body against the hard length of his, arching her back as his hands extended the range of their exploration. When his hand massaged the sensitive skin of her inner thigh through her pantalettes, Spring responded with a soft sigh of pleasure.

"Cursed, restrictions!" Jonathan complained. "Why must you wear such armor? You're trussed up like a Christmas turkey and quite safe from ravishment except by the most determined hand."

Jonathan laughed and kissed her, drinking deeply from the sweetness of her mouth. "But I, my love, am just such a determined hand."

Lifting himself from her, he quickly reached beneath her skirts and removed the offending garment. For a moment he held the pantalettes aloft, waving them like a victory flag. Then, quickly losing interest in his trophy in favor of a more pleasurable reward, he tossed then onto the empty seat at the other side of the coach.

"And now, my lovely," he whispered as he settled himself between her thighs. "You had some doubt as to my ability in our present situation, I believe?"

"Never for a moment," Spring answered as Jonathan filled her and began to move so that the sway of the coach accentuated his powerful thrusts.

A growing intensity engulfed them, pushed higher, coiled tighter until, like an overwound clock spring, it broke around them, quickly pushing them toward the brink.

Chapter Twenty-Three

A light mist fell, and fog shrouded the streets. The thick, gray, overcast sky blocked the sunlight. Jonathan drew back the curtain covering the coach window and peered out.

He kept his gaze on the scenery passing outside, allowing Spring privacy to repair her appearance. He smiled as the soft rustle of satin and lace as she smoothed the material of her skirts reminded him of how she came to be in such a state of disarray.

Instantly his pulse increased, and his loins tightened. He was amazed at the impact just thinking of Spring had upon his body. Even after just making love to her, he still desired her. The disarray of his own clothing had been easily dealt with, but the disarray she caused in his mind and body were not so easily quelled.

This mission he was about required he have all his wits about him. His uncle would act swiftly, given an opening. His own life as well as Spring's depended on his keeping his concentration and not allowing his uncle any advantage.

It called for his undivided attention. He had not counted on fate pushing the stakes even higher by placing Spring in the middle of this situation. At least one good thing had come from this quest. He would never have met Spring had he not come to England.

The first half of the quest to recover his birthright and leave his uncle destitute had been the goal his barrister had been set to task and which Mr. Brownstone was even now close to achieving. The other, revenge for the murder of Edward Tollersley, would be harder to achieve.

But Jonathan had not given up on the quest. And now, the death of Captain Smith had been added to the tally, as well.

How many others were there no one knew about? How many times had his uncle killed for his own gain? Soon, the truth would be known, and the debt paid in full. Jonathan allowed the curtain to fall into place as the familiar shape of Brownstone's townhouse appeared in the fog ahead of them.

As the coach stopped, Jonathan turned to Spring, allowing his gaze to take in the sight of her as she busily patted her hair into place. A small smile played upon her lips, and her cheeks held a slight flush. As if feeling his gaze upon her, she lifted fringed lids, revealing crystalline eyes in whose depths reflected all the love he could ever wish.

In that moment, Jonathan wanted nothing quite as much as to pull her into his arms and reward the trust and confidence she had placed in him with all his powers of love and devotion. She was so lovely, so desirable, so trusting. It took his breath away when she looked at him with her love and desire plainly visible in her eyes.

That his uncle had sought to harm her, to break her spirit caused Jonathan's ire to rise to fever pitch. There was so much that Marcus Tollersley must pay for, and pay he would Jonathan vowed as he gazed deeply into the eyes of his wife.

"Ready?" Jonathan asked, watching as she gently stroked the wrinkles from her skirts.

She smiled. "We have to do this?"

"Yes, but it won't take long."

"Then well go to Grandmother's?"

"Actually, she should arrive here any moment."

"Grandmother, here?" she exclaimed. "But, how?"

"There's no time for explanations now, my love. We have things to do."

Spring fell silent, but tiny lines wrinkled her brow in a slight frown as she tried to make sense of what was happening.

"Soon, my love," Jonathan reassured. "In just a little while all will be revealed. But for now, we must hurry. Time is of the essence."

"But surely Wyndridge would not try to harm us in London?"

"His lordship has killed before and will not hesitate to do so again. We cannot afford to make the mistake of underestimating him."

"But with so many witnesses, surely he would not be so stupid as to try anything."

"There are men who would take the risk for a price, and I'm quite sure my uncle knows them."

Spring shivered. Would the earl go to such extremes to stop them? Suddenly, Spring realized it was not just their marriage that the earl sought to stop, it was Jonathan.

Knowing the evilness of Marcus Tollersley from firsthand experience, she understood there were no limits to the lengths he would go to prevent Jonathan from winning his inheritance. He would fight to stop Jonathan with every means at his disposal.

When the coach came to a full stop, Jonathan opened the door and swung himself smoothly down. With a smile of reassurance, he reached up to help Spring down. He lifted her easily, swinging her gently in his arms before allowing her to slide slowly down the length of his long frame.

Spring found that she was unsteady on her feet when they touched the ground and was glad for Jonathan's support as he pulled her into the shelter of his arm. He brushed a soft kiss across her forehead and then turned toward the house.

A gas light flickered on the portico beside the entry door that stood open. In the light of the lamp a man beckoned them toward the open doorway.

"This way, my lord."

"Thank you, James. He is expecting us, I believe?"

"Indeed, my lord. This way, please."

Jonathan guided her along the hallway. Following the man who had admitted them to the townhouse, they paused while he stopped at large double doors and rapped once upon the gleaming wood then opened the heavy doors and ceremoniously announced them.

"The Earl and Countess of Wyndridge."

"Enter, please."

Mr. Brownstone, seated behind a broad leather topped desk, stood and came around the desk as they entered the room.

An older man with wide girth and a thatch of wild grey hair stood at the window. He turned as they entered, and the penetrating look from his small black eyes focused on Spring.

Who is this man?

He studied Spring with equal curiosity.

"So, this is Lady Spring." The older man spoke in a deep scratchy voice that carried a hint of an asthmatic wheeze. "Knew your father, fine man. Damn shame what Tollersley did to him."

"Lady Spring, please forgive my lapse, I had forgotten you haven't met my partner, Thomas Bailey," Mr. Brownstone said, casting a glance at the older man.

Spring smiled as Brownstone and Bailey exchanged a quick nod in acknowledgement of their disgust with the earl. With the introduction taken care of, Jonathan escorted Spring to a chair close to the fire, and the men turned to business. Spring spread her hands toward the fire's warmth, enjoying its feel on her chilled hands. With her gaze fastened intently on the flames flickering in the grate, Spring listened with little attention to the conversation that the men carried on.

"My lord, all is moving according to schedule."

"Good, and you have the necessary papers ready for us to sign?"

"Of course, of course," Brownstone answered. "And with the copy of the marriage writ attached, the contract becomes quite binding."

"Good," Jonathan returned. "We won't have that to worry about, at least. If he can't access the Lansing funds, then he will be at a disadvantage."

Spring's interested picked up as she heard her family's name brought into the conversation. She turned her gaze from the cozy fire to the strong familiar lines of her husband's face as Brownstone continued.

"The Chancery Court has frozen his accounts in London as well as Brighton and Chichester. His next move, of course, will be to tap the Lansing holdings, but with the agreement that he signed fully executed, he will be blocked from that, as well. I believe his only option will be to stand and fight.

"Yes," Jonathan answered, "but will he fight in court or try some other nefarious plan?"

"It doesn't matter," Bailey interrupted with a toss of his shaggy grey head. "This time we are forewarned. Security will be so tight he'll not win again."

"You're a good friend, Thomas," Jonathan said.

"Edward was my friend, and I never believed that fool's tale of his being a highwayman."

Jonathan nodded.

"Once the court has ruled on the evidence, it is just a matter of clearing up the small details. Your uncle will be ruined."

"You're sure he has nothing else to fall back on? Nothing at all?"

"Nothing. The Lansing estates were his last hope, and now with this marriage those are lost to him. You have him where you want him, Jonathan," Thomas Bailey explained.

"Not yet, but soon," Jonathan warned.

AS SPRING LISTENED to the exchange, a slow chill spread over her. A deathlike coldness settled around her heart, and her chest ached so that taking the smallest breath seemed an enormous task. Jonathan had married her to block his uncle's access to her family's fortune, not to protect her from Marcus , but to put one more of the pieces of the puzzle into play.

Jonathan had known all along about the agreement which Mr. Brownstone had so carefully crafted to protect her family from Marcus Tollersley. She had explained to the highwayman in detail how her father's barrister had secured the agreement with the earl during one of those late-night visits to her room at Wyndridge Hall.

Was that all that mattered to her husband? Had he married her only to thwart his uncle? Had he ever really loved her at all? Spring felt color rise in her cheeks as she remembered with embarrassing clarity how she had freely given her love, her trust, and her body to Jonathan.

No, her mind screamed silently. It could not be true. He loved her. He had told her so repeatedly. Maybe a part of Jonathan loved her, she acknowledged sadly, but he could not possibly love her in the way she loved him. His being consumed by the need for revenge against his uncle left no room for the kind of love she held for him.

She knew he wanted her, desired her physically, but the emotional binding that tied her soul to his forever was somehow lacking in Jonathan. He was not, she realized sadly, able to return her love with the same unlimited devotion she held for him. She was a piece of the puzzle, a strategy, a prize to win. That was all her love represented to Jonathan.

Sadness settled upon her like the heavy hand of grief as she mourned the passing of something wondrous. Never again would she feel the mindless, overwhelming, consuming love for Jonathan. It was forever frozen away in the cold chamber that had become her heart.

So easy, she had made it so easy for him. Not that she had wanted to marry Marcus Tollersley. Nothing could have been further from the truth. But she had wanted so very much for Jonathan to love her and need her in the way she loved and needed him.

From the hallway a noise arose, and Spring recognized the familiar sound of her grandmother's voice. It should have been reassuring. It should have made her feel secure and safe.

It did not.

Nothing could melt the coldness that had settled around her heart. Something wonderful and loving and caring had died within her. In its place was now an empty void nothing could fill.

She ached in every part of her body, but especially in the region where her heart shrank away from the coldness entrapping it. She trembled violently as sure knowledge of her plight spread icy tendrils along her spine. Jonathan did not love her. He had pursued her, had married her only to thwart his uncle.

The walls of the room closed in around her and the air that had been so pleasantly scented by the fire in the hearth was now oppressive. Just drawing a breath was a struggle. Her head pounded, so she closed her eyes against the pain. She raised a hand to her forehead as darkness swam around her. When she opened her eyes, the room swirled crazily, and she realized she was on the verge of losing consciousness.

Would it be so terrible to surrender to the darkness again? There was no pain there, and the knowledge of Jonathan's duplicity might not follow her into the void. In the darkness she would be safe from the terrible knowledge that Jonathan did not love her and had only intended their marriage as a parry to thwart his uncle.

"What's this?" Lady Phoebe exclaimed as she entered the study, and her gaze took in the appearance of her granddaughter. "What has happened my pet, are you ill again?"

Lady Phoebe turned to Jonathan, her expression thunderous. "Look here, the child is near to fainting! What have you done to her?"

Jonathan's startled gaze quickly left Lady Phoebe's outraged visage and came to rest on Spring. Instantly, his expression changed to tender concern as he crossed the room and knelt at Spring's side.

"My dear, what is it? Are you unwell? Why did you not say something?"

Spring straightened her back and folded her hands in her lap. She neither wanted nor needed his pity. Refusing to meet his gaze, she turned her attention to Lady Phoebe, who hovered over her like a large grey bird defending its nestling.

"I'm fine, grandmother," Spring answered, avoiding Jonathan's obvious concern. "The trip was just more tiring than I had thought it would be. I need a good night's rest, that's all."

"Of course, my pet," Lady Phoebe cooed, patting Spring's hand.

Lady Phoebe shot Jonathan an accusing look that spoke volumes. Obviously, she did not believe her granddaughter's distress was caused by fatigue, but, clearly, she was unwilling to discuss the matter in front of an audience.

Jonathan appeared at a loss to explain his wife's sudden illness. He took first one then the other of her hands and rubbed them between his hands, but Spring barely felt the touch of his warm skin on the pallid coldness of her own.

"Spring?" he asked.

"I'm fine, it's just a chill."

"Then perhaps some brandy to warm you?" he asked in concern as he touched her cheek, gently stroking it with his fingers.

Spring nodded, avoiding Jonathan's eyes. Her mind swirled with images from the last few weeks. The nightly clandestine visits to her room by the highwayman. The image of Jonathan when they had been introduced at the ball brought the sting of tears to her eyes. The way he had held her as they had danced. Had he ever cared for her, or was it all part of his plan.

Jonathan left her side and returned immediately with a snifter of brandy that he placed in her hands. His own hand lingered on hers as if she did not have the strength to lift the goblet.

Spring could not bear his touch for another moment. How dare he act as if he cared about her when his only interest was in keeping his uncle from gaining access to her father's estate? She pulled her hand away from his, lifted the glass to her lips and sipped the brandy. Its burning brought tears to her eyes. At least she thought the brandy caused the tears. She coughed as the alcohol nearly took her breath away.

"I'm... fine... now," she stammered as the brandy burned a path down her throat and started a small fire in her stomach.

"Drink the remainder. It'll warm you."

"Please, don't let me interrupt. Continue with your business. Grandmother is here now, so I will be fine."

"I'm sure the gentlemen won't mind waiting while—"

"No," Spring cut in more sharply than was necessary. "Continue with your business, it is after all, the most important thing. Perhaps I might lie down for a bit? I'm sure that I'll feel much better in a moment."

"Of course, my lady," Mr. Brownstone rose from his seat behind the heavy teak desk and moved to offer Spring his arm. "My wife would be honored for you to use her parlor, I'm certain. Come, my dear, it's just across the hall."

Taking the arm Mr. Brownstone offered, Spring allowed him to direct her to the parlor, a small room decorated with a woman's comfort in mind. He led her to a small settee pulled close to the fireplace. Across one end, a colorful Afghan had been spread across its overstuffed cushions. At the other end, a small pillow with a neatly embroidered hunting scene reposed against the armrest. A small table nearby held several of the new women's magazines that had lately become all the rage.

Spring sat on the soft cushions, slipped off her shoes and lay back upon the settee. With a nod of approval, Mr. Brownstone took the Afghan and covered Spring while Jonathan pulled an armchair closer and motioned for Lady Phoebe to take a seat beside her granddaughter.

"And now, my lady," Mr. Brownstone began, clearing his throat before he continued. "If you're comfortable, we shall conclude our business."

"I shall be fine, Mr. Brownstone. Thank you for your concern. Please don't let me keep you away from your work."

Spring picked up one of the magazines from the table and began to peruse its pages.

With a look of confusion, Jonathan turned an imploring look toward Lady Phoebe.

"It's probably just the shock of all that's happened." Lady Phoebe sought to relieve the anxiety mirrored in Jonathan's features. "I'm sure that once this is all settled and she's had a few days of rest, she'll be herself again, my dear."

"Undoubtedly," Spring answered, staring blindly at the magazine in her hand and knowing that never again would she be the same.

"We will conclude this business as swiftly as possible, my dear," Jonathan reassured her as he turned back to his business.

Spring did not acknowledge his words.

Chapter Twenty-Four

Spring stared into space for a moment, ignoring her grandmother's attempts to engage her in conversation. Her mind was lost in thoughts of the information she had overheard. How could she have been so blind? Worse yet, how could Jonathan have used her so hideously?

Tears stung at the back of her eyes. Spring forced them back. She would not shed more tears for what she had lost. She understood Jonathan's need to avenge the murder of his father. She understood his desire to claim his inheritance. What she did not understand was his reasons for proclaiming to love her. Surely, he knew she would have gone along with his plan to thwart the earl's plan. She would have welcomed any method to escape marrying the vile creature, but what she could not forgive was his proclamation of love.

Was it really necessary for him to pledge his undying love? Such a careless disregard for her, manipulating her into falling in love with him. He was her very first love, and now he was the source of her first heart break.

It would have been so much better had he simply approached her with a plan to thwart his uncle. They could have entered into a marriage of convenience. That would have served them both well, and her heart would not have been at risk. From now on, she would protect her heart.

Their marriage, based on secrets and a clandestine agenda, could still serve them both. With their marriage, her mother and the twins could continue to live their comfortable life. They would not be turned out of Lansing Hall.

Spring squared her shoulders, gave a tiny shake of her head, and steeled her resolve. She could do this. She could play her part. She just needed to protect her heart. Now that she knew Jonathan's true intent, she would not be so foolish as to open her heart to him again.

For a moment, her gaze strayed across the hallway to Jonathan where he sat engrossed in conversation with Mr. Brownstone and Thomas Bailey. For just an instant all the pain that assailed stung her eyes as they lingered on him. She quickly pushed it away, squared her shoulders and turned to her grandmother.

"Shall we go?"

"My dear, I'm not sure, I mean..." Lady Phoebe hesitated.

"Actually, I'm feeling much better now," Spring insisted. "The brandy has quite chased away the chill."

Lady Phoebe was still not convinced. "Should not we wait for your husband to complete his business?"

Spring rose.

"My husband can manage his business without my presence. My usefulness does not require my attendance to his business."

Spring turned and quickly crossed the room. At the doorway, she paused and turned back to her grandmother, who appeared fraught with confusion.

"Mother must be beside herself. 'Tis better that we go to her at once."

"But, my dearest," Lady Phoebe tried again. "I'm not certain Jonathan would think it wise for us to go without him."

"Nonsense, we shall be quite safe at home. His lordship would not dare to harm us there. Besides which, I am now married to Jonathan. I no longer hold any appeal for his lordship, I am quite sure."

"But Jonathan—"

"Can follow when he has finished his business. If he wishes." The bitterness that crept into Spring's voice left her grandmother searching her face carefully for some clue as to its source.

For a moment, Spring's gaze focused on her husband's back. He had left the chair and now paced deeper into the room where he stood focused on his conversation with the two barristers. Love for him swelled inside her until it became an almost constant ache in the region of her heart.

He did not love her. He desired her, had taken her as his wife, but it was not love that had driven him to do so. No, far from it.

Revenge. The only thing that mattered to Jonathan was his quest to make his uncle pay for the wrongs he had committed. But what of Jonathan? What price would he pay for the ends that he so fervently sought? For that matter, what price would she be forced to pay, as well?

Resolutely, Spring squared her shoulders, whatever the price, she would pay it.

Just as Jonathan's quest was to recover his birthright and punish his uncle for his crimes against his father, her quest was to ensure the safety of her family.

By marrying Jonathan, she had accomplished that feat. Regardless of the ache in her heart, she must keep in mind the need to protect her family. She could endure anything as long as they were safe.

She might endure, but she did not have to be a party to it, as well. Determined, she turned her gaze back to her grandmother.

"You've had the coachman wait?"

"Actually, I hired a hansom cab," Lady Phoebe answered. "Maria took the coach, just in case the house was being watched."

"But you did have the man wait, of course?"

Lady Phoebe gave her granddaughter a look that said *how dare she consider otherwise.* "Certainly."

"Then I suggest we return home at once," Spring insisted.

Spring turned toward the front door and hurried down the hallway without waiting to see if her grandmother followed.

Lady Phoebe caught her at the door. "I brought a cloak for you," Lady Phoebe said, motioning for the doorman to retrieve the garment.

Pulling the cloak closely around herself, Spring gathered the hood about her face and quickly made her way to the hired equipage. Lady Phoebe followed in her wake. When they were comfortably ensconced in the dim interior of the hansom cab, Lady Phoebe gave the order for their departure.

In silence, they passed through the streets of London. The familiar sounds of the city closed in upon them as they passed unrecognized and unhampered through the crowded streets.

Soon Spring picked out the familiar sounds of Mayfair, the part of London that she considered home when the family occupied the London townhouse.

She relaxed against the worn cushions, letting fatigue and disappointment wash over her.

She closed her eyes against the tears that threatened to fall. Her head ached, but it was little discomfort compared to the pain that gripped her heart.

Winning me was simply a means to an end for Jonathan. He married me, not because he loved me and wanted me as his wife, but because our marriage would foil his uncle's attempt to take over the Lansing estate.

She should be grateful for his rescuing her family from the scheming grasp of Marcus Tollersley. And she was grateful. Grateful he had prevented her forced marriage. She felt gratitude for all that Jonathan had done for her. But why then did her heart feel like it was being trampled beneath the hooves of a runaway team?

Why? Because I wanted more, so much more from Jonathan. I wanted him to need me, to desire me, to love me beyond anything else.

But his entire being seemed caught up in his quest for revenge, and she doubted that anything could be as important to Jonathan as his need to achieve that end.

Spring sighed and turned her attention to the scenery passing outside. A tear trembled on the lashes of one eye and then slid slowly down her cheek. She lifted a hand and brushed it away.

"What is this? You insist we leave without Jonathan, and now you are upset?" Lady Phoebe exclaimed.

"It's the stress," Spring insisted, hoping her grandmother would accept that feeble excuse.

Resolutely, she wiped away a second tear and turned what she hoped was a bright smile on her grandmother.

For a moment as Lady Phoebe continued to study her carefully, Spring doubted her grandmother would be willing to allow her to escape without a more thorough explanation. At last, she appeared to have mentally reached some decision and let the moment pass uncontested.

Evening had fallen, casting long shadows over the passing landscape when the cab carrying Spring and her grandmother turned on the street to the Lansing townhouse. Lifting the curtain, Spring peered out the window. They were only a few blocks from the townhouse. Soon she would be home. Her life would return to normal, or would it? How could she know what was normal now that she was Jonathan wife?

The house was exactly as she remembered, nothing had changed. Spring followed her grandmother into the parlor.

Lady Phoebe pulled the bell rope, and instantly a maid appeared. Her grandmother ordered tea prepared. In record time, the pot was prepared and delivered to them.

Spring gratefully accepted the cup her grandmother offered. She added a generous amount of sugar then sipped the rich fragrant brew. Its warmth slowly seeped into her chilled body. Warmth spread in the cold region of the heart, and with it the pain returned.

"You should rest." Lady Phoebe placed her cup on the tray beside the teapot and turned to Spring. "I've had a room prepared for you and Jonathan on the second floor," Lady Phoebe said as she studied her granddaughter with serious eyes. "The blue room at the end of the gallery. If you should need anything, you have but to ring."

"Thank you, Grandmother," Spring said stiffly.

"Yes, thank you, Grandmother," a familiar voice added from the doorway.

Startled, Springs turned around, expecting to see anger written on his familiar features but found instead the familiar unreadable facade she had come to the detest. Only his eyes were expressive as their gaze captured hers. For a moment, the room spun crazily around her. Spring felt she was falling, spiraling into the ebony depths of his eyes as he held her gaze.

Jonathan stepped forward and took Spring's hand. "Come, my love, you should rest as your grandmother has said."

The time has come to clear the air. Spring led the way up the stairs. She must tell Jonathan that she had no intention of standing in his way. She was home now, safely in her grandmother's house, so she would no longer need his protection. Their marriage need not interfere with his plans.

Across the ocean in America, no one would know of it. There was no reason for him to make changes in his life because of her. Although he had used their marriage to checkmate his uncle, there was no need for him to continue with the pretense. She realized now that he had intended to stop her marriage to Marcus Tollersley by whatever means necessary. Now she must find the words to explain that she understood their marriage was no more than a business arrangement, that she did not expect anything more of him.

Her mind raced with a jumble of mixed emotions as she turned toward the room prepared for them, the room she was to share with her husband. How strange the word sounded.

Did Jonathan think they would continue as before now that the real reason for their marriage had been revealed to her? And why would he not think that? They were married, and she had proved to be totally susceptible to his attentions. She had fallen into his arms as easily as any strumpet.

What exactly was it that Jonathan expected of her? What did he intend their marriage to be?

Chapter Twenty-Five

Spring stopped before the door to the blue room, and Jonathan reached around her to open it . When she stepped inside, Jonathan followed. When she heard the soft click of the lock as Jonathan closed the door behind them, Spring turned nervously to face him.

He took a step closer. His eyes held concern as they caressed her features.

"You should have waited. We must be careful. Marcus will have alerted his men by now."

"Grandmother was anxious to return home, and I did not wish to...to interfere with your business arrangements." Spring hated blaming her grandmother but could not bring herself to admit the truth.

"Our business," Jonathan corrected softly as his gaze slowly caressed her. He stepped closer still.

Unable to hold his gaze any longer, Spring tried to turn away, but his hand on her arm prevented her. She felt color rising in her cheeks and sought to hide the familiar heat that rose in her body as his gaze slowly traversed her figure. His eyes seemed to smolder as they came to rest for a moment on the gentle slope of her breasts.

"Your grandmother said you should rest," Jonathan said, and his hands began to work the tiny buttons at her back. "Let me help you with your gown."

She fought to suppress the tingle of desire that began in her body when Jonathan's fingers grazed her skin. She shivered, struggling to deny the need that rose within her as his hands moved to push the gown from her shoulders.

His fingers moved expertly over her tight muscles, working out the tension they found there. A tremor ran along her spine as his hands worked their magic.

"You are cold?" he asked as he bent to touch his lips to the smooth skin of her shoulder. "Shall I build a fire?"

Cold? Not when his touch heated her body to fever pitch, she thought with self-disgust. She had never felt warmer than when his hands were touching her. His lips against her skin sparked fire throughout her system. Just his touch was enough to have her consumed by burning liquid desire. Could he not feel how her flesh burned beneath his touch?

"No," she finally managed in a stiff little voice that sounded unnatural even to her own ears.

He gripped her shoulders and turned her slowly to face him. One hand caught her chin lightly and lifted it so that she had no choice but to meet his gaze. Whatever he wished their marriage to be, there was no doubt as to his desire for her at that moment.

"My love, I should let you rest," he whispered. "But I find I can't resist your charms."

His head descended slowly, and his lips claimed hers. His touch was gentle at first, tentative, coaxing, seeking a response from her.

"Then don't resist," she whispered when his mouth moved to the tender skin beneath her ear.

With a low groan, his mouth returned to hers. As her lips parted slightly beneath his, he became more aggressive, pressing his case further, demanding and receiving more. His arms closed around her, pulling her tightly against his body.

She could feel the rapid beating of his heart as his chest pressed against her breasts. She felt the relentless pressure of his manhood against her belly, even through the fabric of her gown and underskirts.

He kissed her long and hard, completely stealing the breath from her lungs and the strength from her limbs. His hands worked their magic, and soon she stood bare beneath his heated gaze. Lifting her, he continued their kiss as he carried her to the bed.

Holding her in his warm embrace, Jonathan bent, placing one knee on the bed to lower Spring gently to the mattress. He deepened the kiss as his hands began a leisurely exploration of the gentle curves of her figure. Lightly skimming over her smooth pale skin, his fingertips trailed fire along her electrified nerve endings. In his arms, Spring's body burned with need. She pressed herself against his length, her hands moving to the buttons of his fine lawn shirt as she sought to remove the barrier between them.

"Not yet," he said as he captured her questing hands between them.

Carefully, tenderly, delicately Jonathan made love to her. His hands found the secret places of her desire, sparking flames in her blood and sending her senses reeling. Arching her back, Spring called out his name, imploring him to stop the torture and make her his again.

She felt rather than heard the soft chuckle deep in his chest as he continued his teasing. His lips traveled a torturous path along the column of her neck and then feathered small kisses across her shoulder before dipping lower to taste the sweetness of her breasts.

Spring felt she could stand the tension his touch evoked no longer without losing her mind. Her entire body felt scorched by the flames his touch conjured. When she thought she would surely die of pleasure, finally Jonathan lifted himself from her.

Spring cried out her disappointment at his desertion, but in a matter of seconds, he was back gathering her in his arms. This time there was no barrier between them. His skin burned against hers. His naked body against hers filled her with an even greater sense of urgency as she responded to his touch.

When Jonathan's hand moved down to the juncture of her thighs, she moaned in pleasure and opened herself willingly to him.

"So warm and ready," he whispered against her throat as his fingers gently probed the inner core of her, sending spiraling pleasure through her body. Spring lifted her hips, offering herself as his fingers curled into her, bringing such pleasure she could not hold back a low moan as her body convulsed around his fingers.

"God, how I need you," he said and lifted himself above her.

"Yes, now. Now," Spring implored him, shifting her hips and arching herself upward, seeking him.

Still, he held out, teasing her with the pressure of his desire moving against her womanhood. She moaned deep in her throat, a soft mewling sound that brought Jonathan to the breaking point. He shivered, still resisting.

"I'll die if I don't take you now," Jonathan grated between clenched teeth as he thrust himself deep within her.

Spring received him gladly, sheathing his length with the heated moisture of her desire for him. She matched his movements, bringing her hips upward to meet each thrust. Her fingers laced in his hair as his mouth consumed hers. His tongue played a leisurely game of touch and tag with hers as his body branded her with his possession.

His hands captured hers. His fingers threaded gently with hers as he lifted his head and kissed the knuckles of each hand, gently suckling at a finger here and there. Finally, his mouth returned to hers. Spring felt as if she were about to splinter into a thousand sparkling shards of pleasure as he tensed then plunged deeper, spilling himself into her.

She spun wildly out of control as torrents of pleasure washed over her with the intensity of her release matching his.

It's always like this. Spring drifted back to reality. The touch of Jonathan's hands made her forget everything but him. If she had any doubt about how Jonathan felt toward her, she had no doubts of his desire for her.

There was no way she could ever doubt his desire. She could doubt his love, yes. She could question his intentions, maybe. But never ever would she doubt his desire. *Perhaps that is enough for a beginning.* She drifted off to sleep.

Jonathan stood for a moment, watching Spring sleep. The counterpane he had pulled over her had slipped down so that one rosy nipple peeked tantalizingly toward him with each breath she drew. Her left hand rested beneath her head, while the other reached out as if seeking contact with him. Her golden hair was free and spread about her, covering the pillow like a mass of spun gold.

Jonathan's heart constricted with love for her. She was so lovely, so innocent, so trusting. He would like nothing so much as to return to the bed. He ached to take her into his arms and give in to the temptation she represented.

But he had things to do, business he must finish. Tomorrow the Chancery Court would hear the evidence Bailey had gathered. Soon the court would rule on his suit against his uncle.

Jonathan dressed in the dim light and left the room. He did not allow his gaze to stray back to Spring, for he knew how sorely tempted he would be. He had to keep his mind clear and his thoughts on the danger about them. Already his infatuation with her had almost cost her life and had gotten Tobias injured. If he continued to allow his desire for her to rule his judgment, he could get them all killed.

Resolute, Jonathan left the room, closing the door behind him. No matter how desperately he now wished otherwise, he had unfinished business to attend. Marcus must be dealt with. He had sworn to avenge his father, to right all wrongs. He could not abandon the quest now.

Jonathan took the colt revolver from his coat pocket and checked the cylinder to be sure it was loaded. He had to be careful. Marcus would have men watching for him. He hurried down the hallway, leaving Spring sleeping peacefully.

Dust had fallen over the city when Jonathan left the Lansing household and stealthily made his way through the streets of London toward his aunt's home.

They would be worried about him. He let them know he was back and safe. Although his aunt and uncle did not know the entire story of his reason for coming to England, they were sure to have suspicions as to the reason for his visit. Soon they would know the truth. Soon everyone would know the truth.

"My dear," Lady Sarah exclaimed, opening her arms to him. "I have been quite beside myself with worry. You seemed so upset when you left."

Jonathan embraced his aunt, kissing her gently on the cheek before he stepped away.

"You should not have worried. I have been quite safe, I assure you." It was only a small lie.

Lady Sarah's eyes narrowed. "And what was it that kept you away for so long? Surely there could not have been that many horses for you to inspect. You have neglected me dreadfully, Jonathan. I have had a devil of a time explaining your absence to all the hostesses who had been extending invitations."

"I have been about the business of acquiring a wife," Jonathan answered without ceremony. "Don't you think Grandmother will be pleased?"

"A wife!" Lady Sarah exclaimed. "Who? How?" The lady appeared quite flustered with his news. "Jonathan, you should not tease me so."

Jonathan smiled broadly. "I am not teasing you, dearest aunt. I have this very day taken a bride. That was what you and

Grandmother had intended to happen during this trip was it not, dearest?"

Lady Sarah's mouth dropped open an inch as she gaped at her nephew. Then she had the good graces to look mildly embarrassed at having been found out. "Jonathan?"

"Yes, Aunt?"

"Do not keep me in suspense," she insisted. "Where is this wife of yours? And more to the point, who is she?"

"She is resting at her grandmother's home. We have had a long, tiring trip."

"Jonathan," Lady Sarah threatened.

"Yes, Aunt?"

"Enough of this foolishness, who is she?"

"Lady Spring Melanie Lansing, of course." Jonathan winked at his aunt as if to say, was there ever any doubt?

"But how?" Lady Sarah questioned, pinning Jonathan with an insistent gaze. "It was put about that Lady Spring was to marry the Earl of Wyndridge."

"And so she did," Jonathan answered.

"But I don't understand," Lady Sarah said, looking as if she might swoon at any moment. "You just said you married Lady Spring. Now you say she is married to the earl. Jonathan, you are not making any sense at all."

Taking his aunt's hand, Jonathan led her to the settee before the fireplace in the downstairs parlor. He patted her hand gently as he took in the concerned and confused expression on his aunt's face. He made sure she was comfortable and even spread a small blanket over her lap before he seated himself beside her. She looked up at him for a moment. A look of annoyance crossed her countenance. He patted one small hand where it fidgeted with the blanket spread across her lap.

"There are certain things about my background of which you are unaware," Jonathan began. He closed his eyes for a moment and took a deep breath. He studied the concerned expression in his aunt's wide eyes before he continued. "I think it best that I begin explaining from the very first."

"Yes, please do," Lady Sarah agreed. Her puzzled expression grew stronger, drawing her brows together.

Still, Jonathan did not begin at the beginning, but with the death of his grandfather and his discovery documents that revealed his father had been the Earl of Wyndridge.

Lady Sarah sat spellbound as Jonathan continued with the tale. A tear slipped slowly down her cheek as he told of his father's murder and his mother's grief. When he had finished his story, Lady Sarah took a deep breath then embraced Jonathan.

"I knew your mother was terribly distraught at the death of her husband, but I never realized she feared for your life, as well. How horrible for her. It isn't any wonder she kept your identity a secret. And your grandfather would have preferred you to never come to England. I remember how Father bragged about you in his letters, but I always wondered why he refused to allow you to be educated here. I can see now that he feared losing you to your heritage."

"I am an American," Jonathan answered solemnly. "He need not have feared that I would have preferred England to America. Once I have dealt with this business, Spring and I will return to America."

"Of course, my dear," Lady Sarah patted his arm gently. "But still, I can understand how he might have feared losing you. He had lost one daughter to England already, and you were all he had left of Elizabeth."

Twenty-Six

JONATHAN NODDED. HE knew that both his mother and his grandfather had tried to protect him by keeping his parentage a secret.

It had been from Tobias that he had learned the story of Wyndridge and the twin brothers. He had learned to love the one and hate the other, just as Tobias did.

At the time, he had not known that one man was his father, the other is uncle. He had not realized that the stories Tobias told were those of his father's boyhood. In his own way, Tobias was trying to give him the gift of knowing his father.

"How soon will this be settled?" Lady Sarah questioned.

"Soon, the Chancery court will hear the case tomorrow," Jonathan answered.

Lady Sarah studied him carefully. "You realize, of course, that Wyndridge will not lose easily? He will prevent your winning, by any means necessary, if he can."

"I know," Jonathan answered. "I will be careful." He tried to reassure his aunt. "Besides, I now have more reason than ever to survive," he said, thinking of Spring.

He smiled broadly at his aunt. "And now, I must go."

He stood and turned toward the door.

As Jonathan approached the door, there was a crash from the direction of the front hall. A familiar voice threatened bodily harm to the man standing in his path.

"Unless you're wanting to lose your teeth, ye'll get out of my way," Tobias threatened whoever sought to deny him entry into the Meldon household.

Jonathan quickly stepped to the front hall. "It's alright, Toombs." Jonathan spoke from behind the outraged Butler. "You do recall Mr. McDonald is with me. Please help me get him up to our room."

The Butler turned stiffly with a look of disdain on his face. "Of course, Master Sinclair."

Jonathan caught Tobias as he swayed, pulling the good man's arm over his shoulder and catching him around the waist with the other arm. Jones took the small portmanteau that Tobias had dropped to the floor. "This way, Sir."

Supporting Tobias' weight, Jonathan followed the butler down the hallway and then up the stairs to the suite of rooms given over for his use. When Jonathan had helped Tobias to the bed, he turned to Toombs who hovered near the door.

"Send for a doctor," Jonathan instructed as they removed Tobias' boots and helped the older man into bed. "And fetch hot water and clean towels, as well.

Jonathan knelt beside his friend and began to slowly unbutton the shirt where a dark stain had spread across shoulder. Tobias' skin when Jonathan touched it felt hot and dry.

Fever. The word scorched across Jonathan's mind, burning into his brain. His hands hesitated for a moment in indecision then stripped away the soiled shirt and removed the bandage covering his shoulder.

"You should not have come so soon," Jonathan scolded the older man as he poured cold water from the pitcher on the washstand into a large ceramic bowl. He searched the drawer of the chest beneath the bowl and found a clean towel.

"Couldn't let you go on without me. Besides, 'twill take more than one bullet to stop me." Tobias answered with a grimace as Jonathan began to apply the cold towel to his heated skin.

No, it would not. He had almost lost his friend. Had that bullet been one inch lower, he would most assuredly be dead now.

Jonathan rinsed the towel and applied it again.

"Damnation, that is bloody cold. Are you trying to kill me?" Tobias complained.

"Have to get the fever down. The doctor should be here before long. He will probably do worse than this. He might even have to bleed you."

"If ye think I'd be lying 'ere and letting 'im put those blood suckers on me, you can just think again." Tobias argued.

Jonathan laughed. The fever could not be too bad if Tobias remembered his aversion to leeches. Jonathan continued to apply the cold towel over Tobias' protest.

When a young boy brought a bucket of hot water and clean towels, Jonathan swathed the cold towel across Tobias' forehead, wondering what was keeping the doctor. Surely in a city the size of London a doctor could be easily found.

Tobias's fever broke as Jonathan continued to apply the cold towels. If only Tobias had waited a few more days before attempting the journey. With more time to heal, there would have been less chance of the wound becoming infected.

It was the chance of infection that worried Jonathan. He had seen it so many times, usually with the same result. He shook his head, clearing away those thoughts. He vowed he would not allow anything to happen to Tobias.

Finally, the doctor arrived. He removed the bandage Jonathan had applied, cleansed Tobias' wound, and applied a fresh bandage.

"The infection is not too bad," the doctor said, handing Jonathan a small packet of powder. "Give him this powder four times a day and try to keep him still."

Jonathan turned to Tobias. "You're to stay in bed."

Tobias only snorted.

"He should be fine in a week's time, if the fever doesn't go up again," the doctor said as he left the room.

Jonathan followed the doctor into the hallway. "Whoever attended him did an excellent job. The wound is not festering. He should be up and about in a few days, but try to make him rest all you can."

"Of course, doctor."

The doctor studied Jonathan for a moment. "Dangerous things, these hunting accidents. Be more careful what you shoot at next time."

Jonathan's eyes narrowed slightly, and a muscle tightened in his jaw. "You can be sure," he said in a quiet voice threaded with steel. "the next time I pull the trigger I'll be quite certain of the target, doctor."

For a moment, the doctor appeared disconcerted at Jonathan's response, then with a stammer he reminded. "Yes, well, see that you are, young man."

When the doctor departed, Jonathan returned to Tobias' side. He poured the prescribed dose of the powder into a glass and added water. Helping Tobias sit up, Jonathan held the glass to his lips.

"God awful stuff, that," Tobias complained as he finished the medication.

Jonathan smiled. "It's good for you. Now try to rest. I'll be back to check on you later."

Jonathan touched Tobias' forehead one last time and was relieved to find his skin cool to the touch and slightly damp. The fever had indeed broken.

Jonathan planned to head for Mr. Bailey's office once he had his friend squared away. He had left their meeting immediately upon realizing Spring had left with her grandmother. Now he must finalize the plans for the court appearance the next morning.

With one last caution to his friend, Jonathan left Tobias' room and made his way to the stable behind his uncle's house. He heard Diablo whinny as he approached. Jonathan patted his pocket to be sure he had remembered the small lump of sugar the stallion would be expecting.

Diablo whinnied again. Jonathan whistled to acknowledge him. When he entered the stable, one of the lads stood at the front of the stallion's stall offering him a carrot. The young man turned as Jonathan approached.

"He a fine one, he is." The lad fed Diablo the carrot as he reached to stroke the white blaze on the stallion's chest.

Jonathan gave the sugar lump to the youth. "He has a bit of a sweet tooth," Jonathan said, reaching for the bridle hanging on a peg over the feed bin.

Once saddled, Jonathan mounted Diablo and headed toward Mr. Bailey's. He and the barrister needed to go over all the writs filed regarding his inheritance case. Once that was complete, he would check on Tobias, and then he would be free to return to Spring.

At the thought of Spring, Jonathan felt the familiar tightening in his lower regions. Soon, very soon, they could be together and not worry about Marcus any longer.

Still, they must be careful, Jonathan reminded himself as he turned toward Holborn and Mr. Bailey's office. He must keep his focus narrowed. He must not allow himself to be distracted. The result could be disastrous for all those depending on him.

Jonathan knew he must apply his attention to the issues at hand by keeping his focus steady on the coming confrontation with Marcus. He reinforced his determination to be strong.

Still, he found his mind wandering back to Spring. He was anxious to have this business finalized so that he could return to his wife and begin their new life together.

Spring realized she was alone in the big bed even before she was fully awake. The vibrancy, the power Jonathan evoked around them with his very presence was missing. She stretched leisurely, wondering what had disturbed her sleep. From the dressing room came a muffled sound. Spring smiled. *Jonathan.*

She rose quickly, certain it had been the noise from the dressing room that had awakened her.

Her dressing gown lay spread across the foot of the bed. She pulled it on. Belting it tightly around her narrow waist, she approached the dressing room door. With a bright smile, Spring opened the door, looking around the small room expectantly.

Nothing. The room was empty. Only the slight wafting of steam rising from the tub placed in the middle of the room gave away the fact that anyone had been there.

Spring glanced at the small ornate clock on the dressing table and realized she barely had time for a quick bath before time to dress for dinner. She dropped the robe and stepped into the warm water in the tub.

As the soothing heat eased the tightness from her tired body, she wished she had time to linger but knew dinner would be served exactly at eight.

She must not be late. Her grandmother would worry, and Jonathan would expect her to join them. Besides which, cook would be terribly put out if dinner were delayed because of her.

Spring bathed quickly then stepped from the tub and wrapped herself in the large towel left on the chair nearby. She hurried back into the bedroom. There was a soft rap at the door before it opened slowly. Spring tucked the end of the towel into the valley between her breasts and turned, expecting to see Jonathan.

"Milady," Bridgett, her grandmother's maid, said from the door. "Lady Phoebe thought you might like me to assist you."

"Yes, thank you," Spring answered.

"Lady Phoebe suggested that you might like to wear the yellow silk. I've laid it out, milady," Bridget ran on as she held the gown up for Spring's approval.

Standing quite still, Spring waited while Bridgett gathered the undergarments laid out beside the gown. She stepped into the linen and lace drawers the maid held for her. Once they were in place, Bridgett tied them at her waist. Next came the corset with its stays that cinched in her waist, and the cage crinoline that would support the skirts of the yellow silk gown.

With the gown properly smoothed into place, Bridgett began to work on Spring's hair. Brushing it until it shown, she then coaxed it into ringlets that hung down her back. She added a matching yellow ribbon to hold the mass in place then stood back to survey her handiwork.

Spring quickly thanked Bridget for her help and then dismissed her. Jonathan would be waiting. She smiled warmly as she left her room and started toward the stairs.

A familiar excitement coursed through Spring at the thought of Jonathan, her husband. She remembered the way he held her and loved her this afternoon. Those thoughts brought a blush to her cheeks deepening their color.

Is he downstairs, even now, waiting for me? Spring paused at the top of the stairs.

Expectantly she hurried down the steps and down the wide hall into her grandmother's parlor. The smile that graced her features faded just a little when she saw only her grandmother seated before the fire. Disappointment coursed through her as she registered the fact that Jonathan was absent.

"My pet," Lady Phoebe exclaimed when Spring entered the room. "Are you feeling better since your nap? Yes, I can see your color has quite improved."

"I'm fine, grandmother," Spring answered softly.

Once again Springs gaze traversed the room. Where was he?

Jonathan left Bailey's office, convinced that everything was in order. Thomas Bailey had worked on the case for months. When the

Chancery Court convened on the morrow, it should take very little time for them to hear the evidence. Then all that would remain was for the court to render its decision.

Confident, Jonathan strode to where he had left Diablo tethered. Soon, he could return to Spring, but first he must check on Tobias.

It was going on eight when Jonathan arrived at his aunt's house. He left Diablo in the care of one of the grooms. Inside, he stopped by the kitchen and asked for a dinner tray to be delivered to him before he made his way up to the room he had formally occupied at his aunt's house.

The moment Jonathan opened the door of the room he knew his friend's condition had taken a turn for the worse. Tobias fought the bedcovers, flailing out with limbs made wild by fever as he struggled against some unseen foe, a demon summoned by his fever induced dream.

Jonathan hurried across the room and tried to quiet the thrashing man, fearful that his agitated movements would reopen his wound.

"Easy, old friend," Jonathan soothed.

Tobias' fever bright eyes opened and stared unfocused up at Jonathan. "'E's dead," the tormented man whispered. "Tried to protect 'im, to keep 'im safe."

Tobias reached up and caught Jonathan's arm, his boney fingers biting sharply into Jonathan's flesh as the delirious man struggled to sit up.

"'E's evil, that one. Killed 'is own brother, 'e did." The fever bright eyes closed, and the old man fell back exhausted upon the bed, only to begin thrashing about once more.

"Got to save Drew," the old man whispered. "Canna let 'im win again."

"Rest easy, old friend," Jonathan soothed. "He will not win this time."

Moving over to the dresser, Jonathan poured cool water into the basin and began to apply wet towels to Tobias' feverish body. Their coolness seemed to chase away the demons, quieting the wild thrashing.

When a kitchen maid delivered the tray of food cook had sent, Jonathan thanked her and ate his meal quickly before turning back to his task of caring for his friend.

Through the long hours of the night, Jonathan kept his vigil. He applied towel after towel, until just before dawn the fever broke, and Tobias slept peacefully.

Jonathan breathed the sigh of relief, and only then did he realize he had not sent word to Spring of what had detained him. She would be worried. She had no idea where he had gone.

He wanted desperately to go to her, needed to hold her and make love to her. That would have to wait. Even now, Thomas Bailey would be awaiting his arrival. Soon they would go to Lincoln Inn Hall where the hearing before the Chancery Court would begin.

Had he been able to bring criminal charges against his uncle in the death of his father, Jonathan would be heading for the Old Bailey. Instead, since the case was a civil action, it must go through the Chancery Court, which convened at Lincoln Inn Hall.

Thomas Bailey had assured Jonathan that Lord Lyndhurst was the logical choice to hear the motion Jonathan was entering. Hoping, since he was an American by birth, Lyndhurst might be more sympathetic toward the case.

Jonathan was not so sure. His lordship had been in England since a very young age and might, Jonathan feared, lean to the opposite extreme. Thomas Bailey reassured Jonathan of Lord Lyndhurst's fairness and his diligent nature. As Lord Chancellor, the man had, Bailey pointed out, not hesitated to entertain the interlocutory application to secure the funds of the Wyndridge estate.

While both Lord Langdale and Sir Lancelot Shadwell were judges of the Chancery, as well, Bailey preferred to direct the motion in Jonathan's case to Lord Lyndhurst.

Jonathan had acceded to his barrister's suggestion, trusting that the good barrister knew best.

After a quick bath using the tepid water from the ceramic bowl, Jonathan quickly dressed and made his way down to the kitchen. He crossed to the cook's table and grabbed a chunk of bread and a piece of cheese before he hurried out the door.

He found Diablo saddled and waiting for him in the stable yard. Jonathan fished a coin out of his vest pocket and tossed it to the lad holding Diablo's reins.

Thomas Bailey insisted on taking his brougham carriage when Jonathan had suggested traveling on horseback might be faster. Reluctantly, he fastened Diablo's leads to the rear of the brougham and climbed into the carriage beside Bailey. At least Thomas Bailey's driver could make sure no one tried to take his horse. Jonathan smiled at the thought. Anyone trying to steal Diablo would be in for a rude awakening.

They made their way through the narrow streets of the old city toward Lincoln Inn Hall. After leaving the coachman with the brougham and Diablo, they entered the Lord Chancellor's court.

Jonathan expected to see his uncle's glowering continence when they entered the courtroom. Instead, there was only his uncle's barrister, Benedict Edward Goodwood, Esquire.

The two men of law acknowledged each other with a quick nod then adjourned to their respective places in the courtroom.

Jonathan thought impatiently of Spring and wished the proceedings over so he could return to her.

The court was assembled and called to order. Jonathan listened to Thomas Bailey make his case to Lord Lyndhurst.

The documents recording the marriage of Edward Tollersley and Elizabeth Sinclair were entered into evidence with Jonathan's father's death certificate and Jonathan's birth record.

"These documents could be forged," Benedict Goodwood objected. "Your lordship, I move to dismiss these charges, if this is all the plaintiff has to offer."

Thomas Bailey leveled his steady gaze on Goodwood then turned back to Lord Lyndhurst "If it pleases your lordship, please refer to the bill addressed to the Lord Chancellor of one March. Your Lordship will recall we do have other evidence."

"Pray continue," Lord Lyndhurst instructed.

Smiling, Thomas Bailey took a leather wrapped bundle from the table before him. He unwrapped it to reveal an aged book which he extended toward the court. "This is the log of the China Star for the year 1813, in it is duly recorded the marriage of Edward Tollersley and Elizabeth Sinclair."

"Objection, your lordship." Goodwood was at once on his feet. "What proof is there that this is the log from the China Star? It, too, could be a forgery."

"We are prepared to call a witness to confirm the book is from the China Star, your lordship."

"Overruled," Lord Lyndhurst returned. "Please proceed."

"While it is true that Captain Fisher of the China Star was recently murdered," Thomas Bailey turned a scathing look on Benedict Goodwood with those words. "His wife is here and is willing to testify this is the log her husband had kept in his possession until recently, when it was given over for evidence in this matter, your lordship."

"Call your witness."

Mrs. Fisher entered the courtroom and gave her evidence while Goodwood glowered at her. He had no questions for her when his turn at cross examination came.

Next came the former governor of Nassau, who had met Edward and Elizabeth during the time their ship docked in Nassau for repairs after being damaged and blown off course by a storm in the Atlantic.

The list of evidence was long and impressive. When Thomas Bailey had finished, the opposition could only stammer that Edward was dead, and thus Jonathan could not possibly be Edward's son. Therefore, Jonathan Sinclair had no claim upon the Wyndridge title.

Goodwood offered evidence in the form of letters from the mayor of Savannah, who reported, upon receiving an inquiry into the whereabouts of Edwards Tollersley, that the young man had died tragically on arrival in Savannah, the victim of a robbery attempt.

"Your lordship," Goodwood continued. "There was no mention of his leaving a wife, nothing was said about there being an heir. My grieving client, shocked at the untimely death of his brother, was forced out of family duty to assume the title."

Benedict Goodwood turned an accusing gaze toward Jonathan. He lifted a hand and flicked his fingers toward Jonathan before returning his gaze to Lord Lyndhurst. "This impostor cannot be allowed to disrupt the life of her majesty's loyal servant, your lordship," Benedict Goodwood ended his plea on an impassioned note.

Gathering the evidence that had been presented to him, Lord Lyndhurst stood. "This court stands in recess until I have considered the evidence presented."

Chapter Twenty-Six

Spring read the message delivered to her and decided she would not wait for Jonathan to come for her, she would go to him.

Grasping the bell rope, Spring rang for the maid. When Bridgett arrived, she quickly dispatched the girl to summon a hansom cab while Spring quickly bathed and dressed herself. She was not sure where the Chancery Court convened, but the driver would surely be more knowledgeable than she.

The dark facade of the large building was daunting as Spring stared across the street from the safety of the hansom cab. A sense of foreboding filled her as she stared at the tall stately edifice. How would she ever find Jonathan in such a large place?

For a moment, her courage flagged. Still, she refused to surrender to the fear that suddenly came upon her. She quickly paid the driver and requested he wait for her. He tested the gold coin she handed him between his tobacco-stained teeth.

"'O course, milady," he said with a wide grin.

Spring stepped around the end of the cab, wondering where to begin her search. She hesitated, gazing at Lincoln Inn Hall with wide eyes. Straightening her shoulders and stiffening her resolve, she stepped onto the sidewalk just as the large doors opened and a group men spilled out into the street.

Spring stopped, allowing her gaze to travel over the group, seeking a familiar face.

At first glance she did not see him, for he stood at the back of the group with his face bent down as he talked with a man whose black silk robe and elaborate white wig identified him as a barrister of some importance. She watched as Jonathan acknowledged what the man said with a slow smile, shook his hand and started across the street.

Spring raised her hand to wave to him, his name upon her lips. Suddenly a runaway coach barreled down the narrow street. It bore down on the group of men who had just exited the Chancery, but Jonathan in particular as he strode further into the street.

Spring screamed, one hand going to her throat while the other pointed to the frenzied team baring down on Jonathan. His name sprang from her lips as a tortured cry.

"Jonathan!"

Her bones were frozen and fused into a solid mass, and her muscles refused to respond to the urgent message to move, she could only stare at the coach as it careened recklessly toward the man she loved.

Jonathan, hearing her plaintive cry, sensed the urgency of her voice.

Startled, he reacted to Spring's warning. His body responded instinctively, leaping toward the hansom cab. He coiled his long frame and rolled to safety beside Spring as a frenzied team rushed by nearly crashing against the hansom cab.

Shaking all over, Spring knelt beside Jonathan. She reached out a trembling hand toward him.

"Are you all right?" she asked. Tears traced a visible path down her cheeks. Her heart clutched tight in her chest. She had almost lost Jonathan in the same manner as Papa.

Jonathan sat up slowly. "There appears to be no harm done," he assured her as he brushed himself off and smiled at her.

The men who had exited the Chancery with Jonathan gathered around.

"Bloody lucky," one said.

"Dreadful," still another offered as he extended a hand to Jonathan. "The lady saved you from a terrible accident, I say."

Thomas Bailey looked down the narrow street in the direction the coach had disappeared. "Not so sure it was an accident," he said as he straightened his wig, which had become dislodged by his hurried crossing of the street. "Could have been attempted murder."

Spring shivered. "My father was killed in just such an accident."

"Exactly such, my lady," Thomas Bailey answered.

Thomas Bailey turned to Jonathan, who continued to brush debris from his clothing. "You must be careful, my lord. Now that you have come forward, you will be an easy target."

"I shall be more attentive in the future, gentlemen," Jonathan said to the men crowded around. "I have my beautiful wife to thank for my salvation today. I am afraid in my haste to return to her I was quite careless."

Jonathan smiled at Spring. The softness in his eyes as his gaze rested on her made her wonder for an instant if she might not have been mistaken on her evaluation of his reasons for their hasty marriage.

Spring's cheeks reddened as Jonathan's eyes swept over her, bringing awareness of his intimate perusal. When he reached out to stroke her cheek, Spring found herself leaning into his touch.

"But I forget myself," Jonathan continued. "Gentlemen, may I present my wife, the Lady Spring Melanie Lansing Sinclair, Countess of Wyndridge.

Jonathan introduced her to the men who had accompanied him from the Chancery. One, Spring knew from her acquaintance with Lady Sarah, to be a cousin to Jonathan. The other, a Mr. Collins, seemed familiar, also, although Spring could not remember having met him before.

Baron Reinhardt stepped forward, taking Spring's hand. "Lady Spring and I are old friends," Baron Reinhardt said as he lifted her hand and gently brushed his lips across her knuckles.

Spring smiled graciously, blushing as Reinhardt took her hand. Her gaze went immediately to Jonathan, and she found his countenance darkened by a scowl.

Reinhardt finally relinquished her hand, and Mr. Collins stepped forward. "My lady, I am charmed beyond words."

Spring smiled. Jonathan's friends appeared quite gallant. She basked in their approval. Jonathan's scowl grew darker.

"I say," Reinhart began. "You've made quite the catch, Jonathan. Been angling for Lady Spring myself for quite some time. Must say I am quite crushed to hear she has married my best friend."

Jonathan turned his scowl toward Reinhardt. "You, my friend," Jonathan said. "Will recover from the shock the moment Lady Jane Woodwine looks your way."

"Twas it not enough for you to claim one of the most lucrative titles in all England? Did you have to pick our fairest flower, as well?" Reinhardt complained.

Jonathan's scowl grew darker, his lips forming a firm straight line as Reinhardt continued to pay attention to Spring.

"You had best be very careful, my friend," Baron Reinhart began, suddenly serious. "After the evidence presented today, I don't think there is any doubt of the decision the court will reach. The only way for Wyndridge to retain the title is through your death. He will not hesitate to try. In fact, I dare say this was probably his first attempt."

Collins stepped closer and placed his hand on Jonathan's shoulder. "You realize he will not stop with your death. He will leave no loose ends this time. He would have finished it last time had he known of your mother's existence."

Jonathan nodded. Eyes narrowed, he stared down the street in the direction the coach had disappeared.

"I shall be on guard from now on," Jonathan assured his friends as he took Spring's arm and turned her toward the cab.

"Yes, well, think we shall just tag along, all the same," Collins said, nodding toward Reinhardt.

Spring continued to tremble as Jonathan helped her into the hansom cab. He stroked her cheek tenderly. Her hands clutched at the sleeve of his coat as he pulled away. "Wait here while I fetch Diablo," he whispered and patted her hand gently before he leaned in and brushed his lips across hers.

Thomas Bailey called for his coachman. Jonathan untied Diablo. Both Reinhardt and Collins retrieved their mounts and joined Jonathan as he tied Diablo to the rear of the cab.

Once the stallion was secured, Jonathan directed the driver in the box at the top of the cab to return to the Lansing home. Jonathan joined Spring in the cab while his friends rode one on either side as they made their way back through the streets of London.

"Do you think that coach..." Her voice faltered. "Was Wyndridge trying to kill you?" Spring finally managed as the cab continued down the street at a lively clip.

"It might have been a true runaway, but I doubt it." Jonathan kept his gaze trained on the street in front of the hansom cab. The curtain pulled back allowed easy perusal.

Spring shivered.

"It would have been very convenient for Wyndridge to have this settled by my death. He has done it before. So, he would not hesitate to do so again."

Glancing at Jonathan through lowered lashes, Spring studied him carefully. He was much too careless with his own safety she decided as she noted the small tear in his coat and a bruise darkening on his cheek. From now on, she would stay at his side, whether he liked it or not. He had protected her, now she would protect him.

Jonathan placed an arm around her shoulders and pulled her into the shelter of his embrace. He rested his cheek against the top of her head and sighed deeply. "Tobias appeared much better this morning. It was only the stress of the journey that brought on the fever."

"Perhaps we should check on him," Spring suggested.

Jonathan chuckled softly. "You read my mind, dearest. That is where I am heading as soon as I take you home."

"No, take me with you." She turned into his embrace. "Don't leave me."

His arm tightened around her, and his hand caressed her in slow, seductive circles, moving ever closer to her breast. His touch caused a warming heat to flow through her system.

Spring relaxed against Jonathan. If he did not love her, he did desire her. He exhibited a protective instinct toward her, and he *was* her husband. Perhaps with time, he would grow to love her as she loved him.

After seeing him nearly snatched before her very eyes, she knew she could not bear being separated from him. She would love enough for both of them, she decided, settling into his arms and enjoying the feel of his strong body pressed against her.

His lips moved over her hair then caressed her forehead before dipping down to test the outer shell of her ear. "I missed you last night," he whispered as his breath teased the sensitive area at her nape.

Spring snuggled closer as Jonathan's arms tightened around her. With a low groan, he lifted her and turned her so that she sat in his lap. Pulling her close pressed her breasts against the hard wall of his chest. His eyes darkened with desire as his head lowered and his lips claimed hers.

Senses reeling, Spring responded to the urgent demand of his lips upon hers, his mouth teasing and toying with hers. Gently he coaxed her lips to part. When he won access to the inner regions of her mouth, his tongue became more aggressive, invading her very being with his drugging influence. His tongue parried and thrust with hers in a duel of love that left her breathless and clinging to him. Her body yearned for more.

Spring slipped easily into that realm of mindless passion, of utter desire Jonathan's mastery so easily evoked. She pressed herself closer, moved her head to offer him even deeper access to her mouth while one of his hands moved between them to claim her breasts. She felt his touch to the very core of her being as his fingers stroked her passion-engorged peaks through her gown and chemise. Her nipples hardened and peaked, pressing into his palm. She felt, rather than heard, the deep animal-like groan of passion that stirred in Jonathan's chest as his fingers found the tiny rosebud through the material of her gown.

Responding instinctively, she shifted her hips in his lap, pressing herself closer against him, feeling the hard rod of his desire pressed against her buttocks. As she rotated her hips slowly, grinding against him, another impassioned groan rewarded her.

Abruptly his lips left hers. His arms tightened into stiff iron bands, holding her motionless against him.

"Be still, minx," he whispered against her ear. "We've neither the time nor the privacy to continue. If you continue to tempt me, I shall surely disgrace myself."

Spring smiled her pleasure, exulting in thoughts of making him lose control, but remained motionless. It gave her a heady sense of power knowing the impact she had upon him. Just as his touch turned her into a mindless, passion enthralled wanton, her touch rendered him equally defenseless. His desire for her grew to such heights a mere twist of her hips against the hardened spear straining against his trousers sent shivers throughout his body and weakened him to the point of immediate response.

The cab pulled up in front of Lord Meldon's townhouse, so Spring quickly straightened her gown and tidied her hair. Jonathan helped her down, keeping his arm protectively around her as he moved to the rear of the cab to pay the driver.

Both Baron Reinhardt and Mr. Collins dismounted and moved to shield Jonathan and Spring while Jonathan dealt with the driver. Collins untied Diablo's reins and turned the stallion over to the young lad who came around at the sound of their arrival. Jonathan tossed the boy a coin.

"See that he is fed and has fresh water."

"Yes, milord," the young stable hand answered and led the stallion away.

Both Collins and Reinhardt made a big show of checking the area to be sure it was safe before allowing Jonathan and Spring to leave the safety of the cab and move into the open. Jonathan accepted their overzealous behavior, taking it in stride. His lips curved into a slight smile as he pulled Spring closer against his side.

Finally, after assuring that all was as it should be, his friends ushered Jonathan and Spring into the small yard at the front of the Meldon townhouse. The duo watched until Jonathan and Spring were safely in the small, enclosed yard then took their leave.

Chapter Twenty-Seven

The front door opened as they approached, and Lady Sarah rushed out to welcome them.

"Spring, my dear," Lady Sarah gushed. "It is so good to see you. Jonathan has told me the wonderful news."

Turning to Jonathan, she continued. "I have taken the liberty of preparing a room for you on the third floor, since your friend is occupying the former one."

Spring smiled at Lady Sarah, feeling suddenly embarrassed as the older woman embraced her. "We had hoped that such might happen, your grandmother and I, but we never imagined it would occur so quickly."

"Aunt" Jonathan interrupted. "Do you intend to keep us standing here all day?"

"Heavens, how I do go on. It is the excitement, I am sure. So wonderful, young love and all. Made me quite forget myself," Lady Sarah tittered . "Do come in, please." She motioned them inside and guided them to the downstairs parlor.

"I'll just ring for tea," Lady Sarah said, urging them to take a seat.

Once the maid had departed with her mistress' request for tea, Lady Sarah became quite serious. "Now, tell me about the court. What has happened."

Carefully Jonathan explained.

"Well," Lady Sarah said when he had finished. "I think we shall give a ball in celebration as soon as all this is settled. You know everyone will be clamoring to meet the new earl." She smiled at Jonathan. "Not to mention the fuss that will be raised over the new

Countess of Wyndridge. That will put a few noses out of joint, to be sure."

Lady Sarah turned suddenly very serious. "You know Elizabeth was very secretive about her husband. Even after his death, her letters never hinted at his identity. All she ever said was that he came from a very distinguished family. We thought it might have been some hint of scandal connected with him she sought to hide. She was determined to protect her child, even to the point of giving him her family's name. Now, knowing it was Wyndridge she feared, I can certainly understand her actions. Had the earl learned about Jonathan's birth, I have no doubt he would have moved right away to eliminate the child."

Lady Sarah smiled at Spring as a tear formed in the corner of one eye. "Your aunt would have been the countess had she lived. But had they married, Edward would never have met Elizabeth and we would not have Jonathan, would we?"

"Aunt Marilyn was engaged to Edward?" Spring asked.

"Yes, my dear." Lady Sarah's gaze moved toward the fire flickering in the grate. "Years ago, she was engaged to Edward but died in a hunting accident two weeks before the wedding was to take place. Such a horrible thing. They never discovered who fired the shot that killed her. Left both the Tollersley men distraught, since both men had courted her. But it was Edward she chose."

Aghast, Spring stared at Lady Sarah. Spring had known her mother's sister died young, but she had never heard how Aunt Marilyn had died. Nor had she known Marilyn had been engaged to Edward Tollersley.

"That could explain why Marcus was determined to have Spring," Jonathan said quietly. "It might also point to another murder. If he could not have her, he decided to prevent his brother marrying her. He would not want his brother to marry, since it would move him further away from the Earldom if Edward and Marilyn had a son."

"Wyndridge could have killed Aunt Marilyn," Spring whispered, her voice trembling slightly with emotion.

Jonathan's jaw hardened into a determined line as a muscle twitched slowly in his cheek. "So much to answer for," he grated as he stood and crossed to the window where he pulled back the heavy brocade curtain and peered into the street.

Spring followed Jonathan to the window, placing her hand gently upon his arm. He smiled down at her and pulled her into his embrace.

Across the street a man leaned nonchalantly against the pole of a gaslight. He nodded slightly toward the window and touched the corner of his hat briefly in salute. Alarm spread through Spring to see the man staring at the house.

"Should we call for the authorities?" she asked in alarm.

"No, it's only Collins," Jonathan answered. "Apparently my friends have decided to hover around protectively. I imagine they will tire of it after a while and go away."

Spring felt very much afraid for Jonathan and hoped that Collins would remain on guard.

Jonathan returned the man's acknowledgment then allowed the heavy material to fall back into place over the window. With a deep sigh, he turned toward his aunt.

"How is Tobias?"

"Better this morning. The doctor came by while you were out and pronounced him to be on the mend," Lady Sarah answered.

Jonathan turned to Spring. "We should check on him. I am sure he is anxious to hear what happened at the Chancery."

Jonathan caught Spring's hand and gently urged her to follow him. "If you will excuse us for a moment," he said to Lady Sarah as they crossed the parlor.

"Of course, but the tea will be here shortly, do not tarry long. I am sure Spring must be quite longing for refreshment."

Spring accompanied Jonathan up the wide stairs to the second-floor landing, where he paused for a moment for a quick kiss before continuing down the hall to the room where Tobias was convalescing.

Tobias sat up in bed, leaning against several pillows and enjoying a meal of roast hen, bread, and cheese. He wiped his mouth with the back of his hand as they approached the bed. Sitting up straighter, he pushed the tray of food aside.

"My lady insisted on seeing for herself that you had survived," Jonathan said as they approached. He smiled and pulled Spring closer to his side.

"'tis grateful I am for yer concern, milady," Tobias said as they stopped beside the bed. "And I'd be thanking ye for saving me life, as well."

"You are very welcome, and I must thank you for watching over my husband," Spring returned.

"Been watching 'o 'im since the lad were knee 'igh to a June bug," Tobias answered with a smile toward Jonathan.

"But, please, continue with your meal," Spring urged.

"'ad plenty, thanks, milady."

"You are feeling better?" she asked, anxiously surveying his pale features.

"Aye," he answered. "Don't worry, I'm stronger than one of 'is lordship's bullets. Just takes a bit to fight off its effects, I reckon."

"I reckon," Jonathan echoed with a smile. "You're stubborn enough, anyway."

"Been to the Chancery, then have ye?"

Jonathan nodded and smiled.

Tobias sat up straighter, eyes bright as they searched Jonathan's features. "Well?"

"Thomas Bailey presented all the evidence, and now we await the judgement of the court," Jonathan answered.

"And 'is lordship?"

"He didn't show," Jonathan answered. "But he did arrange a little reception for us as we left the Chancery."

Tobias' eyes narrowed, and his lips became a tight thin line as his hands gripped the counterpane. "Go on, lad."

"A runaway team came down the street just as we left the court. Had it not been for Spring's warning, I would have been run down."

Spring shivered, and Tobias cursed.

"Beg pardon, milady," Tobias said in embarrassment before he continued. "But dammit, lad, I told ye to be careful. Ye cannot let your guard down even for a second, not now. It'd cost yer life, it would."

"I know," Jonathan responded. "I shall be extremely cautious from now on. Collins is outside now. I spotted him from the parlor window. My friends decided to lend their protection, as well."

"'tis good," Tobias grimaced as he tried to lever himself straighter in the bed. "Ye be careful, lad. I'll be out of this bed and watching after ye in a day or so. Until then, just let those fancy friends stay close by. 'is lordship don't care for witnesses, 'e don't."

"We discovered another piece of the puzzle today," Jonathan said and waited for Tobias to respond.

"That being?"

"Lady Marilyn was Spring's aunt."

"Lady Marilyn?" Tobias looked from Jonathan to Spring and back. "The one Edward was to wed?"

"Yes."

"Guess that explains why 'is lordship settled 'is sights on the Lady Spring, then don't it? "'e wanted Lady Marilyn for 'imself, 'e did.

Spring felt a chill flow through her despite the nearness of Jonathan's body at her side. "Do you think Wyndridge might have killed her, Tobias?"

Hatred flared in the old man's eyes, and he struggled to rise from the bed. "Wouldn't put it past 'im. Wanted the lady, 'e did."

Jonathan gently pushed Tobias back to the pillows. "Rest now. You will need all your strength when we face Wyndridge finally."

The old man settled again against the pillows, but he continued to frown as he watched them closely. "Ye will not confront him without me at ye back, lad," Tobias warned.

"Rest, my friend. You will be at my side, I promise."

Leaving Tobias to rest, they returned to the parlor where Lady Sarah awaited them.

"Come," Lady Sarah said as they entered the room. "I am sure you both can use some refreshment." She indicated the brocade covered settee placed at an angle to the wing back chair where the lady sat.

Jonathan watched Spring sip the tea Lady Sarah served her. She accepted one of the small, iced cakes from the tray, as well.

Jonathan tried the tea. Finding it not to his liking, he placed his cup back on the tray. He saw Spring hide her smile behind her cup as she watched him taste the tea.

"We can stay here tonight, but we should send a message to Lady Phoebe." Jonathan smiled indulgently at his aunt.

Reaching for one of the small cakes, he popped it into his mouth, savoring its delicate flavor for a moment before he swallowed and continued. "Perhaps you could arrange to send a note along to her, Aunt?"

"Of course," Lady Sarah answered. "Dearest Phoebe will be quite beside herself with worry." She smiled at Spring. "Your grandmother never liked being excluded. Always wants to be in the center of things, she does. I am sure she is chaffing to hear what happened in court today."

When Spring chewed on her bottom lip, Jonathan wondered why. Was it concern for her grandmother or something else that brought the worried frown to her face. She took a deep breath and sighed, continuing to chew on her lip. "I didn't tell her," Spring whispered. "I did not tell her about it. She was still sleeping when I left, and I did not want to wake her."

Jonathan frowned. "Your grandmother doesn't know where you are?"

"Of course, she does," Spring insisted. "I left her a note. I told her I was meeting you."

"A note?" Jonathan narrowed his gaze.

"I am sure Bridgett told her all about summoning the hansom cab. She is quite the household gossip. Little escapes her attention. She stood beside me as I gave the driver instructions." Spring chewed her lip again. "Of course, she will not have known the reason for my sudden trip, but I had an overwhelming urge to find you."

Jonathan pulled Spring into his embrace. "I am sure your grandmother must have figured it out. We shall send her a message to explain, a letter explaining how you could not wait to see your husband," he teased.

Lady Sarah crossed the room to an ornate desk from which she removed a small lap desk containing pens, paper, and ink. She returned to Spring and placed the writing equipage in Spring's lap.

"You must write to her at once," Lady Sarah insisted. "I will send one of the servants with the letter right away. Put it right into her hands, he will. That way you can be assured of receiving her reply."

Lady Sarah returned to her seat in the brocade upholster wing chair and smiled contentedly, assuming she had settled the matter.

Thank you," Spring whispered as she opened the ink well and dipped in the pen. Again, she chewed her lip, and Jonathan watched as she put pen to paper.

"I think it is time we visited your mother, as well," Jonathan said as he turned toward the window. "She must be informed of our marriage. Do you think she is up to hearing the news?"

Spring smiled and nodded. She folded the letter she had written to her grandmother and placed sealing wax on the fold.

Lady Sarah beamed at Jonathan's words. "But, of course, and I am quite sure Lady Melanie will be delighted with her new son-in-law," she insisted. "Just as I am thrilled with my new niece."

Chapter Twenty-Eight

Three days later, with Tobias insisting himself healed enough to travel, the newly wedded couple began the journey to deliver the news of their nuptials to Spring's mother.

Located in the Midlands between Coventry and Cotswold, her father's country estate had always been a haven of peace and tranquility. Excitement built in Spring when they set off early the next morning for Lansing Hall. Soon she would see Mama and the twins.

They took Oxford Road and quickly left London behind. The hard surface of the city's roadway gave way to local gravel, so the coachman slowed down to save the team. Diablo and the sorrel mare had been tethered to the rear of the coach.

The small entourage kept up a lively banter. Jonathan's friends, Reinhardt and Collins had insisted on accompanying them, as had Lady Phoebe and Tobias.

They traveled comfortably in Rinehart's magnificently appointed coach, but even that became close and crowded after hours on the road. A second, smaller coach loaded with baggage and presents for Spring's mother and the twins followed. Lady Phoebe and her maid, Bridgette, brought up the rear of the caravan in Lady Phoebe's personal coach.

Tobias rode atop Reinhardt's coach with a rifle across his lap, his eyes alert to danger of ambush from Lord Wyndridge. Jonathan had tried to persuade his friend to at least accompany them inside the coach, but Tobias proclaimed himself ready to resume his responsibilities.

"You've decided to return home, then?" Reinhardt asked once he and Jonathan returned to the coach after spending time riding Diablo and the mare.

"As soon as the Lord Chancellor reaches his decision," Jonathan answered. Spring's gaze focused on her husband, sending tiny thrills of excitement swirling in her in her chest. Soon they would leave England and venture across the ocean to America.

"Regardless of the outcome?" Reinhardt persisted.

"Regardless."

"Might visit Savannah myself soon," Collins interjected, smiling at Spring.

Jonathan scowled. "You are welcome to visit our home. I am sure you would discover some business investments to keep your interest whetted for some time," Jonathan suggested, drawing Collin's attention away from Spring.

"Indeed."

A smile tilted the corner of her lips as she noted the scowl on Jonathan's face. Was he jealous?

Spring found Jonathan's light-hearted banter with his friends refreshing. It helped to divert his attention away from his uncle and the danger he posed. Clearly, they were devoted to Jonathan, just as he was to them. It was only when they plied her with their undivided attention that Jonathan became cross with them.

Interesting. Spring studied the trio. Both of his friends were handsome but not nearly so much as Jonathan. Spring mused as she studied them from beneath her lowered lashes.

Collins had a shock of unruly blonde hair that was perpetually out of place, even when he tried to keep it restrained. His eyes were the deep green of the sea on a calm morning, his face masculine and rugged. It was not an unattractive face.

Reinhardt had the aristocratic features that bespoke of his lineage. Both men were of an age with Jonathan. Still, though handsome, neither man could match Jonathan's vestige.

Spring knew both to be popular with the match-making mothers of the Ton. They ranked among the most desirable bachelors, Reinhardt because of his title and pedigree, Collins because of his considerable fortune.

"We will stop soon," Jonathan announced.

Relief flowed through Spring at Jonathan's words. They would stop for the night at a wayside inn just outside of Oxford and continue their journey early the next morning. She had not wished to complain, but the prospect of spending sixteen hours in the coach with barely any time to rest and stretch one's legs had been a bit daunting.

They supped on roast chicken, steak and kidney pie and a rich vegetable soup followed by five-jam tarts and trifles piled high with whipped cream and topped with candied cherries. The meal was exceptional, as was the attention given to their party. Contented and replete, they retired to their rooms for the night.

Jonathan escorted Spring to the room they would share for the night. He had requested a bath drawn for her, and when he opened the door, a large tub filled with steaming water occupied the center of the small room.

He drew Spring into the room, smiling as he saw her delight at the warm bath awaiting her. Urging her further into the room, Jonathan pulled her into his embrace. A deep breath filled his lungs with the arousing scent of his wife. He knew she was tired from the long hours in the coach, as was he, but his body responded ardently to the woman in his arms. He kissed her gently, holding back the sudden need he felt to consume her.

Moving his hands to her shoulders, he moved a step back from her. He schooled his hunger for her to have a care for her needs first.

Slowly his hands drifted down from her shoulders to the first button of the blue coatdress designed for travel. With slow, gentle fingers he freed the buttons, one at a time. Buttons free, he slid the coat from her shoulders then hung the garment across the back of a chair. Next his hands were at the fastenings of her heavy skirt. Nimble fingers made quick work of the openings, and soon the skirt joined the coat on the chair.

He paused to stroke his knuckles down the smooth skin of her cheek, feeling her tremble at his touch. He relished the smooth softness of her skin beneath his hand. His body responded to her closeness. The cloth of his breeches tightened across his arousal

Jonathan turned her gently then worked the buttons down the back of her chemise. His breath caught in his chest as the smooth skin of her shoulders peeked from the parted material. He bent and pressed his lips to her skin and felt a shudder travel through her body. His arms closed around her, pulling her back against his chest.

For a moment he considered pulling her to the bed and burying himself in her soft warmth. He knew she would not resist his advances. The current of attraction flowing between them strengthened every time he held her in his arms.

But their journey had been grueling, exhausting his wife. He could control his needs. There would be other nights. Kissing his way across her shoulder to her nape, then moving up the smooth skin of her neck, he found the soft shell of her ear. His lips played over it, and his teeth nipped at the lobe. He took a deep breath and slowly exhaled against the tender curve of her throat. She shivered and pushed her body tighter against him.

"Your water will get cold. I will check on the horses while you enjoy your bath." He kissed her lips when she turned her head toward him.

"Be careful." She returned his kiss.

"Always, my love." One more kiss later, he left her to finish undressing.

He found Diablo safely tucked into a stall in the stable. The stallion lifted his head and whinnied when Jonathan approached. Tucking his right hand into the pocket of his vest, he produced the small cube of sugar Diablo expected.

After seeing to the comfort of his steed, Jonathan returned to the main room of the inn. He caught the eye of the innkeeper and ordered a pint of ale. Jonathan sat in the corner of the great room, facing the fireplace. His friends, apparently tired and weary after their long day of travel, had retired to their rooms. He pulled his watch from his pocket and saw nearly an hour had passed since he had left Spring to enjoy her bath. By now she was surely tucked into bed and fast asleep. He drained his tankard, rose to his feet, and headed toward the stairs.

Two stairs at a time, he made his way up to the room where his wife slept. He paused at the door, listening.

Footsteps stopped at the door to the room. Spring held her breath, listening. She stilled in the tub, careful that no sound came from within. She smiled as she heard the key being fitted into the lock.

The soft glow of a lamp cast subtle shadows across the small room. The door creaked open, as if the hand gripping it sought to avoid disturbing the silence of the chamber. A smile curved her lips when she saw Jonathan's surprised gaze when he found her still seated in the tub.

"I thought you would have finished—"

"I was waiting for you," she whispered and rose from the tub.

She stood on the small rug beside the tub as small rivulets streamed down her body. She stood straight and tall, watching as his heated gaze traveled up and down her body. A smile tugged at her lips while she watched his Adam's apple bob as he swallowed.

She pointed to the towel the maid had left on the chair against the wall. "Hand me the towel, please."

Instead of handing her the towel, he lifted it and moved to stand behind her. His hands were gentle while he slowly ran the towel over her body. She felt his hot lips on her shoulder as he kissed his way across her damp skin. The towel brushed over her body, chasing the drops of water clinging to her skin.

Finally, when he was satisfied with the job, he wrapped the towel around her torso and turned her in his arms.

Spring tucked the ends of the towel into the valley between her breasts then smiled at him. "And now, husband, it is your turn." She reached for the lapels of his coat and pushed them apart then slid the garment down his arms. She folded it carefully and placed it on the chair.

Next, she reached for the closure of his vest. Soon his vest and fine linen shirt joined the coat. She turned back to him, and for a moment her boldness deserted her as she brought her gaze to the firm muscles of his bare chest.

She caught her bottom lip between her teeth, worrying the tender flesh there as her hand reached for buttons on the front of his trousers. Her hands trembled while she worked the buttons free.

"Allow me," Jonathan said, taking a step back as he bent and quickly removed his boots and stockings. Then the trousers joined the other garments folded neatly on the chair.

Spring's breath caught in her chest as her eyes roved the smooth expanse of his naked body. She lifted one small hand and traced the firm muscled wall of his chest. A small tingle began in her fingertips, ran along her arm, then traveled straight to her belly and lower.

What magic had this the man wrought in her body? She lifted her gaze to meet his and felt heat race up her throat, bringing high color to her cheeks. Embarrassment warred with desire, and she turned away to avoid his gaze.

"The water is getting colder." She motioned toward the tub then turned back to find a smirk lifting the corner of his lips.

Something about the look he gave her set fire to the blood racing through her veins. Heat throbbed as his gaze studied the spot where the towel tucked between her breasts.

He winked and then stepped into the tub and sank into the water.

The infuriating man knew just the effect his perusal wrought in her body. He reveled in bringing high color to her cheeks.

Perhaps it was time that she turned the tables on the exasperating man. Slowly she moved from behind him to stand in front of the tub. Her fingers barely trembled as she reached for the towel ends tucked between her breasts and tugged them apart. She allowed the material to slide slowly down her body then pushed it aside. Folding the towel, she placed it on the floor beside the tub and then knelt on it.

Jonathan's eyes remained riveted upon her the entire time. She watched his Adam's apple move up and down his throat. A small smile lingered on her lips. She leaned forward, pressing her naked breasts against his arm as she reached for the sponge. Pulling her bottom lip between her teeth, Spring soaped the sponge and then applied it to Jonathan's chest.

She took her time, enjoying the feel of his sleek skin where her fingers trailed behind the sponge. She watched the supple ripple of muscle and sinew beneath her hands. As her hands dipped beneath the surface of the water, she heard a low rumbling in his chest. A growl, he actually growled.

A tremor raced through her body at the sign of how her touch affected him. She pushed the sponge across his belly then lower. His eyes narrowed. Their dark depths seemed to almost glow. Sliding the sponge further she followed the hard line of his thigh, first the right and then the left. As her ministration continued, she caught a hint of a smile curving his shapely lips.

One moment she was running the sponge over his strong thigh, the next his hand captured hers and slowly pulled it higher. Then the sponge was free from her grasp and his hand guided hers to the juncture of his thighs. Gently he curled her hand around his hard manhood. Spring gasped. The color in her cheeks burned bright.

Never releasing her hand from where he held it slowly massaging the length of his shaft, his other hand tangled in the hair at her nape and pulled her forward until their lips met.

Emboldened by the pulsing, urgent shaft beneath her hand that spoke of his need, Spring opened her mouth beneath his, her tongue dueling with his. She heard again the growl deep in his chest. His mouth slid from hers and traced across her cheek and down the column of her throat. Spring pressed closer. Her breast flattened against his firm chest.

He rose from the tub, his arms wrapped firmly around her, pulling her into his wet embrace. Spring giggled nervously and pulled away to reach for the towel.

Standing on the small rug, he allowed her to dry the water from his body. Spring captured her bottom lip between her teeth as she concentrated on capturing every rivulet that traced down his chest. When the towel slipped lower, chasing the last of the drips that disappeared into the dark forest at his manhood, that deep sensual growl escaped his chest again.

"Enough," Jonathan said in a raspy voice. He pulled the towel from her hands and tossed it to the floor. In one smooth movement he lifted her into his arms and deposited her in the center of the bed.

The bed creaked in protest as Jonathan rested one knee on the edge then slowly covered her body with his.

When his mouth again found hers, she opened willingly to the demand of his tongue. When his mouth trailed kisses down her throat to her breasts, Spring held her breath for a moment. The fire in her blood increased with each stroke of his tongue, each caress of his hand.

"Wife, you make me weak with wanting." He hands trailed down to test her center and found her wet and warm with need. "If I didn't know better, I would think you planned to seduce your husband."

"Husband," she whispered. "Love me."

"Aye, Love," he answered and moved claim her again.

Chapter Twenty-Nine

Early the next morning, after a breakfast of grilled sausage served with small grilled tomatoes and scrambled eggs, buttered toast with marmalade, and tea, they departed the inn.

After traveling all morning, they stopped at midday to rest the horses and allow the passengers to stretch their legs. Jonathan took advantage of the stop for a few stolen moments alone with his wife.

The shadows of evening had lengthened, and darkness crept slowly across the countryside when at last they topped the last rise, and Lansing Hall came into view.

Spring sighed. Had it really been less than two months since she had answered Mr. Brownstone's summons to London? How was it possible that her life had been so irrevocably altered in so short a time?

The coach rolled to a stop in front of the manor house. Jonathan flung open the coach door then swung down. He reached up and lifted Spring down. He held her for a moment pressed against his chest before he allowed her to slide down the hard length of his frame. His dark eyesfocused on hers held a promise.

"I will be in as soon as I have taken care of Diablo," Jonathan said. He placed a quick kiss on her lips, his hand lingering at her cheek for a moment as he smiled down at her.

Spring smiled up into Jonathan's face, thinking how handsome her husband was. She blushed prettily as his eyes darkened with desire.

"Come, my pet," Lady Phoebe called as she approached from the second coach. "Your mother will be anxious to hear all the news."

When Jonathan turned back toward the coach, his friends joined him.

"I'll take care of Diablo." Tobias leaned down from his spot beside the coachman. "You need to catch up with your wife."

Spring found her mother in the downstairs parlor, seated on the velveteen davenport. Around her on the settee various stacks of papers covered every inch. Her mother looked up as Spring entered the room.

"Dearest," Lady Lansing exclaimed holding out her arms toward her daughter. "You should have told me what Lord Wyndridge was doing."

"Mama," Spring whispered, a painful catch in her throat that forestalled the torrent of words that wanted to spill forth.

Spring hurried across the room and knelt in front of her mother, allowing herself to be gathered into her mother's comforting embrace.

Lady Lansing smoothed Spring's hair back from her face then pulled her closer, gently rocking her daughter in her arms.

"My dearest lamb, what has that evil man done to you?"

"I'm fine, Mama," Spring answered, seeking to reassure her mother.

"I have just been going over the papers that Mr. Brownstone sent."

"You should not worry yourself about these," Spring said indicating the stacks of papers scattered on the davenport. "Jonathan will take care of everything."

"So I've been told."

Her mother studied her intently, so that Spring felt a slight flush steal over her cheeks. Apparently, what she saw written in her daughter's expression gave her cause to wonder, for after a long pause during which she searched Spring face, the lady launched her inquiry.

"Tell me about this young man. Is he as handsome as your grandmother has said he is?

Spring nodding, feeling the flush rise higher on her cheeks. "More so."

"Ah," Lady Phoebe exclaimed from the doorway. "To be young and in love. I had almost forgotten how wonderful young love can be."

The color in Spring's cheeks deepened more.

Her mother frowned, small lines marring her still smooth skin. "How is it that your wonderful young man intends to prevent Lord Wyndridge from taking the Lansing holdings?"

A familiar voice answered from the doorway before Spring could frame an answer. A soft sigh escaped Spring as she turned her gaze toward Jonathan.

"Marcus Tollersley signed an agreement that returns possession of the Lansing holding to you upon the marriage of your daughter to Lord Wyndridge." Jonathan stood in the doorway, flanked by Rinehardt and Collins.

He smiled broadly as he stepped toward the pale woman seated on the settee. He stopped and swept a deep bow. "Jonathan Sinclair at your service, my lady."

Lady Lansing's eyes widened as she took in the three men now standing before her. She cleared her throat, her eyes narrowing just a fraction at Jonathan's bold introduction. After a second's hesitation, she returned to the matter at hand.

"Yes," she answered. "I have here a copy of the agreement." Her thin hand trembled as she patted the topmost paper on the velveteen seat beside her. "But, since that marriage can never be allowed to take place, how then does that help to thwart Marcus Tollersley?"

"I see my wife has not had time to fully explain," Jonathan began.

"Wife?" Lady Lansing gasped. "Spring, are you aware this rogue is married?"

"Well, actually," Spring stammered.

When Rinehardt snickered behind the handkerchief held in his hand, Jonathan shot him a scathing look.

Lady Lansing turned narrowed eyes upon Jonathan. "Sir, how dare you take advantage of a defenseless young girl? You rogue! Were her father alive, he would call you out for this affront!

"Call you out!" Collins echoed, gaining a frown from Jonathan and a hiss from Spring.

Jonathan stepped closer to Lady Lansing. "Your mistrust wounds me, my lady."

"Since her father is no longer with us, I fear I shall have to..."

Jonathan turned toward Spring. Judging from the color rising on her cheeks, she just might explode if he didn't reassure her mother. He turned back toward Lady Lansing. "Things are not as you fear. If you will allow me to—"

"How dare you trifle with my daughter?" Flustered, Lady Lansing did not allow Jonathan a moment to explain, rather turned accusing eyes upon Lady Phoebe.

"Phoebe, were you aware of this?"

Undaunted, Lady Phoebe stepped forward. "I believe I can clear up this misunderstanding," she began.

"Well, do so at once," Lady Lansing snapped.

"Jonathan and Spring were married last week." Lady Phoebe stifled a chuckle. "Marcus will be livid, but there is simply nothing he can do about it now."

"Married?" Lady Lansing repeated incredulously. She focused on Spring, "My dearest, why did you not tell me?"

"I... I—" Spring stammered.

"I believe she was just about to when I interrupted her," Jonathan answered.

As if not quite sure all was as it should be, Lady Lansing's gaze moved from Spring to Jonathan and back to Spring again. She studied her daughter for a long moment. She paused to cough delicately into her lace handkerchief then began firing questions at Jonathan.

"Since your marriage has voided the agreement that Marcus signed, how are we to prevent him from taking possession of the Lansing holdings?"

Without waiting for Jonathan to respond, she continued. "Will you kindly explain how Marcus Tollersley is to be handled."

Rinehardt stifled a grin while Collins feigned outrage.

"There is, of course, the matter of the dowry. Once my husband's estate is claimed by Marcus Tollersley, there will be little left to offer. But perhaps if I sell my jewels?" Lady Lansing, absorbed in her own thoughts, did not spare Jonathan a second to respond to any of the questions she had posed.

"The twins must have a season, as well..."

Jonathan finally cut into the steady stream of rambling.

"My lady, I had no thought of a dowry when I married your daughter. My wife will be quite well cared for without such offering from her family. However, it is because of our marriage that your family will be safe from Marcus Tollersley."

Lady Lansing took a deep breath, as if trying to calm herself. Her hands trembled as she pleated and unpleated the lace handkerchief in her lap. "Safe from Marcus? Pray explain yourself, sir. Do."

Jonathan's hand snaked out to capture Spring's, pulling her closer to his side. He felt her hand tremble as he entwined their fingers. He gently squeezed her hand, offering encouragement. With a sigh, he began.

"Perhaps if we were properly introduced you would begin to understand." He smiled down at Spring and continued. "Jonathan Andrew Sinclair, Earl of Wyndridge, at your service, my lady." He finished with a sweeping bow.

"Wyndridge? But how?" Lady Lansing questioned, her confusion mounted rather than diffused.

"Edward's son," Lady Phoebe supplied the missing information.

"Edward?" Lady Lansing repeated softly.

"I believe you knew my father?" Jonathan asked as Lady Lansing settled into memories.

"What? Oh yes." She exhaled softly. "I knew Edward. He was engaged to my sister, but she died in an accident before the wedding could take place." Lady Lansing dabbed at the corner of one eye where a tear had gathered.

"We have reason to believe her death was no accident," Jonathan said.

"Marcus?" Lady Lansing's eyes widened with shock.

Jonathan nodded.

Lady Lansing studied Jonathan closely, her eyes earnest upon him. "You must not underestimate your uncle," the older woman cautioned. "He will fight desperately to hold that which he considers his."

"I am aware of the deeds that my uncle is capable of. He had my father killed and probably you sister, as well, since she represented a threat to his ambition should she bare Edward an heir."

Lady Lansing nodded. "Yes, I can believe Marcus would have quite rather seen my sister dead than married to Edward. He wanted her for himself, you know."

Spring's eyes widened at her mother's words. She knew, of course, the story of her mother's sister having died in a hunting accident. She had heard the story many times, but until recently she had not considered that the death of her aunt might in any way be connected to the drastic turn her own life had taken in the last few months.

Lady Lansing's gaze returned to Jonathan as she again studied his visage. "You're not at all like your father. Perhaps in character, but your features are different, very different."

"I resemble my mother. It is a trait of the Wyndridge men, I'm told," Jonathan responded.

"So it is," Lady Phoebe confirmed. "I had quite forgotten that trait of the Wyndridge family."

The topic seemingly forgotten, Lady Lansing turned back to Spring. "Your sisters will be so excited that you've come home at last."

"I am quite anxious to see them, as well." Spring smiled. "Perhaps I should go up to the school room and check on them?"

"Then you must run along to see them," Lady Lansing began. Her strength appeared to wane as she spoke. "My dearest, take your young man along as well. They will be quite thrilled to meet him." She paused as if winded.

Lady Phoebe took up the conversation. "You mother and I will chat for a moment, then she must rest for a bit before dinner."

Lady Lansing, having recovered for the moment, continued. "And please, be so kind as to show our other guests to their rooms, as well."

Chapter Thirty

They spent two weeks visiting Lansing Hall. The twins were quite pleased with their new brother-in-law. Beckie declared him Prince Charming who had come to rescue their sister from the evil fiend, while Winnie insisted he was more the knight in shining armor type.

Jonathan smiled and tried to live up to their youthful imaginings. Both Rinehardt and Collins teased him about making further conquests of the Lansing females.

A deep sadness seeped into Spring's soul as they prepared to return to London. Her mother weakened with every passing day. Spring hated having to leave her mother's side, fearing she might never see her again.

But the summons had come from Mr. Bailey. Jonathan had to return to London to receive the decision of the Chancery Court. As much as she hated to leave her mother and the twins, Spring felt she needed to be at her husband's side to support him.

Based on his solicitous behavior during the last few weeks, Spring had decided to trust her husband. She loved him. She was sure if she worked hard enough, she could make him love her in return. She could not bear the thought of being away from him.

She remembered those moments when she'd stood in the street watching the runaway carriage careening toward him and realized she never wanted to lose him, never wanted to live without him. Never. Never could she endure living without Jonathan.

As she relived those heart-shattering moments, Spring realized just how great a loss her mother had suffered with the loss of her father.

Even after receiving word of the court's imminent verdict, they were forced to wait for the hearing to be scheduled. Finally, the long-awaited message arrived. They gathered in the parlor of Lord Meldon's townhouse. Jonathan was grateful for the unwavering support of his wife. Both Rinehardt and Collins had journeyed with them back to London and even now gathered at his side, offering their protection and support.

Jonathan's eyebrows drew together as he read the letter from Thomas Bailey. Lord Lyndhurst, after conducting his own investigation, had reached his decision and would deliver his verdict at two that very afternoon.

"Not to worry, old chap," Rinehardt encouraged as Jonathan re-read the missive. "There is but one conclusion which Lyndhurst could possibly reach."

Jonathan smiled at his friend's enthusiasm. "One would think so," he agreed.

"Quite positively," chimed in Collins. "And for that very reason, it is imperative that you be more cautious than ever."

"Bloody good idea for Bailey to send along a hired coach. With several departing at the same time, Wyndridge will not have a chance to strike," Rinehardt mused.

Three coaches departed the Meldon residence in Kensington, heading toward Lincoln's Inn Hall. Jonathan and Spring traveled in the hired coach with Tobias seated on top next to the driver. Rinehardt's coach led the procession, while Collins brought up the rear.

Still, remembering the last time at the court when Jonathan had nearly been killed, it was with extreme relief that Spring saw them arrive safely at their destination.

They had spent the last few days secluded at Lord Meldon's home. Lady Phoebe had visited often, as had both Rinehardt and Collins.

In fact, it appeared one of those two gentlemen was always underfoot. Plus, there was always the man standing guard outside. Knowing his friends took the threat his uncle posed seriously reassured Spring. Still, the time passed uneventfully.

Just thinking about what Marcus might do made Spring nervous. Marcus Tollersley was not the kind of man to let a thing like the law or morality stand between him and something he wanted. And Marcus Tollersley wanted desperately to hold on to his title and his estates.

The caravan arrived at the Chancery Court and found Thomas Bailey waiting just outside the arched portico. Jonathan stepped down from the coach and turned back to offer Spring his hand. They joined Thomas Bailey where he waited for them.

"Well, my dear," Thomas Bailey brought Spring's attention back to the business at hand. "are you prepared to assume the duties of the Countess of Wyndridge?"

Spring's hand tightened on Jonathan's arm. "I am prepared to be Jonathan's wife, whatever the role."

Nodding his approval of her words, Bailey turned his attention to the small entourage gathered around Jonathan and Spring. "Gentlemen, shall we?" He held open the heavy wooden door and ushered them inside.

Jonathan's hand covered hers where it rested upon his arm. His fingers caressed hers gently, their touch both sensual and reassuring. When they entered the courtroom, Jonathan pulled Spring close to his side, sheltering her in his embrace. He smiled down at her, and Spring offered her smile in return.

Once they were all gathered in the Lord Chancellor's court at Lincoln's Inn Hall, a door opened at the rear of the courtroom, and a tall thin man wearing a black robe with a white collar and bands. On his head he wore a short white wig. Jonathan leaned down and whispered. "Lord Chancellor Lyndhurst."

Lyndhurst began without delay. "It is the finding of this court," Lord Lyndhurst began, pausing to look out over those gathered before him. "That a marriage, regardless of its unusual circumstances, took place between Edward Tollersley, Earl of Wyndridge, and Elizabeth Sinclair, and it is further found that Jonathan Andrew Sinclair is the legal heir of Edward Tollersley by his wife, Elizabeth Sinclair, and as such is the rightful holder of the Earldom of Wyndridge."

Spring's attention drifted away as Lord Lyndhurst continued to render his judgement. Jonathan had won. Marcus was defeated. It was over, or was it? What would Marcus do now?

When the court session ended, Jonathan spoke in a hushed voice to Thomas Bailey, then approached Benedict Goodwood.

"Tell my uncle that I have decided not to seek any further revenge against him. I am aware, as are all these present in this courtroom, that he arranged my father's murder, as well as several others. For that may he be consigned to the hell he has created for himself. He is to be off Wyndridge lands within a week's time and never set foot there again. If he returns, I will not be so lenient the next time."

Tobias approached Jonathan, exclaiming at Jonathan's words. "No, Drew, ye cannot mean to let 'im go after all 'e's done!"

"There are some things more important than revenge," Jonathan said as he pulled Spring into the shelter of his embrace.

Tobias shook his head in quiet disbelief.

"We will return home as soon as things are settled here. "Don't you long to see the Savannah River again, old friend?

"Aye, that river does run in my blood after all these years, I reckon," Tobias answered.

Chapter Thirty-One

A round of parties, fetes and balls were announced in honor of the new earl and his beautiful countess. Spring watched with pride as all the women's eyes followed Jonathan when he crossed the room, while Jonathan bristled with barely restrained jealousy as young dandies clustered around, seeking favor with his wife.

More than ever, Jonathan was determined to take Spring home to Savannah and away from the attentions of all the London Dandies.

They stayed with Lady Phoebe in the Lansing townhouse but visited Lady Sarah often. Tobias, now fully recovered from his injury, accompanied Jonathan whenever he went out. The days slipped by, and soon the day of their departure was approaching. There were only a few details to attend to at Wyndridge Hall, and then they could sail for America.

Jonathan, Tobias, and Collins left early one morning. Fear gripped Spring as they rode away, because she knew their destination to be Wyndridge Hall. She shivered, feeling a chill sweep over her at the thought of Marcus Tollersley and what would have been her fate had not Jonathan saved her.

When they were gone, Spring set about packing. It would be best to keep busy, she decided as she felt loneliness settle around her. She missed Jonathan and could not wait for his return. The time crept by, one day following another, and still Spring could not shake the dark cloud that had settled upon her with Jonathan's absence.

Finally, on the fourth day, just before noon, Lady Phoebe summoned Spring to join her and Baron Rinehardt for lunch.

"My pet," Lady Phoebe began once Spring had taken her seat at the table. "We should go shopping while Jonathan is away. You need new gowns and slippers, everything, in fact, before you leave for Savannah. You do want to make a good impression, don't you?"

"Jonathan said we must stay here until he returns." Spring pushed the food around on her plate, her appetite having deserted her.

"Nonsense, we shall be quite safe, I'm sure," Lady Phoebe insisted. "Baron Rinehardt will accompany us."

"But Jonathan said we should—"

"I will not allow Marcus Tollersley to hold me prisoner in my own home," Lady Phoebe answered and turned to Jonathan's friend. "You will accompany us, won't you, sir?"

The Baron, having assured Jonathan he would watch over the ladies until his return tried to dissuade Lady Phoebe, but the woman would not be put off. If he did not accompany them, then they would go alone. Reluctant, he agreed to accompany them on their shopping trip the next afternoon.

It is nice to be out of the house. Spring thought as the coach rolled noisily through the streets of London to the smarter section of the shopping district. The streets were crowded with carriages of every kind, while the sidewalks were awash with people.

Tension coiled inside Spring, and she felt a sense of foreboding. Jonathan had not wanted them to leave their safe refuge.

The coachman stopped outside Lady Phobe's favorite dressmaker's shop, and Baron Rinehardt courteously helped both women down from the coach. He then escorted both into the dress shop. He stood around for a few minutes then excused himself to wait outside while Spring and Lady Phoebe admired several gowns ordered by the daughter of a foreign diplomat who failed to complete the purchase when her father was recalled unexpectedly.

One gown of rich jade satin, accented with wide rows of French lace and tiny pink rosebuds, particularly caught Spring's attention.

Her grandmother, seeing her interest. quickly encouraged her to try on the gown.

"My pet, it would be perfect for you, and I doubt it would take much alteration to make it fit perfectly. Why not try it and allow Madame to note the alterations needed?" Lady Phoebe urged.

The dressing room at the rear of the establishment was cluttered with bits of fabric tossed carelessly over the floor. Mirrors lined the walls with only a door in the far corner to break up the reflection. With Madame Elaine's assistance, Spring quickly changed into the jade gown. The skilled fingers of the dressmaker quickly made the necessary tucks with pins so that the garment fit Spring's figure as if it had been made for her. Spring smiled as she surveyed herself in the mirror. Jonathan would love the gown. Its rich jade deepened the green of her eyes, while the soft fabric cast subtle shadows across her pale skin, giving it the iridescent glow of mother of pearl.

"It is perfect," Lady Phoebe acknowledged with a bright smile.

Madame Elaine brought out a second gown of rich chocolate with beige underskirts.

"This one is perfect for you, my lady," Madame said to Lady Phoebe.

"Well, I hadn't intended to purchase anything for myself," Lady Phoebe hesitated as her fingers lovingly caressed the satin and lace.

"But my lady—"

Spring escaped while Madame Elaine made her case convincing Lady Phoebe she indeed needed the brown satin gown.

In the dressing room Spring struggled to free herself from the jade gown. Finally, it slipped to the floor, and she reached for her own gown, pulling it quickly over her head and down her body. Reaching behind her she began to fasten the tiny buttons as far as she could reach, hoping soon Madame would return to help her.

In the mirror Spring watched as the door to the alleyway slowly opened. Shock reeled through her system as Marcus Tollersley stepped into the dressing room holding a gun in his hand.

"Quiet, one sound and you're dead," he grated as he advanced toward her.

Spring backed away until her body pressed against the mirror on the wall. Horror welled inside her, threatening to escape on a scream. She fought down the shriek that tightened the muscles in her chest, making it hard to breathe. If she screamed her grandmother and Baron Reinhardt would come immediately and Marcus would not hesitate to kill them.

Above all, Spring cautioned herself she must keep her head. She must not panic. Hatred blared within her as she faced her tormentor.

"What do you want?"

"You, for starters. What is truly mine. All the things your husband has stolen from me."

"You're mad," Spring whispered. "You cannot possibly get away with more murders."

He stepped forward, gripping her arm and dragging her toward the open door.

"Why not?" he asked. "I always have before."

He pushed Spring through the door. His fingers dug deeply into the flesh of her upper arm as the barrel of the gun pressed into her ribs. She would not, could not scream, she told herself as he half pushed half dragged her down the alley. He would not use her resistance as an excuse to murder her grandmother or Reinhardt.

His voice from behind her was a harsh whisper. "Edward was not the first, of course. Marilyn was the first, and it was so easy. I warned her not to choose Edward, but she would not listen. She loved him, she said." Marcus laughed harshly as he continued to push Spring ahead of him along the alley.

"Then Edward, he should have died as a highwayman. He never could resist a dare. It was easy to set him up."

Marcus continued to push Spring ahead of him along the alley. She stumbled along, feeling rocks from the alley cut into her feet through the thin slippers which were not meant for such abuse. Slime and all manner of filth filled the alley. They turned the corner and then another and before long Spring became hopelessly lost in the maze of narrow, crowded streets and alleys.

"But he died, just the same, just took a little longer to see it finished." His fingers tightened painfully upon her arm, causing Spring to gasp. "And then your father, he laughed when I offered for you. Thought his precious daughter was too good for me."

Spring shuddered at the revelation. "You killed him," she accused through clenched teeth.

"Of course. He tried to defy me. No one defies the Earl of Wyndridge. He had to be eliminated, just as Captain Fisher did. Now Jonathan and you will be, as well. You see, I am the Earl of Wyndridge. No one defies me. No one."

"You're mad," Spring repeated her earlier accusation. "You cannot expect to get away with this."

"Why not? My nephew will surely come to the rescue of his young bride."

Spring shivered, knowing that Marcus was right. He had but to wait. Jonathan would deliver himself into Marcus's hands.

I must do something, anything. She had to stop Jonathan from walking into Marcus's trap.

They turned another corner and were met by a throng of people. She felt Marcus's grip upon arm slacken slightly. He was going to kill her, there was no doubt, and he intended to kill Jonathan, as well.

She could not allow him to use her to lure Jonathan into his trap. She must act now before it was too late, Spring cautioned herself as they became enveloped in the crowd.

Taking a deep breath, Spring stiffened her arm. Then she jammed her elbow back sharply so that it connected suddenly with her captor's chest. His grasp weakened as a great woosh of air left him. She yanked her arm out of his grasp.

She lifted her skirts and fled. She ran, not caring which way she went. Only knowing she must put distance between herself and Marcus.

When finally she dared stop for an instant to catch her breath and get her bearings, she realized she was again on Oxford Street near the intersection of Tottenham Court Road. Spring turned onto that street, hurriedly looking over shoulder and seeing Marcus still in pursuit of her. She found a narrow alleyway obstructed by an enormous coal cart. Flattening herself against the wall, she squeezed around the cart and then continued down the alley.

Hurrying on, not caring about the filth that soiled her slippers and splashed upon her skirts, she rushed down the alley. A suffocating stench rose from all directions. Spring turned into another alley where the uneven, muddy ground became even more hazardous from soapy water and other household slops. Everywhere hung the feted odor of a veritable cesspool.

Above her head, all manner of tattered laundry hung on poles across the alley and dripped their fetid water down upon her head. All around her naked, dirty, half-starved children clung to mothers who were hardly better off. The men, dressed in rags, looked upon her with much the same wary fearful expression she cast upon them.

She stopped for an instant, thinking she must have died and been cast into hell. Looking over her shoulder she saw Marcus still bearing down upon her. With a cry of distress, she resumed her flight.

"Here, here," an urgent voice whispered. "Quickly, before he catches you."

Spring turned toward the voice and saw a hand motioning from the doorway of a basement hovel. She quickly stepped inside.

There was no air. The small room gave barely enough room for Spring to stand upright. The walls were damp and the floor earthen. From one corner of the small space, five pairs of small eyes studied her, while a man, himself so thin he was barely more than a skeleton beneath the rags upon his frame, pushed the door shut. He moved to the small window covered by a soiled and torn cloth.

He pushed the tattered cloth away from the broken window and peered out.

"He's still out there. You'd best hide here for a spell, milady."

Spring backed into a corner, pressed herself against the wall, then crumpled slowly to the floor.

"Where am I?" she asked when her heart had slowed enough to allow her to speak.

"St. Giles," he answered, letting the soiled cloth fall back into place.

The Irish Quarter! Spring had read articles about the horrors and degradation that its inhabitants suffered, but she had never believed it could possibly be as bad as the reports had suggested.

Spring shivered. It was worse. The smell was horrible, filth covered the ground, and the people were starving. All around were signs of extreme suffering inflicted upon these poor hapless creatures.

And outside, there was Marcus. Here, in this tiny little room with its wasted inhabitants, was her only refuge from him.

Strangely, as she looked around herself at the curious eyes trained upon her, Spring felt safe. Gathered together in a clutch, Spring counted five children. She could not determine their ages, since their small bodies were stunted from lack of food and other hardships. On a pallet in the other corner of the room, a woman lay very still and silent.

"Quiet now," the man whispered and signaled for the children to move. "He's coming this way."

At a quick signal from the man, five small, wasted bodies threw themselves upon Spring. She fought back a scream as they covered her body protectively with their own thin frames.

Spring heard the door as it was shoved open, heard Marcus's words as he ordered the man out of his way.

"Looking for a woman. Lifted my purse, she did," Marcus said as his eyes searched the darkness of the tiny hove. The children huddled closer together. One whimpered as Marcus moved closer, his booted foot kicking toward them.

"No call to abuse my children," the man defended from the door. "Only woman here is my wife, and she's too sick to leave her pallet."

Marcus crossed to the spot the man indicated and peered down at the woman. With a sniff of disgust, he turned and exited the hovel. The man pushed the door closed behind Marcus and signaled for the children to move aside.

The five pairs of curious eyes again bore into Spring as she sat up. There were four boys and a girl. All were nearly naked. Their clothing hung in ragged tatters about their painfully thin frames.

How can they exist like this? Spring shivered. She watched as the man continued to watch out the window.

"He's gone on down the alley, could come back though, better you should remain here for a while," he said as he turned away from the window.

"I didn't do it," Spring whispered through teeth that had begun to chatter.

The man studied her for a moment. "Don't expect ye did," he finally answered.

"He was going to kill me," Spring whispered, suppressing a shiver.

"Looked like he'd just as soon kill you as look at you, he did. Why?"

Spring blinked at the man. "Why?" she parroted.

"Was he going to kill you just for the pleasure of it, or did he..."

"And power," Spring added quietly.

"Best we send word to your husband so he can come and collect you. Where do you live?"

Chapter Thirty-Two

Jonathan had finished his business at Wyndridge as quickly as possible. He'd met with the tenants and dismissed the caretaker and housekeeper. He would hire new staff who would owe their loyalty to the Sinclairs of Wyndridge, not to Marcus Tollersley.

That accomplished, they had ridden for London. As they neared the Lansing townhouse, Jonathan smiled to himself. Spring was waiting. She would not expect him to have returned so soon, but three days away from her was more than he could tolerate. He chuckled to himself as he realized he was turning into quite the adoring husband.

Several coaches stood in the roadway outside the Lansing house, Jonathan frowned. Guests, he could not take Spring into his arms and carry her to their bedroom for the homecoming welcome he had imagined for the last two hours. But as soon as their guests departed, he would pull her into his arms. He forced his attention back to matters at hand.

Of a sudden, a sense of urgency filled Jonathan. Dismounting, he tossed Diablo's reins to Tobias and bounded up the steps to the townhouse, two at a time. The sense of urgency grew stronger. Something was wrong, very wrong.

The door opened before he touched it. Lady Phoebe threw herself into his arms, weeping. Jonathan caught her and managed to prevent them both from toppling backward down the steps by sheer force of effort.

"Jonathan, oh Jonathan," the distraught woman moaned. "She's gone, that vile man has taken her!"

A large hand closed around Jonathan's heart and squeezed it painfully. His breath caught in his chest and held there, refusing to be expelled.

"Spring," Lady Phoebe moaned the word with her last bit of strength and collapsed against Jonathan's chest.

Lifting her in his arms, Jonathan carried her into the house, crossed to the parlor and deposited her upon the brocade sofa. His gaze swept the room. Rinehardt sat in a chair with a towel held to his head, a doctor tending a gaping knife wound in his left arm. Rinehardt lowered the towel, exposing a second wound as he turned toward Jonathan.

"Sorry, Jonathan," Rinehardt said with a groan as the doctor continued the line of neat stitches closing the wound on his arm. "Took me by surprise." He raised the towel to wipe away a trickle of blood that oozed from the cut on his temple.

"He took her out the backdoor of the dressmaker's shop. Lady Phoebe didn't realize she was gone until I stumbled in."

"He probably would have killed her if she had come in on him," Jonathan said through clenched teeth as the muscle worked in his jaw. "How long?" Jonathan asked.

Rinehardt squinted toward the small ornate clock upon the mantle.

"Damn, if I can focus on the thing. What time is it?"

"Just past six," Jonathan answered.

"Been about three hours," Rinehardt answered.

Collins cursed, and for the first time since he'd arrived, Jonathan remembered his other friend. "She could be dead by now."

No, Jonathan told himself resolutely. If she were, he would know, because with her death the most important part of Jonathan would die, as well.

"We must search for her," Jonathan began.

"But where, Jonathan?" Collins asked. "We have no idea where he has taken her."

From the doorway Tobias took in the scene and let go with a low string of curses. "'E's taken 'er, then?"

Jonathan nodded.

"'E won't kill 'er, not yet," Tobias said in a low harsh voice. "'E'll use her to get to ye, Drew. That's why 'e's taken 'er."

Jonathan turned toward his friend. If anyone knew the workings of the deranged mind of Marcus Tollersley, it was Tobias.

"If he wants me, I'm here," Jonathan answered.

"Aye, but we've got to make sure 'e doesn't keep the upper hand. We've got to stay one step ahead of 'im, that's what."

"He has my wife. How can we hope to gain the upper hand?"

Tobias turned to Rinehardt. "It was 'imself what attacked ye?"

Rinehardt nodded.

"Reckon as 'ow 'is lordship's 'aving to do 'is own dirty work, now that 'is funds 'ave been cut off. That should work in our favor. Four against one, it is."

From the front of the house there came the sound of a scuffle, then a torrent of curses rent the evening air. A screech that would have done any banshee proud split the air and echoed throughout the house.

"What the hell?" Jonathan shouted.

In the hallway, Jacobs battled a dirty, skinny scruff of a boy who could have been anywhere from ten to fifteen years old. His thin body made it impossible to discern his age.

"What goes on here?" Jonathan shouted. "Do we not have enough trouble? Must we be beset with street urchins, as well? Jacobs feed the boy and toss him out."

"Her ladyship sent me, milord." The boy pulled away from Jacob's grasp and pulled himself up to his full height. He pushed out his thin chest and lifted his chin stubbornly.

Jonathan, who had turned toward the parlor, pivoted in one swift movement and pinned the boy to the spot with narrowed eyes.

"Who sent you?"

"The lady, the one the man chased, only my pa, he hid her."

Jonathan found he had to clench his hands to keep from throttling the boy. How dare Marcus send this pitiable bit of baggage to lure him into his trap? He caught the boy by the arm and propelled him into the parlor. Over his shoulder, he ordered Jacobs to bring food for the malnourished urchin. He harshly pushed the boy into a chair. Jonathan stood before him, his stance daring to the child to try to escape.

"How much did he pay you to come here?"

"Who? No one paid me. The lady said you'd give me a coin or two for my troubles, though."

Jonathan cursed. Catching the lad by the arm, he lifted him nearly from the chair. "If anything happens to my wife I will kill you slowly with my bare hands, do you hear me?"

The lad shook his head, his eyes wide and round with fear.

"Now, where is he holding her?"

"I done told ye, she's with me folks." The boy shrugged out of Jonathan's grip and rubbed his thin arm where Jonathan's fingers had bitten into the tender flesh. "Said as how you wouldn't believe me, she did."

"Did she?"

The boy nodded and dug in the pocket of his tattered trousers. "Said I should give you this." He held out his hand. Spring's wedding ring winked in the candlelight.

A shudder ran through Jonathan as he retrieved the small circle of gold from the boy's hand. Spring would not lightly have parted with it. But Marcus could have taken it from her. He closed his hand around the cold golden band, feeling that hand within his chest tighten again around his heart and twist.

The lad straightened his shoulders and lifted his chin defiantly. "Said to tell you 'twas from the highwayman's lady."

Jonathan smiled softly and slipped the ring on his little finger. Spring was alive. She had escaped yet again from the clutches of Marcus Tollersley.

"Quickly," Jonathan ordered as Jacobs returned with a tray of food. "The lad is but skin and bones. He is likely to pass out before we get the information we need."

"Wasn't weak when he tried to force his way past me in the hallway," Jacobs complained. "Was all I could do to hold the scamp. I swear he tried to bite me, he did."

"I tried to tell ye I'd a message from her ladyship. She told me not to leave once I got into the house, she did. Said you'd try to toss me out, but I shouldn't let ye do it." The boy's lower lip poked out in defiance, but its slight quiver ruined his defiant look.

Jonathan moved a step closer to the child. "You saw the man chasing my wife?"

The boy nodded, his eyes narrowed on Jacobs as he moved closer. "He forced his way in the door, looking for the lady, but we hid her, we did."

"And my lady, she is unharmed?" Jonathan asked.

"Except for having all me brothers and sisters climbing over her. His lordship weren't about to touch the likes of them, he weren't. Never suspected the lady was beneath our squirming bodies."

Jacobs placed the tray on the small table that Jonathan had pulled over in front of the boy. The child's eyes widened at the sight of more food in one place than he had ever seen in his short lifetime. It was more than his entire family consumed in a week.

The urchin reached hungrily for a piece of bread and shoved it into his mouth, then quickly followed it with a piece of cheese and a slice of meat. He gathered assorted vegetables and stuffed them into his mouth, as well.

"Slowly, don't choke yourself, lad," Jonathan cautioned. "You still have to show us where my lady is hiding."

"St. Giles," the boy answered through a mouth packed with food.

Lady Phoebe, who had finally regained her senses, sat up and gave a low moan. Hearing the dirty, starving urchin's words, she fell back again in a dead faint.

"Christ," Rinehardt echoed her distress.

Jonathan narrowed his gaze on his friend, questioning. "What is St. Giles?"

"The vilest place on earth," Tobias answered from where he hovered near the doorway. "Filled with the very dredges of the earth, with no hope for help in this life. St. Giles is the Irish Quarter."

When the boy had filled his small stomach to near explosive proportions, he looked at the remaining food enviously.

"My Ma," he said. "She's been sick since she lost the last babe. If she could have some of this food, it'd help her gain strength."

"Of course," Jonathan answered. He pulled the tablecloth from the small table then quickly bundled the remaining food into it.

Placing the bundle in the boy's hands, Jonathan laid his hand on the lad's shoulder as he studied his face intently for a moment. "If things are as you've said, my friend, I swear your family will never go lacking food again."

The boy's pinched face broke into a wide grin. "Milady is safe with my pa. He will not allow the man to take her."

Jacobs continued to hover near the door. Jonathan turned toward him. "Have the horses brought around. Two fresh mounts and Diablo."

Jonathan turned to Rinehardt, who endeavored to stand. "No, stay here with Lady Phoebe, just in case there is any trouble here. We've no to time waste. We must go to her before Marcus finds her."

He turned to Collins and Tobias, "Gentlemen, shall we go?"

With the boy seated in front of Jonathan, they started off at a rapid gallop toward St. Giles. The young boy gave directions as they quickly arrived at the intersection of Oxford and Tottenham Court.

"'Tis too narrow for horses, once we get to Bainbridge Street. 'Tis no more than a narrow alley," the boy said.

They reached the place where Oxford joined Tottenham Court almost at a right angle. Here the boy directed them to turn.

"Stop here," the boy instructed when they had traveled no more than a handful of minutes. "We'll have to go on foot the rest of the way."

The boy slid easily down from Diablo, and Jonathan quickly followed as did the other two men.

"Stay with the horses," Jonathan told Tobias as he handed the older man the stallion's reins. "Better keep a sharp watch for Marcus. He could still be in the area."

"Aye," Tobias answered gruffly. "'Tis sorry 'e'll be if I see 'im after all 'e's done."

"This way," the boy said as he tossed the food bag over his shoulder and turned into the alleyway.

It was just after they had squeezed past the coal cart that the stench hit them. "God in heaven," Collins muttered. "What is that foul odor?"

"'Tis the stench of the Quarter," the child answered.

They walked behind the boy single file, trying to miss the stagnant pools of evil, soapy water and other household slops that covered most of the narrow alley. Overhead, rows of wet sopping clothing dropped fetid water down upon them. Everywhere small children huddled naked and malnourished. The squalor was more than one could bear.

Jonathan tried to put the thought of Spring here in this horrid place out of his mind, but still it persisted. All around, the odors of death and decay festered. He could only imagine her horror at finding herself lost in this mess. *Soon, she will be safe. I will see to it.*

They followed the small lad through the maze of back alleys, a veritable rabbit's warren of hidden squalor. The stench was overpowering. Jonathan looked back and saw that Collins had pulled his handkerchief out and held it over his mouth and nose. Intent on keeping up with the child as he scurried through the maze, Jonathan hadn't dared to take time to do the same.

"Here, 'tis here," the boy announced and turned toward a small doorway leading to a basement hovel.

At once, Jonathan was alert to the danger. He caught the lad just as he was about to disappear through the narrow doorway. If the boy got away now, they might never find Spring. He turned to Collins.

"Stay here, it could be a trap." Jonathan glanced over his should toward his friend and was reassured by the man's quick nod.

Chapter Thirty-Three

S pring had cleaned the hovel as best she could in the hours since Marcus had given up his search for her. She had tended the sick woman, cleaned her up gently with the meager means available to her. Mr. O'Shey had smiled as Spring sought to help his wife. The children huddled nearby. Every now and then, the youngest, Eileen, would reach out to touch the hem of Spring's gown or to lift a golden curl and let it slip through her fingers.

The O'Shey's had offered to share their meager meal with her, but Spring had refused. She would not be here much longer. Jonathan would come for her. She tried not to allow herself to think that Jonathan might still be at Wyndridge. These people needed every crust of bread they managed to procure. Spring knew the crusts of bread were like as not stolen or ferreted from the trash dump behind some restaurant. Her heart went out to these people who, with all their own trouble, had been willing to protect her from Marcus.

Spring was sitting talking with Mrs. O'Shey when the small door of the hovel flew open. The children at once gathered around her, seeking to hide as they had earlier.

A large shadow filled the doorway. Something about it was familiar, less frightening somehow. She struggled to push the children aside.

"Where is she?" a familiar voice demanded.

"Jonathan!"

Pushing the children gently aside, Spring flung herself across the room and into Jonathan's arms. Her momentum almost carried them through the open doorway.

"Easy, Love," Jonathan soothed as he regained his balance and pulled her closer into his arms.

"Pa's looking for the other man," one of the children volunteered. "Don't want he should come back and find the lady."

The young boy who had guided Jonathan to Spring crossed the room and knelt beside his mother. He gently unwrapped the parcel of food and offered it to her.

"See here what I brought ye?" he said, "Ye'll get yer strength back now, for sure."

"The children, give it to the children," she whispered.

Jonathan crossed the room with Spring held protectively in the shelter of his arm. "There's plenty more where that came from Mrs.—" Jonathan stopped as he realized he didn't know the woman's name.

"O'Shey," a deep voice spoke from the doorway. "Thomas O'Shey, and this is my wife, Aine."

Jonathan turned to face the man who had entered the hovel, extending his hand toward him.

"Sir, I am forever in your debt. You have without doubt saved the life of my wife."

The man studied Jonathan carefully in the dim light. "Don't sound English."

"American," Jonathan answered.

Thomas O'Shey smiled broadly. "Rather risk me life saving the wife of an American than a Englisher, any day."

"You have my profound thanks, Mr. O'Shey."

"Little enough to do for a lady in distress. And she has been kind to my misses while she's been here." Thomas nodded toward Spring. "Glad you're safe, milady."

Jonathan pulled a pouch from his vest and held it out to Thomas O'Shey. The man stood looking at it for a moment, then his gaze moved to his wife and children.

Finally, he shook his head. "O'Shey's don't take charity."

Jonathan nodded. "Then let me pay the lad for the work he has done." Jonathan emptied the pouch into his hand. "Sinclairs always pay their debts," Jonathan said as he dropped the coins on the cloth between the boy and his mother.

The boy quickly looked toward his father. O'Shey slowly nodded his assent. "Reckon the lad did earn the money."

"That and more," Jonathan agreed.

Jonathan's gaze swept the hovel, taking in the children huddled in the corner and moving on to Mrs. O'Shey on her pallet. Then he turned back to O'Shey and looked the man up and down. He pulled Spring tighter against his side.

"I find myself in need of a new caretaker for my estate." Jonathan's gaze again swept the children. "My uncle has not kept the place up to my standards. There is much work to be done. It will take a strong family to take care of Wyndridge Hall and the stables. A family with many strong lads. Do you think there might be such a family in the area?"

"There might be such a one," O'Shey answered cautiously.

"It'll take a large family with," Jonathan gazed again at the cluster of children in the corner then back to the lad sitting at his mother's side. "at least four lads to help with the stables and perhaps a girl to help with the housework. Of course, the family will have to relocate. But they would have a home for as long as they wanted it, and all the food they could ever eat."

With effort, Aine O'Shey lifted herself off the rags that made up her pallet, fixing her gaze on Jonathan. "Reckon we might be just about what you'd be looking for, might we not, milord?"

Jonathan smiled at the woman, nodding. He produced a card from his pocket and handed it to O'Shey.

"Take this to the office of Mr. Bailey in Whitehall. He will make the arrangements for your journey to Wyndridge. Later, when your family is stronger, if you should wish it, I will arrange passage for you to America."

"You are too kind, milord," Aine O'Shey whispered, gazing at Jonathan through tear washed eyes.

"Your family risked much for my wife. That is a debt I can never repay." Jonathan turned toward the doorway where Collins waited. "We must go now. My lady has been through much this day. If there is anything you need, you have but to ask Mr. Bailey, and it will be provided. My thanks to you and your family again, Thomas O'Shey, for the aid you have extended to my wife."

The lad left his mother's side and stood beside his father. "I'll show you the way back through the back allies. Don't want you to be getting lost with milady."

When they emerged from the dingy alley, Jonathan lifted Spring into his arms and strode quickly back down the narrow passage. The lad, followed by Collins, led the way. Thomas O'Shey covered their backs as they passed back through the dismal quarter, then along Bainbridge alley and back out onto Tottenham Court.

"Ye found 'er," Tobias exclaimed as they emerged from the squalor of the Irish Quarter.

"Was there ever any question that he would?" Spring asked confidently.

Jonathan lifted Spring upon Diablo's back then hurried to mount behind her. He wheeled the great stallion around and held tightly to the reins when Diablo pranced, impatient to be off.

His gaze settled on Thomas O'Shey. "You and yours are welcome on my lands, be it here in England or America. The choice is yours," Jonathan said just before he put heels to the stallion and led his small band down Tottenham toward Oxford Street.

He tightened his arms around her protectively. His jaw clenched, and his eyes narrowed. Tobias had been right. It would not be over until Marcus Tollersley was dead. They could not leave their quest unfinished, after all.

Spring felt Jonathan's arms tighten around her possessively. He pulled her against his chest. His chin rested on the top of her head as they rode along in silence. She laid her head against his chest, listening to the strong beating of his heart. There had been a moment when she was certain she would never feel Jonathan's arms around her again, never hear the gentle beating of his heart or the tenderness of his voice against her hair. A tear rolled down her cheek and splashed on his hands where they held the reins.

Strength, she needed strength. She did not want Jonathan to see how close to breaking she had been. She forced the tears back, managing to stop the hiccup that threatened to reduce her to further tears. She must think of her grandmother. How very afraid she must have been when she realized Marcus had taken her.

"Grandmother, she must be so frightened," Spring whispered. "Marcus threatened to kill grandmother and Rinehardt. I was so afraid for them."

"Your grandmother is fine. Rinehardt is recovering. He stayed with her to protect her in case Tollersley returned."

"Recovering?" Spring asked, looking up to search Jonathan's face.

"Tollersley attacked him and left him for dead. By the time Rinehardt came too and ran into the shop, you were gone."

"Marcus was going to use me to get you. I couldn't let him do that, so I ran." She took a deep shuddering breath. "I couldn't—"

"It's over. You're safe now, Love," Jonathan whispered against her hair.

She felt his warm breath stir the hair at the side of her face, felt its caress against the shell of her ear. She snuggled closer against his chest, turning her head to press her ear against it, listening to the strong beating of his heart.

She touched his right hand where it held the reins then let her fingers trail over the back of his hand. Her fingertips traced the blue vein beneath his tan skin. He passed the reins over to his left hand then captured her hand with his.

Their fingers intertwined. She felt the small gold band on his little finger and smiled. He gave a slight squeeze to her hand then lifted it to his lips. Spring trembled as his lips skimmed the surface of her palm. She pressed her hand against his cheek.

"Is it really over?" Spring asked, searching Jonathan's face.

"You're safe now, Love." Jonathan kissed her cheek and rubbed his nose against hers. He curled her hand against his chest, his hand holding it in place.

When they returned to the Lansing townhouse, Jonathan carried Spring inside and up to their room. He ignored her protest that she could walk. He ordered a bath prepared and stayed to assist her with her toilet, then he tucked her safely into bed. Once he had seen her safely to bed, Jonathan sat beside her for a moment, gazing down at her. Slowly he removed her wedding ring from his finger and slid it back on hers. He lifted her hand and kissed the ring as if to lock it in place.

Spring reached up to touch Jonathan's face. Her fingers lingered on the firm line of his jaw as her eyes focused on his. There were many things written there, not the least of which was anger.

"It's not finished," he said softly. "I thought we could just walk away from it, but it will never be finished as long as Marcus lives."

Spring nodded slowly as tears gathered in her eyes. Jonathan lifted her hand and kissed her palm, then he slowly folded the fingers of her hand over the spot. He sat beside her until sleep claimed her.

When Jonathan returned to the parlor, a frown deepened the lines on his forehead, and his lips set in a firm straight line. Spring had fallen asleep shortly after he had tucked her into bed. He had wanted to remain with her but knew there was much to be done.

They must devise some new plan to draw Marcus out into the open, but what?

Tobias stood near the window, gazing out into the eerie light cast by the gaslight. He turned when Jonathan entered the room.

"She's all right, then?" Tobias asked as Jonathan moved to the side table and poured himself a brandy.

"Tired but unharmed."

"It's my fault," Rinehardt said. "I should have been more alert. I just didn't think he would be so bold as to try something in the middle of London."

"He's desperate. We must not underestimate him, again," Jonathan answered quietly.

"Aye, that be true," Tobias agreed.

"Then we must draw him out, make him come to us," Rinehardt suggested. "Set a trap for him and be damned ready when he falls into it."

"My thoughts, exactly," Jonathan responded.

"What do you propose?" Collins asked.

Jonathan looked from one to the other of his friends, letting his gaze linger for a moment on each before going on to the next. He swirled his brandy in the crystal goblet then downed it in one long draft before he spoke.

"Gentlemen, I think it's time to live up to my new station in life. It's been quite a while since we spent the night taking in the clubs. Are you up to it? I feel like celebrating my inheritance. It's time the Earl of Wyndridge was properly introduced to London society."

"Up to it?" Collins exclaimed. "My dear chap, we wrote the book on carousing, or had you forgotten?"

"Yes, yes, quite the thing to do," Rinehardt agreed.

"Like as not ye'll get yerself killed," Tobias scoffed.

"Not as long as you're on guard, my friend." Jonathan clapped Tobias on the back. "I trust you implicitly."

For the next week Jonathan, Collins and Rinehardt spent their nights circulating from club to club, taking in the nightlife. It was, Jonathan declared, a party to celebrate the restoration of his rightful inheritance. While they caroused, Tobias lingered in the shadows, waiting and watching.

They began at White's then went on to the Reform Club and on to the infamous gambling den of Crockford's on St. James Street. Everywhere they went, they were obnoxiously loud, and money flowed as freely as the spirits. They returned home late in the morning, reeking of alcohol, tobacco and perfume from their time in the infamous finishes or long taverns filled with prostitutes and young dandies.

Chapter Thirty-Four

Thus, the pattern for their evenings was set, Jonathan fell into the carousing with his friends, drinking, gambling and finally moving on to the long rooms. Jonathan drew the line at the selection of a prostitute at these flesh markets. He watched as the fashionable and wealthy young men chose their mistresses. He was quickly tiring of this scene and longed to spend quiet evenings at home with his wife, but for her safety as well as his own, he dared not give up before Marcus took the bait.

By the fifth night, his head ached from too much spirits, and his eyes smarted from the tobacco smoke, while his senses recoiled at the fetid smell that lingered in the Finish.

Despite their best efforts, Marcus did not make a move against him. After the botched attempt to abduct Spring, *Marcus might even have left the country*. Jonathan nursed his glass of brandy and scanned the crowded gaming room of White's.

Mirrors everywhere reflected the scene, while wide French windows opened onto the terraces that held tubs of beautiful summer flowers. A thousand gas lights glittered brilliantly, their candle power enhanced by the mirrored walls.

Every night Jonathan and his entourage made themselves conspicuous by their ribald laughter and heavy consumption of alcohol while Tobias kept watch.

SPRING HAD HAD ENOUGH. She was grateful for Collins' and Rinehardt's support of Jonathan's cause, but enough was enough.

Every evening they appeared at her grandmother's door, and every evening Jonathan disappeared with them.

The first time or two, Spring had rationalized it away. Jonathan had won his case against his uncle and deserved to spend some time in celebration. She had pretended not to notice when he had returned past five in the morning, reeking of tobacco, spirits and cheap perfume. But night after night they followed the same pattern. It was getting to be more than a body could endure.

As dusk fell over the city, they left dressed for an evening's entertainment. She watched from her window and saw Jonathan, Collins and Rinehardt climb into the Baron's coach and rumble away. Within moments, Tobias followed on horseback. Always the same pattern.

Spring had risen early in the morning and waited at her window for their return. The early morning air held a slight chill, and she sat huddled in the window seat. She pulled her robe tighter around her as she waited.

The coach rumbled down the street, stopping before the Lansing townhouse. Jonathan, Collins and Rinehardt tumbled out and arm in arm they staggered toward the townhouse singing a riotous ditty and generally having a grand time. From the shadows across the street, Tobias materialized and followed them into the house.

Something about the scene nagged at Spring. Something wasn't right. The pieces just didn't quite fit. She had seen the revelers return with her own eyes, yet something told her all was not as it seemed.

All day Spring puzzled over her husband's behavior. Why had he suddenly turned into such a libertine? Had he always been such? No, she would have sensed it, would have known. Jonathan had not been a rake. Granted, Rinehardt had a notorious reputation as such. And Collins' name had been touched by more than one breath of scandal. Was it indeed possible that Jonathan thought his newly acquired station in life required him to have a reputation as a rake and libertine? Albeit a married one?

No, something more was going on. Why, if they were simply going out carousing, did Tobias follow every night? Why was Tobias left to follow under cover of darkness? Had Jonathan suddenly become so class conscious that his friend was no longer good enough to accompany him?

No, Spring refused to believe Jonathan had become so callous. He would not slight his friend. There had to be some other explanation.

On the fifth morning as Spring watched the familiar scene, it finally became clear what she had been missing. As Tobias materialized from the shadows and followed Jonathan and his friends into the townhouse, it suddenly dawned what she had been missing.

Tobias was the rear guard. Jonathan was setting himself up as bait to draw Marcus out into the open. Spring whirled away from the window and marched down the hall just as Jonathan, Collins, Rinehardt and a fourth man unfamiliar to Spring entered the townhouse. Standing in the shadows at the top of the stairs, she listened.

"You can stay here until you're able to find lodgings," Jonathan said to the newcomer. "I'm sure Lady Phoebe won't mind."

"Deucedly kind of you, cousin," the younger man answered.

"Think nothing of it, cousin." Jonathan smiled as he turned to follow Rinehardt and Collins into the parlor.

"Damnation," Jonathan grated, his voice unaffected by drink. "I thought surely he would have made his move by now."

"Might be out of the country by now," Collins suggested.

"No, he's here," Jonathan answered. "At times I can almost feel his eyes on me, feel the hatred of his gaze."

"Christ," the fourth man that Spring didn't recognize whispered, "Did you see what they did to that poor woman?"

Rinehardt laughed, but it held a hollow sound. "Mattimore, my dear chap. That poor woman was well paid for her trouble. She knew what she was getting into when she went there. She's a fancy piece, just like the others. Beautiful but a paid whore, just the same."

Spring gasped, forcing her fist against her mouth to suppress the heated words that rose to her tongue. Where had these men taken her husband?

"Heard talk of those places, but never been to one before," young Mattimore said. "There must have been at least a hundred of them all lined up and displaying their wares."

Collins reached over and clapped Mattimore upon the back. "'Tis educational for you then. You're of an age to know all about the gin palaces and Finishes of London. But just remember, we've work to do. Don't get caught up in the entertainment. We don't want to get Jonathan or ourselves killed."

Spring shrank back into the shadows. Get Jonathan killed? What exactly were they doing that was so dangerous?

Quietly she slipped back to her room and pretended to be asleep when Jonathan came to bed.

He had bathed and changed his clothing so the smell of tobacco and spirits and cheap perfume that had filled the hall were gone. He smelled of soap and masculine energy, instead.

Spring protested, feigning sleep and slowly opened her eyes as if from a deep sleep when Jonathan pulled her into his embrace. Wherever he had been, whatever he had been doing, it was she that he had returned to, her body that he held close and caressed as the sun rose casting pink shadows across their room.

All thoughts fled her mind as Jonathan pulled her into his embrace and slowly coaxed her mouth to open beneath his. One hand found her breast, his nimble fingers tugging and squeezing at her nipple bringing a moan from her throat. Then his hand slid down, molding the shape of her waist and down to her hip. His fingers slowly gathered the soft material of her gown and began inching it upward.

"I missed you," he whispered as he trailed kisses across her cheek.

"I'm sure you were busy with your friends." She felt his lips curl into a slight smile against the flesh of her neck.

"They are not you, wife."

"Then perhaps you shouldn't have gone out with them." She let the slight sense of hurt weigh in her words.

"Nay, Love. I do what I must but always long to be here with you." He pulled the gown up and over her head then rolled to cover her body with his. All thought of what Jonathan and his friends were up to fled as he claimed her with fervor. Her world narrowed to Jonathan and all rational thought fled, driven from her consciousness by Jonathan's skilled caresses.

Later, once Jonathan had left her bed, Spring stretched and turned to gaze out the window of her room, watching minute dust specs float in the shaft of sunlight filtering through the lace covered window.

What had Jonathan and the others been up to that could put their lives in danger if they were not careful? The idea that Jonathan was exposing himself to danger caused Spring's protective instincts to come to the forefront.

If Jonathan was in danger, then she must do something to protect him.

A plan began to form in the back of her mind as she surrendered to the lure of sleep caused by her nightly vigil waiting for her husband to return.

Jonathan held his drink and gazed around the long room with narrowed eyes. This was their last stop of the night. It was the most sordid part of the pattern they had established. Known as the Green

Palace, this particular gin-palace was the most notorious of all the Finishes of the West End. Here, for a price, a gentleman could enjoy anything from the charms of the city's loveliest courtesans to a handsome young lad. High stakes card games that could, with a shuffle of the deck, see a fortune change hands and a man ruined.

Watching the depths of depravity that men sank to sickened Jonathan. Night after night he had watched as the scene unfolded around him. There was no lack of entertainment in the gin-palace. Money could purchase anything, all manner of amusements were offered those regular clients of the palace with the coin to pay.

A favorite entertainment was the plying of a particularly beautiful courtesan with spirits until she fell down dead drunk on the floor. Then to the uproarious laughter of the *so-called* gentlemen, all manner of drinks were dumped upon her prostrate form until the satin of her gown remained a blotch of colors and sordid stains. Of course, as Rinehardt quickly pointed out, the courtesan in question had been well compensated for her part in the farce. But still, Jonathan felt the rise of bile in his throat at the sight.

Forcing his gaze away from the crumpled form on the floor, Jonathan let his gaze travel across the room to where a very young dandy, slight of form and fair of face, stared with wide transfixed eyes at the unconscious woman on the floor.

Everywhere they had gone this night, Jonathan remembered seeing this particular young dandy always lingering close by. The boy was dressed in a fine coat of a deep blue hue and embroidered waist coat. His trousers were well tailored, showing off a well-turned leg, and upon his head he wore a tam that matched his waist coat. Jonathan felt a strange sense of familiarity, yet he was sure he had never met the lad.

The boy looked barely old enough to be out of the schoolroom, let alone frequent the most notorious gin-palace of London. If the lad was not careful, he would find himself the object of the attentions of some of the palaces' less savory clientele.

Jonathan had noticed several men known for their perchance for a handsome face casting glances in the boy's direction already.

Maybe he should warn the shaveling, Jonathan thought as he watched the wide-eyed youth for a moment longer. His eyes met the lad's for an instant before the lad's gaze dared away and he quickly hurried away into the crowd. Maybe the lad had realized the precarious position he was in, after all. Jonathan felt relieved as he turned away in search of his friends.

Allowing his gaze to sweep the room, Jonathan spotted Rinehardt at a gaming table in the connecting room. From the pleased look on his friend's face, Jonathan surmised he was having a profitable evening.

Collins stood close by, watching the card game. The man across the table from Rinehardt threw down his cards and pushed his chair away from the table as Rinehardt pulled the pile of chips across the table with a slow calculated smile.

Rinehardt rose as Jonathan approached.

"Baron Longley, may I present my friend, Jonathan Sinclair, Earl Wyndridge."

Longley looked Jonathan over slowly before greeting him. "Wyndridge? Of course, I heard about the case. An American, I believe?"

Jonathan inclined his head slightly, acknowledging Longley's words.

"Your uncle was not pleased by the Lord Chancellor's decision, I dare say," Longley said as he continued gazing at Jonathan.

"No doubt," Jonathan agreed. "Have you seen my uncle recently?

Longley thought for a moment, placing one finger beside his cheek as he studied Jonathan. "Yes, I seem to remember almost colliding with him as I entered White's this evening. He seemed in quite a hurry. Almost ran me down, he did."

Jonathan, Collins, and Rinehardt exchanged knowing glances. Maybe their quarry had not escaped them, after all. Excitement coursed through Jonathan. Perhaps soon their quest would be over, and he could return his full attention to Spring.

It was nearing five in the morning. Soon the gin-palace would be closing down. Jonathan saw Mattimore where he had been enjoying a fine Havana cigar. His younger cousin had been flirting with a beautiful, young courtesan. The woman wore a sparkling gown, the bodice of which curved so low the pink crests of her nipples were visible above the last row of lace clinging to the smooth white skin of the mounds of her breasts.

At a glance from Jonathan, Mattimore crushed out his cigar and moved to join Jonathan.

Several clients of the gin-palace were too much in their cups, and Jonathan watched in disgust as they were dumped into the cellar to sleep it off. Others, those still able to mumble out an address in their thick intoxicated voices, were bundled into waiting carriages or hired cabs and sent away.

Jonathan looked around for the young dandy, but the lad had disappeared. Was he even now with some beautiful courtesan, or had the lad himself fallen into the clutches of some fashionable gentleman with unsavory desires?

Jonathan pushed the idea from his mind. The lad wasn't his responsibility. The dandy had found his way around the secret nightlife of London so he could damn well find his own way back to the polite side of London society. At any rate, it wasn't his concern Jonathan told himself as he turned to his friends.

"Gentlemen," Jonathan said to his comrades. "Shall we go?"

Chapter Thirty-Five

Jonathan felt the hair at the nape of his neck stand on end. Would tonight be the night his uncle took the bait? He scanned the shadows where the gaslights did not reach. Was that a movement? Johnathan's eyes narrowed as he searched the darkness. This was the most vulnerable part of their trek. If Marcus was going to strike, it would be now.

The coach had been purposefully left more than a score of yards from the entrance of the log house. They made a clean target as they walked down the darkened street toward it. Marcus would have the perfect chance as they walked beneath the gaslight.

They had nearly reached the coach when a shape separated itself from the darkness. At once, Jonathan stiffened, and his friends at his side did likewise. Suddenly all were at attention. A second figure materialized and before the first had a chance to act, it crumpled lifelessly to the ground.

They ran to the spot where Tobias stood over his prey.

"'E's not dead." Tobias said as Jonathan knelt beside the prone figure. "Not yet, anyway."

Mattimore leaned closer. "Is it him?"

"Can't tell," Jonathan answered. "It's too dark to see his face. Bring a lantern from the coach."

"Careful," Tobias warned as they crouched over the prostrate form.

In a moment, Mattimore returned with the lantern and held it high so the light shown on the prone figure.

Jonathan's eyes widened as he recognized the distinctive coat, the tam, and slim figure.

"Damn," Jonathan cursed softly.

"It's not 'im?"

Jonathan shook his head as he caught the thin shoulders and slowly turned the small figure face up in the lantern light. "It's not Marcus."

"It's not Marcus," Jonathan repeated.

But 'e's been slipping around after ye all night," Tobias grated. "I watched 'im."

"Well, let's have a look at him, shall we?" Rinehardt declared, urging Mattimore to hold the lantern closer. "Why is he wearing that stupid tam?"

Catching the offending hat, Rinehardt pulled it from the boy's head and a riot of golden curls spilled free.

Jonathan groaned. He had known there was something familiar about those wide green eyes that kept seeking him out.

"Lady Spring," young Mattimore exclaimed as Jonathan pulled the crumpled form into his arms. "Why those are my clothes!"

The younger man sputtered as he pointed toward the prone form. "She is wearing my new suit!" He pointed toward the coat. "What is wrong with wearing a tam?" He turned an accusing glare toward Rinehardt. "It's all the rage in Paris this season."

He reached out to brush a bit of dirt off the sleeve of the coat. "Had it made in Paris and planned to wear it to my aunt's ball."

Rinehardt snickered. "Afraid you're going to have to find something else to wear to the ball." He snickered again. "Beside which, I think Lady Spring wears it much smarter than you would have."

"Of course, I will compensate you for their loss." Jonathan's gaze never left the face of the woman in his arms. "My tailor will be glad of the business. He is the best in London."

"What the 'ell?" Tobias exclaimed as he moved closer to see the crumpled figure in Jonathan's arms.

"Our little trap has snared the wrong rabbit," Collins said as he stared down at the unconscious figure in Jonathan's arms.

"Quite."

"Ye should've told the girl what ye were about," Tobias said.

Jonathan met that comment with a glare. Without a word, he lifted Spring and carried her toward the coach.

"Quickly," Jonathan ordered. "We must get her away from here before anyone recognizes her."

Rinehardt, Collins and Mattimore followed Jonathan to the coach while Tobias left in the opposite direction. Jonathan held the unconscious form of his wife in his arms as the coach traveled rapidly through the empty streets. She moaned once but still did not open her eyes.

"Not a word of this to anyone," Jonathan warned his friends.

Rinehardt smiled as did Collins, while Mattimore blushed.

"Not a word," they all agreed.

"Would appear your bride—" Collins began but was cut off.

"Has had an accident. She fell down the stairs at the Lansing townhouse. We found her when we returned to the house."

Jonathan carefully felt the back of Spring's head and found a large lump the size of a hen's egg. He tested the skin carefully but found no dampness. The blow had rendered her unconscious but had not drawn blood, probably due to the tam with all her hair tucked underneath. *How hard had Tobias hit her?*

Jonathan held the limp figure of his wife in his arms.

Her breathing was steady, but her color, for what he could see in the dim light of the coach, was pale. Though she did not appear to be in any danger, she would probably have the devil's own headache for a couple of days.

He stroked the tangle of golden curls away from her face. It would serve the minx right if she did. She'd had no business going out alone, much less following him through all the gaming hells and debauchery that she had.

The coach stopped in front of the Lansing townhouse, and all attention focused on Jonathan and Spring as he lowered her tenderly to the seat of the coach. He glared at his companions.

"Not a word of this," he hissed. "Do you hear? It never happened."

"Of course," both Collins and Mattimore answered with sheepish grins.

"Gentleman's honor," Rinehardt added.

One after the other the three men stepped down from the coach, standing guard as they waited for Jonathan to emerge.

Jonathan swiped a hand across his face. He leaned closer to Spring and touched her throat feeling for her pulse. He found it strong and even. He smoothed a hand down the fabric of the frock coat covering Spring's slight form. He smiled. The minx, what exactly had she thought she was doing?

Only then did Jonathan reach to pull the tam back on to Spring's head, tucking those golden curls beneath it carefully before he lifted her gently into his arms.

"Leave your drunken friend where he is. We have a score to settle," a voice said from the shadows beside the coach.

Jonathan stiffened.

"All of you, put your hands up where I can see them," Marcus demanded as he moved forward. The gun in his hand was trained on Jonathan's back. "Back against the coach and keep your hands in the air," he instructed the others.

Jonathan quickly lowered Spring back to the coach seat, praying the tam stayed in place, hoping she did not regain consciousness. He quickly moved to the door of the coach, using his body to block the view inside. If Marcus thought her to be just some dandy in his cups, then she, at least, might survive.

"Hands up," Marcus ordered again as Jonathan turned to face him. The older man waved the gun threateningly at Jonathan.

"Now see here," Rinehardt began, his voice slurred. "You can't treat my friend like this."

"I say," Collins chimed in, stumbling toward Marcus drunkenly. "Do you know who we are?"

"Yes, uncle," Jonathan picked up the taunting as he lurched from the door of the coach, stumbling off the step and barely managing to catch himself as he landed on the street before Marcus. When he straightened in front of Marcus, he held a gun in his hand as did his friends. "These are my friends."

Unaffected by their ploy, Marcus centered his attention on Jonathan.

"I'm going to kill you."

"Like you had my father killed?"

"No, this time I will do it myself."

"You can't do this," Mattimore insisted. "Too many witnesses."

For an instant Marcus turned an evil glance toward the Viscount. "Dead men don't talk." He kept this gun trained upon Jonathan the entire time. "Now drop your weapons and be careful about it, one slip and I'll put a hole through *Earl Wyndridge's* chest." His voice held a contemptuous snarl as he said the words.

When Jonathan moved, Marcus returned his attention to him, the gun centered on his chest.

"Wouldn't care for the odds, myself," Collins said slowly. "Four to one, don't be a fool, man. Put the gun down."

Marcus raked them with his dark gaze. "I'll shoot him," he jabbed the gun toward Jonathan's chest. "first."

"That would still leave three, odds are against you," Collins taunted.

Jonathan moved with lightning speed toward Marcus, but the older man had anticipated his attack He raised the gun and brought it down across Jonathan head. Jonathan stumbled to the side, for an instant stunned by the blow.

Marcus again trained the gun on Jonathan's chest.

In the split second that Marcus's attention was distracted, Tobias materialized from the shadows. He held Jonathan's revolver confidently in his right hand.

"Now, yer bloody lordship," Tobias spoke softly. "Ye drop the gun or prepare yerself for 'ell."

"You've lost," Rinehardt said softly. "Why don't you just let it go?"

"I don't bluff," Marcus said as he cocked the pistol he held aimed directly at Jonathan's heart.

Spring regained consciousness just as Jonathan stepped from the coach. She recognized Marcus' voice at once. A cold chill swept through her. Terror crystalized in her chest. Her breath lodged in her. Her eyes refused to focus for a moment, then finally the scene came into focus. Through the window of the coach, she saw Marcus Tollersley pointing a gun at Jonathan's chest. She heard the words that passed between Marcus and Jonathan. She heard Jonathan's friends when they tried to talk Marcus down.

This was her doing, her fault. Because she had wanted to know what her husband was up to, her curiosity had brought disaster down upon their heads. Because of her, Jonathan had dropped his guard, because of her, he would die.

Carefully, slowly she turned her body on the seat and inched closer to the coach door. Desperately, she tried to think of something to do. Some way to protect Jonathan from the hatred that consumed his uncle.

For a second, when she heard Tobias' voice, she hoped the tables might turn in Jonathan's favor. But with the ominous click of Marcus' pistol, she knew Jonathan's life was forfeit. Marcus would die but would take Jonathan with him.

Without stopping to think what her actions might mean, Spring launched herself from the coach. A blood curdling scream ripped from her throat.

"Noooo!" she screamed, throwing herself in front of Jonathan.

A scream rent the air, and two shots rang out.

Jonathan had no time to react. One second Tobias and Marcus were at a Mexican standoff, the very next instant Spring plowed into him, pushing him out the way of Marcus' bullet.

The report of Tobias' gun blared with deadly accuracy. Marcus crumpled slowly to the ground a look of disbelief colored his features. His smoking gun dropped from his lifeless hand.

Jonathan's arms closed around the thin figure in men's clothing that draped across him. His hand encountered something warm and wet.

"I love you," Spring whispered as her eyelids fluttered closed.

"Bloody hell," Jonathan groaned as he swept her into his arms. "Get at doctor fast," he ordered as he turned and strode toward the house, taking the steps two at a time in his haste to get Spring inside.

Collins commandeered the horse Tobias had left at the edge of the yard and set off at once, while Tobias moved to retrieve the gun that had fallen from Marcus' hand. Young Mattimore stared in wide eyed horror at the limp figure on the street.

"Should send for the authorities, I suppose," Rinehardt said as he walked around the fallen man and followed Jonathan toward the house. Mattimore quickly followed.

"Is it bad?" the younger man asked as he followed Jonathan into the house.

"Can't tell until I get this blasted coat off," Jonathan answered as he turned into the bedroom he shared with his wife. A moment later he lowered Spring to the bed.

"Light the lamp," Jonathan ordered, and Mattimore moved to do so, but his trembling hands fumbled the effort.

"Here, let me do it." Rinehardt took the lamp from Mattimore's shaking hands. Soon a soft glow filled the room.

Jonathan leaned closer to Spring. Her breath shallow, eyes closed, and all color had drained from her face. Jonathan prayed silently.

He stripped the coat from her, exposing the spreading bright red stain growing across the white silk shirt she wore. Jonathan swore.

"Get some towels," Jonathan instructed as he caught the fine material of the shirt and ripped it from top to bottom. "I have to put pressure on the wound to stop the bleeding."

Chapter Thirty-Six

It seemed like hours before the doctor arrived. Jonathan sat on the corner of the bed holding a towel to the wound in the upper left section of Spring's back. Each time he lifted the cloth, the gush of blood resumed. So much blood. With each beat of her heart, her life's blood oozed from the wound. Jonathan kept pressure on the wound, hoping to stem the flow.

Fear knotted in his stomach as he pressed the towel to the wound. Spring remained deathly still. Jonathan was afraid, more afraid than he'd ever been in his entire life. The knot of fear in his belly tightened, moving upward to squeeze the breath from his lungs. It lingered there, forming a tight band around his heart. She had to live. He could not live without her.

The doctor arrived and cleared the room, except for Jonathan. He hadn't even noticed that Rinehardt and Mattimore still hovered nearby as he withered in his own private hell, a hell of his own making. He should have set her free. It was his fault she had been injured, his selfishness that brought her to this.

Jonathan raked a hand through his dark hair and moved to watch the doctor as he probed the wound with shinny instruments. Jonathan felt the pain as sharply as if it were his own flesh beneath the doctor's forceps.

"Got it," the doctor announced triumphantly, holding the bullet toward the lamp.

The doctor sprinkled a yellow powder over the wound then used his needle to draw the wound closed. He placed clean gauze over the wound then applied a bandage over Spring's shoulder and around her torso.

"She's lost a lot of blood, but the bleeding has slowed," the doctor said as he wiped blood from his instruments then placed them back into his case.

"She will live," Jonathan whispered. It was not a question but an order.

The doctor studied Jonathan's set features for a moment then slowly nodded his head. "Yes, I rather think she will, but keep her as still as possible for the next few days. If the bleeding starts again, well..." He looked at Jonathan again. "Just keep her still."

"Thank you, Doctor," Jonathan said as he moved closer to the still figure on the bed.

Kneeling beside the bed, he took her small hand in his and held it against his lips as he prayed silently for her to return to him. He stroked the golden curls away from her face, his heart breaking. He lay his head beside hers on the bed, entreating, begging her to come back to him.

"I'll check on her later this evening," the doctor said as he placed a small vial on the dresser. "Give her this for the pain. It will help her rest."

"Thank you, doctor."

From the hallway there came a loud commotion followed by shouts and oaths.

The doctor looked at Jonathan and winked. "I'd give Lady Phoebe a dose, as well."

With that he collected his bag and left the room quickly. The doctor sought to escape the wrath of the older woman who was rapidly bearing down on the room.

"What is this? What has happened?" Lady Phoebe burst into the room. "The authorities are prowling all over the house! They say Marcus is dead, and my granddaughter is injured."

Jonathan stood and stepped forward.

"Out of my way, I demand to see my granddaughter!"

Lady Phoebe tried to sidestep Jonathan, but he caught her arms, holding her in his firm grip. "Why wasn't I summoned at once?" she demanded as she struggled against Jonathan's grip.

Jonathan sighed. "Because, my dearest lady," he began. "there was no time. Besides which, you would only have become hysterical."

"Hysterical?" Lady Phoebe turned on Jonathan. "I have never had a fit of hysteric in my life. I've buried two husbands and my only son without a hint of it. If you persist in keeping me from my granddaughter, I assure you the fit I throw will not be from hysterics." Lady Phoebe pulled herself up to her full height of five feet and glared at her grandson-in-law.

"She's unconscious," Jonathan said as he moved aside so that Lady Phoebe could see Spring. "It was just as well, because the doctor had a difficult time extracting the bullet. The pain would have been unbearable."

"My pet," Lady Phoebe murmured as she knelt beside the bed. "What have they done to you?"

Jonathan flinched at her words. He moved to the window. A light mist had begun to fall. "She saved my life, but it very nearly her cost own." Jonathan's voice choked off. He hung his head, his shoulders drooping with the weight of the world upon them.

Pulling a chair close beside the bed, Jonathan sank into it. He buried his head in his hands. All his fault, this was all his doing. How many mistakes could one man be held accountable for? Certainly, his were mounting up by the minute.

"Explain yourself," Lady Phoebe demanded. "How came my granddaughter to be in this state?"

Jonathan lifted his head, shaking it slowly. "It's a long story," he whispered.

"And we shall have plenty of time to hear it," Lady Phoebe answered.

Hands clenched into fists, Jonathan stared down, focusing on his hands where they hung between his knees. Slowly the story spilled out of how night after night, they had set traps for Marcus, only to catch Spring instead. When at last the tale was finished, Jonathan raised his head.

"We were distracted when we found it was Spring who had fallen into our trap. My only thought was to get her to safety before anyone discovered her identity." He expelled a long sigh.

Lady Phoebe gave him a pointed look, urging him to continue.

"Marcus chose that moment to strike." He unfurled his fists then clenched them again. "The bullet she took was meant for me."

Lady Phoebe, seated on the bed beside Spring, reached over to caress her granddaughter's forehead before she turned her gaze back to him.

"'Tis lucky for you then that she was there, is it not?"

Jonathan stared at Lady Phoebe, beginning to wonder if the old lady was indeed unhinged. "She was almost killed." His teeth clenched together, almost trapping the words.

"And had she not been there you most assuredly would be dead now," Lady Phoebe met his stare unflinching.

"I would not have put my wife in such danger," Jonathan grated.

"Nor would she have wished you to be in such danger. But once you'd set upon that course, she must have felt she had no choice but to try and protect you."

"Protect me?

"Yes, and it's best you remember that in the future. 'Tis no simpering lass you've wed, but a woman of courage and strong heart. She can and will protect those she loves."

"Courage, yes," Jonathan agreed as he lifted Spring's hand to his lips.

"It was no small thing she was willing to do for her family. You know, of course, that Marcus orchestrated the whole mess. Even to having my son killed. I suspected as much. I could not stand by and allow him to marry my granddaughter. That was why I saw to it that the fever lingered."

"You?"

"Of course," Lady Phoebe confirmed. "It was a simple matter of putting a few drops of the special potion that Aaron supplied into her tea, just enough to bring on the fever. She was never in any real danger, of course."

"I warned her not to eat or drink anything because I suspected someone of trying to poison her," Jonathan answered.

"I know," Lady Phoebe answered. "But, by then Marcus had returned to London, so there was no need to continue with the illness."

"I never would have allowed my uncle to wed her," Jonathan said quietly.

Lady Phoebe smiled, reaching over to pat his hand gently. "I realize that."

Jonathan shivered. "I find myself forever making vows, bargaining for her life. This time I've promised to set her free."

"And what if *she* does not want to be free?"

Jonathan raised hopeful eyes to Lady Phoebe.

Spring stirred, and a soft moan escaped her lips, she could bear no more. One never profited by eves-dropping. The ache in her heart exceeded the pain that ravaged her body. Why did Jonathan want to send her away?

Why did her body ache? Where was she? What had happened? She tried to move but gasped when pain shot through her. Memory returned swiftly with the pain.

"You're not supposed to move," Jonathan said as he gently pressed her back to the bed. "The bleeding could start up again."

"Could I turn on my side?" She tried to move, but it felt like a hot branding iron shot through her shoulder. She winced in pain, her face pale and drawn.

Jonathan stood and carefully slipped his arm under her. He turned her tenderly to her side then placed a pillow at her back to support her.

"Much better." She smiled wanly, unable to contain the low moan of pain the movement caused.

Lady Phoebe, after assuring herself of Spring's return to the land of the living, even if a painful return, puttered around fussing over her granddaughter. "My pet, do you think you might be able to drink some broth? I'll go right away and have it prepared for you."

Spring closed her eyes, relieved that her grandmother had left. Her frenzied movement around the room had made Spring dizzy.

Once Lady Phoebe had departed, Jonathan appeared at a loss as to what he should be doing, then finally he turned to the dresser and lifted the small vial the doctor had left. He poured a small dose into a glass and added a splash of water. He returned to the bedside and held the glass to Spring's lips.

"For the pain," he coaxed.

Spring looked at Jonathan questioningly as she slowly drank the potion he held for her.

Jonatan smiled sadly. "You saved my life and almost lost yours."

She thought she saw a tear in his eye, but he blinked rapidly, and it was gone. She reached out and took his hand. He turned his hand in hers, entwining their fingers. Her other hand twisted in the sheets as she remembered his words when he'd told her grandmother of his vow. Still, she needed to know what had happened after she'd lunged to save Jonathan.

"Marcus?"

"Dead."

Lowering her gaze to the bed where her fingers twisted in the smooth sheets, she waited for him to say the words that would set her free.

Free? Did he not realize she would never be free again? That her heart, her very soul would be his forever? How noble he made it sound. He was doing it for her, he claimed.

Her fingers withdrew from his, and her hand fell back to the bed. Both hands clenched into fists. The least he owed her was honesty. If he didn't want her as his wife, he should be man enough to tell her. Vow, indeed.

Lady Phoebe returned with a small tray containing a cup of steaming broth. She placed the tray on the small table beside the bed then cast a glance from Spring to Jonathan. She slowly shook her head, causing Spring to wonder if she sensed the tension filling the room.

"The constable is still prowling around downstairs. I expect he'll want to speak with both of you." Lady Phoebe smoothed Spring's hair back from her face.

"Later," Jonathan said firmly as Lady Phoebe exited the room. He rose from his chair and moved to close the door behind Lady Phoebe.

"Now," he said as he returned to Spring's side.

She held her breath, not now, not yet. She did not think she could stand to hear the words quite yet. She squeezed her eyes tightly closed and held her breath. She'd just hold her breath until she passed out, then he couldn't say those words.

Chapter Thirty-Seven

Gently he took her in his arms, being careful not to disturb her shoulder. His lips touched hers lightly then more possessively as he deepened the kiss. She responded to his touch pressing herself closer to him.

"You're not to move, Love," he whispered as his lips gently tasted her ear lobe. "Doctor's orders."

"But—" He silenced her objection with another kiss.

"I must properly thank you for saving my life," he said as he trailed kisses down her throat and across her uninjured shoulder to the place where the bandage impeded his progress. "And then, I would like to know why my wife was roaming around London dressed as the most fetching young dandy I've ever seen?"

His lips traced the path back up her neck and to the shell of her ear where he paused to test its delicate pink outer rim with his teeth. She tried to lift her hand to his face, but he caught it. Again, entwining their fingers.

"No, remember doctor's orders." He kissed across her cheek to the corner of her lips. "You must remain very still."

"Not very likely," Spring answered, suppressing a chuckle. "When you kiss me, my body has a mind of its own."

Jonathan held her so that her head rested on his shoulder and her injured arm was supported on his chest. He held her protectively in his arms. His lips pressed light kisses on her forehead and across her hair as his fingers gently caressed the smooth skin of her arm.

A shiver passed along her body. "Cold?" Jonathan asked.

"No, I am quite comfortable in your arms, thank you." She sighed and snuggled closer. "Forever," she whispered.

"Now, wife," Jonathan's voice held mock severity. "What were you doing dressed like that? What mischief were you about?"

His answers would have to wait since the medicine had quickly worked it magic, lulling Spring into peaceful slumber.

A week later, Spring was well on the mend. Her color had returned to normal, and although she tired easily, there appeared to be no infection in the wound.

The doctor allowed her to sit up for a few hours at a time but insisted she wear her arm in a sling to take the strain off her shoulder. Spring happily agreed. Anything was preferable to being bedridden.

Jonathan had been quite solicitous toward her. Still, she chafed under the knowledge that it was his sense of duty and honor that bound him to her, that his real desire was to be free of her. She did not want him to remain with her out of duty but out of love. Her own sense of honor and even more, her pride, demanded that she send him away. But her heart ached at the thought.

As much as it would hurt her to do so, Spring was determined to set him free. She would not have a husband who did not love her.

He came to her at noonday, carrying a tray filled with small sandwiches, sweets, and tea. She watched as he placed the tray on the small table at the window and then beckoned her to come and eat.

Spring seated herself across from him. Hardly touching her own food, she watched as he ate, His large hand competently held the fragile China cup as he sipped his tea. She smiled as she watched him, remembering how little he cared for the amber brew.

Finally, she decided to broach the subject of their marriage. If she had something distasteful to do, there was no point in putting it off.

"I've been thinking," Spring began, moving away from the table to stand by the window.

"Indeed?"

"Well," she hesitated. This was going to be harder than she had thought, and her thoughts had been pretty extreme. "Since Marcus is no longer any threat, there's really nothing to hold you here."

Jonathan arched an eyebrow at her over his cup but remained silent.

"I mean, I certainly appreciate all you've done," she ran on, knowing her words were rambling. "to protect my family and all, but I can see no reason to continue with our marriage, now that the reason for it has been removed, that is."

"No reason?"

"Well, it's," she began, stopped took a deep breath, and tried again, hoping to hold back the tears that threatened to fall. "It's not like you married me for love or anything. I certainly don't expect you to stay with me out of," She faltered and turned to gaze out the window trying to quell the tears that threatened, so that she could continue. "out of duty." *Or pity,* she added silently.

Jonathan placed his cup carefully back on the tray and stood. He moved to her side. His hands moved up to tenderly grasp her shoulders, then one hand moved to her chin and turned her face up gently to face him.

"You do not wish to continue with this marriage?" Jonathan eyes bore into hers, and she felt like she was drowning in their depths.

"It is no longer necessary, is it? Marcus is gone. Your inheritance is safe, as is mine. Why continue if it does not please us to do so? I realize our marriage was a necessary foil against Marcus, but now..."

"And now it does not please you?" His voice, filled with what almost sounded like anger, cut her to the quick.

More than anything in the world. "I had hoped for a marriage based upon love, not duty, honor or intrigue."

Jonathan's hands fell away from her, and Spring had never felt so alone. Bitterness rose in her throat, and she fought to swallow it down. She had begun this and she would see it through.

"If we had married for any other reason than to thwart your uncle's plans..."

Jonathan turned his back upon her, and her heart sank. She was suddenly glad she spoke out first. It would have hurt so much more had he rejected her.

She heard him take a deep breath and his broad shoulders seemed to fall just a bit. His voice, when it came to her, sounded strained. "I've..." His voice broke. Another deep breath, then he started again. "I have not been completely honest with you," he said, his voice but a soft whisper. "The contract that my uncle signed," He stopped and took another deep breath before he continued. "if I had but refused to marry you, you would have been free of Marcus. But I wanted, God help me, I wanted you under any terms. Now it appears my own selfishness has cost me that which I craved the most."

Jonathan quickly left the room, leaving Spring staring after him. What exactly did he mean? He had married her to thwart his uncle's plans, she knew what she'd heard. She knew he had.

Spring flew to the chest and dug out the packet of papers that Mr. Brownstone had given her. She spread them on the bed, frantically seeking the contract that Marcus and she had signed.

She read it through carefully. The last passage caught her attention.

If for whatever reason the Earl of Wyndridge should refuse to wed Lady Spring Lansing, the debt owed to Marcus Tollersley shall be null and void.

"What have I done?" Spring cried as she sank to the floor, tears spilling onto the contract clutched in her hands.

Sometime later, Spring wearily pulled herself up and onto the bed where she sprawled exhausted. She had no more tears, only a deep aching emptiness for what she had lost.

Much later, Spring awoke to the room in total darkness. She lay quietly wondering what had awakened her. There came a flicker of light, and then the lamp on her bedside sputtered to life. A black gloved hand turned the wick low so that it bathed the room in a pale-yellow glow.

Her gaze followed the shape of the hand up past the wrist to the black sleeve and on up to the wide shoulders and finally to the black mask. She held her breath.

The highwayman had returned. But that was impossible, Spring told herself, shaking the last vestiges of sleep from her mind. Jonathan was the highwayman.

He moved without a word to the bed and sat beside her. Catching one of her hands in his black clad one, he pulled her gently toward him. The dark eyes behind the mask flashed with determination.

"I've come to take you away with me," he whispered in that familiar coarse voice as his arms closed around her, pinning her to his chest.

This is madness, Spring melted into his arms. "And what of my husband?" Spring asked as her heart began to thrill triple time.

"Let him speak of duty and honor, it counts for naught. I offer you passion and love."

Spring settled into his arms.

"You are mine," he whispered against her neck as his lips tasted the soft flesh there.

"The highwayman's lady?"

"Aye."

She titled her head so that he had full advantage in his sensuous assault upon her throat.

"And where would we go?"

"Does it matter?"

No. She remained silent.

"America." His lips were a whisper against her skin.

She smiled against his lips as they brushed softly over hers.

"And if my husband should choose to fight for me?"

"He has from the first, but he's not bold enough to just take what he wants." He kissed her deeply. "I am."

"And what do you want?"

"You," he whispered, tightening his arms around her. "Your love, your delightful body, your passion." His hand slipped to her breasts. "Your children."

His hand moved to the buttons at the back of her gown. Slowly he freed her from the garment, then rose to discard his own clothing. When he returned to her all that was between them was the black silk mask and the bandage on her shoulder.

He stroked her body from shoulder to hip lightly with a long black feather. Spring withered beneath its touch. Her body sprang to life as need kindled deep within her. She caught the feather to stop its torment, turning the weapon against its master.

"Why do you carry this feather?" she asked as she trailed it along his ribs. She smiled at his sudden intake of breath.

"It was a black feather that led to my father's downfall. The highwayman was to be just a prank, a lark, something for bored young dandies to pass the time. The highwayman wore the feather in his hat, his calling card. Marcus put it in my father's room to seal his fate. Marcus had planned it from the start. While my father played at highwayman, never really taking anything, save a kiss from the ladies, my uncle saw to it a real highwayman robbed a coach and killed the driver. When my father escaped to America, Marcus sent his assassin after him.

He ran his hand over her side from hip to thigh. Spring trembled in pleasure as he continued to caress her in slow deliberate circles, coming ever closer to her breasts and then dipping down to the golden curls at the juncture of her thighs.

"Jonathan," Spring began.

"Nae, Love," he answered. "'Tis Drew," the highwayman whispered as he fondled her breasts.

Her nipples hardened under his manipulation. She pressed her body closer so that the peak of her breast filled his hand.

"I am afraid I have made an error." She felt him stiffen beside her, his hand upon her breast stilled.

"I accused my husband of not loving me. But now I find I was wrong. He does love me. I'm sure of it, just as I'm sure that I love him."

She thought she heard a soft chuckle.

"He cannot love you more than I," the masked man said as he dipped down to capture a nipple between hot moist lips. He suckled it for a moment then released the passion roused nub.

"Does he make you feel like this?"

"Therein lies my problem, for when you touch me or he does, for that matter, 'tis the same. Jonathan or Drew, highwayman or husband, one blends into the other."

This time she was certain she heard a chuckle.

The highwayman tightened his arms around her. "I love you."

She moved her hand up to pull mask from his face. "And I love you, Jonathan Andrew Sinclair, Earl of Wyndridge, American and highwayman."

Another chuckle.

"Always," she promised as he carefully moved his body to cover hers.

About the Author

Melba is a retired Special Education Teacher holding a Bachelor of Arts in History and a Masters of Education in Learning Disabilities. She spent 20 years in the classroom and loved every moment.

Melba is active in the writer's community, enjoying giving back to that community through service. She is currently president-elect of Outreach International Writers, Inc. an online non-profit writer's organization that has become her tribe.

Melba's southern roots show in her frequent use of y'all and other southernism. When not writing she enjoys traveling with her hubby, cruising (especially in Europe), container gardening, reading, reading and reading some more. She enjoys cooking and trying new Keto recipes.

The chief executive of the household is our dictatorial Pomeranian, Rowdy. He runs the house.

Read more at https://MJFlournoy.com.